SHAMELESS LOVE

"What's happening to me?" Elizabeth whispered.

"What you feel," Chase answered with a reverent awe for her innocence, "is desire, what men and women share when they discover that something special exists between them. Let me show you how wonderful it can be."

Slowly, Chase stood and drew her to her feet, his eyes drinking in her starlit beauty. He pulled her into his arms and pressed his lips to hers, gently, tenderly.

Elizabeth, caught up in the magic of the night, could not bear to deny him or herself. Tonight she was only a woman searching for love. Surrender and desire were all she sought.

His kiss stunned her; liquid fire burned all the way down her trembling body. As his lips grew more ardent, more demanding, she melted against him, weak with yearning.

"I knew from the moment I saw you that you were destined to be mine." His warm breath brushed against her flaming cheeks.

"No," she whispered, frightened by the bold, possessive words. "You must stop, Chase. You are shaming me."

"No," he murmured. His lips traced the sweet pulse at her throat. "I'm not shaming you, Elizabeth Rose. I am loving you, and love knows no shame."

As their lips touched again, a thrill ran through her, and she pressed herself against him, eager to fill the aching emptiness within, to taste the intoxicating joy of his shameless love . . .

FIERY ROMANCE
From Zebra Books

SATIN SECRET (2116, $3.95)
by Emma Merritt

After young Marta Carolina had been attacked by pirates, shipwrecked, and beset by Indians, she was convinced the New World brought nothing but tragedy . . . until William Dare rescued her. The rugged American made her feel warm, protected, secure — and hungry for a fulfillment she could not name!

CAPTIVE SURRENDER (1986, $3.95)
by Michalann Perry

Gentle Fawn should have been celebrating her newfound joy as a bride, but when both her husband and father were killed in battle, the young Indian maiden vowed revenge. She charged into the fray — yet once she caught sight of the piercing blue gaze of her enemy, she knew that she could never kill him. The handsome white man stirred a longing deep within her soul . . . and a passion she'd never experienced before.

PASSION'S JOY (2205, $3.95)
by Jennifer Horsman

Dressed as a young boy, stunning Joy Claret refused to think what would happen were she to get caught at what she was really doing: leading slaves to liberty on the Underground Railroad. Then the roughly masculine Ram Barrington stood in her path and the blue-eyed girl couldn't help but panic. Before she could fight him, she was locked in an embrace that could end only with her surrender to PASSION'S JOY.

TEXAS TRIUMPH (2009, $3.95)
by Victoria Thompson

Nothing is more important to the determined Rachel McKinsey than the Circle M — and if it meant marrying her foreman to scare off rustlers, she would do it. Yet the gorgeous rancher felt a secret thrill that the towering Cole Elliot was to be her man — and despite her plan that they be business partners, all she truly desired was a glorious consummation of their vows.

PASSION'S PARADISE (1618, $3.75)
by Sonya T. Pelton

When she is kidnapped by the cruel, captivating Captain Ty, fair-haired Angel Sherwood fears not for her life, but for her honor! Yet she can't help but be warmed by his manly touch, and secretly longs for PASSION'S PARADISE.

Available wherever paperbacks are sold, or order direct from the Publisher. Send cover price plus 50¢ per copy for mailing and handling to Zebra Books, Dept. 2373, 475 Park Avenue South, New York, N.Y. 10016. Residents of New York, New Jersey and Pennsylvania must include sales tax. DO NOT SEND CASH.

LONE STAR LOVESONG

EMMA MERRITT

ZEBRA BOOKS
KENSINGTON PUBLISHING CORP.

ZEBRA BOOKS

are published by

Kensington Publishing Corp.
475 Park Avenue South
New York, NY 10016

First printing: June, 1988

Printed in the United States of America

This book,
a small momento of thanks,
is for you,
Alice Dyer Cockrum

Prologue

June, 1862
Chalmette, Louisiana

The sky was black with storm clouds, and rain pelted the earth with unleashed fury. The front lawn, once adorned with formal gardens, was now muddy and rutted from the heavy traffic of carriages and ambulances. Since the Federal troops had begun their offensive against New Orleans two months ago, The Rose had been converted into a hospital. Union officers, their bodies covered in raincoats, hats pulled low on their heads, barked commands, and soldiers moved back and forth as they transported the wounded on stretchers.

Standing on the gallery beneath the hand-hewn shingle roof was Elizabeth Rose Barrett, her petite figured camouflaged in a plain brown shift and white apron. Strands of blond hair escaped the chignon to wisp around her face. Beside her stood an elderly black woman.

"You better go see what the major man wants," Feldie said.

"Yes," Elizabeth sighed, "I suppose so."

She hadn't liked Major Emery Watkins from the minute he rode into her yard and took over her plantation. A short, squat man, he was repugnant in soul as well as in body. His faded blue eyes were constantly weeping, and she felt them on her every time she was in the same room with him. He seemed to be playing a game with her in an attempt to wear her resistance down. Visually he disrobed her; blatantly he lusted after her. Elizabeth couldn't control his fantasies, but she refused to let him touch her.

Eventually, Elizabeth turned and walked into the house. When she reached the stairs, her brother rushed out of the dining room, now the operating room, headed for the kitchen at the rear of the house. More hot water and linen were needed. Elizabeth was worried about Johnny. Though he had recovered physically from his war wound, he still suffered from severe bouts of melancholy. Johnny had enlisted for active duty when the war began because honor demanded that he do so, but he wasn't a soldier at heart. Johnny was a gentle man, an artist, destined to create life, not to take it. He returned a shell of a man, his spirit gone.

Elizabeth climbed the stairs and moved down the corridor, not stopping until she reached the linen closet. Slipping the key into the lock, she opened the door. When her arms were laden with Mama's beautiful linen, she turned to see Emery Watkins standing in the door.

8

"I've been waiting for you," he said in his nasal whine, his eyes busily taking off her apron. "Perhaps you didn't get my message."

"I received your message but knew you'd want me to finish my work first." She deliberately stared beyond him.

He pushed through the door, his obese form blocking out the light from the hallway. "True," he murmured.

Elizabeth's palms grew clammy. Keeping her voice calm and trying to step past him, she said, "I'll be in your office in just a minute, Major. I need to take these down to—"

With a lunge, Watkins grabbed the linens from her and threw them on the floor. His flabby body pressed her into the small room until the shelves cut into her back. "I've waited a long time, my dear. You've always eluded me in the past, but now you have nowhere to go."

"Don't touch me!"

"I must," Watkins answered. "I'm being transferred shortly, my dear. I must complete all my business here before I go, and you are definitely part of my business."

He took another step; his square, pudgy hand darted out to rake stubbed fingers down her cheeks. Elizabeth shuddered with revulsion; her stomach lurched and she thought she was going to vomit. She dodged away from his hand, but his arm snaked out and coiled around her; he pressed his bulging stomach against her and began to rub, his other hand grabbing her breast.

His fingers pinched her tender flesh, and Elizabeth

9

groaned as she beat his chest with her fists, but his weight pinned her down and rendered her helpless. Tears tumbled down her cheeks. Her body was entirely covered by his. The walls of the room seemed to be closing in on her. She couldn't get air into her lungs; she was dizzy.

When she felt his wet lips dribbling on her temples moving toward her face, she felt a renewal of strength as well as abhorrence. She forced her arms free and raked her fingernails down both cheeks. Watkins smashed her chin with his fist, cracking her head against the shelves behind. While she was dazed, he yanked the apron from her body and slung it to the floor. Each hand caught a part of the opened bodice, tugged, and buttons flew in all directions. He ripped the material so that her gown parted and slid down her shoulders, exposing her chemise and petticoat. He was breathing so heavily, his chest was heaving. Sweat rolled down his temples and beaded over his upper lips as his eyes feasted on the creamy beauty revealed by the torn clothing.

Elizabeth's hand grazed the shelf, her fingers running over a candlestick. She grasped and swung it, but the blow missed Watkins. Hissing his anger, he slapped her face until blood trickled down her chin and she lolled against the wall.

"I like this. Make me fight some more," he gasped, his groin tightening. He fumbled with the opening in his pants. When he was standing in front of her with only his jacket on, he pawed at the clothing over her crotch like an animal, all the time thrusting his lower body against her tender, bruised flesh.

When she felt the slimy touch of his hand on her

10

maidenhood, Elizabeth screamed, not once, but again and again. Not until she was bereft of the major's weight and heard the thud as he landed against the far wall did she realize that Johnny had come to her rescue.

As she crumpled to the floor, Johnny shouted, "I'll kill you, you son of a bitch. You took one of my sister, but that was only because she was willing to lie with scum like you. You won't lay a hand on Elizabeth. I promise you that."

"Johnny, no!" Elizabeth pushed to her knees. "Watkins isn't worth it."

"No, by God, he's not." Johnny turned to Elizabeth. "But you are."

Seeing the opportunity he had been waiting for, Watkins jerked his gun from the holster and shot Johnny in the back.

"No," Elizabeth screamed, and the entire world seemed to spin around her as she crawled into the hallway to where he lay. "Not Johnny, too!"

Crying uncontrollably, she saw the blood gushing from the wound in his chest, his white shirt quickly turning a dull red. She ripped the material from his body.

"Don't die, Johnny. Please don't die. You're all I have left." She dragged Johnny into her lap and held him. Closing her eyes, she prayed, "Dear, Lord, please don't let him die. Please."

Emery Watkins slowly pushed to his feet. As if shooting a man in cold blood were an every day occurrence, he slipped his revolver into the holster and walked to the closet. Calmly he picked up his breeches, stepped into them, and sauntered down the hall as if nothing had happened.

After Johnny's funeral, Elizabeth brought charges against the major, only to learn that General Butler had removed all municipal authorities and replaced them with Federal officers who were prejudiced against any one associated with the Confederacy. Emery Watkins was not on trial. Elizabeth was.

On the morning judgment was passed, the presiding officer said, "Elizabeth Rose Barrett, we find Major Emery Watkins innocent of the charge of murder. According to the 'Woman's Order' (No. 28), which states that any woman who might by word, gesture, or movement shows contempt for any officer or soldier is to be treated as a woman of the town plying her vocation, we find you guilty of being a whore and soliciting the major's attention. By law we can confiscate your properties for the government."

Elizabeth's expression never changed as judgment was passed, but inside she was crying. Without compassion her brother had been taken from her. Now they were threatening to take her property—the only thing she had left. And she had done nothing but protect herself against rape. She looked directly at Major Emery Watkins.

I promise you that one day I will kill you.

"However," Elizabeth heard the officer say, "because other officers have testified in your behalf we are going to show you clemency. You are free to return to your home. If you're apprehended a second time for leading a soldier on and placing him in the position of having to kill an innocent bystander, you'll

12

be sentenced to two years on Ship Island under federal guard and your property will be confiscated."

That day Elizabeth Rose Barrett learned the meaning of Yankee justice!

Chapter One

February, 1867

A shawl draped around her shoulders to ward off the winter chill, Elizabeth pulled the drapes aside and fastened them to allow the afternoon sunlight to spill into the library. When she heard the light knock on the door, she called, "Come in," and turned to watch a bundled-up black boy enter the room, carrying a small package in a gloved and extended hand.

"Why, Jefferson," she exclaimed, "I didn't expect you until much later. What a quick trip to town you made."

"Sure did." A pleased grin spanning his face, he reached up with his other hand to doff his broad-brimmed hat. "Got the mail by myself at the post office and brought it straight home to you."

"Thank you." Elizabeth smiled at the proud ten-year-old as she took the package from him. "You're

15

really earning your money this week. You're an excellent messenger boy."

"Yep! I reckon I am, Miss Elizabeth." Jefferson nodded his head and answered truthfully with the innocence of youth. He took his gloves off and shoved them into his coat pocket; then he moved closer to the fireplace to spread his hands above the warm, golden flames. He watched as Elizabeth examined the package and scrutinized the writing.

"This makes three letters and one package this week, Miss Elizabeth," Jefferson exclaimed. "And this one comes from Eagle Pass, Texas!"

Elizabeth's soft laughter filled the room. "And now you're showing off, Mr. Thomas Jefferson Barrett."

"Umhum." He nodded his head, totally unrepentant. "Mr. Mathias said it were—"

"Was," Elizabeth automatically corrected, moving across the room.

Irritation flickered momentarily in Jefferson's eyes, but he continued his sentence. "—was all right for me to read what's on the outside of them letters."

"—those letters." The top drawer of the mahogany desk slid open, and Elizabeth extracted a pair of scissors.

Now Jefferson furrowed his forehead. "—those letters. On account of there's no teacher I shouldn't stop reading."

"Because we have no teacher, you shouldn't stop reading."

"Yes'm." His patience tried to the limit, Jefferson sighed deeply. Getting through a sentence around Miss Elizabeth wasn't easy.

"And Elijah is right. The more you read, the better a reader you'll be." Laying the package and scissors down, she opened the drawer of the mahogany desk to pick up a small coin which she handed to Jefferson. "Here you go. You can add this to the money you're saving."

"Thank you," the boy said, quickly depositing the coin in his breeches pocket, but he made no effort to leave the room. Deep in thought, he remained at the desk to watch her open the mail. "Miss Elizabeth," his tentative question floated through the air, and Elizabeth turned to look down at him, "do you think I'll ever be able to speak an entire sentence without you correcting me?"

Elizabeth's lips quivered, but she didn't laugh. The boy was perfectly serious. Understanding his need for reassurance, she again lay her package aside and stooped to embrace him. "Yes, Jefferson," she promised, hugging him tightly, "and that day has already come. You just spoke an entire sentence that was grammatically correct. And speaking correctly is just like reading, the more you practice, the better you'll be."

Elizabeth reached out, took the hat from Jefferson's head and ran her hands through the springy curls, then unable to resist the urge, planted a kiss on his forehead as she hugged him even tighter. When she pulled back, her eyes were bright with unshed tears.

"I know we're not supposed to be hugging and kissing on young boys who are growing into men, Jefferson, but I do love you. You're such a smart little boy."

"That ain't —" Jefferson stopped talking and grinned into Elizabeth's twinkling eyes. He quickly corrected himself before she could. "That's not what Aunt Feldie tells me."

"You can also be trouble with a capital T, Thomas Jefferson. Now, I think it's time you scooted. You have your chores to do."

"Yes'm."

A smile lingering on her face, Elizabeth watched the boy as he raced out of the room. When the door lock clicked into place, she returned to the desk, picked up the package, and finished tearing through the wrapping paper to find a small box which she opened. She pulled a folded letter from the lid. On the bottom of the box, on a bed of white material, lay two gold brooches. Both were exquisite and dainty pieces, one a rose, the other a butterfly.

"Vanessa!"

The anguished cry was a mere whisper as Elizabeth slumped into the chair behind the desk. With shaking hands she picked up the letter, her eyes skimming over the scrawling print. Vanessa wanted to come home but couldn't. Not knowing how much longer she would live, she had returned the two brooches she had taken when she ran away.

When the letter abruptly stopped with a splattering of ink, Elizabeth couldn't believe it. Surely Vanessa wouldn't do this to her; surely not! She searched for an address; she had to know where Vanessa was. To Elizabeth's dismay all she found was the postmark: Eagle Pass, Texas.

The words began to dance across the page and to mock her. Vanessa said so little but alluded to such much. She had broken four years of silence to give Elizabeth an important clue to her whereabouts — the name of a specific town in Texas. With this information it couldn't be difficult to find Vanessa, Elizabeth thought as she continued to gaze at the butterfly brooch.

No matter what Vanessa had become, she was all Elizabeth had left. She had to go to her; she couldn't let her die, too. Elizabeth stood and walked to the window to stare at the gardens below. She was unaware of the brown bleakness of winter around her; she was unaware that afternoon had turned into dusk and that the fire was nothing more than glowing red-orange embers. All she could think about was springtime at The Rose with Mama, Papa, Johnny, and Vanessa . . . the way it used to be before the war.

"Miss Elizabeth!" Jefferson called from the hall as he opened the library door. "Aunt Feldie says it's time for you to get ready for supper."

"Thank you, Jefferson," Elizabeth said. "I'll be right down."

"The study is mighty dark, Miss Elizabeth," he

19

said, peering into the evening-shadowed room. "I can hardly see you. Is something wrong?"

"I received a letter from Miss Vanessa today. Do you remember Miss Vanessa?" Elizabeth asked as she returned to the desk and laid the brooch down to light the lamp.

"Yes'm, I kinda remember her. Is she never coming home, Miss Elizabeth?" Jefferson moved closer and looked at the fragile, glistening pieces of jewelry.

"Yes, Jefferson," Elizabeth declared softly, "Miss Vanessa is coming home. I'm going to Texas to get her."

Jefferson crossed his arms on the desk and rested his chin on them. "Miss Elizabeth," he finally said, "you ain't going to Texas by yourself, are you?"

"I hadn't given that much thought," Elizabeth admitted, not bothering to correct his grammar.

"Then I reckon you better," Jefferson declared and straightened up to look directly into her face. "It's not safe for a woman to be traveling by herself, Miss Elizabeth. You need a man with you, so's he can protect you."

"You're right," Elizabeth agreed. "But the only two men I could take with me are Elijah and Uncle Wally, and both of them are needed here to run the plantation and the mill."

"Yes'm, that's true," Jefferson agreed solemnly.

"What do you think I ought to do?" A smile flirted with the corners of Elizabeth's mouth, and she cast gentle, amused eyes on Jefferson.

"Well, Miss Elizabeth," drawled the lad, "I figure you ought to take me with you."

Elizabeth tilted her head and pretended to consider his suggestion. Finally she burst into laughter and said, "Well, Thomas Jefferson Barrett, that's sorta what I figure, too."

Chapter Two

San Antonio, Texas

Stable stench — damp, stale hay mixed with animal refuse and sweat — assailed Major Chase Daniel as he slung his saddle over his shoulder and walked the length of Muldoon's Livery Stable to the opened door. Water dripped from the brim of his hat, and tendrils of black hair curled over his raincoat collar. Concern and fatigue made his face look as if it had been chiseled from granite. He stared at the inclement weather, unusually dark for five o'clock on an April afternoon, and thought it a correct reflection of his own emotions.

An unexpected cold front had moved in to join forces with an early spring storm. The wind whined around and through the numerous cracks in the make-shift wall; thunder boomed, and as if it were angry at the world, lightning ripped at the blackened sky with its jagged claws. Rain fell in torrential fury on the sun-baked earth, quickly reducing it to muddy pulp.

The black troopers inside the building were oblivious to the raging storm. They were in San Antonio for the weekend—two days of rest and relaxation before they returned to the rigors of frontier military life—and Major Daniel had promised them a good time. Knowing their commanding officer as well as they did, they trusted him to keep his word. They looked forward to a wonderful home-cooked meal and a comfortable bed in dry quarters. While they tended their horses, some of them laughed and talked together; others sang softly.

So that the nine troopers could hear him above the storm, Chase yelled to his sergeant, "Mr. Liberty, I'm going to Beck's House to see if we can get some rooms."

"Yes, sir," the deep-voiced black man answered.

"Beck's House!" several troopers sang in unison, happy and knowing grins crossing their ebony faces as they looked at their commanding officer.

"I would say that includes more than dinner and a bed, sir," another of the men called out as he waved a currycomb through the air.

"Attention, soldier!" Samson Liberty's voice boomed louder than the thunder outside.

Chase looked squarely at George Washington Man who immediately snapped to attention. Without breaking the military stare and without betraying his thoughts, Chase slowly and deliberately fastened his raincoat beneath his chin. Finally he asked dryly, "What else do you have in mind, Corporal Man, besides a dinner and a bed."

"How about a soft, cuddly woman to go in that bed, sir?"

Chase said soberly, "This is getting to be a habit."

"Yes, sir." Corporal Man nodded his head. "It sure is, sir. I just hope it ain't a habit that I break any too soon, sir."

Chase's lips slipped through a grin into a low chuckle. "Very well, Corporal Man, I'll see what I can do about getting all of you a soft, cuddly woman to go in your beds."

"Thank you, sir," the corporal replied with a saucy salute. If it were possible, his smile widened even more.

"Mr. Liberty, you and the men come on over as soon as you have the horses taken care of." A smile still lingered on Chase's lips. "I don't think it'll take you too long to groom and feed the horses, do you?"

The men's no sirs were lost in another clap of thunder, but Chase wouldn't have heard them anyway. His shoulders hunched against the cold blasts of air, he was already sloshing across the muddy plaza in front of the Alamo. He sought momentary respite from the rain beneath the small portico of the elegant Menger Hotel. The storm had cast a blanket of darkness over the city; the windows glowed with artificial light, and the lobby teemed with people, most of them military.

The other officers who had been summoned to San Antonio for the meeting with General Sheridan, Commanding Officer of the Fifth Military District and Colonel J.J. Reynolds, Military Governor, would be quartered at the Menger as guests of the federal government; not so Chase Daniel. By choice he would be staying with his hand-picked troopers at Beck's House, a small unobtrusive hotel on one of San Antonio's side streets. While the owner, Cedric Beck, was a true southerner who only tolerated federal troops, he loved their money and was most accommodating in order to get it. Beck's silence and cooperation were the characteristics which endeared him to Chase.

A greeting rent the air. "Chase Daniel! You old son-of-a-gun! Did you change your mind about staying here with the rest of us?" Captain Jack Stevens walked out of the hotel lobby to stand beside Chase.

A ghost of a smile touched Chase's lips, and he shoved his hat back on his head to show curly, black hair and a tanned, handsome face with lines of strength and determination etched on it. "No, I'm on my way to Beck's. Just stopped here because it was dry."

Jack moved to the edge of the portico and laid his palm against one of the columns to brace his weight. Looking across the street through the heavy downpour, he said, "What did you think about the meeting today?"

Chase shrugged. "All of them are alike to me. We do a lot of talking but resolve little."

Jack nodded and asked, "Do you think the war has touched General Grant in the head? He can't really believe Bainbridge's men are holed up in Mexico, setting up a massive outlaw ring. Reports confirm that Bainbridge and his most trusted officers were killed."

"Nope! The Old Man isn't touched in the head," Chase answered. "You know as well as I do that he wouldn't take the trouble to send me on special assignment down here to investigate if he didn't have strong reason for his suspicions." Chase then lapsed into silence as he stared into the blackened, storm-ridden sky. Eventually he added, "Despite reports to the contrary, Jack, I'm not sure that Colonel Roswell Irwin Bainbridge is dead. You can't kill a man like that so easily." A blast of wind carrying a heavy spray of rain moved Chase and Jack farther back on the porch until they stood in a wedge of light that spilled from the opened door.

"Say it's so," Jack said. "Say Bainbridge is alive and operating out of Mexico. What do you propose to do? Are you and these nine, hand-picked, black troopers going into Mexico to try to apprehend a Confederate colonel and his men who have turned into cut-throats?"

Jack found the idea so preposterous that he grinned. All the time, he watched a slow smile ease across Chase's face—a gesture that was entirely characteristic of Chase Daniel. Chase always did things slow and easy, and seldom failed. Not a word was spoken, yet the major's gesture completely sobered the captain. He saw the flinty resolve in the blue-gray eyes; he heard it when Chase finally spoke again.

"No, Jack," Chase promised, "I'm not going try. I'm going to succeed. I'm going to apprehend Roswell Irwin Bainbridge and his men and bring them back to the United States to stand trial for their war crimes."

Shaking his head, Jack slid his hands into his pockets and hunched his shoulders. He didn't doubt Chase for one minute; one thing for sure, Chase Daniel was as good as his word. "When are you heading out to San Felipe Springs?"

"Monday morning," Chase replied, removing his hat and running his fingers through his hair.

"You were pretty hard on P.S. today, ole boy," Jack accused. "You could have walked a little softer."

"Life has taught me not to be too soft," Chase said, adjusting his hat on his head. "And as a reminder, my friend, General Phil Sheridan wasn't too easy on me." The rain slacked and Chase took the opportunity to leave. He tugged his collar closer around his neck and pulled his hat farther over his

27

forehead. With a wave he said, "See you later, Jack. I need to get to the hotel to see if I can get rooms enough for my men."

Goodbyes were lost in a clap of thunder as Chase buried his hands deeper in his cloak pockets and ducked his head against an unmerciful onslaught of wind and rain. Hurried steps carried him several blocks away from the Menger to a gray, two-story frame building. The front door stood open, and people milled around in the small lobby. A rectangular sign, bearing Beck's name and hanging from one rusted hinge, banged against the post as the wind swung it back and forth. Chase walked up onto the porch and into the lobby toward the short, heavy-set man who stood behind the counter, writing.

"Good evening, Mr. Beck," he said, throwing his saddle bags on the counter top to startle the man.

Cedric's head jerked up and he dropped his pen on the ledger. "Major Daniel!" The proprietor of the hotel rubbed his hands down the front of the bibbed apron that stretched across his protruding stomach. "If this ain't a surprise, sir. I wasn't expecting you until next weekend."

"At the last minute General Sheridan changed the meeting date," Chase explained with an apologetic smile, "so I'm here a week earlier." He pulled his hat off, thick waves falling to soften the gaunt and chiseled features of his face. "The army is famous for last minute decisions and changes, Mr. Beck.

That's the primary reason why I decided to rent my apartment by the month. I know it'll be waiting for me when I finally do arrive. And after the past three weeks of chasing the Mescaleros across West Texas and fighting General Sheridan, I can use some rest. I think I'll die out to the world the minute I hit the bed, which isn't going to be any longer than it takes me to sign in and walk up the stairs." Chase reached for the roster, flipped it around, and wrote his name.

"Well, Major," Beck said, beads of perspiration breaking out on his forehead, his eyes furtively darting around the lobby, as he thought of an excuse to keep Chase from going directly to his rooms, "I—uh—I hate to tell you this, but Mrs. Beck's got your room all tore up, sir." His lips twitched nervously as he watched furrows deepen on Chase's forehead. Hastily the landlord added to his already growing fabrication, "Started spring cleaning before the rains came, and we—uh—we been so busy, she ain't had a chance to get it put back together again."

Chase sighed wearily. This was the way the past week had gone for him. "Thank Mrs. Beck for taking care of my rooms for me, but I'll take them just as they are," Chase said.

"Well, even then," Beck said, stalling for time, "it'll be awhile before Mrs. Beck and I have them ready."

"How soon?" Chase asked, wondering what else

29

could go wrong.

"No less than a couple of hours," Cedric answered. "And while you're waiting, sir, you could have a drink and maybe eat your supper."

Chase nodded. "Also, Mr. Beck, I'm going to need nine more rooms — one for each of my troopers."

Before Chase finished speaking, Beck was shaking his bald head. "On such short notice I can't get that many rooms for you, Major. I'm all booked up. Horse race in town this weekend. Immigrants headed for Mexico and California. Soldiers everywhere."

On another irritable sigh Chase dropped the pen, ink splattering on the counter, and reached into his pocket to pull out a roll of bills which he shuffled in front of the proprietor. "Have you any suggestions?"

Cedric's gaze never left the money; he scratched his head and thought a while. Suddenly he snapped his fingers and exclaimed. "Your men wouldn't be wanting some female company, now would they, Major?"

Chase's eyes narrowed. "That they would, Mr. Beck."

Cedric nodded his head vigorously. "I figured so, sir, and I have just the answer. Why can't they stay at Celeste Doucet's place for the night?"

"At *Le Grande* Casino?" Chase asked.

He was skeptical. This casino catered only to the

most elite of San Antonio society, and soldiers—especially Union soldiers—weren't considered to be a part of San Antonio society. But the idea had merit. Having only been in the casino once, Chase didn't personally know Celeste Doucet, but he knew the reputation of her establishment—clean and honest. Although a saloon and brothel, the casino differed from the mirrored and frescoed liquor saloons in other parts of the city; it boasted no six-shooter brawls or glass throwing. Might be the best place for the men while they were in town! As long as they had a woman and a bottle they would be content and wouldn't be stirring up any trouble.

"Le Grande Casino," Beck repeated. "Just nine months old and already one of San Antonio's most popular casinos, major. When Celeste Doucet arrived and announced she'd be opening the place, people tore into her, but she's a tough lady. She put her casino on West Market Street in one of the most reputable business districts of the town on purpose, and there was nothing those snobs could do about it." Beck laughed. "The newspapers attacked her, but it didn't hurt Madam Doucet. In fact, the articles actually helped her. People went to her place out of curiosity at first. Now they go because of its reputation."

From first hand observation Chase knew Madam Doucet's establishment was elegant; her clientele the richest. *Le Grande* Casino had rooms on the first and second floors for drinking, dining, reading and gambling. The rooms on the third and fourth floor were for special entertainment only, and the price of the entertainment was extremely high.

A wary smile pulled Chase's lips. "You're proposing I send my men, black Union troopers, to *Le Grande* for the night, Mr. Beck?"

Beck leaned forward and lowered his voice to say, "Well, sir, if it was anybody else except Madam Doucet, I'd say no. But she, sir, is a business woman, and she's mighty accommodating."

"For a price?"

Beck nodded and repeated, "For a price. Even though she's from New Orleans herself, she's tolerable of Yankee soldiers—black or white. She's got girls of color working for her, sir. And I might add, for a mighty reasonable price she'd be inclined to let them stay for the night."

Chase laughed dryly. "Is Madam Doucet in such dire needs of customers that she must use you?"

"Simple business arrangement," Beck explained without taking offense. "We help each other along."

"How much is this mutual trade agreement going to cost me, Mr. Beck?"

Cedric pursed his lips and rubbed his chin. "Well, sir, you gotta remember Madam Doucet is a business woman."

"Quite a bit in other words," Chase muttered as he laid the bills on the counter one by one. "Tell me when to stop, Mr. Beck."

Finally Cedric's hand darted out to cover the

growing pile of money. "That'll take care of it, Major."

"You'll work out all the details?" Chase asked.

"Yes, sir," Cedric said and stuffed the money in his pocket. "I'll take care of it personally." He waved toward the saloon. "Why don't you have a drink on the house, Major, and eat you some supper—beef stew with Mrs. Beck's own biscuits. By the time you finish we'll have your rooms ready and your bath drawn."

"Since I have no other alternative, Mr. Beck, I will."

Chase flipped his broad brimmed campaign hat at a jaunty angle and eased out of his raincoat to reveal his blue uniform, the yellow trimming on his jacket and trousers proclaiming him to be an officer in the cavalry. After he had hung the overcoat on the rack, he walked to the saloon. His hand on the top of one of the swinging doors, Chase heard Beck call his name. He paused and turned.

"Are you going to be wanting some company for yourself this evening?" the landlord asked.

Chase hesitated. He was highly selective in his lovers, and preferred not to reduce lovemaking to a business proposition.

"I think you'd enjoy it, Major," Cedric said. "Even though she runs a brothel, Madam Doucet's reputation is mighty good. Her girls are the very best. Why, sir, Madam Doucet just recently bought herself a brand new carriage, imported from Europe. Has a driver she does"—Cedric nodded his head—"who drives the girls when they have engagements away from the Casino." Now he wagged his stubby index finger. "Let me tell you, sir, her girls hobnob with the highest of San Antonio society. And Mrs. Beck told me just the other day that despite what the self-righteous ladies of San Antonio might think, Celeste's girls set the fashion by wearing the latest designs from Europe by way of New Orleans."

Chase hid a smile. A fashion show was not in his plans. But he could use some long-overdue relaxation. "Yes, Mr. Beck, I think I would enjoy some company tonight."

Cedric grinned and bobbed his head. "If I know Celeste, sir, she'll send you some company that you will enjoy! If I may say so, her girls are special. What time do you want her to be here, sir?"

Chase pulled his watch out of the pocket. Six o'clock. "Nine," he replied. "That should give me time to eat and bathe, should it not?"

Beck's bald head bobbed in answer, and as soon as Chase disappeared into the saloon, the little man shuffled from behind the counter. Concern furrowed his brow. "Jonah," he called, moving toward the stairs and beckoning the thirteen year old with a crooked finger, "go tell Mrs. Beck to get some kettles of hot water ready for the major, and tell her we gotta get him rooms ready right now. Move, boy. *Mucho pronto*. Cause when you get through with this chore, I got another one for you." Cedric pushed the boy in the direction of the kitchen; then he moved toward the staircase to mutter under his breath as he slowly heaved from one step to the next.

"I should have known better than to let the major's rooms," he panted aloud, running his palms down the front of his apron in unconscious habit. "That's what I get for feeling sorry for that woman. Should of knowed better. Should of knowed I'd get caught." At the door now, he balled his hand and knocked.

When the small black boy answered the summon, Cedric said, "I need to see your mistress."

"Yes, sir," Jefferson answered, opening the door wider. "Come on in, Mr. Beck. I'll get Miss Elizabeth for you."

Cedric stepped into the room. "Tell her to hurry," he instructed. "What I have to say is mighty important."

"Yes, sir." Jefferson scampered across the room to knock on the door. When Elizabeth replied, he entered the room to find her seated at a small table, writing a letter. "Mr. Beck is here to see you, Miss Elizabeth."

"Did he say what he wanted?" she asked, laying her pen aside and folding the paper.

"No, ma'am," the boy answered. "Just said it was might important."

Elizabeth flexed her shoulders and back, then

35

closed the leather writing case. Picking it up, she stood. Inadvertently her gaze went to the painting that hung on the wall above the fireplace. She had been drawn to it immediately upon walking into the room; it seemed to cast a spell over her. The style was so reminiscent of Johnny's—delicate and fragile, yet strong enough to endure the ages.

The painting was a familiar and beautiful landscape of the deep south with its thick forests, brooks, honey suckles, and dogwood trees. A handsome man, wearing a white shirt, unbuttoned a ways, and brown trousers, tucked into knee-high boots, leaned against the railing of a small bridge. An enigmatic smile curled his lips, and his eyes twinkled. Elizabeth could almost feel the gentle breeze that fluttered through his golden brown hair.

The scene reminded Elizabeth of The Rose; it reminded her how lonely she was and how much she had lost during the war. She missed the plantation and the sugar mill. She missed her family: Aunt Feldie, and Uncle Wally, and Elijah Mathias. She and Jefferson were alone on the Texas frontier, alone in her quest to find Vanessa.

Her gaze landed on her trunk—Mama's trunk—and the crest on the top, a faded red rose. She sighed wearily. Grandpapa Dupree had bought this chest in Paris and given it to his daughter for her trousseau when she announced her engagement to John Whitney Barrett, owner of The Rose Plantation. Now it was Elizabeth's, one of the few possessions she had after the war ended.

"You better hurry, Miss Elizabeth," Jefferson prompted, jarring Elizabeth out of her introspection. "Mr. Beck said it was important. And he's really fidgeting."

Clutching the leather case in her left hand, Elizabeth nodded and hurried into the parlor. She smiled and extended her right hand. "Mr. Beck," — her voice was soft and husky, — "Jefferson said you wished to see me. How can I help you?"

"Uh," Cedric stammered, her beauty startling him as much now as it had when he first saw her disembarking from the stage earlier today. Although she'd taken off her hat, she still wore the green dress that accented her eyes. He caught the tips of her fingers, gave them a limp shake, and dropped them.

Accustomed to being stared at, Elizabeth returned the proprietor's curious gaze without so much as a flicker of her lashes.

Finally Cedric dropped his head. "Miss Barrett, I'm sorry, but I'm gonna have to ask you to give up these here rooms, ma'am."

As if she hadn't heard correctly, Elizabeth stared at Cedric Beck for a few seconds before she repeated incredulously, "Give up my rooms."

"Yes ma'am." Cedric shifted from foot to foot. "Well ma'am the damn—" he broke off immediately and mumbled, "Sorry, ma'am, the Yankees rent these here rooms by the month, and I can only let them when there ain't no Union official in town.

And—well, Miss Barrett, I wasn't expecting any of the Yankees until next weekend, so's when you came in all bedraggled like a lost puppy I was mighty happy to let you have the apartment. But—well—now—they done showed up and want their room."

In order to hide the intense disappointment which swept through her, Elizabeth crossed the room and stood in front of the fireplace, her back to Beck. Reaching up, she laid her writing case on the mantle. "I understand," she eventually said, and well she did understand the man's dilemma. She, too, had made many compromises during these trying years of Yankee occupation.

"Please don't be upset, ma'am," Cedric said, genuinely contrite because he was having to turn her out.

"I'm upset, Mr. Beck," Elizabeth admitted with a sigh as she spun around and leveled her gaze to his, "but not at you, altogether. I fully understand your predicament. Don't worry about it. Jefferson and I can be just as happy in another room as we can be in here. Just tell us where you want us to go and send the boy up to move our trunks."

"Uh . . . uh . . . well, ma'am," Cedric shifted his gaze nervously, "that's just it. I don't have any more rooms available." Out of the corner of his eye, he saw Elizabeth's eyes narrow and her lips thin. Nervously he ran his palms down his apron, and perspiration popped out on his brow.

"You're asking me to find another hotel at this time of night and in this kind of weather!" she exclaimed, her anger getting the upper hand. She'd battled the storm once today in search of lodging; that was enough.

"Mr. Beck," Jonah knocked on the door and yelled at the same time, "me and Odell have the tub of cold water. Mrs. Beck said she'd send up the kettles later. Where do you want us to put it?"

Cedric's head swiveled back and forth as he looked from Elizabeth to the two boys and back to Elizabeth again. "Sorry, ma'am," he muttered, moving toward the door. "I need this room vacated immediately."

Elizabeth had had enough. She planted herself in front of Cedric Beck to stop his escape, folded her arms across her breasts and glared into his face.

"Mr. Beck," she declared, "I understand your predicament and I'm willing to cooperate with you. But you must also understand mine. Until you have a place for me to go, I'll be staying right here. I've already paid for these rooms, and I refuse to be kicked out—especially for a damned blue-belly."

Dammit! Cedric thought, rubbing his palm over his head. He couldn't count the times that Mrs. Beck had shook her finger in his face and warned him about the trouble he could get into if the major ever found out his apartment was being rented out when he wasn't in town. Oh, Lord, why hadn't he listened to her? He had to get Elizabeth Barrett out of the major's apartment because Chase Daniel was one man he didn't want to tangle with. And he had only two hours in which to get her out!"

"Well, ma'am," Cedric said, his hand sliding into his pocket. "I'll just refund the money you've paid, and—"

Elizabeth shook her head. "No, Mr. Beck," she declared, "you're not getting out of this so easily. You won't just refund the money I've paid. I'll stay here in this suite for the night or *until you find me comparable lodging.*"

Cedric wilted in defeat. "Yes, ma'am," he mumbled. "I'll see what I can do."

"That's not enough, Mr. Beck. You *will* do something."

Cedric looked at the woman standing in front of him, no taller than five feet and two inches tall, but she appeared to have grown several feet in the past few minutes. She was a veritable giant. "Yes ma'am."

"Mr. Beck," Jonah asked, "where do you want this tub put? It's might heavy to be holding, sir."

Cedric was so concerned about where he was going to put Elizabeth that he didn't even hear Jonah. He brushed past the child as if he wasn't there and lumbered down the hall, muttering to himself.

"Oh, shoot!" Jonah swore under his breath, slipping one hand out of the ringed handle and slipping the other in; then he turned to Elizabeth who remained standing in the opened door.

"Where do you want me to put this, ma'am?" He tossed his head, a swath of brown hair flying through the air to settle over his forehead and eyes.

"For all I care, young man," she answered, "you can dump it out the window and water the garden."

Puzzled, the boy looked at her. "Why should I do that, ma'am? The garden's getting plenty of water. It's raining outside."

Elizabeth sighed and waved Jonah into the apartment. "Take it to the bedroom." After all, he wasn't at fault for her present dilemma.

When Jonah was gone, Elizabeth paced the floor, refusing to repack her suitcases and prepare to leave. She was determined to hold her ground. If Cedric Beck didn't find her suitable lodging, she would stay right here. Come hell or high water . . . or Yankee! *Damn those Yankees! Would they forever be robbing her of things rightfully hers?*

Jefferson sat quietly. Miss Elizabeth was in one of her fighting moods, and he didn't intend to get in the way. Best to let her work it out of her system in her own way. His eyes moved back and forth between Miss Elizabeth and the big clock on the far wall. The minutes ticked slowly by—ten, twenty, thirty. An hour passed. Then came sharp raps that seemed to explode in the silence of the room. Elizabeth hastened to the door.

Cedric Beck stood there, water dripping from his raincoat. "Miss Barrett," he said, somewhat stiffly, "I've found you a room. You'll be staying with

41

Pearl Gladewater, a friend of Mrs. Beck's, who lives across town."

"Are you providing me with transportation, Mr. Beck?" Elizabeth's green eyes pierced the landlord.

"Yes, ma'am," he answered, rubbing his moist hand over his head. "Now it ain't my buggy, ma'am. I've already let that for the day, but a friend of mine who helped me find you a place to stay offered you transportation. Captain Blake Lowell will be here in about thirty minutes, ma'am, to take you to Mrs. Gladewater's."

As she looked into Beck's pleading eyes, Elizabeth nodded her acceptance. "Very well. I'll be ready. Send someone up to move my trunk, please."

"Sure will, Miss Barrett," Cedric said, heaving a deep sigh of relief. "Also, ma'am, he added, "I'm refunding what you paid me, and to show you how sorry I am this happened, I'm paying for your room and board at Mrs. Gladewater's."

"Thank you, Mr. Beck."

"And if you don't mind, ma'am, Mrs. Beck will be coming up to see that the room's ready for its new occupant. He's . . . uh . . . he's mighty particular. Most of these belongings are his personally, Miss Barrett. And, well, we got to make sure that . . . that everything is in place, ma'am."

Of course, she minded Mrs. Beck's coming up to check out the room for someone else! As if she'd steal something out of the apartment! Elizabeth inwardly seethed. She minded the whole chain of events that were disrupting her day, but she also understood that Cedric Beck was a victim of circumstances as she had been, as she still was. A smile barely touched her lips.

"Tell her to come on up, Mr. Beck. I don't mind because everything is in its rightful place."

A huge grin curved Cedric's face when he turned from Chase's apartment. Maybe everything would turn out all right, after all! Now he needed to make sure the major was given a meal that would keep his interest for the next hour or so. He sure didn't want him sashaying up here too soon.

Supper over, Chase sat at a corner table drinking a glass of wine and mulling over the events of the past week. The two-day meeting in Austin had been a total waste of his time and effort. The trip from Austin to San Antonio had been exhausting. The weather had moved from one extreme to another: The first half of the journey the sun had relentlessly bore down on them, and the heat had been unbearable; he and his men had eaten dust. On the second half, a cold front had moved in, accompanied by a spring storm. He and his troopers had almost been washed away.

Chase's hunger was satisfied; he was dry and warm but plastered with grit and mud. Again he extracted the gold watch. Eight o'clock. It was time to take a bath and relax for the evening. A smile eased across his countenance. He was glad that one of Celeste's girls was coming tonight; he was looking forward to being with a woman — such a wonderful relief from the constant companionship of rough soldiers. As Corporal Man would phrase it, a soft, cuddly change. Chase set the empty glass down and reached for his saddlebags. Before he picked them up, he heard his name called and looked around to spy General Sheridan's aide rushing toward him.

The private stopped when he stood in front of Chase and swiped his forehead in salute. "A message from General Sheridan, sir," he announced, his hand dashing into his breast pocket to extract a sealed letter.

Chase broke the seal and unfolded the paper to read: *The paymaster detail en route from Indianola to San Antonio was robbed yesterday. Captain Terrence Lee was badly wounded in the fracas. The messenger doesn't know if he's still alive. One prisoner was caught and is being held at local jail. Will keep you informed of details.* At the bottom of the page was a personal postscript: *I'm sorry about Terry, Chase. I know how close the two of you were during the war.*

"Thank you, private," Chase said as he refolded the letter. His face was grimmer than it had been earlier in the day. Although Terry was a few years older, he and Chase were the closest of friends and had been for all of Chase's life. Both were orphans who had been reared in Ida Owen's Orphanage in Philadelphia.

As soon as General Sheridan's aide was gone, Chase heaved himself out of the chair, slung the saddlebags over his shoulder and returned to the counter in the lobby. Plans for his evening had changed drastically.

"Evening, Major." Whereas her husband was short and round, Wilma Beck was tall and reed thin. Dressed in homespun muslin of a nondescript brown shade, she reached up to tuck a loose strand of white hair into the small chignon on the nape of her neck. "I guess you're ready to go to your rooms. I'll have Jonah bring up the hot water for your bath. The tub's already up there."

"Thank you, Mrs. Beck," Chase said, "but I won't be staying. I'm going to put my saddlebags in my room, and then I'm leaving."

"Know what time you'll be returning, sir?" she asked. "So's I can have the water hot for your bath?"

"Don't worry about the water, Mrs. Beck. I probably won't be returning tonight."

Although Chase's decision not to remain was rather abrupt—especially after all that Mr. Beck had been through this evening on account of the major—Wilma didn't question him. As long as he paid in cash and in advance, she quietly tolerated the Yankee.

"What about your clean clothes?" she asked.

"Shall I put them in your room while you're gone?"

"That's all right," Chase answered. "Just leave them outside the door in the morning. I won't need them before." He also needed to get word to Celeste not to send the girl since he was leaving. "Is Mr. Beck in?"

"He is, but he's out back at the woodshed right now. Can I do something for you?"

"Tell him to cancel my plans for this evening."

"I will, sir," she answered and walked toward the kitchen. Her hand on the door, she stopped and turned. "Does this mean you're going to want a refund on your money, sir?"

Chase didn't stop as he walked toward the curved stairwell. Over his shoulder he said, "I'll talk with Mr. Beck about it later, ma'am."

Before Chase's boot hit the bottom stair, a woman, without so much as a glance in his direction, haughtily sailed past him. The fragrance of her perfume—light and airy, a breath of springtime—lingered to tantalize his nostrils; her gown brushed against his legs, and he was taunted by the proximity of her.

The woman stood in front of the counter. As if she were waiting for someone, she kept glancing at the door, the light from the overhead lamp glowing in her golden hair—the most beautiful hair Chase had ever seen. It looked like spun gold. Unconsciously he started toward her. Then something outside the room caught her attention, and she turned toward the door but didn't move in the direction. Chase stopped walking when a man entered the lobby and headed directly to the woman. His gaze returned to the woman to see the expectant look on her face when the man neared her.

Chase was bitterly disappointed.

Chapter Three

Dazed, Elizabeth watched the stranger approach. He reminded her of Johnny. Not the moustache, but the thick blond hair and the trim physique. He wore a black coat and gray trousers tucked into knee-high boots. A holstered revolver, hanging low, rested on each thigh. As he neared she realized he didn't look like her brother at all; it was the expression in his eyes that reminded her of Johnny. They were warm brown eyes that laughed . . . like Johnny's did before the war.

"Miss Barrett," the man said when he stood in front of her. "I'm Blake Lowell. I believe you're expecting me."

"Yes." Elizabeth was truly amazed. When he talked, he even sounded a great deal like Johnny.

"I believe you're going to Mrs. Gladewater's," Blake drawled, openly amused at her scrutiny.

"Oh . . . oh yes!" Elizabeth blushed when she saw the laughter in his eyes and realized she had been staring. "I'm sorry," she apologized, "I didn't mean to stare, but you remind me so much of my brother."

"And I thought it was my good looks," Blake teased.

"Quite possibly that, too," Elizabeth added, a twinkle in her eyes.

"If you're ready, Miss Barrett," Blake said, "we'll be on our way."

"Well, to be perfectly honest, sir, I'm not really ready, but this is a situation that didn't seem to honor my sentiments at all," Elizabeth said. "So it's more like ready or not, Captain Lowell."

Lowell laughed. "I can tell you've been talking with the Becks and while I appreciate their referring to me by my title. I'd appreciate it if you'd call me, Blake, ma'am. That's what I go by. The captain was a long, long time ago." He settled his hat on his head.

"When was that . . . Blake?" Elizabeth asked. "The war?"

"No not the war," he replied. "I served in the Texas Light Cavalry, but around here the captain stems from the fifteen years I spent as a Texas Ranger." He grinned—an infectious gesture that demanded a response from Elizabeth. "Now I'm just plain Blake. So ready or not it's time for us to be on our way."

"While I'm not at all happy about being evicted from one hotel at eight o'clock in the evening and having to go out in this weather to another place, I'm much less happy about being evicted so a Yankee can have my rooms."

"Well, ma'am," Blake said, "I can understand exactly how you feel. I share the same sentiment toward Yankees myself."

Elizabeth laughed softly and added, "But since I must evacuate the premises, traveling in a buggy is much more preferable to walking and carrying a huge trunk."

Their low laughter, Elizabeth's musical trill and the man's deep baritone, drifted over to taunt Chase, who was still standing on the lower stairs watching them. He wished he could hear their conversation, but they were too far away and were talking in low tones.

"It's kind of you, Blake, to get out in weather like this and take me to Mrs. Gladewater's."

Blake stared into her face and admitted, "I wish it were kindness that prompted my actions, Miss Barrett, but it wasn't. You see, I'm an improvised ex-Confederate soldier in search of work, and Mr. Beck paid me." His blue eyes twinkled. "Mr. Beck said you were beautiful and had I known he was telling the truth, I would have done it out of the kindness of my heart."

"Thank you for being honest," Elizabeth said, "but I don't think money alone enticed you out in weather like this, Mr. — Blake."

No, ma'am, it really wasn't money alone. I was curious to meet the woman who created such a problem here at Beck's House. He described you as a real southern lady."

"From the sound of your accent," Elizabeth said, "I think perhaps I'm talking to a real southern gentleman."

"Southern I am, but gentleman I'm not so sure about, Miss Barrett. The war has made me redefine many words that used to be standard to my vocabulary. That's one I haven't quite resolved yet. But I am Blake Randolph Lowell from Savannah, Georgia."

Elizabeth smiled at him. "Elizabeth Rose Barrett of Rose Plantation out from New Orleans, sir. I'm so glad to make your acquaintance."

Elizabeth's words warmed Blake, and he stared into her uplifted face. The slamming of a door in another part of the building jarred him. "Now, ma'am," he said, reluctantly breaking the spellbinding moment, "if you're ready, we'll be on our way." His hand lightly cupped Elizabeth's elbow and he guided her out of the hotel onto the porch. He assisted her onto the buggy; then he loaded her trunk and swung Jefferson aboard.

Curious about the woman, Chase took a few steps and ducked his head in order to look through the door at the waiting buggy. A glowing lantern illuminated a bronze engraved name plate: *Le*

Grande Casino. Evidently the woman was one of Celeste's girls. The man most certainly didn't look like a driver? What then? A customer? Chase mulled the question over as he watched the carriage disappear down the street; then he slowly turned, walked across the lobby and up the stairs to his suite.

Quite suddenly he felt alone, very alone. Strange that he should feel disappointed because the woman was a whore.

"This is the second time the Union payroll has been stolen in the past six months." Phil Sheridan sat opposite Chase around a large, round reading table in front of the window. "God only knows I can't spread my men any thinner. We just don't have the manpower to patrol the entire line of frontier." Almost as if he were talking to himself rather than to Chase, he muttered, "Morale is low; the men are ready to get back home to peacetime living. If they don't get their pay, we're going to have more problems on our hands. As if we don't have enough with the Indians and the Mexicans."

"Sir," Chase said, leaning forward in his chair, "do you think perhaps these robberies on our payrolls could be masterminded in Mexico?"

"Dammit, Daniel," Sheridan exploded, his fist coming down on the desk. "I listened to that for two days in Austin. Don't get started on that

Bainbridge nonsense again. Nothing's happened to change my mind."

"Then it ought to have, sir," Chase answered stiffly, "All these robberies following the same pattern, sir. And according to every report, the thefts are carried out with military precision."

"Why shouldn't they be carried out with such precision?" Sheridan countered. "Nearly every male of age fought on one side or the other during the war. And here in Texas the war is far from being over. You agree, Major?"

Chase nodded. While he was in complete agreement with the general, he wasn't going to be sidetracked into discussing the present political climate of the state. "With regard to the outlaws, sir," he said, "look how easily they disappear, as if they're swallowed into the earth. No sign or trace of them. No one ever sees them. Somehow they've got to be slipping back into Mexico."

"I'll grant they're taking refuge in Mexico," Sheridan conceded, "but I don't believe Roswell Bainbridge is still alive. Still less do I believe his army officers are building up a massive outlaw ring." Sheridan sighed deeply, tiredly. "Despite what I think, you're going to persist in believing this, aren't you?"

"Yes, sir," Chase responded.

"Damn those orders," Sheridan exclaimed.

"Now it's more than orders," Chase said, thinking about Terry. "Now it's personal."

"I know how you feel, Chase, but there's nothing we can do but wait." Sheridan stood. "Now, why don't you go out and get yourself a drink?"

"I want to be here when you receive word about Terry," Chase answered.

"Tell me where you'll be, and I promise to send you word the minute I hear something."

Chase smiled grimly. "I'll be back at Beck's House, sir."

Thirty minutes later Chase returned to his rooms. Long strides carried him across the lobby and by the unattended desk. He knew Mrs. Beck was close by; he could hear her voice coming from the kitchen, but he didn't detour to let her know of his arrival.

In his rooms he closed the door and walked into the bedroom to stand for just a moment and gaze at the painting above the mantle. After scrutinizing it from a distance for a few minutes, he sat down on the edge of the bed to pull off his boots and socks. As he unbuttoned his shirt and slipped out of it, he returned to the fireplace.

He reached out, and with his index finger traced the name of the caption on the gold frame: Portrait of Love. Then he looked at the name in the corner: Daniel. Was that his mother's name or the name of the man whom she loved?

As if in a trance, he stared at the beautiful landscape her gifted hands had created when she was pregnant with him. It was the same; always, yet, never was it the same. Every time he thought he had each line, each shade of color committed to memory, he returned to find a new line and a more subtle shade of color. His eyes moved over the exquisite details: the man, the budding azalea bushes that lined the brook, the pink honeysuckles, the dogwood trees in full bloom.

Inevitably it was the man who drew Chase's attention. With a wistful longing in his eyes his gaze returned to him. He touched a lock of golden brown hair that fluttered in the breeze. The man was so real that Chase sometimes felt as if he were about to step out of the painting.

Some time later, he took a cold bath and dried off, but he didn't dress. Wrapping a towel around his midsection, he gathered his soiled clothes, put them in the basket Mrs. Beck provided, and placed both the basket and his boots in the hall as was his custom when staying at Beck's House. In the morning in their place he would find his clean clothes and polished boots. Locking the door, Chase returned to the bedroom. As he walked to the dresser to get a cigar, he draped the towel over the nearest chair. When he returned to the bed, he fluffed the pillows and propped himself up to smoke awhile. As he listened to the steady patter of rain on the tin roof and the occasional blast of thunder, his thoughts wandered from Terry to the strange woman he saw in the lobby, to his return, to San Felipe Springs on the Mexican border, . . .

back to the beautiful woman he had seen in the lobby. Finally he put his cigar out and stretched out, allowing the familiar sounds of the storm to lull him into near sleep.

Elizabeth stood in front of the suite she and Jefferson had shared earlier in the day before Mr. Beck had removed them. Strange how circumstances changed one's feelings and actions, she thought. Earlier she had felt right at home in these two rooms; now, she felt self-conscious. Even though Mrs. Beck had given her the keys and permission to enter the rooms in search of her writing case, Elizabeth was uncomfortable. But she couldn't waste any more time than was necessary. Blake was waiting for her outside in the rain.

She hadn't realized she left her writing case behind until she was unpacking her clothes at Mrs. Gladewater's home several hours after she arrived. She was surely glad Blake had stayed for a long visit after supper. When she told him about her case and its sentimental value, he had insisted on returning her to Beck's House immediately so that she could get it.

She twisted the key in the lock and pushed open the door to step into the room. The blaze in the fireplace had died to embers which didn't cast enough light into the room for her to see clearly. Moving across the parlor, she reached for the lamp that hung on the wall and extracted a match from the tin container that hung next to it. She struck one, the acrid smell of sulphur permeating the room and lingering longer than did the bright explosion of light. She lit the lamp, and holding it in her hand, moved toward the fireplace.

Abruptly Chase sat up on the bed and sniffed a time or two. He smelled sulphur, but he hadn't used a match to light the cigar. Where was the odor coming from? he wondered. The walls were thin, he reasoned; it could be coming from any one of the rooms on the second floor.

But Chase was wary. Life spent in a foundling's home had taught him to be prepared for any situation, especially the worst. War had reinforced all the lessons learned during childhood. Quietly his feet touched the floor. Instinctively, he reached for his breeches; then he remembered: *His uniform was in the hall.* He knew someone was in the adjacent room; his sixth sense—that sense of survival—assured him of that. He didn't take the time to rummage through the wardrobe for clothes; he grabbed the towel from the back of the chair and wrapped it about his midsection. With a stealth and grace born of years of experience, he silently crossed the room and pulled the revolver from his holster.

His fingers closed over the knob and he opened the door to see a small figure, bundled up in the swirling folds of a hooded cloak, standing beneath the lamp. Water tip-tapped to the floor to puddle around her feet.

"Who are you and what the hell do you think you're doing in here?"

Embarrassed at having been caught in his apartment, Elizabeth had no thought but to obey the man's question. "I'm Elizabeth Barrett," she said, flinging off her hood. "I'm here to—" She said no more. The expression of wonderment that replaced the anger on Chase's face stopped her short.

Without her answering, Chase knew who she was and what she wanted. This was the same woman he'd seen in the lobby earlier. He'd never forget her beautiful hair; it was the color of winter sunshine. The lamplight lingered on it, spinning the yellow strands into pure gold. The length was coiled into a knot, but loose curls formed a natural halo for the woman's face. Her eyes were framed with thick, curling lashes; they were so innocent as to be provocative. She seemed almost angelic but couldn't be. He recognized her as the whore from Madame Doucet's place.

"Well, hello, Elizabeth Barrett," Chase drawled. "Although I wasn't expecting you, I'm glad you're here."

Elizabeth's gaze moved over Chase's near naked body—not the first she'd seen, having been a nurse—but this one was different. It was five feet ten inches of muscle, deeply tanned from exposure to the sun. It was vital and alive.

Elizabeth licked her dry lips and said, "Really, I didn't just barge in." Her face was so hot with embarrassment, she wondered that it wasn't glowing like the embers in the fireplace. "Mrs. Beck gave me the keys and permission to enter your rooms—"

Mrs. Beck hadn't given Cedric his message after all, Chase thought. She must have been worried about his demanding a refund. While a part of him was irritated at the landlady's underhandedness, another was glad. He needed a woman tonight; he needed one badly . . . and just anyone would have done. This woman would more than do. Already he could feel his groin tightening.

"You don't have to explain why you're here," he said, his voice soft and seductive. "I know." Chase balanced his cigar on the mantle and laid the revolver next to it.

"You do?" Elizabeth asked in surprise and wondered how Mrs. Beck had managed to send word up so quickly.

"I do." When he looked at her again, a smile curved his lips, transforming his chiseled features into dark, rugged handsomeness. For every step he took nearer her, she took one backwards until the wall stopped her.

Chase didn't see the fear in her eyes. He wasn't consciously aware of her resistance. His thoughts centered on the needs of his body, on the desire to forget his sorrow, both his needs and forgetfulness

59

to be fulfilled through the pleasure of her body. His hands slid beneath the swirling folds of the cloak to clamp about the tiny waist. He dragged her into his arms, his mouth moving unerringly toward hers.

On her cheeks Elizabeth felt the warmth of his breath and the faint odor of whiskey mixed with the expensive blend of aromatic tobacco. She shivered with fear and dodged the man's lips, twisting her face to the side. Her hands moved to her waist, and her fingers gripped into the man's flesh as she tried to free herself. Although his clasp wasn't painful, his grip didn't loosen.

"I've waited a long time for a woman like you," Chase murmured thickly, his lips touching her neck. "I like one who has spirit."

The words were so reminiscent of Emery Watkins, Elizabeth was instantly transported to the painful past. She no longer saw the stranger's face. She saw a fat face with watery blue eyes, contorted in his lust. She saw the forehead and upper lip beaded in sweat; she smelt the horrible stench of his body odor. She opened her mouth to scream, but she couldn't scream. Never again could she scream. If she screamed, Johnny would come . . . and Watkins would . . . if she hadn't screamed Johnny would still be alive. Elizabeth was suffocating. Again she was being pressed into the darkness of a linen closet by an ugly, obese body. The room was closing in on her.

She doubled her hands into fists, but she couldn't hit the man. His arms, like manacles, were strapped around her body to lock her flailing arms between them. His long, muscular frame pinned her to the wall. She tried to kick him, but her feet tangled in the cloak. The man's hand caught her twisting face and held it still. At last his mouth captured hers in a burning kiss.

Chase groaned low in his throat. It had been a long time since he wanted a woman as he wanted this one, and for the moment he cared not that she was a prostitute. As long as she was brazen in her advances and responses, was knowledgeable about the needs of men, and was willing to see that these needs were consummately satisfied, he could pretend that she was all she looked to be—an innocent and demure lady. He would enjoy a night of fantasy—a night of forgetfulness.

He lifted his face from hers to murmur thickly, "Dear, God, Elizabeth Barrett, I'm glad you came. Now it's time to go to bed." He smiled. "Time you get what you came here for. Time you give me what I'm wanting and needing."

Elizabeth felt his arms go slack around her and she pushed out of the embrace. To keep from falling to the floor, she flung out her arm, her hand curling around the end of the mantle. Vaguely she was aware of his complete nudity, the towel having slipped from his waist. Elizabeth felt the cold metal of the revolver, and her fear turned into cold resolve. Her fingers curled around the grip and she lifted it. She leveled the gun at Chase, but she saw Emery. She had the second chance for which she had prayed so many times.

Staring down the wrong end of the barrel, Chase's ardor quickly evaporated. As he backed away, he looked into the woman's face, her eyes glassy and distant. "Miss Barrett," he said quietly, "please be careful. That weapon is loaded."

"I should hope so," Elizabeth returned. The revolver—pointed directly at Chase's heart—never moved.

Perplexed by the situation—an entirely new one for Chase—he shook his head and took a step toward the mantle to get his cigar. When he heard the soft click as Elizabeth cocked the revolver, he stopped and held his hands up.

"Stop in your tracks," Elizabeth said coolly, "or I'll shoot you. I have no intention of being raped."

"Raped!" Chase exclaimed. My God! This was the first time he'd been accused of rape—and by a whore! "What is this?" he asked, his eyes narrowing. "A play to get more money?"

Elizabeth's eyes raked contemptuously over his frame. "You don't have enough money to buy me."

Chase laughed bitterly, at himself, at the situation. "The irony of the entire situation, Madam, is that I've already bought you. You're mine for the evening. You know that when you let yourself into my rooms so why this act?"

The man's words left a bitter taste in Elizabeth's mouth, but she refused to give way to shame or mortification. Instead she allowed anger to the forefront of her mind; it was her safest defense.

"Had I known you were in the room," she replied, controlling her temper and using it to her advantage, "I would never have entered. I'm not so desperate for a man or for money, sir, that I must have a man who insists on raping me."

The barbed accusation slapped Chase in the face. He was confused. "Look, lady, you're the one who—" He broke off to stare at her in confusion. She didn't look like a whore. She didn't have their worldliness. He raked his hands through his hair. "What are you doing in my apartment?" he asked.

"As I was about to tell you when you attacked me," Elizabeth said, "I came for my writing case."

Chase was prepared for any answer but this. Disbelief written on his countenance, he could only stare at her.

"I left it when I was here earlier," she explained. "Not knowing that you were going to be in town, Mr. Beck let me rent your room for the weekend," Elizabeth continued. "When I was packing my luggage this afternoon so Jefferson and I could move, I forgot my writing case."

"Where did you leave it?" he asked. When Elizabeth pointed at the fireplace, he turned his head, his gaze brushing the mantle from one end to the other. He turned mocking eyes on her. "Do you think you got your fireplaces mixed up? Or maybe you forgot which room you were in? Or maybe you were concentrating too much on pleasing Jefferson?"

A smile glimmered on Elizabeth's lips. "I admit I was concentrating on pleasing Jefferson, I concentrate on pleasing any man who buys my pleasures, sir, but I was in this room and I did leave my case in here."

"Look, lady," Chase said impatiently, "I don't know what's going on, but I'm tired, and I don't intend to give you one more cent no matter how good in bed you might think yourself to be. Now get out."

His words incensed Elizabeth as well as embarrassed her, but she'd never give him the satisfaction of knowing how deeply he'd touched her. "If you find my writing case, please leave it with Mr. or Mrs. Beck," she said. "It has great value to me. It was a gift from—a special man in my life, and I'd like to have it back." She turned and moved toward the door.

"My gun," Chase said. "I'd like to have it back. It wasn't given to me by a special woman in my life, but it sure as hell has great value to me."

"I'll leave it outside in the hall," Elizabeth replied, her hand curling over the door knob.

"By the way," Chase said as he looked at her retreating figure, "I want you to know that I'm going to lodge a complaint with Madame Doucet."

Elizabeth turned and looked at him blankly. "Don't you mean Mrs. Beck?" she asked.

"Oh, no," Chase returned. "I understand the Beck's very well. They speak the same language called money. But I will have a reckoning with your employer and you'll soon find yourself out on the street without a job."

Elizabeth's hand dropped from the knob, and she turned to lean her back against the door. "I don't know a Madame Doucet, and I have no employer save myself."

She sounded sincere, and — his eyes skimmed her disheveled form again — she had never looked like a whore. Still Chase was puzzled. "But you were traveling in her carriage," he said, "and Beck said —"

"The carriage belongs to Mr. Lowell, my companion," Elizabeth said, then perversely added, "for the evening."

"Aren't you the — didn't Mr. Beck arrange for you to come here tonight to my room?"

"No. Thinking you were gone for the evening and not wanting to take the time to search for my writing case herself, Mrs. Beck gave me the keys to your room."

"Oh, my God!" Chase muttered. She was telling the truth. What a mess!

Never had he wished for clothes more.

Suddenly embarrassed by his nakedness, Chase picked up the towel and wrapped it around his midsection. With a modicum of dignity restored, he strode to the wardrobe in the bedroom and jerked open the doors to pull out a pair of trousers. Feeling less vulnerable, Chase returned to the fireplace in the parlor and reached for his cigar which he jabbed into the corner of his mouth and chomped down.

Jefferson! she had said. *She and Jefferson were sharing these rooms. Who the hell was Jefferson and why the hell do I want to know . . . or care? She was traveling with Mr. Lowell, her companion for the evening, and thought the carriage belonged to him. Who was Lowell?* She might not be the whore meant for him, and she may not work for Madame Doucet, but she had too many men in her life to be a lady!

Chase moved to the table and poured himself a whiskey. He needed one. "Maybe you left your writing case in the bedroom," he said gruffly. "Check in there; then get out of here." He quaffed the drink in one swallow, thankful for the fire that burned down his throat and took his thought off the wanting that was blazing in his body.

The revolver still in hand, Elizabeth walked into the bedroom to stop immediately inside the threshold. Her gaze inadvertently went to the bathtub—such a personnel, intimate object. A damp wash cloth hung over one side; the towel that had so recently been draped around his body, around the most private and sensuous part of his body, was draped haphazardly over the back of the nearby chair. On the dresser across the room sat a razor and shaving mug. The essence of Chase Daniel filled the room.

"Well?" Chase's quiet question seemed to mock Elizabeth.

Slowly she raised her head to encounter his reflection in the mirror. The lines of his face were implacable and sharp. His eyes were steel blades. Indolently he leaned against the doorjamb and folded his arms over his chest. For a moment their gazes locked together, and Elizabeth saw an unidentifiable and frightening emotion swirl in the depths of Chase's eyes.

"Did you find what you were looking for?"

He broke visual contact with her and deliberately let his gaze slowly stray from the tub, to the towel where his eyes lingered, forcing her to remember the feel of his arms around her, the feel of his body against hers, before they finally went to the bed and the rumpled pillows.

"No," Elizabeth felt like there were hundreds of butterflies fluttering in her stomach, and this time it wasn't fear of the man, "I don't see it anywhere. Perhaps I didn't leave it here after all or maybe someone picked it up when they cleaned the room after I left." She forced her boneless legs to move and walked toward the door. "I'll leave now. Thank you for allowing me to look."

When she stood in the living room, Chase said,

"I'm sorry about—about—my mistake." He didn't quite know how to apologize to a woman for having taken her for a whore. "May I see you home?"

"No, thank you," Elizabeth answered quietly. "Mr. Lowell is waiting for me." She wanted him to misinterpret her statement. "I'll leave your gun outside in the hall," she said, easing out the door.

Chase returned to the window, and using one finger he drew the gauzy curtain aside to strain into the night- and rain-darkened street below. Surely enough, the carriage from *Le Grande* Casino was sitting in front of the hotel; the man was waiting for her. Jefferson this afternoon. Lowell tonight. Oh, hell, what did he care. He probably wouldn't see her again anyway.

Without looking back, Elizabeth fled Chase Daniel's room. Down the corridor and stairs, across the lobby, she ran to the safety of the waiting buggy. But she hadn't escaped Chase Daniel. She knew he was standing in the window watching her; she felt the heat of his gaze on her back. As Blake assisted her in boarding, she looked up at the second story. She saw Chase, looking down at her. Their eyes caught and held.

"Did you find your writing case, ma'am?" Blake asked, breaking the spell.

"No," Elizabeth murmured, reluctantly dropping her head. She straightened her skirt and petticoats around herself and burrowed her hands in to the deep folds of her cloak. She smiled brightly and said, "I must have made a mistake about leaving it. I'm sorry I had you return for nothing."

"Quite all right," Blake returned. "I've been doing some thinking while you were gone. I was wondering if you'd mind letting Jefferson work for me tomorrow?"

On edge with the discovery that she was riding in a whore's carriage, Elizabeth said, "What kind of job are you offering him, Mr. Lowell?"

"Grooming horses at Muldoon's Livery Stable," he replied.

"Is that job you work at when you're not working for Madame Celeste Doucet?" Elizabeth asked, having put all the pieces of the puzzle together.

Blake was a little surprised and quite a bit disappointed that Elizabeth knew he was connected with Celeste Doucet. He waited a few seconds before he answered. "The war has forced many of us into trades that we were not trained for, Miss Barrett. Although some would say my career is beneath the dignity of a southern gentleman, I am, at least, earning an extremely comfortable living."

"What about the Rangers?"

"Notice I said that I'm earning an extremely comfortable living, Miss Barrett. The Rangers don't earn much money, they're never comfortable, and their life span is extremely short." He turned his head and looked at Elizabeth. "I'm a part owner in the *Le Grande* Casino. All the gaming tables and equipment on the first two floors are mine. Celeste runs the rest of the operations." He guided the horses around a large mud puddle.

Although the rain had eased, the wind was blowing harder. Elizabeth pulled her cloak more closely around herself and closed her eyes against the biting chill.

"A group of black soldiers is staying at Celeste's place tonight," Blake continued, "and I've agreed to groom their horses in the morning for them. I thought maybe Jefferson would like to earn some money. I wouldn't expose him to anything indecent or immoral."

"If he wants to," Elizabeth answered, "I'll let him help you."

At the plantation Jefferson was accustomed to running errands in order to earn extra money, and now that he had the opportunity to work, Elizabeth couldn't very well refuse. She smiled fondly as she thought about his growing account at the bank.

Silence enveloped the carriage as the team slowly made its way across town for the second time. Elizabeth was saddened by the loss of her writing case, but at the moment that was a secondary worry and grief. Much to her dismay her thoughts were totally consumed with the stranger at Beck's House.

She didn't even know his name. Yet, she knew his body. She knew the feel of his mouth on hers.

She had shared an intimacy with him that she had shared with no other man, but she didn't know his name. His face was firmly etched into her memory, each line, angle, and curve. She remembered how the muscles and contours felt beneath her hands; she remembered the feel of soft black chest hair against her palms. His soap-clean body odor filled her nostrils.

Elizabeth was glad when finally they arrived at their destination. Blake left with the promise to return bright and early the next morning. After Elizabeth had changed into her nightgown, she blew out the candle on the night table and scurried beneath the covers. Tired as she was, she couldn't go to sleep. The strange man whom she met at Beck's House came back to haunt her.

She rose, slipped into her dressing gown, and walked to the rocker in front of the fireplace. Sitting down, she stared into the blaze, but she didn't see the dancing red-orange flames. Clearly she saw the fixity of blue eyes and sharp lines and angles of a masculine face, softened only when the man smiled or laughed. Again she heard the deep, mellow timbre of his voice when he promised to give her pleasure; she shivered.

The thunder clapped, the sound reverberating through the room. As if in a trance, Elizabeth stood and walked to the window. She drew the curtain aside and watched the bolts of lightning as they majestically danced across the sky time after time. She closed her eyes and leaned her forehead against the chilled window pane. The thunder claps heralded a renewal of the rain, but the streaks of lightening reminded her of the electrical current that flowed between her and ... the nameless man.

He was only a stranger; she had only been with him for minutes; yet, he was having a profound effect on her emotions. She had felt loneliness before and had learned to deal with it; not so the hunger that this man had stirred up in her body and the ache of unfulfillment.

Chapter Four

The military doctor, wearing a long white jacket over his uniform, sat beside Captain Terrence Lee's bed at the Menger Hotel. Across the room at the window, Chase stood, watching dawn erase the morning gray from the sky. San Antonio was coming alive; yet, the only sound to be heard in the room was Terry's labored breathing. The hours had crept by since Chase had arrived at his friend's side.

Chase walked around the room finally to stop at the foot of the bed and look down at the sallow face, a mere shadow of the vital, energetic man Chase had known for the majority of his life. Perspiration plastered straight black hair to his head and face. When the bloodshot eyes were opened, they were blank and unseeing. Now they were closed and sunk in blackened sockets.

Chase asked, "Do you think he'll make it, Jasper?"

Hilton Jasper raked his fingers down his thin, beard-stubbled jaws. "Don't hold out too much hope," he said. "Stomach wounds are always critical, and this one is worse than most. Besides, he's lost a lot of blood. He shouldn't have insisted that he be brought here."

Hilton stood and stretched his wiry body. "God, I'm tired. These chairs aren't made to sit in." He walked around the room a few times, stopped, and asked, "You going to stay here?" When Chase nodded, he said, "Good. I'm going to go get a pot of coffee and two cups." At the door he said, "I'll be right back."

Again Chase nodded and moved to sit in the vacated chair and stared at Terry. Instead of seeing the man, however, Chase saw the wiry youth who had been closer than a brother to him. A grin tugged Chase's lips as he thought of all the pranks the two of them had played on the girls at the home and on Aunt Ida. Tears stung his eyes when he thought of their childhood vow never to be separated.

When Terry began to toss restlessly, Chase wrung a washrag out and wiped his face. "Hang in there, old boy," he murmured. "You're a fighter. Remember you're the one who taught me how to fight." Laughing to keep from crying, Chase said, "And you're the one who bet me I wouldn't tie Mary Jane's pig tails together. What a whipping Aunt Ida gave me, and you hid behind the woodpile and laughed at me."

Quietly Chase talked, recounting childhood memories to his friend, talking about anything that came to mind. About thirty minutes later Terry's eyes opened, and he blinked several times. He tried to move, but his body was numb.

"Chase?" he whispered in a weak voice. His vision was bleary and he was unable to focus on the man who sat beside him. "Is that you, Chase? I thought I heard you talking to me."

Chase caught the grappling hand. "It's me," he said.

"Bainbridge," Terry gasped, a spasm of pain causing his grip on Chase's hand to tighten. "I'm sure the outlaws are Bainbridge's men. Military." He coughed and spit up blood which Chase wiped away. "I heard them—" Terry began again but had to stop to draw in several large gulps of air. "— heard them refer to the colonel."

"Don't talk now, Terry," Chase said.

"Got to, Chase. The man . . . who shot . . . me. I had the strangest . . . impression that he recognized me."

Chase smiled. "You were wearing your uniform, Terry?"

Terry tried to laugh but the sound was a death gurgle deep in his chest. "Not the uniform," he whispered, exerting all the strength he had to push up on one elbow and jab his finger against his chest. "Me, Chase. I think he knew me personally, and he thought I recognized him."

Chase eased Terry back down and said, "We'll talk about it when you're better. Not now."

A sad smile pulled the corner of Terry's mouth. "I think that I'm as better as I'm going to get in this world."

Chase leaned forward and pushed the moist hair off Terry's forehead. "Don't talk like that. Remember, we're brothers for life."

"Yeah, I remember." Terry's eyes caught and held Chase's. "Chase, he knew me." He closed his eyes and rolled his head to the side. "Dear God," he murmured, "I wish I could place him. He's the key to this entire puzzle."

"We have another key," Chase said. "A prisoner. One of the outlaws. He's being held at the jail right now."

"Good." Terry sighed. "You question him, Chase."

"We are," Chase assured the captain.

"You, Chase," Terry insisted weakly. "You . . . question . . . him . . ." His words died upon his lips as he lapsed into unconsciousness.

Chase sat in the chair beside the bed until he heard the light kicks on the bottom of the door. He hastened across the room and let Hilton Jasper in.

"Had my hand full," the doctor explained, carrying the metal pot and two cups to the table. "Would have been back sooner but I wanted to brew the coffee myself. Have my own special way of doing it." He looked over his shoulder at Terry. "Any change?"

"He came to briefly."

"Say anything important?" Jasper asked as he poured coffee into the sups.

Chase walked to the window and lifted a hand to rub the back of his neck. "Nothing I didn't already know," he answered.

"Drink a cup of this," Jasper invited. "This is real coffee, guaranteed to put hair on your chest."

Chase took the coffee and unaware of the taste, gulped it down. When Terry thrashed on the bed, he turned to look at his friend; he thought about Terry's insisting that he question the prisoner himself. His boots snapped on the floor as he moved to the table and set his cup down.

"Hilton, if Terry rouses, tell him I've gone to the jail to question the prisoner."

"Already been done," Hilton responded. "Sheridan already had the report."

"I figured so, but I want to question the man myself."

Hilton shrugged. "Whatever you say, Major. I'm just the physician." He leaned over to refill his cup with the steaming coffee.

Chase quickly covered the distance between the Menger and the jail, known as the Bat Cave. He entered the two-story building, spoke with the deputy on duty and was soon ushered into the prisoner's cell. The young man—no more than

77

twenty-one or two — lay on one of the two bunks in the narrow enclosure. His eyes were closed, but Chase knew he wasn't asleep. The body was too alert, ready to respond at the least provocation.

"If you don't mind, Mr. Addison," he said to the deputy, "I'd like to visit with the prisoner . . . in the cell, and alone."

"He's mighty dangerous," Floyd Addison replied. "Killed two soldiers and shot another one in the guts. They don't expect the soldier to live."

"I know," Chase said. "Still I'd like to talk with him alone."

Just like a damn Yankee! Didn't have a lick of sense! Addison nodded and unlocked the cell to permit Chase entry. Then he relocked it and withdrew from the room, leaving Chase and the outlaw alone. As soon as the metal door clanged shut, Chase sat down on the opposite bunk.

"I'm Chase Daniel," he said, reaching into his breast pocket. "Major Chase Daniel of the United States Cavalry." He pulled out a cigar and said, "Care for a smoke?"

"Don't smoke," the man replied, never opening his eyes. "And I don't talk."

"I really didn't expect you to," Chase returned calmly, delving for a match which he struck against the rusted metal bars of the cell, "but telling me your name isn't going to hurt."

"Rod," the man hissed irritably. "Rod Everett."

"Glad to meet you, Rod. Where you from?"

"Chalmette . . . out of New Orleans."

After several puffs on the cigar, Chase said, "You know you'll probably hang for murder."

"Probably so," Rod returned with calm acceptance. "But the way I see it, I didn't murder nobody. I just killed me two or three damn Yankees. Nothing they wouldn't do if given the chance."

Chase crossed his legs and leaned back on the bunk. "Don't guess anybody informed you that the war's over."

Everett bolted up, and his feet thumped to the floor. "This war ain't never going to be over, mister, until we've killed every one of you." He walked to the door. "Now why the hell don't you get out of here and leave me alone?"

"If you cooperate with me," Chase said, "I can save your life."

"Well, blue-belly," the man turned to sneer at Chase, "I ain't cooperating with you cause I don't want your help." He laughed. "And I ain't worried about dying."

"You think the colonel is going to free you?" Chase asked casually, his eyes leveled on the ashes at the end of the cigar.

Color left Rod's face, and he peered suspiciously at Chase. "Don't know anything about a colonel," he finally spat.

Chase saw the man mask the nervousness that nonetheless edged the corners of his lips. He had struck a tender chord. "The soldier you shot in the guts, the one who's alive," Chase watched Rod closely, "he recognized you just as you recognized him."

"Don't know what you're talking about," Rod snapped and wrapped his fingers around the bars of the door and started to shake it. He yelled to the top of his voice, "Come get this man out of my cell before I kill him."

Addison poked his head around the door. "Ready to come out, Major?" he called.

"Give me a few more minutes," Chase answered. He dropped the cigar to the floor, stood, and twisted the toe of his boot on it. "If you decide to cooperate, send for me. I promise I'll save your life."

"Yeah, I'll just bet you will."

Rod stood clinging to the metal bars a long time after the door slammed behind the major. He could feel the hangman's noose around his neck already. Damn Bainbridge! He didn't intend to get him out of jail. He was expendable like all the others. But he had to get out.

Rod slowly shuffled back to the cot and sat down. He had to get back to Mexico. Vanessa's life depended on it. If Bainbridge learned that she was going to escape to the United States and give evidence against him, he'd kill her. He wouldn't care that she had been his mistress for the past three years. In that way Bainbridge and Vanessa were alike—they loved only themselves to the exclusion of all others. Knowing this, Rod still loved Vanessa, and he guessed he always would.

Chase was strapping his guns on in the deputy's office when the door opened. He turned to see the driver of the *Le Grande* Casino carriage enter with a large basket in his hands. The man who had been escorting Elizabeth Barrett!

"Howdy, Floyd," Blake said. "Brought you and the prisoner's breakfast."

"Yes, sir, Captain Lowell," Floyd answered, getting up so fast the chair legs grated across the floor. He reached for the basket. "I know I can trust you and Madame Doucet, Captain Lowell, since the sheriff hired you to serve us meals, but you know the rules. I have to check the contents before they go to the prisoners."

"I understand," Blake replied as he gave Chase a cursory glance, turned his back and walked to the window.

At the door Chase stopped and openly stared at Blake Lowell. His clothing was expensive—an embroidered blue shirt and equally fine riding trousers. His weapon belt hung low, and two matched, white-handled revolvers, butt forward, rested in the holsters that were specially built to the contour of his guns. They lacked a top and exposed half the cylinder and all the trigger-guard. This was no errand boy, and the title of Captain clearly indicated that. But captain of what?

As surely and accurately as he was being sized,

Blake Lowell had already measured Chase — and that was a long time ago, in New Orleans during the war. Of course, Daniel wouldn't know him because he'd been in disguise then as a private in the Union army . . . on his last mission for the Confederate Secret Service, but he remembered Daniel.

Whereas Blake respected Chase Daniel, he didn't know that he'd ever like him. Deep down, he knew they were too much alike; he also knew too much lay between them. Each had chosen to walk a different path — one within the law, the other outside it. The recent war had created chasms that would forever separate families and friends. Perhaps the best description of him and Chase Daniel would be that of worthy opponents.

Chase opened the door and walked out of the room. When the door closed behind him, Blake asked, "Was that Major Chase Daniel?"

"Yes, sir, it was," Addison replied, taking out his lunch parcel and shoving the basket toward Blake. "Wanted to question the prisoner about the robbery of the Union pay wagon."

Blake nodded. "Want me to take this to the prisoner while you eat?"

"Well, yes sir," Addison replied, "that would be right nice of you, Captain. But you'll have to be real careful. He's a mean one."

While Addison stretched to the peg behind him for the key ring, Blake untied the holster thongs around his thighs and unbuckled his gun belt which he exchanged for the cell keys.

"Go ahead and enjoy your meal, Floyd," said Blake. "I'll let myself in."

Chase, returning to the deputy's office to leave a message, opened the door in time to hear Blake's remark. "Where the hell do you think you're going?" His voice blazed across the room as he slammed the door and strode across the floor.

A bland expression on his face, Blake lifted the basket in the air. "To give the prisoner his food."

Chase turned to Addison. "Isn't it your job to feed the prisoner and to make sure that maximum security is kept?"

Addison laid his fork down and slowly rose to his feet to glower across the desk at Chase. "Well, sir," he drawled, "I reckon it is, but seeing as how this is Captain Blake Lowell of the Texas Rangers"—an honest assumption on Addison's part, his philosophy being once a ranger, always a ranger, "I don't reckon it's gonna hurt none if he carries the man his food. I did check the basket, Major."

A smug smile pulling his lips, Blake held the basket toward Chase. "Do you want to check it and me?"

Again they exchanged a long, hard look. Finally, Chase shook his head and waved. "Go ahead," he said, then looked at Floyd. He heard the door open and close and knew Blake was in the cell block. "I came back to tell you that if the prisoner should ask for me, send word immediately."

"Okay," Floyd answered absently as he slid down in the chair and attacked his food with hearty appetite.

Angry because the deputy seemed to be ignoring him and his request, Chase said, "Please relay the message to your relief."

His mouth full, Floyd mumbled, "Okay."

Blake's footfalls echoed through the long rectangular room. He stopped in front of the occupied cell. "Brought your breakfast," he said to the man who was feigning sleep.

Rod bounced off the bed to the bars, and his eyes rounded. "Well, you took long enough!"

"Lower your voice," Blake ordered in a cold voice, "or you won't be alive a minute longer."

"Yeah," Rod snarled, "and how do you propose to do that?"

"Like this," Blake replied.

Before Rod knew what had happened Blake's arm snaked through the bars, curled around his neck and pinned him to the door. He felt the sharp point against his stomach and knew Blake Lowell was holding a knife to him.

"A fine damn mess you've gotten us into with your bungling," Blake said. "Killing two Yankees and wounding a third. Just know this, Everett, before I let you give me away and spill information about the colonel, I'll kill you."

"I wasn't." Rod sniffed and backed off. "I just don't like being questioned by them damned Yankees. Droves of 'em. And this last one I don't like, Lowell. God! but his eyes seem to drill into your very soul."

"No, Everett," Blake contradicted, "they don't seem to; they can drill to your very soul. You'd better be extremely careful around Chase Daniel."

"Oh, God!" Everett whined, his fingers curling around the bars of the cell. "Keep him away from me."

Blake unlocked the door and moved into the cell with Everett. "You should have thought of this when you killed the soldier," he said, then asked, "Why did you react so stupidly, Everett? We certainly didn't need all this attention focusing on us right now."

"The two I killed were in self-defense," Rod explained. "Then I looked over and saw the captain. Although I knew he was one of the ones who had been chasing us during the war, I wouldn't have shot him, but he recognized me, Blake. He knew I was one of Bainbridge's men. I had to shoot him."

Blake nodded and watched Everett empty the basket on the bunk and wolf down his breakfast.

His mouth full, Everett asked, "What's the plan for my escape?"

"Don't know," Blake answered. "I haven't received word from the colonel yet."

"It better be soon," the prisoner said, between bites, " 'cause these soldiers are gonna want to hang me real quick and they won't care whether I get a trial or not."

"You should have thought of that before you killed Union soldiers," Blake returned unsympathetically.

"If it comes to that, Lowell," Everett promised, waving a piece of bread through the air, "I'll spill my guts."

"No," Blake said, "you won't spill your guts, Everett, and that's a promise."

The two men exchanged long, meaningful glances, Blake's eyes so dark they looked like polished glass, hard and slicing. Rod Everett tried to outstare Blake, but he couldn't. He finally dropped his head.

"Who's got the strong box?" Rod asked.

"Celeste," Blake replied. "Monday morning I'm taking it to the ranch."

Rod laughed. "You're going to use this to your best advantage, aren't you? You can't wait to take my place in the brigade, can you?"

"Yes, to the first question, and no, to the second," Blake answered.

Rod's laughter turned into a snarl. "I pray to God that Bainbridge refuses to see you, Lowell. I hope you never get to see his face."

"I will," Blake promised quietly.

The door opened and Addison yelled, "Is everything okay down there, Captain?"

"Just fine," Blake returned. "I'm gathering the utensils up now. I'll be out directly." To Rod he said, "We'll have you out of here as soon as possible. If you keep your mouth shut, you'll come out alive. If not, you're a dead man!"

All the way back to the Menger, Chase thought about Blake Lowell. Naturally he was curious about him because he was the man who was with Elizabeth Barrett last evening, but Chase's curiosity was aroused for another more important reason. He intuitively felt as if he knew the man. The shell or recognition was there even though he couldn't quite see the core yet.

He walked through the lobby of the Menger and up the stairs to Terry's room. When he entered, he saw Jasper hovering over the bed. Clustered around him were several other officers, among them Phil Sheridan.

"He's gone," Jasper announced flatly and pulled the sheet over Terry's head.

Chase's boots thudded heavily on the floor as he moved from the door to the bed. He pushed past the officers and yanked the sheet down. For long minutes he stared at the dead form of Captain Terrence Lee. He wasn't aware that all the others melted out of the room, leaving him alone with his friend.

Tears ran down the rugged cheeks. "I'll find Bainbridge and bring him back, Terry. He'll stand trial for all he's done. I promise you."

Chase left the Menger and walked to the nearest funeral parlor where he made arrangements to have Terry's body shipped back to Philadelphia for burial. He knew Aunt Ida—the woman who had reared him and Chase at the foundlings' home—would want to have Terry close by. Now the difficult part came; he had to sit down and write the letter, telling Ida Owens that Terry was dead. Chase had written many such letters during the war, but the task never became any easier.

The letter written and delivered to the soldiers who would accompany the body home, Chase returned to his apartment. His grief was so great he never noticed the beautiful day around him. Not a trace of the storm remained in the sky; the sun, a brilliant orange globe in the eastern sky, was magnificent, the clouds white and fluffy, the sky blue. Even so, the day was brisk and cool, unusually so for April in Texas, and called for a fire.

Bringing his clean clothes in from the hallway, Chase knelt in front of the fireplace to rake the cold ashes aside and stack the kindling. On top he laid the logs. Then he saw a flash of gold as the sunlight reflected off something behind the wood box. Curious, he laid the last piece of wood on the fire and leaned forward to investigate the metallic gleam. Wedged in a crack between the box and the wall he found a black leather writing case. In the bottom right hand corner were gold embossed initials: ERB. Elizabeth Barrett. Lightly rubbing his thumb over the letters, he wondered what the R stood for.

Although it brought little consolation at the moment, Chase realized she had been telling the truth. Her writing case was proof of that. Again he saw the image of the woman whom he'd found in his apartment the evening before, and for the hundredth time he wondered what she was really like.

He felt the warmth of embarrassment climb his face. He had acted like a damned fool. And he was jealous as he could be of the other men in her life—the engimatic Jefferson, the suspicious Blake Lowell. Chase imagined all the fire and passion that he and Elizabeth could have generated, and to think of it being wasted on a man like Lowell!

Chase stood and slapped the black leather against the palm of his hand. Returning Elizabeth's writing case would give him reason to leave the confines of his rooms and he wanted to see her again. A visit with Elizabeth Barrett would satisfy his curiosity and maybe put thoughts of her out of mind. Perhaps it would take his mind off Terry's useless death.

Chase sighed. He'd been too long on the frontier, too long without a woman. That's why he was preoccupied with Elizabeth; that's why he thought she was so outstandingly beautiful. With a shrug he dismissed last night's obsession with the woman. Drink had probably dulled his wits. Surely no woman could be as lovely and desirable as he had thought she was. Yes, he decided, the light of day would cast her entirely different, and he most assuredly wanted to see the difference.

Eager to be on his way, Chase strode into the bedroom and changed clothes—a stripped waistcoat and a black coat to match his gray trousers; a black neckerchief, the tying of which he spent a great deal of time. Entering the lobby, he found the landlord behind the counter.

"Good morning, Major." Cedric stopped shuffling through a stack of papers long enough to look up. "My, my, but you're gussied up this morning. Where are you headed so early?" He took off his spectacles and laid them on top of the papers.

"To Parker's Funeral Parlor," Chase said. At Beck's uplifted brows, he added, "My best friend died last night. I'm sending his body home."

"I'm sorry, sir."

Unable to talk about Terry without a lump forming in his throat, Chase nodded.

"Anything I can do to help?"

"I need someone to take care of the horses," Chase answered briskly. "I doubt the troopers have anything but women on their minds at the present."

"No, worry, sir," Cedric replied with a wave of his hand. "I thought about that and have already taken care of it for you. We figured your men would be needing their rest this morning, so's me and Celeste figured that into her overall cost. She has a young fellow working for her who does grooming when her patrons stay overnight."

"Thank you, Mr. Beck," Chase said, "but I'm not sure I want a young boy to look after our mounts. I had to fight all the way up the General Grant, and only after threatening to reign my commission did I get something better than nags for my troopers."

Chase was truly a cavalryman and as such knew the horse was his not valuable weapon and dearest friend, his most trustworthy companion. In order to be an effective trooper, man had to become one with his mount. This oneness was achieved by living with the animal every day and by recognizing its needs and caring for it. Chase didn't trust his horses to the care of anyone but their owners.

"Don't worry none," Cedric assured him. "Captain Lowell is Madame Doucet's partner, and he assured me he would oversee the job hisself."

"Captain Lowell?" Chase was not a little irritated and puzzled over this. Everywhere he turned he was running into *Captain* Blake Lowell. He knew Lowell was no hackney driver or errand boy, and he certainly wasn't a stable hand. "Who is this man?" he demanded.

"Why, he's Captain Blake Randolph Lowell, sir." Cedric fairly beamed and said proudly. "Captain of the Texas Rangers before the war and served in the

Texas Light Cavalry during the war, sir. Won several medals for distinguished service, sir. He gave you Yanks a run for your money.

"Originally from Georgia," Cedric said, warming to his subject. "His family owned a large plantation, but he decided to find his fortune out west and came to Texas. That was one of our best days, Major. Yes, sir," Cedric ran his hand over his slick head, "I reckon Blake Lowell knows more about guns and knives and horses than any man in Texas. So's don't you worry about them horses," Cedric assured him the second time. "Blake's a good ol' southern boy, and he knows how to take care of 'em. He understands their importance."

Chase nodded. For the moment he would accept this explanation of Blake Lowell. He certainly didn't want to arouse too much speculation by appearing to be overly interested.

"As usual you're more than efficient, Mr. Beck. Thank you." Chase laid the writing case on the counter. "I found this in my room this morning. Lodged in a crack behind the wood box. Do you recognize it?"

"No, sir, I don't reckon I do," Cedric said, turning and twisting his head to better see the case.

"How do you suppose it happened to be in my room?" he asked.

"Well, now . . . I don't rightly know, Major." Cedric picked up his spectacles and hooked the thin wire over his ears. Then his eyes focused on the letters in the corner. "ERB," he mumbled, breaking out in heavy perspiration. His sins had found him out and come back to haunt him!

"Any idea what the letters stand for?" Chase prompted. Cedric Beck took a long time in answering. Finally, in a small voice he said, "Yes, sir. They probably stand for Elizabeth Barrett. I imagine this case belongs to her."

"Who is Elizabeth Barrett?" Chase's expression and tone were bland; not so his eyes. They glinted with purpose and interest. "And what would her case be doing in my apartment?" Leaning on an elbow, Chase braced himself on the counter and scrutinized the landlord.

Cedric began his explanation with a deep sigh. "Miss Barrett, best I can tell, sir, is from Louisiana. Owns a large sugar cane plantation and mill down there. Well, yesterday she came in by stage from New Orleans."

Chase felt as if he were standing in front of Elizabeth Barrett naked again, and the feeling brought the warmth of shame to his face. He was mortified by his actions of the night before. Why hadn't he given her an opportunity to introduce herself and to explain her presence in his apartment before he made the assumption that she was a whore? *Because you wanted her to be a whore,* a small voice replied. *Because you wanted her!*

Remember, the voice of justification added, she said she was staying with Jefferson, and you saw her with Lowell. So she can't be such a lady after all, can she?

Cedric mopped his face with his apron and resolutely kept his eyes lowered to the case. "Thinking you wasn't coming until next weekend, I sorta rented out your apartment to her, sir." Now he lifted his head and said hurriedly, "Felt sorry for the two of them, Major. What with the storm and them being so far away from their home. I plumb felt sorry for the little tyke."

Chase's interest was thoroughly aroused now. He retrieved the writing case. "What little tyke?"

"Why, the one that travels with her," Cedric answered. "Ten-year-old boy. Jefferson, I believe she calls him."

Chase was so relieved he laid the chest on the counter again. Jefferson was a child! "No one else is traveling with her and the boy?" he asked.

Cedric shook his head and answered, "As far as I know it's just her and the boy."

"You're sure she's not traveling with a man?"

"Oh, no, sir," Cedric replied, puzzled by Chase's interrogation. "Only man she's been with since she's been here is Blake when he took her over to Mrs. Gladewater's last night."

Chase believed what Beck was telling him; the man had nothing to gain by lying. Why then had Elizabeth allowed him to believe the worst of her by perpetuating his misconception?

"If you'll leave the writing case with me," Cedric

suggested, "I'll make sure Miss Elizabeth gets it, sir."

"Thank you, Mr. Beck," said Chase, "but I believe this is a task I must perform. Looking at it, I would say it's quite expensive and must be quite important to her. You said she was staying at a Mrs. Gladewater's?"

"Yes, sir. That's the only place I could send her on such short notice when you arrived."

"Ah, yes, back to that," Chase drawled, his tone deceptively quiet. His blue eyes speared Cedric to the wall. "I don't appreciate your renting my rooms when I'm away, Mr. Beck, but," Chase lifted a hand to silence the landlord when he started to apologize for his actions, "I can understand why you did it. My only regret is that you didn't tell me when I came in." Chase's voice lowered to a wistful thoughtfulness. "Yankee I may be, Mr. Beck, and a soldier of the Federal Army, but I'm no less a human, no less a gentleman than any man who calls himself a Southerner. I would not have allowed you to evict the woman from the room and send her out on the streets by herself to find other lodging in good weather, much less bad."

"Oh, no, sir," Cedric said, lifting the tail of his apron a second time to wipe his face, "I didn't kick her out. Blake carried her in the carriage they just bought. Real fancy, sir. Straight from New Orleans."

When Cedric saw Chase's brow furrow, he hastily

said, "Yes, sir, Blake came and got her and the boy and carried them over to Mrs. Gladewater's himself. And, Major"—Beck didn't want to lose Chase as a customer; he was one of the few whom he could count on to pay his bills in cash—"I reimbursed her the money she'd given me and paid for her room and board at Mrs. Gladewater's myself."

"Under the circumstances that was the least you could do, Mr. Beck. I do not want a repeat of this situation again."

"Yes, sir," Beck muttered, relieved that Chase wasn't any more angry than he was.

"Now, give me the directions to Mrs. Gladewater's."

"It's way on the other side of town," Cedric told him as he wrote the address on a sheet of paper. "If you don't want to get muddy, you'll need to hire a buggy."

Chase put the address into his pocket and headed for the dining room. As he ate breakfast, he thought about Elizabeth Barrett's deception, and his curiosity was further aroused. How could he have been so wrong about her . . . or was he? One thing he knew for certain: she wasn't one of Madame Doucet's girls. *She definitely wasn't Jefferson's girl!* According to Beck, Lowell merely transported her and Jefferson from Beck's House to the Gladewater residence. All of Chase's preconceived ideas of her seemed to be unfounded and unwarranted. This bothered him and embarrassed him; he owed her an apology. And by damn he would give her one.

His purpose silently restated and reaffirmed, Chase reached out to pat the writing case. He drank the last of his coffee, dropped his napkin on the table, and stood to stride through the lobby to the waiting buggy. In a matter of minutes he had driven across town and was hitching the horses to the lone post. He opened the white picket gate and walked up the boardwalk to the large veranda to knock.

Eventually Pearl Gladewater opened the door. "Yes," she said suspiciously, peeping through the crack and looking the stranger up and down. "What can I do for you?"

"I'm Chase Daniel, Mrs. Gladewater, right now a resident of Beck's House."

The door opened a little wider, not so Pearl's eyes. They remained narrow, wary slits, and she said nothing.

"Mr. Beck informed me this morning that Miss Elizabeth Barrett is staying with you."

"And if that's true?" Pearl snapped, indisposed to give out any information to a stranger—and a Yankee at that, judging by his brisk accent.

Chase held the writing case up so that Pearl could see it. "I found this and have reason to believe it belongs to Miss Barrett. I would like to return it to her, if I may."

The door swung open and Pearl extended her hand. "You can leave it with me," she instructed.

97

"I'll see that she gets it if it's hers, and if not, I'll return it to Cedric myself."

Chase dropped his arm to his side, the writing case resting in the crook of his hand. "Thank you, ma'am," he said, careful not to offend Mrs. Gladewater, "but I don't reckon I can do that. You see, I feel personally responsible for Miss Barrett's having been evicted from my rooms, and I would like to give her an apology along with her writing case."

Pearl studied the young man standing in front of her. Despite his being a Yankee, he looked her in the eyes when he spoke; and his eyes were honest.

"Well, young man, I reckon I can see your point. And I also reckon Miss Barrett would want her property back, but she's gone."

Chapter Five

Staring at the rock pavilion in the center of the park, Chase sat in the buckboard and listened to the lively music of the German band. He had already been to the funeral parlor to say his final farewell to Terry and to talk with the soldiers who would escort the body back to Philadelphia. On his return to this side of town, he had dropped by the livery stable to check on the horses . . . and, out of curiosity, to meet little Jefferson. Chase chuckled quietly. The boy was all right. He'd left his horse in the care of the youngster.

Chase had seen Lowell, and again was puzzled that he was performing such menial tasks. Chase wasn't certain who or what Lowell was, but he knew he was no lackey, not with his credentials. He was an ex-Texas Ranger, a man who had given distinguished service to his country during the War Between the States. Blake was familiar to Chase; he felt as if he ought to know him. He was one of the greatest enigmas Chase had encountered in his life, and while Chase admired certain characteristics of the man, he also distrusted him.

Shifting in the seat, his hand grazed the writing case to bring his thoughts back to Elizabeth Barrett and to remind him of his purpose in being at San Antonio's Music Pavilion. Although his first meeting with Elizabeth had been inauspicious, he was glad that he'd met her last night. He was even happier to be seeing her again today and considered himself fortunate that she herself had encouraged such a visit. After all, she was the one who asked him to return her property should he find it. And he had found it. Leaping down, he tucked the case under his arm and strode toward the building.

"Welcome to Music Pavilion," an usher said. "If you'll follow me—"

"Thanks," Chase said, "but I'm looking for someone in particular. "Yes, I think I see her."

His eyes landed on a woman who sat on the second row from the stage. Because she was wearing a hat he couldn't be sure it was Elizabeth. She turned, and he saw her profile—the golden curls that framed her face. Yes, that was the woman who had been in his apartment last night.

Chase pushed past the usher, moved to the outer aisle and walked the length of the building, stopping only when he reached the second row of seats. He glanced at Elizabeth as he scooted into the chair next to hers, but she didn't see him. She was thoroughly engrossed in the music.

He had wondered if he would be disappointed when he saw her in the natural light. He wasn't. If anything it enhanced Elizabeth's beauty. The early morning sunlight cast her in an ethereal loveliness; the golden curls wisping around her face were like a halo. A sash—the same shade of green as her eyes—accented her tiny waist. Everything about Elizabeth Barrett suggested intelligence, breeding, and gentleness.

Leaning so that his lips were merely inches away from her ears, leaning so close that his nostrils filled with the elusive scent of her perfume, Chase said, "I love polkas, don't you?"

The minute she heard his deep voice, Elizabeth's eyes flew open and her head turned. Astonishment froze the features on her face when she saw the man from Beck's House—the man who was responsible for her eviction. She couldn't believe he was sitting here beside her in the Music Pavilion . . . as if nothing untoward had happened the night before.

At first Elizabeth was angry. Then she was curious. She wondered at the coincidence of their meeting here; she wondered if perhaps he had thought of her as much as she had thought of him. Then she didn't wonder at all. She was heady with the odor of his herbal cologne; her skin was atingle with excitement. She was thoroughly caught up in the man.

How different the morning cast him. He wasn't as harsh or brooding. Though the lines of his face were sharp and angular, they seemed to be tempered with a tenderness Elizabeth hadn't noticed last night. For all his toughness, she felt an aura of gentleness — a soul-deep gentleness — about him.

"What a coincidence," Elizabeth said. "Our meeting here like this."

"No coincidence," he answered, smiling at her start of affront. "I came to see you."

"I have no desire to see you," Elizabeth said. "Leave at once."

"This is a public place. You can't order me away as if I were a servant," Chase answered, a small smile lifting the corners of his mouth. "Besides I wouldn't go even if you could."

Grabbing her parasol and reticule, Elizabeth said rather haughtily, "Well, I can."

Before she could rise, a young couple with two small children sat down on the other side of her, blocking her escape. Elizabeth heard Chase's soft laughter and turned to glare at him. Then with a determined tilt of her chin, she returned her attention to the stage. Her back stiff, she held her parasol and reticule in her lap, her hands folded over them, and would have gazed straight ahead but a tiny hand patted hers. She looked down into the biggest and brownest eyes she had ever seen. The little girl couldn't have been more than four years old.

"My name's Ellie Jessup," she said, staring into Elizabeth's face. "What's yours?"

"Elizabeth."

"Who's he?" Ellie leaned across Elizabeth's lap and pointed at Chase.

Slowly Elizabeth's head turned and she stared into Chase's face. "I don't know," she murmured.

Without taking his eyes from hers, he answered, "Chase. Chase Daniel."

Although her heart was thumping at a furious pace and she was tingling all over, Elizabeth quickly turned her head and broke the visual caress; she refused the intimacy Chase initiated. She wanted nothing whatsoever to do with him.

Unaware of the music that filled the pavilion, Chase sat for a long time, first watching Elizabeth talk softly with Ellie, then the child as she played quietly in between the seats. The child's question continued to ring in his mind.

Who was he? He couldn't answer that himself. Oh, he could give a name. Anyone could do that. But who was he?

He knew only what Aunt Ida had told him about his mother. In autumn of 1836 a young, unmarried and pregnant woman calling herself April arrived at Mrs. Owen's home, asking for and receiving shelter. Keeping to herself mostly, April revealed hardly anything about her past or background. She told Aunt Ida that the father of her child loved her but was unable to marry her. She would say no more than this. The following August, April gave birth to a baby boy. Her only legacy to her son had been two paintings. A miniature self-portrait of herself that he kept with him at all times and 'Portrait of Love,' signed Daniel.

Aunt Ida and raised Chase and he loved her dearly, but that love didn't diminish his desire to know his own family or to discover his family name. He felt as if a part of him was missing. He couldn't help but wonder why his father had refused to give him a name, and at times he was angry at and blamed his mother for dying and leaving him alone and for never talking to Aunt Ida. As a child he had daydreamed about having a family like other children; other times he cursed the fate that took his family from him. Though great, Aunt Ida's love had not been enough to slack that yearning to find his other self.

Chase had no family name to carry on. Because of the name on the portrait Aunt Ida had called him Danny, but when he was old enough he had chosen his own. Choosing your own name, he had told himself, was one of the advantages of being a bastard. He chose Chase because it meant the hunter and he liked the sound of it . . . and because he would always hunt for his family name.

He chose Daniel because it was the name on the portrait of the man and he wanted that to be his father's name. Because he wanted Daniel to be the man in the portrait.

Chase learned at an early age that life is hard for a bastard.

Chase was so deep in thought he wasn't aware the concert was over until he heard the shuffle around him and realized people were moving out.

"Miss Barrett," Chase said, rising to his feet as Elizabeth smoothed her shawl over her shoulders, "I want to apologize for my behavior last night." He was glad when she stopped her fussing and turned to look at him. "Would you forgive me for assuming the worst and taking advantage of you? I was — I was expecting company, and when you arrived, I just assumed . . ." His words trailed into silence.

The apology pleased Elizabeth, but it was the emotion — a different emotion from the one she had seen last night in his eyes; this one was reserved especially for her — in the depth of those blue eyes that unnerved her.

"It . . . was as much my fault as it was yours, sir. I should never have entered your rooms unannounced or without an escort." A little more at ease with him, she smiled. "How did you know I was here?" The feather of her hat escaped the netting to bounce in front of her face.

He reached out and tucked it back in before he

bent to retrieve her writing case from the nearby chair. "Mrs. Gladewater. It's quite a detailed story that began with my finding this."

"My chest!" Elizabeth exclaimed and reached for it. "Where did you find it?"

"Lodged in a crack somewhere behind and underneath the wood box."

Tears sparkled in the green eyes that lifted to Chase's face. "Thank you so much for returning it, Mr. Daniel. It means so much to me. It was a gift from Johnny, and it took all the money he had. And now he's—" Elizabeth abruptly stopped in midsentence. She was saying too much, revealing too much about herself to this stranger. Again she was overwhelmed by the gentleness in Chase's expression, and the desire she had to wipe his tears away.

At the mention of Johnny's name, disappointment quickly stabbed Chase and he wondered how many men were in Elizabeth's life. How relieved he'd been to learn that she was involved with neither Jefferson or Lowell. Now he had this fellow to contend with, and intuitively Chase knew this one had touched Elizabeth's heart.

"I knew how much stock you must put in your writing case," he heard himself say, "to weather all you did to come back to Beck's House to get it."

"Thank you again, Mr. Daniel." Elizabeth smiled and although she was reluctant to leave him, she made to step past him. "Now, I really must be on

106

my way. Mr. Lowell and Jefferson will be here any moment to pick me up."

"Miss Barrett," Chase spoke tentatively; he remembered what a spitfire she was when aroused — "when I stopped by the stables to check on the horses this morning, I—I took the liberty of telling Mr. Lowell that I was coming to the concert myself and that I'd drive you to Mrs. Gladewater's."

Elizabeth could only stare at the man in stunned silence. If he knew who Blake was, he also knew about Jefferson. She was angry and embarrassed that he'd caught her in an outright lie. At the same time she was excited that he had dared to assume she would ride home with him. To say the least, her emotions confused and frightened her. Last night he had touched only her body; from that she would quickly recover. Today he had touched her heart; that she would never forget.

"Don't you think, sir," she finally said when she regained use of her voice, "that you were being rather presumptuous, assuming I would ride with you before you asked?"

"Perhaps I was being presumptuous," Chase answered in that same quiet voice, "but at the time I didn't think so. You see" —the blue eyes caught hers—"I didn't want to be alone this afternoon. I wanted company; I wanted a chance to get to know you better. Please reconsider and let me take you home."

Elizabeth searched Chase's eyes to find shadows of sorrow and wondered what demons were driving him. She wanted to ask but felt that would be an invasion of his privacy. Most grief was personal and didn't need to be shared.

"Thank you," she said, "but I'll walk." She would be far safer away from Chase Daniel, she decided. Yankee or not, this man was far too dangerous for her to be around.

Her gown brushed against Chase's legs when she turned and moved across the pavilion onto the lawn. All that remained to taunt the man was the elusive fragrance of her perfume. Chase slowly followed her out of the building.

When Elizabeth stood on the grounds, she looked dismally at the street, a muddy quagmire. If she walked home, she would ruin both her shoes and her dress and the trip would take her a long time. She really didn't relish a walk under such conditions, but neither did she relish riding with him.

"Miss Barrett," she heard Chase say from immediately behind her and jumped as his voice entered the private sanctuary of her thoughts.

"—don't leave yet," he said. "I'd like to talk to you a little longer, please."

His hand lightly touched her elbow, and Elizabeth felt as if she'd been burned by five tongues of fire. She felt the heat of his touch throughout her body. Looking at him again, more studious this time, she decided he was a charming man and indeed a persistent one; she reckoned that he wasn't always this patient and soft. Commands and demands rolled off his tongue more readily than requests.

"All right," she agreed faintly. Nothing could possibly happen to her if she lingered on the lawn and . . . talked with him.

"First," he said smiling, "I'm Chase Daniel. When we see each other again, I want you to know me."

Elizabeth felt breathless at his announcement. It was confident, almost arrogant. "What makes you think we'll see each other again, Mr. Daniel?"

"I believe in fate," he returned simply. "You didn't leave your writing case by chance nor did you show up in my room last night by chance. That was by grand design, Miss Barrett."

Elizabeth chuckled. "More like human frailty called forgetfulness . . . or fear . . . or anger, Mr. Daniel."

"I'm sorry about the fear and the anger," Chase said. "Last night I was too upset to pay any attention to what you were saying. Really, I was too embarrassed. Only this morning did I realize the true circumstances of your leaving Beck's House. I want you to know I'm truly sorry you were put out. Had I known Beck had rented the room to you, I wouldn't have allowed him to displace you. I would have found quarters elsewhere."

At the moment Elizabeth wasn't at all concerned that she'd been evicted from Beck's House. If she had allowed herself, she could have drowned in the lake-blue eyes that were more startling than beautiful. Gentle was her acceptance of his apology. "I believe you, Mr. Daniel, and I accept your apology; however, none is really necessary."

His fingers tightened around her lower arm. "I would very much like the opportunity to wipe last night out of your mind. I'd like for you to get to know the real Chase Daniel."

"Thank you," Elizabeth declined, "but I'm not going to be here long enough for us to become better acquainted. I'm leaving in the morning to join my sister at Eagle Pass, and I really must be leaving. I have many things to do this afternoon." Quite gently but also firmly Elizabeth removed her arm from his grasp, feeling oddly alone and unsteady when his hand left her arm.

"Miss Barrett, I didn't intend to be presumptuous when I told Lowell that I would bring you home from the concert. It was the action of a desperate man who wants to get to know a lovely young lady better."

His words gently wrapped around Elizabeth's heart to tie her to him with a bond she couldn't fight. When he tugged the invisible string, she stepped closer to him.

"Last night, Miss Barrett," he said quietly, "you

110

deliberately led me to believe you had many men in your life. You led me to believe Jefferson is a man and that you had spent the afternoon with him in my rooms. You also allowed me to believe you were spending the evening with Lowell."

"Yes, I did," Elizabeth answered, flushing beneath his piercing gaze and feeling a tinge of guilt. "And under the same circumstances I would do it again, sir. Considering that you were attempting to—to—"

"—seduce," Chase filled in.

Elizabeth lifted a brow, but her body burned with memories of Chase's sweet touch. "Considering that you were attempting to seduce a lady, what did you expect me to do? How else was I going to protect myself?"

Chase felt uncomfortable; this was the first time a woman had pointed an accusing finger at him, the first time one had felt as if she needed to be protected from his advances. Because of the circumstances surrounding his birth he had always been cautious in taking a woman. Never had he forced one; never had he persuaded one against her will. Elizabeth was right. He had lusted at first sight and had given her no time for explanation; he had prejudged her. Words had been her only defense. He reached up and ran a finger around his collar which seemed to be getting tighter by the minute.

"Perhaps you had reason to act as you did last

night, Miss Barrett," he sincerely conceded, "but after I apologized and explained my actions today, why didn't you tell me the truth?"

Elizabeth felt all her composure and resistance slipping away beneath the man's persistent attack. Yet, she continued to fight, to protect her heart. In a voice that was so low Chase had to lean forward to hear her, she said, "Mr. Daniel, I don't owe anyone an explanation or an apology for my behavior, much less you. I didn't assault you; you assaulted me. And, Mr. Daniel, I may or may not have a . . . a lover. That, too, is my business."

"That's quite true, ma'am," he agreed, a certain ache in his heart if that should be the truth. Fleetingly he wondered about Johnny—the one who had given her the writing case. After a lengthy pause he said, "If you'll excuse me, I'll be on my way." He tipped his hat and turned, striding toward his buckboard.

Elizabeth didn't want to travel with him; she was afraid to, but neither did she want him to leave. What did she want from him? she asked herself. Did she want him to beg? She watched the stretch of material across his shoulders as he walked and knew Chase Daniel wasn't a man to beg anyone.

She realized he was leaving her . . . to get home quite by herself. She looked at the rain-soaked streets and thought of the too few boardwalks between the Music Pavilion and Mrs. Gladewater's house and knew she had two choices: ride home with Chase Daniel, or walk through the mud and slush. She looked down at her silk dress. She darted one more quick glance at the street.

"Mr. Daniel," she called and watched as he stopped walking to turn around, "I've changed my mind. I would like for you to take me to Mrs. Gladewater's."

Elizabeth drew her breath in sharply as Chase continued to regard her as if he were considering her offer, as if he might refuse. His expression never changed, and this irritated Elizabeth. She had wanted some indication that he was pleased with her decision to ride with him.

"Then come along, Miss Barrett."

When Elizabeth reached his side, he caught her arm lightly in his grasp and guided her to the buckboard. Again the touch was like a red-hot brand to Elizabeth, searing through the material of her clothes to burn her flesh. She gasped.

When he heard her quick intake of breath, Chase instantly apologized. He didn't realize that he was holding her so tightly. "I'm sorry. I didn't mean to hurt you."

"You haven't hurt me," she managed in a broken voice, wondering if she'd find that his finger marks had burned through the material to brand her skin when she took her gown off. "I simply wasn't expecting to be manhandled like this."

Desire surged through Chase in such proportions he could hardly contain himself. This woman affected him as none other ever had. Her remarks, whether innocent or calculated, excited him. And he thought for a maddening few seconds as she let him walk away that he wouldn't get to take her home.

"Ma'am," he said in a low, husky voice, "please pardon me for saying this, but when I've manhandled you, you'll know it, and it sure won't feel like this."

Elizabeth cursed the emotions that clashed within her. She cursed the man who had caused her to lose control of her highly organized life. How could she be so frustrated with him at the same time that she was so attracted to him. She pretended outrage at his remark but thrilled to think of his handling her.

"Mr. Daniel, you'll never get the chance to manhandle me," she returned quietly. "After all, sir, you are a Yankee and I am a Southerner, one of the few things which stand between us."

"Yes, ma'am," he agreed congenially, "I am, and you are, but I'm also a man and you're a woman."

Despite the excitement that surged through her, Elizabeth wanted to wipe that grin off his face.

Holding her no longer than was absolutely necessary even though he wanted to, Chase effortlessly swung her up on the seat. While she settled her petticoats and crinoline, he gathered the reins, climbed in the buckboard and sat beside her.

"Well, Miss Barrett," said he with a certain

degree of smugness, looking ahead and clucking the horses, "since we're going to be in such close confines, I suggest we get better acquainted."

He turned to stare into the parasol that Elizabeth flipped into his face as she settled it on her shoulder. On the other side, Elizabeth smiled.

Chapter Six

Chase slowly and carefully guided the horses through the muddy thoroughfares of San Antonio. "This is one of the oldest cities in Texas," he said to Elizabeth's parasol when he drove into Military Plaza, "and has a beautiful Spanish heritage. Although Americans began coming in during the early 1800's, it retains its Spanish touch." He pointed. "The Spanish Governor's Palace."

Elizabeth gazed curiously at the low squat buildings, made mostly of stone and adobe. Built around the Spanish town square, the buildings carried the architectural design of their early founders. Cantinas, general stores, livery stables, dance halls and saloons, the plaza was filled with vendors, plying their goods. The odor of cooking food filled the air to make Elizabeth realize how hungry she was.

Chili stands were on the south side of the plaza; on the east were the fresh vegetables; eggs, poultry, and butter were sold on the north; and on the west, serried ranks of wagons stood, bulging with hay, piled high with wool or hides. Here, on the ground, sat the Mexican vendors.

"Look, Mr. Daniel!" Elizabeth shouted, the parasol coming down as she pointed.

Chase pulled the horses to a halt.

"Aren't they beautiful?" she exclaimed, wonder in her voice.

"Who or what?" Chase asked dryly, his gaze slowly moving across the line of Mexican vendors, old men and women who were selling chili peppers and tamales, and across to the women who stood in front of small wicker bird cages.

"Please," Elizabeth turned a pleading face to him, "let's get closer. The songbirds are so beautiful. They remind me of the one my brother bought me when I was a little girl."

Before Chase could move the buggy, one of the women, wearing a large black scarf that covered her head and shoulders, picked up two wicker cages and walked toward them. "Would you care for a songbird, *señorita?*" she asked. "I have canaries, mockingbirds, and cardinals."

"Oh," Elizabeth breathed, looking from the cardinal to the canary. "They are so beautiful." As if he knew he were on display, the canary hopped about on his perch, cocked his head, and blinked

117

his eyes at her. When he opened his beak and warbled, she squealed with delight. "I must have this one. He reminds me of Yellow Bird."

"Then you shall have it," Chase said. As he reached into his pocket for the money, the Mockingbird seller walked to his side of the buggy and set the cage down.

"No," Elizabeth protested, when he handed the woman a bill, "I can't accept a gift from you, sir. I don't even know you."

"Of course, you can," Chase returned. "Let it be my apology—a peace offering." He paused and smiled, his eyes once again caressing her face. "And you do know me, I introduced myself to you at the Music Pavilion. What better place to meet?"

Unable to look into the awesome beauty of his eyes, Elizabeth lowered her head. "Thank you, Mr. Daniel. This is very kind of you."

And calculating, Chase thought with a twinge of guilt. *Every time you look at that bird I want you to think of me.*

"What do you plan to name the canary?" he asked.

"I'll have to think about it," she replied. "It has to be something special."

Chase turned his head to grin at her. "Because I gave it to you."

She lifted her head to settle twinkling green eyes on him. "Because I allowed a Yankee to give it to me."

118

"Are we back to that again?" Chase asked, a slight degree of irritation in his tone.

Afraid to look at him for fear of what she'd seen in his eyes, Elizabeth peered at the beautiful bird. "I don't know that we'll ever get away from that, Mr. Daniel."

Chase's mouth thinned in disappointment, but he said nothing. He concentrated on driving through the growing crowd that gathered in the plaza despite the rain and muddy streets.

As they neared Commerce Street, Elizabeth asked, "What building is that?"

"The courthouse," Chase answered. "Known locally as Bat Cave because they have to periodically rout out the bats. That part of the building to the back is the old Spanish *presidio* revamped into the jail."

Elizabeth gave a cursory glance to the building, but her interest waned quickly. She turned her head and looked in delight at the tamale, enchilada, and chili wagons that lined the street, their vendors singing out their menus.

When they reached Miss Gladewater's house, Chase nimbly leaped from the wagon, jumped over a puddle of water, and tied the horses to the post. Before Elizabeth could disembark, he was at her side, his hands again at her waist. This time she was prepared for his gallantry, but again he surprised her. He didn't swing her around and set her down; he held her protectively in his arms and easily carried her onto the veranda.

Had she wanted to, Elizabeth couldn't have fought him. Her hands were filled with parasol, writing case, reticule, and bird cage, and she was crushed against his chest. More, she was prisoner of her own emotions, at the moment directly responsible to them, and they would not allow her to resist. She heard the steady thump of Chase's heart; she felt his chest expand and contract with each breath he took. She smelled his cologne, the same he'd had on last night . . . when he thought she was a whore.

"I don't want you to ruin this pretty little dress," he said, his breath fanning against her temples.

When he set her down, Elizabeth's hat was askew, the feather bobbing in her face. Her breath came too quickly, and her heart beat too erratically — a condition that seemed to afflict her when she was in Chase Daniel's presence, and one that irritated her to no end. For the past six years she had kept her emotions under rigid control; her life had been orderly. She was perplexed to find that her emotions had suddenly gone truant over a bounder such as this.

She stumbled backwards until she fell against the wall. After she set the wicker cage down, she reached up to straighten her hat and brushed the feather aside. With as much dignity as she could muster under the circumstances she said, "Good-day, Mr. Daniel. Thank you for returning my writing case and for bringing me home." Her voice softened measurably. "And thank you so much for the canary." *Every time I see him I'll think of you,* she thought.

"You're welcome." Chase took off his hat and a thick wave fell across his forehead. "Miss Barrett, likely as not we won't see each other again. And since I've already rented the buckboard for the day, it would be a shame to waste it. What do you say to a truce for today? I'd like to take you for a buggy ride."

Elizabeth wanted to spend the day with Chase; his company was charming, and she found herself able to forget her worries and her loneliness when she was with him. She was surprised when she realized she hadn't once thought of Vanessa this morning, and finding her sister was Elizabeth's primary concern. Elizabeth was also startled by and afraid of the feelings Chase was able to arouse in her.

Through all her years of her nursing she had remained immune to men; the incident with Watkins had served only to strengthen her resistance. Chase Daniel was different. So easily he had shattered her line of defense and was walking directly toward her heart. This Elizabeth wouldn't allow. Her heart belonged to her alone; she would give it to the man of her choosing, and Chase Daniel was not of her choosing.

Although he was curious about her thoughts,

Chase patiently awaited her answer.

Eventually Elizabeth said, "I agree it's a shame to waste the buckboard, Mr. Daniel, but—"

"Land sakes alive!" Pearl Gladewater interrupted when she walked onto the veranda. She was looking at the wicker basket. "What is this?"

Elizabeth whirled around, her gown rustling against Chase's legs, to stare at her landlady. "My canary," she answered. "Mr. Daniel bought it—I—"

When Chase saw Pearl's eyes narrow disapprovingly, he quickly came to Elizabeth's defense. "Miss Barrett bought it from one of the Mockingbird Seller's on Military Plaza," he said.

"Well," Pearl grumbled, her gaze shifting from Chase to the canary, then to Elizabeth, "just don't let any of that bird seed get on my floor. Birds are a nasty lot, I always say. So you're going to take Miss Barrett for a buggy ride?" she said.

"I am if Miss Barrett is willing." Although Chase answered Pearl, he was looking at Elizabeth.

Pearl threw Elizabeth another disapproving gaze. "Can't say that I would approve of this if I was your maw, but I don't reckon you'd consider it any of my business."

"No, Mrs. Gladewater," Elizabeth said, drowning in those lake-blue eyes, "I don't think it's any of your business."

"Won't be," Pearl retaliated, "so long as it don't tarnish the good name of my house."

As if Pearl Gladewater had never spoken, Elizabeth said to Chase, "Miss Barrett is willing."

A hand on her hip, Pearl turned to Chase and drawled, "Well, I reckon I have enough victuals cooked so's you could eat with us. Mind you, you might as well pay me as Cedric Beck. I could use the extra money."

"That sounds reasonable to me," Chase answered, wishing he had Elizabeth all to himself, wishing he didn't have to share her with anyone. "I thank you for the invitation, Mrs. Gladewater. I'd love to stay if it won't be any trouble to you."

"No trouble as long as you can pay for the meal," Pearl informed him. "And I'd like to see the money first." She turned to Elizabeth. "I'll be taking Mr. Daniel into the parlor while you're putting your stuff up."

"Thank you," Elizabeth murmured, turning to dart down the hall and disappear into her room.

As soon as she deposited her paraphernalia on the reading table, she shut the door and leaned against it. Closing her eyes, she emitted a long sigh and welcomed the privacy of her room. She didn't understand her thoughts concerning Chase Daniel. He was virtually a stranger; yet, she felt an undefinable drawing to him. A drawing that was kin to a bonding. She reckoned him to be a bounder, but rather than its turning her against him, it excited her.

Last night he had thought she was a whore and had treated her accordingly; yet she couldn't forget the feel of his hands nor the tantalizing brush of his cigar and whiskey-scented breath on her body. Involuntarily she pressed her fingers against her mouth and remembered the play of his lips on hers, the rough-but-gentle-pressure as they slanted and opened hers, the sweet thrust of his tongue as it explored and sought out all the secret places in her mouth. She felt a pang of yearning, and her lower body ached anew.

"Miss Elizabeth," Pearl called from the hallway, "I'm serving Mr. Daniel some lemonade. Would you like to have some?"

"Thank you, Mrs. Gladewater, I believe I will," Elizabeth answered, glad her thoughts had been interrupted.

She didn't have time to be preoccupied with a man like Chase Daniel. Without trying, he was already making inroads into her mind and thoughts. Next came her body. Her eyes inadvertently strayed to her bed. As surely as she was standing here, she knew Chase Daniel's intentions. They included taking her to bed, and as she realized how easy it would be for her to agree, she began to understand the degree to which this man incited her emotions.

For the second time in a matter of minutes, a battle waged within Elizabeth. She couldn't lose sight of her purpose in coming to Texas. She had to find Vanessa, nurse her back to health, and bring her home. This was not the time or the place for her to become involved with a man or to explore these newly found sensations Chase Daniel was able to arouse.

Peeling off her gloves, Elizabeth walked to the dresser on the far side of the room and laid them down. She slipped the shawl from her shoulders and draped it across the back of a chair. She pulled the pins from her hat and set it on the dresser.

She was perplexed at the ease with which the major had insinuated himself into her life in such a few hours. Already she felt as if she knew him. Her mind raced back to her first meeting with him, and she recalled that even under those distasteful circumstances she didn't feel the revulsion for him that she'd felt for Emery Watkins. At first, she had been frightened of Chase, but a deep-seated part of her seemed to recognize him and had immediately responded to him and his touch.

Loneliness, Elizabeth, a small inner voice explained. *You're attracted to this man because you're lonely. You're far away from home and the people whom you love and trust.* She heard Aunt Feldie saying, *Be careful, girl. You're extremely vulnerable . . . and remember men are a selfish lot. They take and never give. They want a woman for only one purpose. Remember, most men have two women in their lives: a mistress for sex; a wife for babies.*

Elizabeth heard another knock on the door followed by Pearl's shout, "Don't tarry in there too long, girl. You got that Yankee in my parlor to keep company. I only invited him to dinner because of you."

Elizabeth grinned. She knew why Pearl Gladewater had invited Chase to stay and it wasn't because of her. "I'll be out as soon as I freshen up a bit."

"I'll tell Mr. Daniel," Pearl called. "And don't let that bird scatter seed all over this room."

"I won't, Mrs. Gladewater," Elizabeth promised.

Filling the basin with water, Elizabeth doused the wash cloth, wrung it out, and pressed it against her flushed face. Then she combed the tendrils of hair that framed her face; the chignon of curls she left untouched. She retied the green ribbon at the collar of her dress.

As she stared at her reflection in the mirror, she wondered what had happened to the Elizabeth Rose Barrett who controlled her life with an iron hand, whose entire existence was predicated on cold logic. Her trip to Texas had certainly been eventful and was as upheaving to her life as the war had been, albeit in a different way.

Her acquaintance with Chase Daniel was redefining the parameters of her thinking. She was much more flexible and less judgmental. Because of her emotional response to Chase Daniel, Elizabeth could sympathize with Vanessa. She understood more fully her sister's motivation for running away with Rod Everett. At least, Vanessa had eloped

126

with a man whom she'd known for several years; whereas, Elizabeth was drawn to a stranger she had known for only a few hours.

"Miss Elizabeth!" Pearl called quite loudly this time. "Your lemonade's ready, and Mr. Daniel is waiting for you in the parlor."

"I'm coming," Elizabeth answered.

Before she turned from the dresser, she picked up a sprig of green grogram and wound it through her curls. Her smile began to inch slowly into her eyes. How long had it been since she'd enjoyed the company of an exciting man? How long since she'd had a beau? Too long! What would it matter if she were to enjoy Mr. Daniel's company today? She would be leaving in the morning and would never see him again. She laughed aloud, exhilarated with her daring.

Chapter Seven

Wondering if Elizabeth ever planned to make an appearance, Chase stalked around the parlor like a caged animal. He drank his glass of lemonade, a brew he'd never learned to appreciate fully, and looked at the pictures and paintings that hung on the wall; he picked up and inspected all the decorative dishes and figurines. Finally he stopped walking to stand in front of the window and gaze into the yard. His ears perked when he heard the soft thud of a closing door and the light footfalls of a woman.

He turned to see Elizabeth framed in the door, her face radiant and lovely. She was smiling — her entire being was smiling — and her eyes were glittering. She wore emeralds on her ears, but compared to her eyes, they had no luster or beauty. Chase felt a knot in his chest as he looked at her. She was indeed one of the most petite women he'd ever seen; yet, she had strength of character that gave her added stature. She aroused an emotion in him that he'd never felt before, and he knew at that instant he would do things for Elizabeth Barrett that he'd never contemplated doing for any other woman. The admission was downright scary.

"I'm sorry to have kept you waiting, Mr. Daniel," Elizabeth said, moving into the parlor.

"It's quite all right," Chase replied, a teasing lift at the corners of his mouth. "I love sitting in parlors by myself staring at the wall decorations."

Elizabeth smiled and dropped her eyelids to allow dark curling lashes to brush against her cheeks; but she did not lower her head. Well versed in sociably acceptable coquetry, she openly flirted and allowed him to see the blush of pleasure tint her face.

The whisper of her gown as she walked was one of the sweetest sounds Chase had ever heard. When she settled herself on the settee, he sat in the chair next to her.

As if they were courting, Elizabeth picked up the pitcher and looked at Chase. "Would you care to have another glass of lemonade, Mr. Daniel?"

"Please," he answered, although it was the furthest thing from his thoughts. Maintaining eye contact, he dared her to share his fantasy. He would care to hold her in his arms and kiss her lips; he would care to undress her, slowly, to reveal her lovely flesh. Then just as slowly and as carefully, he would make love to her. He would push any thought of other men out of her mind.

Elizabeth held the pitcher up, but she didn't fill the glasses. She was captivated by the enigmatic gleam that flickered in Chase's eyes. She was surprised that blue eyes could be so mysterious and alluring. Right now they reminded her of blue tongues of fire—beautiful but dangerous. She was too caught up in her game of make-believe to heed warnings—whether they be conscious or subconscious. Furthermore, she reminded herself, she wasn't going to be around Chase Daniel long enough to suffer any consequences.

Chase was disappointed when she lowered her smiling face and presented him with the crown of her head, covered in shining curls and green ribbon. His gaze shifted and he watched her pick up the glass and pass it to him. He deliberately let his fingers brush hers as he took the drink. Her hands were beautiful to behold, smooth like satin and as soft to the touch.

"Where are you from, Mr. Daniel?" Elizabeth asked, sitting back on the small sofa and sipping her coffee.

"Philadelphia," he answered.

"And what are you doing down here?" she asked.

"I'm working with the government," he replied, loathe to let her know that he was a soldier, even more loathe to let her know he was a special agent for Grant. He didn't want to see the revulsion in her eyes that he'd seen in so many as he'd traveled through the South after the war's end. Neither did he want her to think he was a carpetbagger.

"And in what way are you connected with the government?" she asked as she sipped her drink.

Chase shrugged. "Engineer of Frontier Defense," he answered, calling the title out of a dusty corner of his memory. "General Grant wants me to make a study of the number of forts we need to protect the line of settlements from Indian incursions."

"Commendable," Elizabeth replied. "However, from what I've observed, the Union army seems more interested in bilking the South than in defending southern citizens from Indian incursions."

"Reconstruction government is difficult at the best, ma'am," Chase replied stiffly.

"I'd hardly call it a reconstruction government, sir," Elizabeth retorted. "It's more like a perpetuation of military destruction. Only now we southerners have no recourse. Vanquished, we must yield ourselves to Yankee domination and injustice which is enforced by soldiers, carpetbaggers, and scalawags."

Elizabeth could easily get vehement when she thought of occupational government! She would not soon forget the hurt and disgrace she had suffered at their hands. Forever she would be branded a whore thanks to General Butler's Federal

Court.

Chase's lemonade was suddenly quite tart. He set his glass down and leaned forward. "Miss Barrett, could we please change the subject?"

Elizabeth wished it were as easy to erase the past from her heart and memory as it was to change the subject. And changing the subject was an easier task for a Yankee than a Southerner. They were not the vanquished. Elizabeth leaned forward to set her glass next to Chase's.

"I can't pretend the war didn't happen, sir. I can't pretend the Union army didn't abuse the people of Louisiana."

"I'm not asking you to pretend," Chase said. "I'm asking that we not discuss it, that our friendship be predicated on something more substantial than prejudices stemming from the war. Can we not like each other simply because we are two people? Perhaps because you're a woman and I'm a man?"

Elizabeth didn't get to answer Chase's question. The gate slammed and Jefferson bounded up the boardwalk with a shout. "Miss Elizabeth, I'm home."

Before his feet hit the bottom step, Elizabeth was on the veranda. "Get to the back porch and wash off before you come into the house, young man," she instructed, hands on her hips. "You smell just like a stable and from the looks of your breeches and boots you've hit every mud puddle between

132

Muldoon's and here."

"Oh, no, ma'am," Jefferson said, the laughter in the depth of his dark eyes belying the grave words, "I missed one or two."

"Hello, Jefferson," Chase said over Elizabeth's shoulder.

"Hello, Major Daniel," the boy said, his eyes lighting up. "Took care of your house just like you told me to. Used the stable body brush and sponge, then the curry you gave me. And I had his shoes checked."

"Sounds like you did a good job to me," Chase said.

"Yes, sir, I did," Jefferson announced. "Mr. Lowell said I was a good worker, and he didn't have to go over any of the horses after me." His eyes widened in astonishment when Chase handed him a coin. "All this for me?" he asked. "And you ain't even checked my work yet!"

Chase grinned. "All that because I care for my horse," he answered, "and I trust you to give me an honest day's work." With a wink he added, "If Mr. Lowell said you did a good job, I'll take his word for it. Besides if you didn't, I know where to find you."

"Get around to the back, Jefferson," Pearl called from the kitchen, "and get them dirty clothes off and take yourself a bath. The tub's on the porch. When you finish, I have your dinner ready."

With a wave and a grin, Jefferson disappeared

133

around the house and Elizabeth and Chase returned to the parlor.

"You're curious about Jefferson, aren't you?" said she.

"No, it's you that I'm curious about," Chase replied. "What are you doing out here by yourself?"

Elizabeth moved to the table and picked up her glass of lemonade. While she wasn't thirsty, she wanted something to do with her hands. She took a sip and swallowed before she said, "I've already told you, Mr. Daniel, I came out here to visit with my sister."

"Where does she live?" he asked, the quiet words compelling Elizabeth to lift her head so that her eyes met his.

"Eagle Pass," she answered.

"That's a long and dangerous way from here," he said. "Too long and dangerous for a lady to travel by herself. The town is located on the Rio Grande River directly on the Mexican border and right now it's full of riffraff and outlaws. You ought to have a man traveling with you."

"Thank you for your concern," Elizabeth said softly and sincerely. "But I don't want a man traveling with me. I've learned to take care of myself. Except for Jefferson, I've been alone for many years now, Mr. Daniel. That's why I must reach my sister. She's the only living relative I have."

"The war was hard," Chase said.

"Hard and cruel," Elizabeth answered practically, thinking about the Union occupation of New Orleans in those bitter first years under General Butler. "It killed my parents, my brother, and many of my friends; it cast my sister on the other side of the world. It destroyed an entire society—the good with the bad. My life and home are a shell of what they were five years ago, Mr. Daniel."

"Are you bitter?" Chase asked.

"No, I'm angry," Elizabeth said. "Resentful of and angry toward those who come to take advantage of the South in her plight." Tears in her eyes, she looked up at Chase. "A loving and understanding reconstruction would be so much better for our displaced black people. In the end, Northern reconstruction will hurt them as much as if not more than it's hurting the plantation owners now."

Chase wanted to take Elizabeth into his arms and hold her close. He wanted to dispel her fears and fight her dragons. His desires written in his eyes for Elizabeth to see, she swayed toward him. Chase's arms extended . . . but they never curled around Elizabeth in an embrace. He heard a buggy rumble to the side of the house and frowned.

"Blake's here," Pearl called out from the kitchen. "We'll be eating soon."

Pearl's shout broke the magic of the moment. Elizabeth hastily looked away from Chase, took a step backward and brushed her hands down her skirt. Suddenly uncomfortable with the intimacy which she had allowed to develop between her and Chase, she rushed to the table and picked up the glasses and pitcher.

"I'll take these to the kitchen," she mumbled.

Chase moved to the window and was standing there when Blake Lowell walked into the room. He turned and nodded his head. "Mr. Lowell."

"Mr. Daniel." Blake nodded and moved to sit on the settee.

As before when he'd first met Blake Lowell, Chase was assailed by the feeling that he knew the man, not the name perhaps, not even the face. Years of war and subsequent danger on the frontier had given Chase an instinct, a second sense, which warned him of impending danger. Chase intuitively recognized Blake Lowell, but he wasn't sure yet if he were friend or foe. He hoped he was a friend; he'd hate to have him as an enemy.

Chase heard the rustling and knew Elizabeth had entered the parlor before he heard her say, "Hello, Blake. It's so nice to see you again." Slowly he turned to watch her eyes light up when Blake stood and took her hand in his.

Blake said, "It's nice to see you again, Miss Elizabeth. I've been looking forward to this all day."

"Thank you," Elizabeth murmured, then added on soft laughter with daring flirtation — a luxury she hadn't enjoyed since before the war, "After all we've been through together, Blake, let's not stand

136

on ceremony. If you insist on my calling you Blake, I insist on you calling me Elizabeth."

Blake looked at her tiny, delicate hand. "Elizabeth." He made the word a caress.

Chase was furious. Furious at Elizabeth for openly flirting with Blake Lowell. Furious at Blake Lowell for being such an appealing man and for appealing to Elizabeth. Furious at himself for caring.

Then, as if compelled by the draw of a magnet, Elizabeth turned her head and looked at Chase, who stood contemplating her and Blake across the room. He wasn't frowning, but Elizabeth saw the gray shadow of disapproval, perhaps dislike, on his face; she was pleased. In fact, she was exhilarated at the thought of both men being interested in her, and both men were!

She returned her attention to Blake and said, "I was disappointed when you didn't come to pick me up."

"Well, ma'am," Blake leveled a meaningful stare at Chase, "seeing as how Mr. Daniel and you had already made plans to go buggy riding after he brought you home, I didn't want to interfere."

The smile was instantly wiped off Elizabeth's face as she silently iterated Blake's words. She turned to look accusingly at Chase. While she was pleased that he was a man who took matters into his own hands when he knew what he wanted, she was also irritated that she had played into the same hand. How easy it would be for her to fall under Chase Daniel's spell. With a shiver of anticipation she recalled his promise: she would know when she had been manhandled by him.

She turned back to Blake. "That was so kind of you," she said. "You're such a gentleman."

The meaning of her statement was not lost to Chase as Beck's words returned to haunt him: "Blake Lowell's a good, ol' southern boy." Evidently a "good ol' southern boy" was what Elizabeth wanted.

"Come and get it," Pearl called. "Dinner's on the table, and I want to eat while it's nice and hot."

"May I escort you to the dining room, Elizabeth?" Blake asked, intentionally edging Chase out.

"Thank you, Blake," Elizabeth answered, "but I need to talk with Mr. Daniel . . . alone, please."

Blake glanced at Chase. Then he nodded his head and moved into the hallway. Only the echo of his boots on the hardwood floor broke the silence in the parlor.

Elizabeth walked to the window where Chase stood. "And you accused me of deception earlier today, Mr. Daniel?"

"I didn't lie," Chase said. "I told Lowell the truth. That I was going to deliver your writing case to you and would bring you back to Mrs. Gladewater's."

"Did you tell him that you intended to take me for a buggy ride this afternoon?" she asked.

"Yes," he answered without hesitation, "but I had no control over your answer. That was for you to decide. I asked and you agreed to go."

Elizabeth's eyes stayed, probing, appraising, trying to read behind the chiseled strength of Chase's face, but she was unable to ascertain what he was thinking. One thing she did know, she was disappointed that he had tried to manipulate her. However subtle his maneuver might be, Elizabeth still labeled it manipulation. No matter how much she wanted to spend the day with him, she would not allow anyone to control and direct her actions, especially not a Yankee. Too many years of being on her own and accountable only to herself guided Elizabeth in her decision.

"Thank you so much for inviting me," she said, "but I don't think I'll be going for that buggy ride after all, Mr. Daniel. I like to feel responsible for my own decisions. Somehow I feel as if you've pushed me into this one." Turning, she walked out of the parlor.

Chase's first inclination was to leave, but he'd never been one to run from an unpleasant situation. He had been wrong to be so presumptuous, but he had simply wanted to spend the day with Elizabeth. When he was with her, he tended to forget the anguish of Terry's death. As he stepped into the dining room, he saw Pearl and Blake sitting at opposite ends of the table. He sat across from Elizabeth.

139

"Saw them soldiers bringing in a prisoner early last night," Pearl said, passing the platter of fried chicken. "Looked like a young boy. Guess you got to see him when you carried the victuals over to the Bat Cave this morning?"

"Yes," Blake answered, "I saw him." He and Chase exchanged even glances. "That's where I first saw *Major* Daniel." Another calculated stab by Blake.

Chase heard Elizabeth's gasp of surprise, but he never looked up from the platter as he speared a drumstick. Blake was laying all his cards on the table, Chase thought, and it was definitely a winning hand.

A smile of triumph touched Blake's lips. "Deputy Addison told me that you are a major in the *occupation* army, sir. Is that right?"

"Yes, Mr. Lowell, I'm a major," Chase admitted. He knew Lowell had deliberately set the stage for this small revelation in hopes of lowering him in Elizabeth's eyes. He looked at her and silently pleaded with her to understand. "But I'm not part of the occupation army. I'm in the cavalry and am assigned to assess the number of forts needed along the frontier for defense against the Indians."

"Who was the boy, Blake?" Pearl asked, disinterested in the conversation between Blake and Chase. She was more interested in gossip she could swap with the neighbors. "Anybody we know? I didn't get a good look at him."

140

"Rod Everett," Blake answered.

"Rod Everett?" Elizabeth said the words so low no one heard them. She raised her head and stared at Chase.

Chapter Eight

"Rod," Pearl mused. "No, I don't think I know him."

Rod Everett. Rod Everett.

Elizabeth sat in stunned silence, the name spinning in her mind, totally obliterating all coherent thought. The blood rushed out of her body to leave her cold and clammy and nauseated. She felt as if she had been turned into a statue; she wasn't aware of any life processes within her own body; she was vaguely aware of those who sat around her. This couldn't be *Vanessa*'s Roderick Everett!

"Are you all right, Miss Barrett?" Elizabeth heard Chase say anxiously.

Turning blank eyes toward him, she murmured, "Yes, I'm fine." Not quite composed yet, she wiped her hands on her napkin and reached for her glass of water.

"You're as white as a sheet, girl," Pearl declared, squinting down the table at Elizabeth. "If I didn't know better, I'd think you'd seen a ghost."

A ghost from the past, Elizabeth thought as she swallowed the water, *and not a pleasant one from the sound of things.* Retreating in silence, she smiled feebly.

"Can I get you anything?" Chase asked.

"No, thank you," Elizabeth answered. "I'm fine really."

More interested in hearing about the prisoner than she was about the state of Elizabeth's health, Pearl said, "I guess the young fellow who was arrested was a Southerner."

"Yes, ma'am," Chase answered absently.

He was concerned about Elizabeth. Her face was ashen, her eyes shadowed with pain. She smiled, but he saw no laughter on her countenance or in her eyes.

"I knew it!" Pearl exclaimed. The force of her hand coming down on the table and the rattling dishes brought all eyes to focus on her. She looked at Chase and accused, "That's all you blue bellies can do is pick on our innocent young men and accuse them of crimes they didn't commit."

Visions of Terry dying in the hotel room swam in front of Chase's eyes. He stood so quickly the chair grated against the floor. His personal grief pushed him to self-defense. He was tired of people treating him as if he were less than a human. So he fought

143

for the North, so the North won! That didn't exclude him from the human race.

"First, ma'am, let me say my belly isn't blue. Second, let me assure you this man isn't an innocent. Innocents don't shoot three men in cold blood like Roderick Everett did."

Oh, God, no! Elizabeth silently cried. Hiding her hands in her lap, she gripped them together tightly. *Vanessa cannot be a part of this; she isn't an accomplice to Rod's crimes.* Elizabeth knew Vanessa had been promiscuous, but promiscuity was an immorality that involved only the degrading of your own body. It couldn't be compared to stealing and killing — gross transgressions against mankind. Elizabeth couldn't bear to think of Vanessa as an outlaw . . . or a murderer.

"And," she heard Chase say, "one of those men whom Everett killed, Mrs. Gladewater, was my closest friend."

"Well," Pearl drawled, "there ain't no need for you to take it so bad. Might as well sit down and finish your meal. You paid for it."

"I'm finished, thank you" Chase said coolly, his gaze settling on Elizabeth, who was still pale from her shock. "Goodday, Miss Barrett."

Although Elizabeth was still having difficulty regaining her composure, she was embarrassed by Mrs. Gladewater's rudeness.

Elizabeth rose and said, "I'll see you out, Mr. Daniel."

Silently they walked out of the room and down the hall. At the front door she laid her hand on his arm and said, "I'm sorry about the death of your friend and about the way Mrs. Gladewater spoke to you."

Chase smiled and covered her hand with his. "As you pointed out earlier, Miss Barrett, we are what we are."

"But that doesn't mean that we have to be cruel to one another. Or that we falsely accuse."

"No, it doesn't mean that we have to be cruel, but somehow that's the way we humans seem to cleanse our heart of sorrow," Chase said. He lifted his hat from the rack in the hallway and held the crown in his left hand as he smiled at Elizabeth. "It's been a pleasure meeting you, Miss Barrett. Good-day until I see you again."

Elizabeth smiled sadly, sorry to see him go. Getting to know Chase Daniel would have been pleasant. Still she wouldn't invite him to stay longer, nor would she reconsider going on a buggy ride with him, a pleasure she would enjoy immeasurably . . . a pleasure she didn't have time for now. Her purpose in coming to Texas loomed in front of her. She had to find Vanessa, and even more than before, time was of the essence.

His hand on the door knob, Chase paused to study Elizabeth; every feature of her beautiful face he visually traced. Again he wondered what had been said or done that triggered such a reaction from her. In a matter of seconds all the laughter and joy had been erased from her countenance. Now she was preoccupied; her eyes were darkened with what appeared to be grief.

"Is something wrong?" he was compelled to ask, still concerned with her strange behavior at the dinner table.

Elizabeth didn't immediately answer. Too much had been thrown upon her shoulders too quickly. She contemplated telling Chase about Vanessa and Rod and asking him to let her talk with the prisoner. But second thought assured her that she couldn't get caught up in his gesture of kindness. She liked Chase Daniel; she could like him even more. While she trusted him, she didn't trust the uniform he wore. Chase Daniel was a cavalry officer, and his loyalty belonged to the Union.

She smiled. "I guess the trip from New Orleans is catching up with me. I'm rather tired."

"New Orleans is quite a ways from here," he said.

"In Chalmette really," Elizabeth supplied. "Just below New Orleans."

Chase stored the fact in the back of his mind, but at present he was thinking only of his disappointment in leaving Elizabeth and the possibility of his never seeing her again—a thought he couldn't readily accept. Abruptly he asked, "Do you believe in fate, Miss Barrett?"

Caught off guard by the sudden change of subject, Elizabeth stared into the blue eyes for a second

146

before she stammered, "Well, yes, . . . I guess I do."

"I do, too." Chase's smile held promise in its slow curl. "I promise you we'll be seeing each other again." Without another word, he flipped his hat on his head, turned and walked out of the house.

Elizabeth ran to the window and watched him descend the steps. She heard his soft whistle as he walked across the lawn to the buggy. Although she had refused to spend the afternoon with him and was reluctant to see him go, she was also relieved. One way or another she was going to the Bat Cave to visit with Roderick Everett.

Once Chase sprang into the seat of the buckboard, he swept the house with a smile. Seeing Elizabeth framed in the window, he lifted his hand, waved and called, "As the Mexicans say, Miss Barrett, *hasta luego*."

Until we meet again. The words were his promise.

"Why don't you go on into the parlor, Blake," Elizabeth heard Mrs. Gladewater say as she gathered the dishes from the table in the dining room. "Me and Miss Elizabeth could do with some company this afternoon. Stay for supper and I reckon I'll sell you my leftovers so's you kin take them to the jail."

Blake laughed. "That sounds like a good deal, Mrs. Pearl."

Elizabeth's heart thumped with excitement. Blake Lowell was the answer to her dilemma! He was a Southerner; she could trust him . . . more than she could trust a Union officer. When she heard Blake

147

walk into the room, she turned, her gown rustling around her feet.

"You are indeed an interesting man, Blake," she said sincerely. "A man of many facets."

Again Blake laughed. "Are you telling me that I'm a jack of all trades and a master of none, Elizabeth Barrett?"

"No," she returned, crossing to the platform rocker to sit down, "I wonder why a man who was a captain in the Texas Rangers and who served in the Texas Light Cavalry during the war would be half owner in a brothel."

"Casino." Grinning, Blake wagged a chiding finger at Elizabeth as he sat down on the settee across from her.

"A matter of semantics," Elizabeth retorted, chuckling with him. "And a ploy to get me off the subject."

"Right on both counts," Blake answered. "I don't like talking about myself."

"Painful memories," Elizabeth guessed.

Blake nodded. "My entire family was killed during the war." *My mother and sister were raped before they were killed.* "All our belongings of value were stolen, and our home burned to the ground. I have nothing left to go back to but sorrow. A planter without a plantation ceased to be a planter." A sad smile tilted the corner of his mouth. "That's me."

"You could have returned to the Rangers," Elizabeth said softly.

"I could have," Blake answered, "but I didn't want to. At the end of the war I was thirty-five without a cent to my name. I decided it was time for Blake Lowell to amount to something. So Celeste came up with this idea of a casino that I liked, but I didn't want to stay in New Orleans. The frontier's in my blood."

"So you compromised," Elizabeth said. "You opened the casino in San Antonio and now have a thriving business."

"Well, together Celeste and I opened it," he admitted honestly. "She financed it, but I manage the gambling tables. From what I've earned, I've bought half interest in the place. Some accuse us of charging exorbitant fees for the services we render, but we render excellent service. The casino's reputation is based on honesty."

"Why the food contract to the jail and the stable service?" Elizabeth asked.

"Not a contract," Blake answered, his grin widening. "Celeste and I don't charge the city or county a cent for providing this service. This is part of our responsibility as citizens of San Antonio and Bexar County."

"Again I detect a play on semantics," Elizabeth said. "I would call this bribery—"

"A matter of good business," Blake interrupted. "If we keep the authorities happy, they tend to listen to complaints about our business with a sympathetic ear. You could call it mutual cooperation, and it's well worth the cost."

"On the way home from the pavilion, Chase showed me the Bat Cave and said it was an historic building."

Blake pursed his lips and shrugged a shoulder. "Could be." He wondered in what direction the conversation was traveling. Elizabeth was an intelligent woman; he didn't figure her to play games. "I don't keep up with things like that."

"The back part is," Elizabeth continued, "the part where they keep the prisoners. Chase said this was once the—the old Spanish *presidio*."

"Yeah," Blake said, "I reckon it is. They've sorta redone it."

Elizabeth leaned forward. "Would you take me with you tonight, Blake, and let me see the jail?"

Blake contemplated Elizabeth for a long while before he asked, "Why? And don't tell me it's because you're interested in historic buildings. I don't believe that for one minute. Also I know it's not because you want to spend more time with me."

Elizabeth trusted Blake more than she trusted Chase, but experience had taught her to be wary. Still she realized that she must confide in him if she were going to enlist his help. Lowering her voice so that Pearl wouldn't overhear her, she said, "I think I may know Roderick Everett."

Blake's eyes narrowed. This was a development he hadn't foreseen. Elizabeth's presence at the jail could create a predicament from which he couldn't easily

150

extricate himself. "How would you be knowing Everett? He's an outlaw, a cold-blooded murderer."

"So I've already heard," Elizabeth answered. "Still I believe he's the man with whom my sister eloped."

"This fellow isn't married," Blake said, then realizing he'd stumbled, he hastily added, "or so he said."

Her heart plummeted to the floor, but she steadfastly held on to hope. That was all she had left. "Even if he didn't marry her, he might know where she is," Elizabeth said. "They were heading for Mexico. Roderick told Vanessa there was a fortune to be made down there."

"Maybe he left her in Mexico," Blake reasoned. He'd known Everett for over a year and had never seen him with the same woman twice. He'd certainly never heard him mention a Vanessa.

"I must see Rod, Blake," Elizabeth insisted. "I must know if this is the same person. If he is, he can tell me something about Vanessa."

Because she was driven by desperation, Blake knew Elizabeth would see Everett with or without his help. Blake's best interest lay in helping her. He certainly didn't want Everett spilling his guts to Elizabeth . . . for her sake as well as his.

"Please, Blake," Elizabeth begged. "You can take me with you tonight when you deliver supper to the jail. My sister may also be in San Antonio."

Blake doubted this, but he knew it wouldn't do any good to say so to Elizabeth. "All right, I'll take you." The words were an extension of Blake's sigh.

"But I don't know if you'll get to see Everett. He's a Federal prisoner, Elizabeth, wanted for the murder of three soldiers. Do you know how serious that charge is?"

Oh, yes, Elizabeth thought, *I know how serious the charge is. I've had dealings with Yankee injustice before.* In answer to Blake's question she only nodded.

"Also," Blake added, "the man is dangerous."

"If this is the Roderick Everett who ran away with Vanessa," Elizabeth said, "I know him. He's a boy who—"

"If he is, he's no longer the boy you knew," Blake said. "He's a man, a hardened killer who will use whomever he has to in order to accomplish his goals." He scooted to the edge of the settee and reached out to take her hands in his in a warm, friendly grasp. "Do you understand all I'm saying?" When she nodded, he said, "You must believe it and act accordingly."

Two deputies were on duty at the jail. One of them, Manuel Candello lounged against the wall, looking out the window at the activity in the plaza. The other, Stillman Algernon, sat behind the desk, shuffling through papers.

"Evening," Blake said, a basket looped over each arm. "Ready for supper?" He held the door open for open for Elizabeth.

"Evening," Candello said, hastily straightening up and brushing his hands through thick, blue-black hair. "I am glad to see you," he said in a soft Spanish accent as his eyes ran appreciatively over the diminutive blonde standing beside Blake.

A pleasant grin spanning his thin face, Stillman Algernon unfolded six feet and five inches of lean, lanky frame. "Howdy, Captain." He, too, only had eyes for Elizabeth.

"Gentlemen," Blake said, "this is Miss Elizabeth Barrett." He led her into the office and set the baskets on the desk in front of Algernon. "Miss Barrett," Blake's hand swept to one of the deputies, "this is Manuel Candello and Stillman Algernon."

Elizabeth smiled. "Good evening, Mr. Candello and Mr. Algernon. I'm pleased to meet you."

"Good evening, *señorita,*" Manuel said.

"Howdy, ma'am." Algernon dipped his head and resettled the cud of tobacco in his cheek.

"She's from New Orleans," Blake continued, "and is mighty interested in seeing our historic Bat Cave."

The three men looked at one another and laughed. They saw nothing of interest in the building.

"Do you mind if I show her around," Blake asked, his request innocent enough, his tone quite casual.

Elizabeth's heart was beating in her throat; she could hardly breath because of her excitement. She eagerly awaited the deputies' answer.

153

"Well, now, Captain," Algernon said, his gray eyes flashing to Candello's, "that's a little out of the ordinary, ain't it?"

"It is, but then her request is a mighty unusual one," Blake returned evenly. "And she won't be here to see the building by the time the prisoner is gone."

Stillman rubbed his chin and thought. "Well," he finally drawled, "Don't reckon I mind none you opening the door and letting her see into the cells, but I don't rightly think I can let her go in."

"What if I go in with her?" Blake suggested. "Or one of you." He pulled the linen off the top of the basket and began to set the food on the desk. "The one who remains out here can check the baskets."

Algernon now eyed the food with much the same appreciation as he had Elizabeth. He was hungry, and he did love Mrs. Pearl's fried chicken and biscuits. Besides it couldn't hurt to let the captain take the little woman in to see the cells. Nothing the prisoner could do.

"We'll have to check you for weapons, Captain," Algernon said, "and you ma'am, will have to leave your purse out here. Also, captain, we'll have to leave the door open, so's we can hear everything the prisoner says."

"Stillman," Blake said quietly, "you and I fought side by side for fifteen years in the Rangers, and we fought together in the war. Does that count for anything?"

Stillman's eyes lowered beneath Blake's gaze.

154

"Yes, sir, Captain, I reckon I can trust you."

Elizabeth's stomach was churning by the time she and Blake walked through the door. She was glad for the reassuring touch of his hand on her elbow as they moved down the corridor between the barred enclosures.

"Whatever you do," Blake admonished in an undertone, "don't let the deputies know that you're an acquaintance of Everett's. That could get you in trouble — big trouble."

The prisoner was lying on his bunk when Elizabeth and Blake stopped in front of his cell. Because it was late evening and no lamps were burning, Elizabeth couldn't distinguish the man's features but she didn't recognize him. His dark hair was long and unkempt, his face darkened with several days' beard growth. If this were the Roderick Everett whom she knew, four years had made a difference in his appearance.

Everett gazed curiously at his visitors and wondered who the pretty woman was and what she was doing with Blake. At the moment, however, his concern was centered on his escape from this jail. That Yankee major had spoken the truth when he told him he faced a hangman's noose. The U.S. Army wouldn't let him off with less.

Everett swung his legs over the cot and asked, "Did you bring my supper?"

Blake nodded and urged Elizabeth closer to the cell. "I did. The deputies are checking it out. They'll have it to you in a minute." He glanced toward the door and said in an undertone, "I brought someone to see you. Miss Elizabeth Barrett from—"

"Elizabeth," Everett exclaimed and immediately lowered his voice when Blake grimaced and waved his hand at him. Everett bounded to his feet and rushed across the cell.

"Rod," Elizabeth whispered, "it is you." Relief swept through her body in such proportions that she felt faint and caught the bars in both hands. She blinked back the tears.

"Elizabeth," Rod said again, his eyes moving over her face as if to assure himself it was really her. For a moment both of them were assailed with memories of the past. "What are you doing here?" he eventually asked. Why he asked that question he didn't know. He knew the answer. It was that damned letter *La Mariposa* had him mail from Eagle Pass.

"I'm looking for Vanessa," she said, keeping her voice low, her gaze sweeping back and forth between the door and Rod. Urgently she asked, "Where is she Rod? Where's Vanessa?"

"I don't know," he mumbled, and he didn't know where Vanessa was.

Beginning with her name, the Vanessa he knew changed when she crossed into Mexico to meet and to marry the aged *hacendado,* inheriting his entire estate when he died only a year after their marriage. She had been known as *Dona* Belinda Mariposa de Silva for so long Everett had ceased to think of her as Vanessa, and he was sure that no one else ever thought of her by her given name.

"I don't know where Vanessa is," he said. Her name felt strange to his lips. He shook his head and looked at Elizabeth in puzzlement. He had begged *La Mariposa* not to send the package and the letter. Whereas Vanessa had changed, Rod knew Elizabeth hadn't. She was crusader from the top of her head to the very bottom of her toes, always out to save a lost cause.

Although he wanted to tell her the truth about Vanessa, he didn't dare. He couldn't risk her life; besides she couldn't do anything for *La Maripo* — Vanessa. Besides Vanessa would never forgive him if he directed Elizabeth to her. They must never learn of Elizabeth's presence in Texas or her life would be in danger also.

"I haven't seen her since we arrived in Mexico four years ago," he lied.

"You've got to know — " Elizabeth lowered her voice when she felt Blake's hand on her shoulder, " — where she is." As Rod continued to shake his head, she said, "The two of you are not — not married?" She gripped the bars tighter as her spirit flagged.

Everett glanced nervously at the door and raked his hands through his tousled hair. "No," he laughed bitterly, "Vanessa and I didn't get married. She met a Mexican *hacendado* and married him soon after she arrived in Mexico. He had more money to offer

157

her than me. She wasn't willing to wait 'til I got my fortune."

"Whom did she meet?"

"About seen everything there is to see?" Algernon called from the door.

Elizabeth looked from Everett to the deputy and back to Everett. "Whom did she meet?" she demanded.

"Just about through," Blake answered. His hand clamped around Elizabeth's arm and he gave it a tug.

Elizabeth gripped the bars all the tighter and stayed where she was. She had to know the name of the man Vanessa was with.

"Don't know how to pronounce his name," Rod said, his gaze not quite meeting Elizabeth's. "It's a real long Spanish name. Vanessa changed hers to Spanish also. I didn't stick around after they married."

Elizabeth thought she had become acquainted with every facet of despair during the past six years, but she discovered today that she hadn't. Time was running out, and she knew she wouldn't get another chance to question Rod. She also knew he was lying to her.

Blake caught her shoulders and pulled a little harder this time. "We've got to go," he breathed in her ears, "before they get suspicious."

"No," she cried, lifting tear-stained cheeks to him, "I must find out."

158

"I don't know anything, Elizabeth," Rod whispered. "I don't know the man's name. I don't know what I'd tell you if I did."

"What name is Vanessa going by?"

"Elizabeth," Rod said, performing the first good deed that he could remember for the past six years, "go home and leave Vanessa alone. She's changed; she doesn't belong to your world anymore." *And you sure as hell don't want to become a part of hers. The war isn't anything compared to the world that Bainbridge has created in Mexico and plans to bring to the United States.*

"She'll always be my sister," Elizabeth cried softly, clinging to the bars, her heart breaking as Everett turned to walk to his cot and lie down. Blake caught Elizabeth's arm.

"Is everything okay down there, Captain?" Stillman asked, walking to the door and peering into the cell room.

"Yep," Blake answered, "everything's fine. Miss Barrett thought she saw some of the original structure and we were looking at it. We're on our way out now."

"No," Elizabeth whispered.

"Yes," Blake said and jerked her down the aisle. As they walked toward the office, he said in an undertone, "Dry your tears, Elizabeth. These deputies are trained lawmen, and they know how to read faces. Don't let them know anything."

Elizabeth was adept at hiding her feelings. She

159

nodded, digging through her reticule for her handkerchief which she used to wipe her face. When she reached the door, she looked over her shoulder at the prisoner who lay on his bunk in the same position as she had left him.

"Well, ma'am," Algernon said, "the captain here will take you on a tour through the rest of the building. Me and Candello have got to feed this prisoner now."

"Thank you so much, Mr. Algernon and Mr. Candello, for allowing me to see what remains of the Spanish *presidio,*" Elizabeth said, caring less about the stones and mortar that held this or any building together. "The architecture is reminiscent of the Spanish heritage of New Orleans." On and on she talked, unaware of what she was saying to cover the tears and disappointment in her heart. How close she had come to finding Vanessa, yet how far away she was. Slowly Vanessa was slipping through her fingers.

Although neither deputy was interested in the architectural history of the building, they listened attentively as she spoke.

Blake moved to lean against the desk where the baskets sat. "Well, boys," he said, when Elizabeth finished, "if you've got all your food out and are finished with Mrs. Pearl's basket, I reckon I'll take it back to her."

Nodding his head, Algernon turned to look at Blake. "Tell Mrs. Pearl we rightly appreciate the supper." He chuckled quietly. "Ol' Floyd's gonna be upset cause he missed this."

"He's working tonight?" Blake asked.

"Yep, him and Thurman 'til three in the morning when Johnson and Gravitt relieves 'em."

Chapter Nine

The lamp light did little to soften Chase's facial features as he stood glaring at the two deputies who stood in front of the desk in the jail office.

"We was wrong to allow Captain Lowell to see the prisoner," Stillman Algernon confessed, his eyes never wavering from Chase's, "but he didn't do it, sir. Captain Blake Lowell ain't responsible for this!" His gaze swept to the blood stain on the floor of the sheriff's office. "No matter what you think, the captain wouldn't of killed Floyd no way. They was friends, Major. They rode together as rangers."

"No, *señor*," Candello quietly agreed, supporting Stillman, *"El Capitan* would not do this."

Chase was frustrated. His only lead to the robbery and possibly to Bainbridge was gone. Everett had escaped, sometime between eleven and three. The relief guards were the ones to discover the escape.

"Outside of you," Chase was quickly losing his patience, "Blake was the only one who had access to the prisoner. He was the only one who could have given Everett a knife."

"Well, sir," Stillman walked across the room and spat out the opened window, "we made him leave all his weapons out here, sir, and we searched him to make sure he wasn't carrying any concealed ones on him."

He purposely omitted telling the major about Miss Barrett's visit. First of all, he didn't reckon the young lady had anything to do with Everett's escape. Second, he and Candello were in enough trouble for letting Captain Blake in to see the man and he was afraid if General Sheridan discovered he and Candello had openly violated one of his orders, he would show them no mercy.

"I searched the baskets myself, *señor*," Manuel said, careful to keep his testimony in agreement with Algernon's. He would honor his friend's silence about the woman's visit. "There was no way a knife could have been hidden in it."

"But somehow someone managed to get a knife to him," Chase murmured as he walked to the door and looked at another blood·stain on the floor outside Everett's cell. "The prisoner called Thurman to the cell, managed to grab him and slit his throat. Taking the keys off the dead man's body, he unlocked his cell and slipped into the office to take

163

Allison unawares and slit his throat . . . or, someone came into the office, found Allison alone and killed him, then killed Thurman."

"Well, now," Stillman drawled, raking his fingers down the side of his mouth, "I don't rightly know who might have come up to see Floyd, seeing how late he was on duty."

Stillman ambled across the room and peered out the window into the darkened morning. He was as interested in finding out who helped Everett escape as the Major, and he was willing to cooperate every way he could. He had known Floyd Addision for nearly twenty years.

"Is this the basket the food came in?" Chase asked, moving to Stillman's desk.

Without turning to look, the man nodded.

Chase picked up the basket and examined it. When he set it back down, he noticed something sticking out from under the bundle of wanted posters. Shoving them aside, he found a length of green ribbon—the same kind of ribbon Elizabeth was wearing on her dress when he had seen her last.

Dear God, Elizabeth has been here. Chase hurt; his chest contracted until he thought he would suffocate. *Elizabeth recognized Rod Everett's name today at lunch. My God! Is she involved with Everett? Did she slip him the knife?* Chase found the thought repugnant. Still he couldn't divorce himself from the idea that she knew Everett. Something continued to nag him. A small fact about Elizabeth and Everett he should remember but couldn't. Unobserved by either deputy, Chase picked up the ribbon and tucked it into his pocket.

"No one else came to see the prisoner?" he asked quietly.

Stillman paused a few minutes before he lied outright to the Major, but he saw nothing to be gained by mentioning the lady's name. "No, sir."

Jack Stevens opened the door and walked into the office, shaking his head. "Nothing," he said to no one in particular as he entered. "We can't find a sign of Everett. No telling where he's holed up at or where he's gone."

Chase figured he was either holed up at *Le Grande* Casino or he was on his way to Mexico, but he said nothing. Sheridan wasn't willing to listen to him; and he wasn't willing to scare Everett any more than he was now. What information Chase had he'd use to find Bainbridge himself.

"You find anything?" Jack asked.

"Same as you. Lowell brought their supper about six." Chase waved at the deputy, "Candello checked the basket himself and took the prisoner his food. But the ones who can answer our questions are dead."

Stevens nodded. "I'll guess I'd better get over to the Menger and make my report to the General. He's going to be madder than hell about this. What about you?"

"Have him send for me if he wants to see me. I need to think awhile."

Outside the Bat Cave the two men separated. Stevens walked toward the Menger. Chase lit a cigar and stood in front of the building to gaze into the star-studded sky. An elusive piece of information kept flitting through his mind, here one minute, gone the next, but never staying long enough for him to get total recall . . . something that connected Elizabeth with Roderick Everett.

A methodical man, one accustomed to filing information and to finding solutions to problems, he stood there smoking and sorting through all the facts he could recall about Elizabeth. Always he came back to her plantation in New Orleans, Louisiana. Suddenly the answer came; he snapped his fingers and threw down his cigar. Both Elizabeth and Everett were from Chalmette, Louisiana.

He started walking and didn't stop until he was in front of Pearl Gladewater's house. He didn't want to wake the old lady, but he did want to talk with Elizabeth before anyone else discovered she'd been at the Bat Cave. He eased on the porch and moved to the window he guessed to be hers. His fingers slipped between the pane and the casement, and he raised it slowly and quietly.

He slipped into the room, waited a moment until his eyes adjusted to the moonlit room, and walked to the end of the bed. As he gazed at the slumbering woman, he decided that Elizabeth Barrett was easily the most beautiful woman he'd ever seen. Even in sleep she was beautiful.

She was lying on her left side, her blonde hair a tangled web of silver around her face that rested in the palm of one hand. The right arm stretched the length of her body on top of the sheet that was pulled over her breasts. In the moonlight he saw the smooth and creamy shoulder. Chase fought the urge to reach out and caress it.

Wanting a woman wasn't a new experience for Chase, but wanting one to the exclusion of all others was. He had the strangest feeling as he gazed at Elizabeth Barrett that she was a woman who would keep his interest for a long time. Despite her maturity, she had an air of innocence that intrigued him. She also had an aura of mystery that concerned him.

Elizabeth breathed deeply and turned over on her back, pushing the cover down to her waist. Chase gazed at her small breasts, revealed through the thin material of her nightgown. He felt a warm stirring in his groin.

Reluctantly he turned and looked around the room for Elizabeth's white dress. He found it lying on the back of the slipper rocker in front of the fireplace. With two strides he crossed the distance, picked up the dress, and found the ribbon missing from the collar.

Silently he returned to the bed. Leaning over, he clamped his hand over Elizabeth's mouth at the same time that he said, "It's me, Miss Barrett, Chase Daniel. Please don't be frightened. I have my hand over your mouth to keep you from crying aloud and waking anyone."

Elizabeth's eyes opened wide, and her scream was muffled by the strong hand that bit into her cheeks. Her hands came up and clawed at the offensive binding, but Chase didn't relinquish his hold.

Chase could feel her accelerated heartbeat. "I'm not going to hurt you," he promised in a low voice, wishing his body didn't respond so readily to her proximity. "I just want to talk with you, and I didn't want to awaken Mrs. Gladewater."

Elizabeth couldn't imagine what was so important that Major Daniel wanted to talk with her at this time of the night and had compelled him to sneak in through the window. She stopped her fighting and stared at him over the hand that still capped her mouth. She shivered when his elbow accidentally grazed her breast. She wished her stomach would quit turning somersaults.

Chase sat down on the side of the bed and gazed into those shadowed eyes. He watched the frenetic beat of her pulse and thought she was frightened. "Don't be afraid," he whispered. "I'm not going to hurt you."

Elizabeth nodded to reassure him.

"If I remove my hand, will you promise not to scream?"

Elizabeth nodded her head. She wouldn't dream of screaming and awakening Pearl Gladewater. The last thing she wanted was that woman to find a man in her bedroom. She would find herself on the streets again. The minute Chase removed his hand, she reached down and grabbed the sheet and tucked it under her chin.

What's so important that you had to talk to me at this time of the night?" she asked, her voice softening when she realized how it seemed to thunder through the silent house.

"It's not night," Chase replied in hushed tones, his eyes caught in the golden cloud of hair that tangled in riotous curls around her face, giving her an air of vulnerability. "It's four o'clock in the morning."

"Still too early for you to come visiting, Major Daniel." Her eyes darted beyond his shoulder to the curtains that were blowing in the gentle breeze. "And especially through the window."

Chase made no comment. He pulled a match out of his pocket and lit the candle on the night table. Then he sat down on the bed beside Elizabeth.

"Why did you visit Rod Everett at the jailhouse?" When Elizabeth didn't answer, he handed her the length of green ribbon.

Elizabeth's breath caught deep in her stomach; she felt the muscles in her chest contract. This time the somersault were caused by fear, not by Chase. "Did the deputies tell you?" she asked.

169

Chase shook his head. "No, I found it at the jailhouse."

"Many women wear ribbon," she murmured, forcing a calmness into her voice she was far from feeling. "What made you think it was me?"

"The ribbon is missing from the dress you wore to the concert yesterday morning," he said. "And I know that both you and Everett were from Chalmette, Louisiana." When Elizabeth made no comment, he said, "Tell me why you went to see the prisoner."

"Why should I?"

"Because Everett escaped about two hours ago and killed two deputies. You could be an accomplice to their murder."

"Mr. Algernon and Mr. Candello?" Elizabeth asked in a shocked whisper.

"No, Addison and Thurman."

"Does anyone else know about my visiting the jail?" she asked.

"I told no one," Chase replied. "Please tell me what you were doing there. Maybe I can help you."

Elizabeth wanted to tell Chase the truth, but six years under an occupational government, those first turbulent years full of bloodshed and injustice by the conquerors, had taught her to guard her tongue. New Orleans had been fraught with informers—some of whom a person considered to be his closest friend. She was also well acquainted with Yankee injustice. Ironically, the same wheels of justice seemed to be rolling over her once more.

"I'd feel more comfortable in my dressing gown," she said and pointed to the foot of the bed. "It's down there."

Chase reached behind him, picked up the wrapper, and handed it to her. When she didn't immediately turn loose of the sheet behind which she was hiding and continued to stare at him, he turned his back and walked to the window.

He heard the bed squeak as she stood up, the gentle swish of material, and imagined the way she looked standing there in her nightgown, the candlelight filtering through the gauzy material to silhouette her body. He had the greatest urge to turn around and look at her, but too much was at stake for him to risk it for a moment's pleasure. He had lost Everett, but maybe he had gained another lead that was far better.

As Elizabeth slowly buttoned the shift, she thought of what she would say to Chase. Disinclined to lie and fearful of the judicial system under the military governments, she would tell him the truth, but only as much as was necessary to convince him of her innocence. She liked Chase, but she had no reason yet to trust him.

"Why haven't you told anyone that I visited Roderick?" she asked.

"Because I didn't want circumstantial evidence to get you involved in a lengthy investigation."

"Thank you," Elizabeth said quietly, truly

171

touched that Chase had thought enough about her to ask for her explanation before he judged her and before he involved her.

"Roderick Everett lived in Chalmette," she said. 'I hadn't seen him since July, 1862. He was only a boy, frightened of war and devastated by the collapse of the only society he knew. Unable to cope, he deserted the army and was on his way to Mexico to seek his fortune."

"I would have judged him to be older than you," Chase said and turned to see her standing beside the night table, the candle light glowing in her golden hair.

"He was in years," Elizabeth answered, "but not in maturity. Rod was always looking for the pot of gold at the end of the rainbow. When he left Chalmette in 1862, he thought he'd found it."

"Was he more than a friend?" Chase's interrogation had gone beyond the investigative to the personal level. Chase, the man, was interested in her answer.

"No," Elizabeth answered with a sad gentleness, "just a friend who was a victim of the war. You see, it's difficult being on the losing side."

Chase's heart went out to Elizabeth. He yearned to take her into his arms and hold her. "Why didn't you tell me this at dinner yesterday? Why didn't you ask me to take you to see him? I would have."

"I should have," Elizabeth admitted. "But you see, I haven't learned to trust the . . . occupying

. . . government yet. I've found it to be harsh and unjust." She paused and looked at him. "I'm just now beginning to have confidence in it."

Her confession touched a tender cord in Chase. He watched as she nervously brushed her hand through her hair.

"Well, Major Daniel," she said, "where do we go from here? Am I under arrest?"

Instead of answering, Chase asked, "Did you slip Everett a knife?"

"No."

"Did Lowell?"

"Not while I was with him."

"Then you're not under arrest," Chase replied quietly.

"Do you believe me?" Elizabeth asked, wishing she could see his face more clearly but he was standing beyond the circle of light.

Chase moved closer and caught her hands in his. "Yes, I believe you."

The confession was Elizabeth's undoing. It reached deeper than mere caresses. Overwhelmed by the sensations that rushed her body, she looked down to see her smaller hands completely covered with his larger, calloused hands. The roughness felt good to Elizabeth. The gentle pressure gave her strength, as well as reassurance.

In comparison to his sun-browned hands, Chase thought, hers were creamy white. Leaning over, he kissed her gently on the forehead and felt her tremble beneath his touch. Inadvertently she swayed closer to him, and her breasts, free from the confines of undergarments, brushed against his chest. Chase felt a tightening in his loins and cursed himself for being ten-thousands kinds of a fool.

For the first time in her life Elizabeth was consumed by lust. She wanted far more than the whisper light brush of his mouth on her head. She wanted him to possess every inch of her body. She wanted all of Chase Daniel, and she wanted him to have all of her. Sheer willpower forced her head down. She kept her face lowered, for her desires were written there for Chase to read and she mustn't let him. She would not let him know the power he had over her.

Chase cursed the moment; while he wanted so much more than a kiss, he dare not take it, else he would push Elizabeth farther away, else she would think she was buying his silence with her body.

"Yes," he repeated, "I believe you," and his breath felt like thick honey as if oozed over her fevered skin.

"Do you really believe her?" Jack Stevens asked as he paced back and forth across his room at the Menger.

"I want to believe it," Chase answered.

Jack's eyes narrowed and he studied his friend. "Are you involved with her?"

174

"No." *But I wish I were.*

Jack flexed his shoulders and said, "All right, Chase, I'll send to New Orleans and get all the information on her I can, and I promise to keep her name out of the investigation as long as I can."

"Longer than that," Chase told him. "I don't want her name connected with Everett's in any way, and I don't want the report sent to anyone but me." Chase looked at his friend. "Promise, Jack, you won't show it to anyone else but me."

Jack sighed but nodded. "I promise, Chase. As soon as I get the information, I'll send it directly to you wherever you may be." He suddenly grinned. "God help me if Sheridan ever finds out about this."

"I'll take the blame," Chase told him. "If the information is something he should know, naturally I'll show him, but I don't want to take a chance on losing her. She's the only lead we have now, so we can't take a chance on anyone knowing that we're aware of her friendship with Everett. I want her to continue her journey to Eagle Pass."

"Which is right on the Mexican border," Stevens mused, "where Everett was supposed to have found his fortune." After a moment's silence, he asked, "How do you propose to keep her under surveillance?"

"My troopers and I will escort the mail stage."

The captain laughed shortly. "You think of everything."

175

"I try," was Chase's dry reply.

"You think she might be involved with Bainbridge?"

"She could be."

"Now the picture is clear," Jack said. "For a minute, there, Chase, I thought you were turning into a mortal like the rest of us and were interested in the woman for herself."

Chase smiled and shrugged nonchalantly, unwilling to let his friend know he'd spoken the truth. He *was* interested in the woman for herself.

Chapter Ten

From her seat inside the lobby of the Plaza House Monday morning, Elizabeth watched the stage driver and the young man who rode guard tighten the straps that held the baggage to the top of the mail coach—the fourth time they had done this within the past hour. She surmised that they were as impatient to be on their way as were the passengers who lounged inside the hotel. She glanced at the elderly couple and their teenage son, Proctor Horn, the obese reporter who was pacing the floor, and the young black woman sitting across from her.

"Just how long are we going to be delayed?" Horn muttered the question to no one in particular and expected no answer as he sat down next to Elizabeth and squeezed her further into a corner.

With the toe of her shoe she gently nudged the

scarf-covered wicker cage over so that it sat in front of her, and she leaned down to see that Jefferson was still curled up and asleep beneath the long settee. When she raised her head, she encountered the sympathetic smile of the black woman sitting across from her.

"Mr. Ingram," the man next to Elizabeth called out when the driver stamped into the room, "just how long are we going to be delayed?"

"Don't know, Proctor," the driver retorted curtly, wiping his sleeved arm across his forehead. "Can't leave until the rest of the army escort arrives." When he heard the groan of protest, he said, "I understand how you feel, but them's my orders."

"And when will the escort get here?" Horn demanded, a growing belligerence in his tone. "We're already two hours late. I'm supposed to be in Castroville by tomorrow. At the rate we're going, I won't be there by next week." He twisted from side to side, pressing Elizabeth into the wall, as he searched for his handkerchief.

"If ya'll want to, you can go into the dining room and get yourself a cup of coffee while we're waiting," Ingram announced to all the waiting passengers and proceeded to pull off his leather gloves as he sauntered across the room. "That's what I'm going to do, and," he muttered under his breath, "I'm gonna be a'adding a lot of whiskey to that coffee. Makes the trip a lot faster and the ride more pleasurable."

"It's outrageous to charge us twenty dollars a seat, DeWitt." Mopping his perspiring face with the handkerchief, Proctor Horn rose and followed the driver. "You can't guarantee to get us where we want to go on time."

"Well, now I can guarantee that you'll get to your destination as well as anybody else. Just can't guarantee the time, Mr. Horn. But if you don't like the way this here stagecoach is run, my advice is to write about it in the newspaper and find other transportation," the jehu drawled amicably. "Besides, it ain't my fault that the prisoner decided to escape from the Bat Cave last night."

"You know as well as I do that—" Horn's words trailed into silence as he and the driver disappeared into the dining room.

Glad the man was gone, Elizabeth heaved a sigh of relief and scooted over. She and the woman sitting across from her smiled at each other again.

"I'm Elizabeth Barrett," Elizabeth said.

"Joy Franklin," the black woman replied. She held a small portmanteau in her lap.

"How far are you traveling?" Elizabeth asked.

"Ft. Clark."

"You're married to a soldier?"

Joy laughed softly and shook her head. "I'm a schoolmarm and I've been hired by the government to teach the black soldiers how to read and write. My first assignment is at Ft. Clark."

"How marvelous!" Elizabeth exclaimed.

"Are you going to one of the forts?" Joy asked.

"No, I'm on my way to Eagle Pass," Elizabeth replied, "to see my sister."

When they lapsed into silence, Elizabeth opened her reticule, took out the small box that housed the two brooches and opened it. She delicately fingered the butterfly and wondered about Vanessa. During the entire journey from New Orleans, Elizabeth had whiled away her hours in wonderful daydreams of life at The Rose after Vanessa returned. She had imagined her sister's wanting to come home, their working side by side to restore the plantation to its former glory, and bringing back to it the grandeur the war had taken away. They would give beautiful balls once again; they would court and someday marry.

Yesterday, after she had seen and talked with Everett, Elizabeth realized her dreams were wishful thinking. In her fantasy she was selfishly creating the person she wanted Vanessa to be. Last night she had faced reality. Vanessa was her own person and had a right to choose the kind of life she wanted to live. Elizabeth had given up the idea that Vanessa would ever return to The Rose. Now her desire was to see her again and to visit with her, to learn and accept this new Vanessa.

Elizabeth wondered why Vanessa had neglected to tell her of the marriage and her change of name. Was Everett right? Vanessa really didn't want to be found. In returning the brooches she was breaking the last ties with Elizabeth and The Rose. Elizabeth couldn't accept this explanation. Vanessa was really ill or she was in some kind of trouble. Perhaps, she, too, was involved in criminal activities like Rod. Concern turned into deep-seated worry. She would find her sister, Elizabeth promised herself. She would!

Tired because she'd gotten little sleep last night, she closed her eyes and leaned her head against the back of the settee. She thought about her early morning visit with Chase and smiled. They were even, she decided. When they first met, he thought she was a whore; she thought he was like Emery Watkins. Both of them had been wrong.

Chase was different from the majority of Union officers with whom she had been in contact; he was kind. He didn't jump to conclusions and form judgments based on circumstantial evidence. Take last night for instance, when he found her ribbon, he didn't immediately bring down the gavel and pronounce her guilty. He gave her the benefit of the doubt; he came directly to her for an explanation. For that she was grateful.

Before he left her room, he had returned her ribbon to her and assured her that all would be well. He promised he would keep her name out of the investigation. Later a note had been delivered in which he admonished her to tell no one—absolutely no one, including Blake Lowell—that he knew of her visit to the jail. That would be his and her secret. The note ended with *hasta luego*. The words seemed so personal and intimate to Elizabeth; they were a caressive promise.

With no effort at all, Elizabeth could hear Chase's deep, rumbling laughter; she could see the craggy face softened with a smile. Lost in new and wonderful fancies about Chase, Elizabeth wasn't aware of the people milling around until she felt a hand on her shoulder and heard a masculine voice softly say, "Elizabeth."

For a second her heart pounded furiously against her chest, her breathing quickened, and her expectations soared. Her dream manifested itself. Chase Daniel was here. When she looked up to see Blake Lowell, expectation turned into disappointment.

"Blake," she murmured, "how nice to see you."

Although Elizabeth liked Blake and was not displeased to see him, she yearned to see the darkly handsome face of Chase Daniel; she wanted the hand that rested on her shoulder to be Chase Daniel's. She had told Chase she didn't want to know him better, but that was a lie. She did. As much as she loved Vanessa and wanted to see her again, Elizabeth was reluctant to leave Chase and continue the search.

She especially wanted to see him one more time before she left for Eagle Pass; she wanted to thank him for believing her. Even now her gaze went past Blake as she sought out that familiar physique among all those army-blue uniforms. A black trooper walking by, tipped his hat and smiled. Elizabeth returned the greeting. Odd, days ago she despised that uniform and transferred all her hatred to the men who wore it. Now, she found herself thinking steadily about a man who not only wore the uniform but who was the epitome of everything that uniform symbolized . . . everything she thought she hated.

"May I sit down?" Blake asked.

"Of course," she said and immediately scooted over. As she looked at Blake, she wondered how she could have ever thought he looked like Johnny. Now that she knew him better, he didn't resemble her brother at all. *But,* an inner voice of conscience nagged, *Blake Lowell is the man you should be daydreaming about instead of Chase Daniel. You share a common heritage; both of you were born and reared in the South. Yours is a cultural bonding, such as you and Chase will never share. You'll never cross the gulf that separates you and Major Chase Daniel, no matter how much either of you desires it!*

"I guess you head about Everett," Blake said.

Elizabeth nodded. "Mrs. Gladewater talked about nothing else this morning. She doesn't seem to think he's such an innocent southern boy anymore. Both of the deputies were killed, we heard." When Blake nodded, she asked, "What do you think they'll do with Rod if they find him?"

"They've already found him," Blake answered.

183

"Beside the Castroville road. His belly filled with lead."

"Oh, my God," Elizabeth exclaimed, her face blanching.

Blake caught her hand in his and squeezed gently. As much as he wanted to tell her that he'd been the last person to see Everett alive, he didn't dare. Already Chase Daniel suspected him of killing the man. While he was guilty of taking his body and dumping it on the Castroville Road, he hadn't murdered Everett.

All night Blake had contemplated telling Elizabeth about Everett's deathbed confession: Vanessa, now known as *Dona* Belinda Mariposa de Silva, had been Bainbridge's mistress for the past three years. She was tired of the life she was living and wanted to return to the United States to give evidence against Bainbridge. Everett, totally obsessed with the woman, was returning to Mexico to rescue her.

Until Blake found out more about Bainbridge and his mistress, until he verified Everett's story for himself, Blake decided to keep the information to himself. He didn't want to get Elizabeth involved in something unnecessarily, and he didn't really trust Everett. Everett had never been a close companion of truth.

"I'm sorry Everett didn't know anything about your sister," he eventually said.

"Me, too," Elizabeth replied.

Lowering his voice so that no one could overhear him, he said, "Don't worry about being implicated in Everett's escape. No one knows you visited Everett. Neither Stillman, Candello, nor I told the soldiers."

"Thank you," Elizabeth murmured, remembering the secret that she and Chase shared. She feared that somehow she was getting entangled in a web of deceit.

"Elizabeth," Blake said, "I want you to know I'll be looking for Vanessa. Will you describe her for me?"

Everett smiled. "Better than a description of her, I'll show you a painting." She withdrew the miniature from her purse and handed it to Blake.

"She's lovely," he finally said, his eyes taking in her dark beauty. He looked up. "The same green eyes as you."

"Like Papa's."

Blake returned the portrait and said, "I came here this morning for another reason, Elizabeth."

Elizabeth looked at him in surprise.

"I had to see you again," he said, "not to tell you about Everett or your sister, but for myself."

Blake Lowell was a gentleman, Elizabeth thought as he spoke, polished and debonair. And he cared for her. But he didn't stir her senses as did Chase Daniel. His presence didn't drive her to distraction. He wasn't the substance of her dreams; he didn't bring excitement and anticipation into her life. Her

185

heart didn't soar at the thought of seeing him again; it didn't plummet to the bottomless abyss when she mistook him for someone else.

"For the first time since the war," Blake confessed, his clasp tightening, "I've found something that I want desperately." The brown eyes that stared directly into Elizabeth's were somber and serious.

Elizabeth couldn't misunderstand Blake's statement, nor did she pretend to. Neither could she let him assume that she returned his feelings. She gently withdrew her hands from his. "I like you very much, Blake, and I enjoy your company. I hope you'll always be my friend."

"Nothing more than friendship?"

"No," Elizabeth answered.

"Another man?"

Yes—the thought flashed through Elizabeth's mind with clarity—it is another man. A man whom she met for the first time the night before last. No matter what Chase Daniel felt for her, she knew he was the first man—the only man—to touch her heart.

Her hesitancy was Blake's answer. "I was afraid of that," he admitted and with a sad smile added, "It's Daniel, isn't it?"

"Daniel?" Elizabeth repeated, her eyes widening with astonishment. She was startled that Blake knew.

Blake nodded his head. "Has to be Chase Daniel," he returned. "Can't be someone back home.

No man who cared about you would let you come out here by yourself to search for your sister."

Elizabeth didn't confess her growing feelings for Chase; that was a secret she shared only with her heart. She said, "No matter who the man is, you of all people should know that each of us has things which we must do by ourselves. Finding my sister is my task and mine alone."

A sad smile curved Blake's lips as he stared at her. "Be careful, Elizabeth," he admonished. "The frontier is a rough place, tough on men, hell on women."

A black trooper stepped through the door of the Plaza House and yelled, "All of you who are riding Santleben's mail coach to Castroville, Ft. Inge, and on to Eagle Pass, please board. We'll be leaving in ten minutes."

Elizabeth turned to look at the man. His campaign hat sat at a jaunty angle on his mop of curly black hair, and his thumbs were hitched into his weapon belt, his legs straddled. If ever she had seen the massive oak with roots so deep that it could never be budged she saw it now. This man was six feet five inches in height, possibly taller; his shoulders were broad and tapered into slim waist and hips. Tough muscle-hardened legs tightly stretched his breeches. Although he spoke to all the passengers, his gaze was directed at the black woman who sat across from Elizabeth.

DeWitt Ingram clapped his battered hat on his

head as he bustled into the lobby. "Does this mean that we're finally ready to go, Sgt. Liberty?"

"Yes, sir," the trooper answered.

"Lonnie," Ingram yelled to his young assistant, "open the door and let's load 'em up."

Elizabeth bent down and shook Jefferson. "Get up," she said. "It's time for us to get going."

The boy slowly opened his eyes and blinked; then he rolled from under the settee.

"I'll take the valise and bird cage," Elizabeth instructed. "You carry your luggage and get on top of the stage."

"Yes, ma'am," Jefferson answered, quickly setting his hat on his head.

She turned to Blake. "I guess this is good-bye."

"I'd like for it to be *hasta luego.*"

No, it can't be, Elizabeth thought. *Hasta luego belongs to Chase.* His face superimposed itself on Blake's; dark blue eyes stared into the secret coffers of her heart.

"I'll be riding out that way," Blake told her. "I'll look you up."

Elizabeth nodded.

"Everybody aboard who's gonna get aboard?" Lonnie Pickard's voice rang through the vacating lobby.

"I have to go," Elizabeth said, turning and reaching for the bird cage.

"Here, I'll carry these," Blake said, leaning over to pick up her portmanteau at the same time that

188

Elizabeth did. They bumped heads and began to laugh. They were so engrossed in their laughter, neither Blake nor Elizabeth was aware of Chase's approach until he coolly said, "Good morning, Lowell, Miss Barrett."

Elizabeth flinched away from Blake and raised her head to look at Chase in surprise. She couldn't keep the color from flushing her face as she thought about the secret between them. Somehow it bound them together in an intimacy that was far more sensual than that created by love-making.

"Good morning, Major," Blake said, his tone as frosty as Chase's.

"Guess you heard about the prisoner's escape last night?"

"Yep," Blake answered.

Elizabeth allowed her eyes to move from the tips of Chase's mud-caked boots up the tight stretch of army-blue pants and tunic with their yellow stripes, to the white campaign hat, pulled low on his furrowed brow, not quite concealing his questioning eyes. His gloved hands were planted firmly on lean hips—in that deceptive pose that seemed to be so indolent and casual. But which could be so different, Elizabeth thought.

"Did you also hear about his death?"

Blake knew Chase was pushing him, hoping to send him over the edge. He inhaled deeply and waited a moment before he answered, "Yes, Major, I've heard all the details several times. I'm sure you

189

know that I spent the past three hours being interrogated by Captain Stevens."

The two men stared at each other for length before Elizabeth broke the uncomfortable silence. She prayed that Chase's coming had nothing to do with her visit to the jail. Now that she'd talked to Rod she felt renewed urgency to find Vanessa. Although she was frightened of the answer, she asked, "To what do we owe the pleasure of your company, Major? Surely you didn't come just to tell us about Everett's escape and death."

"No, ma'am," Chase answered as he searched her face for a hint of her thoughts, "that's not why I came at all." His eyes narrowed as his gaze slid over to Blake who stepped closer to Elizabeth, and although he didn't touch her, his stance was protective and loving. "I'm here because I'm the officer in charge of the military troop that is escorting this stagecoach to Ft. Inge."

Relief whooshed through Elizabeth. "You'll be riding with us," she exclaimed. She was delighted that he'd be traveling with them. They would have more time together.

"I'll be riding with you," Chase returned, his lips lifting in a smile.

Haunted by Chase's continued promise of *hasta luego,* she asked, "Did you know you would be with the escort this—the last time I saw you?"

"No," Chase answered softly, binding her to him with those mesmeric eyes. "Everett's escape and death changed my plans . . . to my advantage I might add." He paused fractionally and said, "But I would have seen you again no matter what."

"Major," DeWitt Ingram stomped into the lobby, "let's get a move on. Passengers are irritated, and I'm already about three hours late. We got a lot of miles to cover and a short time to do it in."

"Are you ready to board?" Chase asked.

"Just about," Elizabeth returned. "Please give me a few minutes to say good-bye to Mr. Lowell privately."

Chase stared at her for a few moments before he nodded his head and walked off. He was irritated with Elizabeth's request.

"Thank you for being my friend, Blake," she said and reached for her portmanteau and Gloria's cage, but Blake shook his head and held on to them. "I don't know what I would have done without you."

"Beck would have found you another driver," he said and chuckled.

"But that driver wouldn't have been my friend."

When they reached the stage, Blake said, "Remember, Elizabeth, anytime you need me, I'll be there."

"That's a pretty big promise," she countered with a smile, her gaze inadvertently going to Chase who leaned against one of the porch pillars, his expression closed.

"But one that I mean." Blake set the bird cage

191

and the portmanteau inside the coach; then his hands circled Elizabeth's waist, and he easily swung her in. He said lowly, "Also, remember I'll be looking for your sister."

As Elizabeth nodded and smiled, she saw Chase scowl.

Blake closed the door and said, "I'll be seeing you around." He stepped back to stumble against Chase who had moved to stand immediately behind him.

The two men gave each other another long, hard look.

Finally Chase called, "Sgt. Liberty, take 'em on out. I'll catch up with you later. I have some more business I need to attend to before I leave."

The black trooper nodded and lifted his hand to flick the edge of his hat in salute. DeWitt Ingram's "Giddy up!" echoed through Main Plaza; his whip cracked through the air, the traces snapped, and the coach creaked as it abruptly lunged forward.

Jefferson held on to the metal railing of his seat with one hand and to his hat with the other. Elizabeth tightly clutched the scarf-wrapped wicker cage and her portmanteau; Joy, sitting next to her, clung for dear life to her luggage. Crowded onto the seat with the two women was the teenager who was disinclined to talk to anyone including his parents who sat across from Elizabeth. The youth crossed his legs, rounded his shoulders, and pulled his hat over his face. Across from Elizabeth, Proctor Horn sat beside the boy's parents who were traveling to their oldest son's farm about ten miles out of San Antonio.

Elizabeth leaned her head out of the window and gazed at the two men who stood side by side in the plaza.

Chapter Eleven

Chase and Blake stared at the beautiful face framed in the coach window until the stage disappeared onto Commerce Street headed toward Castroville. Without moving, Chase asked, "Did you take Everett his supper last night?"

Blake rocked back on his heels and put his hands in his back hip pockets. Staring at the cloud of dust, all that remained to remind him of Santleben's Mail Coach, he said, "I've already answered these questions, Major."

"I want to hear the answers again," Chase said. Two nights in a row he had gone without rest. He was tired and irritated. Seeing Elizabeth acting so cuddly with Blake hadn't helped his disposition any at all, and Blake's attitude was a further irritant. "Did you take Everett his supper?"

"Yep," Blake sighed.

"What did he talk about?"

"He didn't talk, Major. He was a prisoner, not my friend."

"What was Deputy Addison?"

Blake's eyes momentarily clouded with regret. "Floyd was my friend," he said. Then he whirled around. "I know what you're getting at, Major, and you can dismiss it right now. I carried all the prisoners their meals but that doesn't mean I killed Addison or helped Everett escape. No matter how justified I might have thought the boy to be in the killing of the three Union soldiers, I wouldn't kill my friends nor would I have placed their lives in jeopardy. Just about anybody here"—he waved his arm around, taking in the whole of San Antonio— "would have gladly aided and abetted Roderick Everett. The majority of us have no sympathy whatsoever for Yankees, so why pick on me?"

"I'm not picking on anyone," Chase returned with a sigh. "I'm following due process of law, Mr. Lowell. The army payroll was stolen, three soldiers were murdered, and two deputies were murdered because of Everett's escape. The person who helped Everett escape either committed the murder himself or is an accomplice, and I have reason to believe that the person who perpetrated this crime has no loyalty to any cause—be it southern or northern—else he wouldn't have murdered the deputies since there was no cause for their deaths."

Blake said nothing and Chase continued. "Yester-

195

day morning when I went to visit Everett, I noticed that you and Addison were quite chummy. He had no qualms whatsever about letting you go in to the prisoner by yourself."

"And he had no reason to have any qualms," Blake answered. "He knew he could trust me. Last night when I carried Everett his supper," Blake said, deliberately neglecting to tell him that Elizabeth accompanied him, "Deputies Candello and Algernon were on duty. Candello was the one who inspected the basket of food and believe you me, he went through it thoroughly. In fact, he's the one who carried the basket in to Everett." Blake was silent for a few minutes, then added, "Addison and Thurman came on duty at eleven. My guess is that someone came to visit them, and that someone is responsible for Addison's death and Everett's death."

"Someone who Addison and Thurman knew and trusted," Chase said. "That's the only way he could have gotten close enough to slit his throat with a knife."

Again Blake nodded.

"Who could that someone be?" Chase mused.

"I don't know, Major," Blake said, "but I sure wish the hell I did. Then I could get you and the entire army off my back!"

"Are you going to be around?" Chase asked.

"Here and there," Blake answered.

"Mostly where?" Chase demanded, his question more personal than investigative.

As if he read Chase's mind, Blake grinned. "Mostly where I want to be, Major." He lifted his left hand and brushed the tip of his hat. "Now, I'll say good-day, sir. Hope you have success in finding your murderer." Easily he swung into the saddle of the Arabian and rode toward Commerce Street, leaving in his wake velvety laughter that coiled mockingly around Chase who watched the flank of the horse, with the distinguished markings, until Blake disappeared.

Mid-afternoon Ingram stopped the coach to let the couple and their son off; then he drove a few miles farther to stop at a small stream of water and allow the horses to drink. The remaining passengers, Joy, Elizabeth, and Proctor Horn, hot and dusty, gladly disembarked and moved upstream from the horses to drink themselves. Jefferson, not in the least worried about the dust and grime, took a quick drink and darted off to explore the new territory.

"I'm so glad we stopped," Elizabeth said to Joy as they knelt beside the stream and splashed water on their faces and neck. "I feel as if I've been baked alive." She reached back to pull her damp clothing from her back.

Afterwards the two women sought refuge from the heat in the shade of the short, scrubby trees scattered across the rolling hills. They talked quietly together while the jehu and Lonnie rehitched the stage, and Proctor walked around, grumbling to whomever would listen.

"Are you ladies ready to return to the stage coach?" Samson's deep, rich voice came from behind Elizabeth.

Joy looked up at him and smiled. "I would much prefer not to return to the coach," she replied. "I'd love to be on a horse riding the open plains like you're doing."

Elizabeth smiled to herself. Samson was lost in Joy's beautiful chocolate brown eyes.

"If I had an extra mount, ma'am," he said, "I'd certainly let you ride.

"I think that could be arranged, Mr. Liberty," Chase said as he crested the small incline immediately behind them.

Although she was kneeling, Chase's words caused Elizabeth to whirl around so fast she lost her balance.

"Major," Samson said. "I'm sure glad to see you, sir. I wasn't expecting you to join us so soon."

"Finished my business sooner than I expected," Chase said, his eyes directly on Elizabeth who was rising to her feet. Looking at her but speaking to Samson, he said, "I don't mind riding the rest of the way to Castroville in the stage. I'll visit with Miss Barrett if she doesn't mind."

Elizabeth looked from Chase to Joy's and Samson's expectant faces. While she wanted to ride with Chase, she didn't want to appear too eager. Lowering her head and brushing the twigs from her skirt, she said, "I don't mind your riding back in the stage, Major; however, I'm afraid you'll find me poor company. Since I didn't get too much rest last night, I'm afraid that I'll be napping some this afternoon."

"Then I shall be quiet and allow you to get some rest. My pleasure will be watching a beautiful lady in repose."

Elizabeth searched his face to see if he were teasing her; he wasn't. His eyes were swirling with that enigmatic emotion that tended to devastate her nervous system. She couldn't stand the verbal caress, fraught with sexual undertones. Even with Proctor Horn riding with them, she and Chase Daniel were going to be entirely too close in that coach.

As they returned to the stage, Chase walked close enough to Elizabeth that their arms almost grazed . . . but not quite. She didn't know what she would do if he touched her. His very presence put her on edge; his touch would push her over. Yet, she yearned to feel his hands on her.

As if he could read her mind, Chase turned when they reached the stage, caught her waist and swung her inside. Her hands automatically landed on his shoulders. For long minutes they stared at each other, the only two people in the world. She pushed back in the seat and watched as Chase boarded.

"Tell you what," Proctor said — his jacket and waistcoat long ago discarded — as he peered inside the coach, "I'm gonna ride up there with the boy. It's got to be cooler than riding in the coach." He fanned himself with his wet handkerchief.

"There's plenty of room," Elizabeth said. While she wanted to be alone with Chase, she was afraid to be alone with him. She had no defenses where he was concerned; her heart was exposed; her emotions susceptible.

Proctor mopped his face. "There's room," he agreed, "but I still think I'll ride atop." And up he went.

Looking out the window because she didn't know what to say to Chase, Elizabeth watched Ingram make the last inspection of the coach before he climbed into the driver's seat.

Chase leaned over and pulled the cover from the wicker cage. "Have you named the bird yet?"

Ingram's "giddy up" echoed through the air and the stage lurched to a move.

Elizabeth watched the tiny canary cock its head to the side and burst into song. "I'm calling him Gloria."

"You're calling *him* Gloria?" Chase asked dryly.

Elizabeth nodded and her lip automatically lifted into a smile. "His full name is Glorious Burst of Song."

Chase leaned back, folded his arms over his chest, and looked at her blankly for a few second. "I'm sure there's a connection somewhere that I'm missing."

Elizabeth shook her head. "None. I'm simply

200

going to call him by the Latin word for glorious—
gloria."

Chase grinned. "A special name for a special bird."

Elizabeth laughed. "He awakened me as the first ray of sunshine hit the room with a lovely burst of song. I lay there listening to him for the longest time thinking about home."

"Chalmette?" Chase asked, enjoying the reflective softness of Elizabeth's countenance.

"Chalmette," she said. "The Rose is surrounded by beautiful rose and azalea gardens. And right now they're in full bloom; the air is filled with their perfume. The birds are singing, and the butter-flies—" She smiled. "That's why I wanted Gloria; he reminded me of home. Vanessa will love him."

"Vanessa is your sister?" Chase asked. When Elizabeth nodded, he asked, "How did she end up out here?"

Elizabeth was silent for so long Chase didn't think she was going to answer. Eventually she said, "My father was a colonel and after he was killed in the war, my mother had no desire to live. Father was her entire life. That winter she contracted pneumonia and died. My older brother," her voice grew faraway, "John Whitney Barrett, II, came home soon after-wards, badly wounded and suffering from melan-choly."

Tears welled up in Elizabeth's eyes. "He wasn't meant to be a soldier. He was an artist, a gentle man

201

who wanted only to create life on canvas. Johnny was never the same again."

Although Chase's heart was lightened to learn that Johnny was her brother, he also shared her grief. He had seen many such men broken by war. "Is Johnny waiting for you at The Rose?" he asked.

The tears rolled down Elizabeth's cheeks. "Yes," she whispered, "he's waiting for me. He's buried in the pear orchard beside Mama."

Chase wanted to take Elizabeth in his arms and hold her, but he wasn't sure what to do. If she had been any other woman, had he been wearing anything but this uniform he would have followed his heart's desire, but he was afraid of ruining this moment of truth and revelation between them. He compromised by reaching out and clasping her hands in his. He squeezed them gently and reassuringly.

"He escaped dying in the war," Elizabeth said. "He died because he was protecting me against unwelcome and unsolicited advances from a Yankee major who was in charge of the hospital in my home. Major Emery Watkins."

Chase listened as Elizabeth poured out the story in lurid detail. When she was through, his eyes were darkened with pain and anger at the injustice; he hurt with her. "I'm sorry," he murmured but the words seemed so trite and ineffective.

The moment of deepest grief past, Elizabeth pulled her hands from Chase's clasp and fumbled in her pocket for a handkerchief. Wiping her eyes, she said, "I overcame my sorrow through work. After Watkins was transferred, I worked with the new commanding officer until the house was no longer needed as a hospital. Then I started working to rebuild The Rose."

"Nothing but a child yourself," Chase said.

"Hardly a child," Elizabeth responded. "I was twenty-one. I guess that's why I adjusted better to the harsh reality of war. Vanessa never did. Neither did Rod. Vanessa and Rod ran away to Mexico where they thought they could find happiness."

Chase felt a tingle of excitement. Another piece of information to connect Everett with Bainbridge. Perhaps the link that freed Elizabeth from suspicion and bound Vanessa with Bainbridge. "How long has it been since you've seen your sister?" he asked, refusing to think about the possibility of Elizabeth's being involved.

"Five years," Elizabeth replied. "She was seventeen when she left; she'll be twenty-one now. Quite a young woman."

"And you're twenty-five."

Elizabeth leveled green eyes on him. "Twenty-five. How old are you?"

Chase chuckled. "Thirty."

"I'm sure you're wondering why I'm running around unmarried and without children," she said.

Chase shrugged. "Most women your age are generally married with several children," he agreed.

203

"I've spent the last seven years of my life rebuilding everything that you Yankees destroyed and tried to wrest from me. Finally, Mr. Daniel—" she inadvertently wagged her index finger in Chase's face.

He caught her hand in his and said, "Please call me, Chase." When she looked as if she were about to protest, Chase said lowly, "Please."

She nodded and pulled her hand from his clasp. "Finally, sir," she compromised, "I have rebuilt my plantation so that we're breaking even. Not making any money, but, thank God, I'm not losing it either, and I'm not in debt above my ears to carpetbaggers."

"So now you can give your attention to courting?" Chase said.

"Yes," Elizabeth drawled as if the idea were new to her, "I can now give my attention to courting, Mr.—"

"Chase," he said.

When Elizabeth made no effort to repeat his name, he said, "Please say it, Miss Barrett. You'll find that it's not that difficult to pronounce." He reached out and lifted her chin with the tips of his fingers. "Look at my mouth and listen to me." He exaggerated his lip patterns as he slowly pronounced his name. "Now let's see if you can do it."

Elizabeth swatted at his hand, but he caught that one also and held it against his leg.

"I'll turn you loose when you say my name."

"Blackmail," Elizabeth murmured.

Chase nodded. "What can you expect," he said lightly. "After all, I'm a Yankee."

"Chase," she whispered and liked the feel of it on her tongue so much that she repeated it. "Chase Daniel."

"May I call you Elizabeth?" he asked.

Drowning in the lake-blue eyes, Elizabeth moistened her lips—totally innocent of the provocativeness of the gesture—and nodded her head.

"Elizabeth," Chase whispered. "Elizabeth Barrett." He wanted to pull her into his arms and to make love to her, but he dared not move, lest he frighten her away. "What does the "R" stand for?"

"Rose."

"Elizabeth Rose Barrett."

"I was named after the wild roses that grow around the plantation," she explained. "Climbing roses. Up a trellis outside my bedroom, their fragrance wafts through the open window to permeate the entire room. I have a mahogany four-poster bed with a white canopy, bedspread and bolsters. Every night Aunt Feldie turns my covers down and puts a red rose on my pillow."

Chase easily envisioned Elizabeth's bedroom, so much so that his fantasy ran as wild as the roses that grew outside her window. By closing his eyes, he could see a beautiful woman lying on those satin coverlets, her blonde hair swirling around her face.

"Do you ever wear your hair down?" he asked abruptly.

"Not too frequently," Elizabeth answered. "It's easier to take care of when I'm working if it's up."

"I'd love to see it down," he said and wondered what it would feel like to brush his fingers through the silken tresses. When he felt the heat slowly moving through his body to settle in his loins, he shifted his legs and asked, "Who's Aunt Feldie?"

"A black woman," she answered, "born to Grandpapa in slavery. She and her husband, Wallace, still live at the plantation. Aunt Feldie is the housekeeper and Wallace runs the sugar mill."

"How long do you plan to visit your sister?" Chase asked.

"I'm not sure," Elizabeth replied. "In her latest letter she told me that she had been sick. I'll remain as long as it takes for her get the strength to travel."

"Travel where?" Chase asked.

"I'm taking her home," Elizabeth said.

"She's ready to return, I take it," Chase said.

Elizabeth tilted her head, a tad defensively. "She belongs at The Rose, Mr. —"

"Uh-huh," Chase said, wagging his index finger back and forth in front of his face.

"Vanessa's a lady," Elizabeth repeated. "She belongs at The Rose. That's her home as well as it is mine."

"That may be the way you perceive it, Elizabeth," Chase said, "but that may not be the way it is. If Vanessa didn't want it four years ago, what makes you think she's going to want to return now?"

"The war's over," Elizabeth said. "We're rebuilding the South."

"That is your life," he said, "but it's not Vanessa's."

"You can't possibly know what Vanessa's dream may be," Elizabeth exclaimed. "You don't know her."

"But I know people," Chase answered, and he thought he had made a good assessment of Vanessa. "Vanessa ran away because she awoke to find her dream turned into a nightmare. She won't find life in the South any different when and if she returns than it was when she left. She can never recapture those pre-war years. The South has changed, Elizabeth. For better or worse, it has changed. It will never be the same again. Perhaps your sister will never find her dream back in the bayous of Louisiana."

"I've found mine," Elizabeth argued.

"No," Chase said tenderly, "you created a new dream in the New South. You didn't give in to despair and sorrow; you battled the elements and won. You're a strong woman, Elizabeth Rose Barrett."

"Thank you," Elizabeth whispered. "Thank you for everything."

Chase moved so that he was sitting beside Elizabeth. He clasped her hands, leaned over and gently pressed his lips against hers. When he felt her tremble, his first impulse was to take her into his arms and kiss her deeply and thoroughly, but he didn't react impulsively. Elizabeth was innocent. He must move carefully and slowly. Ignoring the flames of desire that leaped through his body, he reluctantly pulled his lips from her.

The gentleness and restraint of the kiss shook Elizabeth to the very depth of her soul. It affected her more than the passionate one she had shared with Chase the first night she met him. For a fact, she knew Chase Daniel was the man to whom she would open the door of her heart willingly.

Looking at her tremulous lips, Chase murmured, "Thank you, Elizabeth Rose."

For a long time they sat there holding hands, laughing and talking together.

"Major!" Samson called, riding back to the stage at break neck speed, Joy close behind. "Messenger from Castroville. The bank has been robbed."

Ingram pulled the stagecoach to a halt, and in a matter of minutes Chase was mounting his horse, and Joy was in the coach.

"Three of 'em," the messenger from Castroville said. "Wounded one in the shoulder, but they got away. Sheriff's got a posse and they took after 'em."

With an economy of words, Chase divided his men into two patrols: one would accompany him to Castroville; the other, under the leadership of Samson, would escort the stage. Chase doffed his hat at Elizabeth. "Thank you for a pleasurable, ride, Miss Barrett. I look forward to seeing you again." Then he lifted his gloved hand in the air and waved to his men.

Elizabeth leaned out the window and yelled, "Major Daniel!" When he didn't stop, she cupped her mouth with her hands and yelled the second time. "Chase!"

The major halted at the top of the crest and looked over his shoulder.

"Be careful."

A slow, easy smile slid across Chase's face. "I will, ma'am, and that's a promise."

Chapter Twelve

As the afternoon sun sank in the west, the stage coach rolled down the last hill to cross the Medina River and stop in front of Vance's Hotel and General Store in Castroville. Elizabeth had never been more pleased to see a day's travel end than she was today. She was fatigued and covered in grit; her clothes, wet from perspiration, were plastered to her body. Yet her smile reflected her happiness. She was concerned about the danger Chase faced in trailing the outlaws and eagerly anticipated her next meeting with him.

"Guess you heard about the bank robbery, Mr. Ingram?" one of the stable boys asked as he ran and grabbed the traces.

"Sure did," DeWitt answered, spitting over the side of the wagon. He climbed down from the driver's seat as Lonnie leaped to the ground on the other side and ran to open the coach door. Ingram rubbed his hand across his mouth. Grinning, he reached out, knocked the boy's hat off, and ruffled his shock of red hair. "We lost part of our escort because of it. I'll just bet you robbed that bank, Martin, just to see if I'd make it without them soldiers."

"Oh, no, Mr. Ingram," the boy protested amidst laughter as he playfully scuffed with the jehu, "I wouldn't do that because that's where I'm keeping my money. Besides"—a gust of wind caught his hat and sent it spinning through the air, and he took out after it—"I don't have a horse of my own, and my ol' mule certainly can't outrun those horses of Major Daniel's."

"Sure couldn't, Martin," DeWitt replied. "That's for sure." He lifted his head and scratched his chin and neck.

Martin looked at Lonnie and grinned. "Amelia's been all dressed up today, Lonnie. She figured you'd be riding guard, and Maw figured you'd be hungry tonight, so's she and Amelia cooked supper for you—if you're a'mind to come." The boy giggled. "I told Maw you might not want the food, but you'd eat it just so's you could be with Amelia."

"Reckon I'd like to have supper with your family," Lonnie answered, and when Ingram threw back his head and guffawed, the guard's face turned red.

211

"Well, Mr. Pickard," the jehu said, "I see you have your plans already made for the evening."

Lonnie grinned and nodded his head. "If you don't mind, sir?"

"Nope," DeWitt said, "don't mind a'tall. Just make sure the coach and horses are taken care of first."

"That'll take hours," Lonnie complained.

"Yep, it will for sure if just one of you does it. However" — Ingram rolled his eyes and looked suggestively at Martin and Jefferson — "if you hire you some help, you'll be finished real quick like, boy. Now as for me, I got to get a bite to eat." He patted his stomach. "I'm real empty."

Martin looked at Lonnie, and the two of them exchanged a secret smile. Both knew DeWitt Ingram was headed for the nearest saloon with the cheapest liquor. Food wasn't one of his primary needs. He believed a man would die of dehydration quicker than he would from hunger.

"Make sure you're here on time in the morning, boy," Ingram warned. "I'll be pulling out without you, if you ain't, and I won't pay you one cent."

"Yes, sir, Mr. Ingram," he said.

Ingram then turned his attention to the passengers. "Ladies and gentlemen," he announced loudly, making a point to extract the big gold watch from his pocket as Proctor Horn stiffly climbed down, "I'll be pulling out at six in the morning. If you're planning on making the next leg of the journey with me, I would advise you not to be late. Lonnie, here," he jerked his head in the guard's direction, "will unload your luggage and take it to your rooms. Let him know your plans for tomorrow. He'll need to come by at five to start loading 'em up. You can spend the night here at Vance's Hotel or at one of the other hotels in town—take your choice—but this is as far as I'm taking you. You'll walk the rest of the way or hire a buggy."

A shrewd businessman with an ear open for an opportunity to make money, Jefferson had overheard Ingram's conversation with the guard. On the ground now, he said to Pickford, "I'll help you with the horses, if you want. I groomed the soldiers' last night, and the major said I did a real good job."

Lonnie's long face perked up instantly. "Well, yes sir," he drawled, "reckon I do need some help."

As Jefferson discussed the terms of his employment with Lonnie, Elizabeth and Joy disembarked for the night, soon to be settled into adjacent rooms on the second story of the inn. By nightfall Elizabeth was completely refreshed; she had bathed and changed clothes and washed and dried her hair. When she went to coil it into a chignon, Chase's words whispered in her ear. Remembering Chase's kiss, she reached up and traced the shape of her mouth that automatically curled into a smile that settled in her green eyes. She would let her hair hang down for him.

213

Humming, she brushed her hair from her face and tied a ribbon in it. She did this several times, getting a little exasperated when curling tendrils refused to be cramped behind the bow. Finally she sighed and let the recalcitrant locks wisp around her face.

Opening the door, she walked onto the veranda and sat in one of the rocking chairs. As she waited for Jefferson to finish his chores so they could go eat their supper, she gazed at the beautiful and tranquil Medina River lined with the majestic cypress and pecan trees. Beautiful gardens, filled with blooming flowers, decorated the back lawn. A cool, evening breeze brought the fragrance of the flowers to Elizabeth and brushed the loose tendrils of hair against her temples and cheeks.

When she heard the heavy thud of booted feet, her heart began to leap in anticipation. Making sure she kept her gaze straight ahead so Chase wouldn't think she'd dressed up for him or that she eagerly awaited his return, she nervously reached up and straightened the collar of her dress. She felt to make sure the ribbon was in place in her hair. She pinched her cheeks and lightly kneaded her lips with her teeth to ensure soft color.

"Evening, Miss Barrett." Samson's deep voice came from behind her across the long veranda.

"Good evening, Sergeant," Elizabeth replied, striving desperately to keep the disappointment out of her voice, hoping her heart would resume beating again. She turned her head and smiled. "I suppose you've come to see Joy."

"Yes, ma'am," he said, doffing his hat. "Figured we'd eat some supper together." Three or four long strides put him in front of Joy's room, and he knocked. "You're welcome to come with us if you want to, ma'am," said he.

"No, thank you," Elizabeth returned at the same time that Joy opened the door and walked onto the porch. Although she did want something to eat, she didn't want to intrude on Samson's and Joy's evening. "I'm waiting for Jefferson. I need to make sure he has something to eat. I'll get something later."

When Elizabeth saw Joy, she said, "That dress is lovely. Yellow is so becoming on you."

Joy laughed. "You're just saying that because yellow is your favorite color. Gloria is evidence of that."

"She might be saying it cause it's her favorite color," Samson said, "but it's true, Miss Joy. You sure do look pretty tonight."

Joy's brown eyes danced with happiness, and her voice had a wonderful breathless quality when she said, "Thank you, Sergeant Liberty."

Elizabeth stood and moved to the railing as the couple headed for the stairs. Unable to contain her curiosity any longer, she called, "Sergeant Liberty, have you seen or heard from Major Daniel?"

"No, ma'am." Samson stopped at the top of the

215

stairs, turned and looked at her with question.

"I just wondered if he'd apprehended the bank robbers," she said. "I'm worried about him."

"I don't think so," Samson said, "else he'd be back. You want me to give him a message when I see him?"

"Oh, no, thank you," she hurriedly returned. "I'm just concerned." She dismissed them with a wave. "Have an enjoyable evening."

Not long after Samson and Joy left, Elizabeth saw Jefferson rushing up the lawn from the river.

"Miss Elizabeth," he yelled as he scampered up the stairs, "can I sleep with Corporal Man and the rest of the soldiers?"

"Where are they sleeping?" Elizabeth asked.

"Down the river away in a large grove of trees," he said excitedly and pointed. "And they asked me if I wanted to bed down with them."

Elizabeth smiled. She could see no reason to deny his request. Since the troopers were escorting the stage onto Uvalde, they would be getting up at the same time as she in the morning and would see that Jefferson was with the coach at departure time. "I suppose you do?"

"Oh, yes, ma'am," he said. "I'll sleep on one of their bedrolls just like them. Why, Miss Elizabeth, they're real soldiers. Some of them fought in the war—" Realizing what he'd said, Jefferson abruptly hushed up.

"Some of them fought in the war and now

216

they're out here fighting on the frontier to protect the settlers against Indians and outlaws," Elizabeth continued smoothly.

No matter how destructive the war had been to her private world, she knew it had also destroyed the evil institution of slavery on which the entire economy of the South had been founded. It had paved the way for a better society and economy. In the immediate aftermath of war, people had difficulty seeing this because of the debris. Once that was cleaned up the South would rebuild herself — stronger and healthier this time.

"Never feel guilty about the part your people played in the war between the states," Elizabeth told the boy. "Not only was this a fight for independence for them but it was a search for integrity and manhood." She laid her hand on Jefferson's head and smiled fondly. "And the search has just begun, Thomas Jefferson. That's why I want you to get the best education possible. You have a responsibility, a heavy responsibility, to bear now. You must lead your people out of slavery into equality."

Jefferson listened patiently, nodding his head the entire time Elizabeth spoke, but the minute she finished, he said, "Can I spend the night with them, Miss Elizabeth?"

Elizabeth laughed at Jefferson and realized that her message was beyond the ten-year-old's comprehension at the moment. "Yes," she answered, "you *may* sleep with them tonight. What are you going to do for supper?"

Jefferson grinned. "Eat with them. We're going to cook it over a fire, Miss Elizabeth. I'm going to eat just like a soldier." A far-away look in his eyes, he said, "You never can tell. Maybe I'm not going to school back east and become a doctor. I might become a soldier like Sergeant Liberty and Corporal Man."

"You have plenty of time to decide," Elizabeth answered.

"Yep," Jefferson returned, skipping down the stairs two at a time, "I reckon I do. Goodnight, Miss Elizabeth, I'll see you in the morning."

"Good night, Jefferson," she called to the running boy.

She returned to the rocker, but now that she was by herself she was restless, she was hungry, and she was lonely. She didn't want to sit out here; she wanted to do something, and she wanted to do it with somebody . . . with Chase Daniel.

She heard a door open and shut, and Proctor Horn, freshly bathed and dressed, stepped onto the veranda and walked to the railing.

"Mr. Horn!" Elizabeth said pleasantly. "I'm surprised to see you here."

"Why?" he asked, looking at her quizzically.

"I don't know," Elizabeth returned. "For some reason, I thought you would be staying elsewhere."

Horn laughed. "No, my dear lady, although I

must pick up this bill myself, I'll stay in hotels while I'm gathering material for my articles. The places my newspaper finds for me aren't altogether to my liking. Vance's Hotel suits my purposes just fine."

Proctor's stubby fingers caught the length of gold chain that dangled from his waistcoat pocket and extracted his watch. When he clicked the lid back in place and returned the watch to the pocket, he said, "I don't mean to be taking liberties, Miss Barrett, since we only met this morning, but knowing you're a woman by yourself and have no escort, I'm offering to take you to dinner, ma'am."

Elizabeth's face lit up. She didn't relish an entire evening in Proctor Horn's company, but then she couldn't tolerate the idea of spending the entire night hungry. All things considered Horn's company was preferable to hunger pains.

"Thank you, Mr. Horn," she answered. "I would love to go with you."

Elizabeth found the trip through Castroville delightful. The Alsatian village was clean and beautiful. The houses, reminiscent of the owner's European ancestry, were constructed of native stone. Much to her surprise, she found Horn's company entertaining. Her evening went by rather quickly.

"When I decided to come out west," he told her as they finished their apple cobbler and fresh cream, "I had a fair idea what to expect from a frontier, but I was totally unprepared for Texas."

"That bad?" Elizabeth asked.

"Worse," Horn replied. "I've slept in houses that were nothing more than stakes firmly fixed in the ground to form the walls and were inhabited with scorpions and insects. The roof was thatched. If it didn't rain, I had a relatively peaceful night, fighting for bed space with only the scorpions and insects. If it rained—" he shrugged his shoulders and both of them laughed.

When they were through eating, Elizabeth and Proctor returned to the hotel. He hastened to his room to complete an article he was working on, but Elizabeth, not wanting to be cooped up quite yet, walked to the river and gazed at the water, glimmering an iridescent silver in the moonlight. She gazed at the hotel and watched as one by one the lights were extinguished. Finally she pushed away from the tree. She had to go to bed. Morning would come early, and a long, hard day of traveling awaited her.

The minute she walked into her room, she smelled the fragrance of the flowers from the gardens below. Fumbling in the dark, she found a match on the dresser. She struck it and lit the candle that spit and sputtered before it finally exploded into soft light. Looking at her reflection in the mirror, she unfastened her dress and slipped out of it. Wearing only her chemise, she picked up the candle holder and walked to the bed. When the circle of the light flickered over the turned-down bed covers, she saw the rose. In her haste to set the candle down, she almost dropped it.

Chase Daniel had been here in her room! Her mysterious visitor bearing a gift had to be Chase! He was the only one with whom she had shared her story of the bedtime rose.

With gentle hands, she lifted the rose and pressed the delicate petals against her face. The thought of his being in her room, of touching her turned-down bed covers assailed all her senses and rendered her mindless and weak with longing. She ran to the window and threw open the wooden shutters. She peered through the moonlight, but she saw no movements; she heard no sound. He was gone. Then a long way down the river, she saw the distant glow of the camp fire. She heard the soft, distant sound of a harmonica and singing . . . laughter . . . and more music.

Never taking time to reason about her actions, she quickly donned her chaste, white wrapper and fastened it down the front. She blew out the candle, grabbed the stem of her rose, and rushed out of the room. Down the stairs, across the lawn, and up the river she scurried, unmindful that the rocky terrain was tearing her slippers to shreds. Breathless, she arrived at the outer edge of the camp and stood for a moment, looking at the black troopers who sat around the fire. She leaned against a tree and listened to the melancholy wail of Corporal

221

Man's harmonica.

When the music stopped and the men started to laugh and talk, her boldness deserted her. She dropped back several paces to wonder what had possessed her to come to the soldiers' camp. She began to question her certainty that Chase had been in her room, that he had left the rose. Anyone could have put the rose on her pillow. The innkeeper. The maid.

Corporal Man began to play again, but Elizabeth didn't stay. She turned and slowly retraced her steps. When she reached the river, she heard a man whistling. She listened for a moment and recognized the tune to be the same as Corporal Man was playing. Her heart began a thunderous beat, and without thinking she moved closer to the water to see . . . to see Chase Daniel standing on the shore.

Chapter Thirteen

A small inner voice urged Elizabeth to leave the river, to return to the safety of her hotel room, but she couldn't. As if she were rooted to the earth as were the trees, she remained in her hiding spot and watched as Chase slipped out of his jacket and shirt. In the pale glow of the moon she saw the broad, muscled shoulders, and the shadowy growth of hair across his chest. He hung his gun belt over a low-hanging limb. Then he shed the rest of his clothing. In an instant he dove into the water, swam several feet and returned to the shore. Slinging his hair out of his eyes, he stood straddle-legged and dropped his hands to his hips.

Though the intimate parts of his body were

shadowed, Elizabeth's imagination was inflamed; she needed not the light of day to recall vividly his exquisite masculinity. At the thought she drew in her breath sharply and fire raced through her body—not the heat of shame but sheer flames of desire that curled in her loins to become a blaze of unsated hunger. She gazed at the glistening beauty of Chase's muscled frame.

Chase stood a moment longer, his eyes piercing into the wooded darkness. He felt as if he were being watched, but he didn't have prickles of alarm. Because he didn't feel as if he were in danger, he quickly dismissed his suspicion. Probably a passerby.

He climbed atop a fallen tree trunk and dove into the river again, the water sliding easily around him, cooling, refreshing, and delightfully welcome after a hard day in the saddle. He turned on his back and let himself float lazily as he listened to the music from the camp.

The bank robbery was still on his mind. Although he and his men had joined the posse in search of the outlaws, they found no trace of the men; they vanished without a sigh. Chase flipped over and dived beneath the surface again. His men were some of the best in the entire Union army; he trusted them, and they were highly trained and skilled, but they, like he, lacked the specialized skill and training of the Southwestern Indians. Therefore, they had been unable to find and follow the outlaws' trail. Chase was sure they had left one, no matter how invisible it might have appeared.

His powerful arms sliced through the water. If he were to rid Texas of the outlaws and the marauding Indians who crossed the Mexican border at will, he must have scouts who were trustworthy and who thought, rode, hunted, and tracked like Indians. But where would he find men like this? That was the question he had posed himself all afternoon. That was the question that remained unanswered.

Defying every code of morality she had been taught, Elizabeth remained in the shadows of the wooded area and watched Chase as he swam. Powerful arms propelled him through the water so easily — powerful arms that not so long ago held her. She looked down at the flower she held. Calloused hands had plucked the rose; gentle fingers had nipped it from the bush; a man with a tender and compassionate heart laid it on her pillow.

Elizabeth protectively cradled the rose in her hand. Ever since she had first met Chase Daniel she had been filled with conflicting emotions. She was aware of herself as a woman, a woman who wanted and needed a man. Why did Chase Daniel have the power to do this to her, she wondered, when he was but one man among many! Yet, when he entered a room he was the only man among many. She was aware of no one else, only Chase Daniel. He and she shared nothing in common. Yet, his mere presence caused her body to tremble with anticipation; it caused her to ache with yearning.

Although an innocent, Elizabeth understood that the basic attraction between her and Chase was sexual. He simply wanted her and had established that the first time she saw him. Far more startling was the discovery that she wanted him, too. And the more she was around him, the greater her desire became. As she watched him bathe, she was tempted to reveal herself, to give herself to him and to satisfy this longing in her soul.

But newly revealed emotions could not so easily override years of convention and morality. Not even the thought that she was far away from home and no one would be the wiser compelled her to move closer to him.

Chase finally stood, lifted his hand to brush his hair out of his face, and waded ashore. Elizabeth didn't think she'd ever seen a man look more magnificent; he looked as if he were sculpted in silver. So compelling was his presence she quickly and irrationally pushed arguments and doubts aside; she unconsciously took a step toward him and in so doing stepped on a twig. The snap broke the mesmeric bonding and jarred her back to reality.

Standing still, lest he hear her, she watched him slip into his undergarments and breeches. He raised his head and looked around. Elizabeth had the distinct feeling that he could see her through the blanket of night. She must get away before he discovered her. Cautiously she backed up, only to hit a low hanging branch, the limb swatting against the trunk of a nearby tree with a dull thud. Whereas only moments before desire had rooted her to the ground, now fear bound her.

Chase now knew he was being watched, deliberately so, and he wondered by whom. He knew it wasn't Indians; he was too close to civilization and the watcher too clumsy. Nor was it one of his troopers; he would have identified himself. Without moving quickly so as not to alarm the onlooker, he reached for his gun belt. Although he didn't feel threatened, he decided to be cautious. He pulled his revolver from the holster and carefully made his way through the trees, straining through the darkness.

He hadn't gone far when he saw a streak of white and heard someone running through the undergrowth. Quickly, reflexively he was in pursuit. In a bright spill of moonlight he spotted the flowing robe and the small figure that ran in the direction of the hotel. Elizabeth! Heat tinged through his body to settle in his loins when he thought of her deliberately viewing his nakedness.

He slid his gun into the holster, and his pace

quickened as he followed his silent observer. He saw her turn her head; she knew he was following her. Then she broke through a clearing a short distant from where he had been swimming, and he could tell that her moon-frosted hair was flowing down her back. She stumbled and fell to the ground, the rose dropping from her hand.

Concerned that she'd hurt herself in the fall, Chase instantly knelt down and clasped her shoulders. At first he could only look at her hair, curling strands of pure gold framing her face, a long curl hanging over her shoulder. He'd swear this was the first angel he'd ever seen.

"Are you hurt?" he asked, bemusement casting his voice low and faraway.

"No," she whispered tremulously and stared into his craggy face. The velvet shadows of night blanketed them in intimate indigo darkness.

His hand loosened its hold on her shoulder, raised and headed toward her hair. The movement startled Elizabeth out of her bemusement. A flutter that could only have been fear started in her belly and sent a throbbing, excited heat into her groin. For a second, she felt lightheaded and giddy. Her entire body was shaking uncontrollably. For the first time in her life, she was close to swooning.

"You're shaking," Chase exclaimed, his voice fraught with concern. Both hands gently tightened on her shoulders and he pulled her closer to his body. "But it's too warm for you to be cold." Then, "You're frightened!"

Hardly were the words out of his mouth than a ghastly thought careened through his mind. "You — you didn't know that was me taking a bath?" He pushed her away so he could see her face. Surely she wouldn't have stood there and watched a stranger!

"I knew it was you," she assured him, letting the warmth of his touch embrace her as she inhaled the clean, fresh odor of his body.

"Why did you run from me?"

She ventured an upward gaze into the shadowed eyes. "I was frightened."

"Of me?" he asked.

"No," Elizabeth silently answered, feeling weakness trickle through her. "Of myself."

She gazed at Chase's muscular chest. She saw the droplets of water glistening on the mat of thick black hair that disappeared below the band of his trousers. She remembered every inch of his magnificent body, and again she was inundated with yearnings that she couldn't yet identify but knew with certainty must be satisfied.

Her confession touched Chase as nothing else could have and filled him with pleasure. He wanted to reach out and touch her, but he was afraid to. Elizabeth wasn't a whore; she wasn't a wanton, nor was she a sexually experienced woman. She was an innocent, awakening to pas-

229

sion for the first time; therefore, he had to move carefully and slowly. If he didn't, he'd lose her for sure. Lose her before he ever won her, and win her he firmly intended to do. He watched her lower her head and reach out with groping fingers until she found her rose.

Cradling it in the palms of her hand, she brought it to her face and inhaled deeply. She felt that same electrical aura around Chase that she had felt the first time she saw him. Unwittingly, she again became a part of that sexual current that flowed from him.

Chase's hand moved to her chin, and he lifted her face.

Reluctantly Elizabeth forced herself to look up. "What's happening to me?" she whispered.

"What you feel," he explained with a reverent awe for her innocence, "is desire, the emotion that a man and woman share when they discover that something special exists between them." Rising, he extended his hands; she raised hers to his. "Let me show you how wonderful it can be, Elizabeth Rose." Her name was a caress that whispered through the air.

Slowly, very slowly so as not to alarm her, Chase drew her to her feet and stood for a moment looking at her, at her glorious hair, each shining strand stroked by starlight. Again moving carefully he pulled her into his arms. He lowered his dark head to hers and pressed his lips against hers in a most tender awakening, the most tender acquaintance of man to woman.

Elizabeth, caught up in the magic of the night and the spell of the soft harmonica music, had no disposition to deny him or herself. Tonight she was only a woman searching for romance and love. Time and logic held no sway; surrender and desire were all she sought.

When Chase had held her in his arms before and had kissed her, Elizabeth had felt the electrical current flowing between them. Yet, this kiss — new with tenderness and fraught with care — stunned her; liquid fire burned all the way down her body, melting her bones. She opened her mouth to make some protest but none would come. Chase took advantage of her confusion to kiss her again. This time his lips were more ardent, more demanding.

Her mouth opened wider beneath his, and the passionate response set Chase's blood to boiling. His arms tightened around her slight frame to draw her closer, and the kiss deepened. When finally he lifted his face, he whispered huskily, "I have dreamed of you coming to me ever since I first saw you in the lobby of Beck's House. I knew from the moment I saw you that you were destined to be mine." His warm breath brushed against her flaming cheeks. "Mine, Elizabeth Rose Barrett."

"No," she whispered. The bold, possessive

words frightened her. They seemed to brand themselves into her soul, truly making her Chase's.

"Yes," he said.

As his fingers lowered to Elizabeth's hips, he realized how scantily she was dressed. No drawers. No petticoats. The flames of passion totally engulfed him, and he held her against him, her small breasts pressing into his chest.

When Elizabeth felt the hard length of his arousal, she began to tremble anew and to shake her head wildly, her hair a rich cascade of waves around her face. "Don't," she enjoined.

"I must," he said huskily. "I must make you mine."

Ineffectually, her hand pulled at his, the movements causing her to brush against him and only serving to incite him further. "You have gone far beyond the bounds of decency, sir." Her whisper was feeble resistance. "You are shaming me."

"No," Chase murmured, exhilarated by her innocence. His lips traced the pulsating cord of her throat. "I'm not shaming you, Elizabeth Rose. I am loving you, and love knows no shame."

"Love, sir?" Elizabeth murmured, her heart beating so hard she knew Chase could hear it, that he could feel each pounding blow. Yet, she found that she had no desire to be free of his embrace. If anything, she wanted to be drawn closer and closer until they were one, until he and she flowed together to become one powerful current, a bolt of white lightening that flashed to dissipate totally the inky blackness of night. " 'Tis more like you've removed the floodgate to passion and desire. I feel as if I'm drowning."

"Passion and desire are the sisters of love," he said.

"I know from experience that not all sisters remain together," Elizabeth returned breathlessly. "Most of them part once they're grown. Which shall you leave me with when you depart, sir? Passion? Desire? Love? All three?" Her voice lowered to a fearful whisper. ". . . or none?"

Despite the answer he might give, Elizabeth couldn't let him go. Her arms circled his back, and her fingers dug into his shoulders. Beneath the softness of her palm, she felt the moist hair and the warm texture of skin. She lifted her face and welcomed Chase's lips that covered her in a fierce, urgent kiss. Leaving her mouth, his lips tasted her chin, traced her jawline, lingered on the throbbing pulse at the base of her neck.

"Elizabeth Rose," he murmured over and over again as his mouth traveled up again to explore the sweetness of her face and neck. He wanted to sweep her off her feet into the intimacy of a safe, private place, to make love to her until both of them were sated. "You ask what I'm going to give you," he said, his mouth nipping her sweet lips. "I shall give you all three, Elizabeth Rose,

233

love, passion, and desire."

As their mouths touched again, as his lips and tongue moved intimately against, then within, her own, a thrill ran through her—a charged thrill that encompassed every fiber of her being. With the tip of his tongue he traced the line of her lips, then surged between them to savor the velvet flower of her inner mouth in a way that made her knees grow weak and her heart thunder.

When his hands began to wander freely over her lower back, Elizabeth raised her arms and locked them around his neck. She pressed herself against him, eager to fill the yearning emptiness of her body.

He pushed away from her and unbuttoned the wrapper and shoved the straps of the nightgown over her shoulders to reveal the sheer beauty of her delicate loveliness. In the moonlight her skin looked like polished satin, smooth and flawless. His fingers stroked the small mounds until the nipples were pert. He lowered his face and caught one in his mouth, sucking gently at first one then the other, to send Elizabeth's emotions reeling. Calming his racing heart, he slowed his motions, until his tongue lazily circled a small, taut nipple, inflaming her whole body with frantic desire.

They were sliding to the ground when the soft, distant music stopped. Clapping and shouting then laughter echoed through the woods. Seconds later the harmonica tones again filled the air with a bouncy tune, and the loud, lusty voices of the troopers joined in the song: *When Johnny comes marching home again! Hurrah! Hurrah!*

Elizabeth stiffened in Chase's arms. The melody first, then the words completely dissipated all passion and desire from her. Tears sparkled in her eyes. Johnny hadn't come marching home; a stranger had. A stranger with dull, vacant eyes and hollow laughter. Hurrah! Hurrah! Johnny had died on the battlefield, long before he was buried beside Mama in the pear orchard!

When Elizabeth looked down to see her gown open, the whiteness of her breasts gleaming in the moonlight, shame and guilt tumbled in on her. Humiliated at her wantonness, she hastily caught the material in both hands and closed the gap. Chase reached for her, but she stepped back.

"Elizabeth," he murmured, his heart sinking as he cursed Corporal Man for playing that particular song at that particular moment, as he cursed himself for having taken advantage of her innocence. Yet, he knew if he had to do over again he would do the same thing. "Please, let me show you the wonders of love."

"No," Elizabeth returned, her voice ragged, her body reacting to the sudden plummeting of her emotions, "don't do this to me! I'm not a loose woman."

"I know you're not," Chase said. "I think you're a desirable woman, and I want to make

235

love to you."

The words were sweet and sounded sincere, but the sleeping giants of fear and morality had awakened. Elizabeth couldn't fight both of them. "I can't," she whispered. "I can't allow you to make love to me. There's too much that lies between us." *And too much heartbreak afterwards when you leave me.*

"If we want to, Elizabeth, we can move anything that lies between us."

Elizabeth shook her head. "It's too late for us, Chase. We come from two different worlds." She turned and fled through the woods. *Besides, in making love to you I would fall in love with you, and I don't think that's what you're offering me. I want a home, marriage, and children, not clandestine affairs and relations. Though I no longer condemn Vanessa for the kind of life she chooses to live, I do not choose to live it myself.*

Chase took out after her but stopped when he reached the hotel. On the moon-drenched lawn he saw the wilted rose she had dropped during her flight. He bent to retrieve it and stood for a moment, holding it, the soft petals reminding him of Elizabeth's softness; then he lifted it and inhaled the delicate fragrance which wrapped him in a sensual, perfumed spell and reminded him of the fragrance of her skin, all musk, all woman.

He glanced at the second story of the hotel to see a pale light filter through the window shutters over Elizabeth's window. The desire to follow her was great. He knew he could love her into submission. He remembered how she had quaked in his arms and knew her denials had not come from her heart. Now, however, was not the time.

Elizabeth would regret such a surrender when she awakened in the morning, and this he did not want. No regrets! No recriminations! He was a patient man, accustomed to getting what he wanted, and he wanted Elizabeth Rose Barrett. He was willing to woo her into his bed.

He looked down at the flower which he held, which was so symbolic of Elizabeth. She was as fragile and delicate as the rose. He could so easily crush Elizabeth beneath the onslaught of his passion. She was a sweet scent to his soul; a fragrant balm to his wounded spirit. She had asked him what he would leave her with when he was finished with his love-making. He knew: He could give her no less than love, passion, and desire following in the wake, but he wasn't prepared to give her marriage — and that's what a woman like Elizabeth Rose Barrett would want.

Chase was confused; he didn't understand his own emotions at all. He had lusted after Elizabeth from the beginning, from the night he saw her in the lobby of Beck's House, and he had decided then to fulfill that desire. He felt a twinge of guilt when he remembered his haste and nonchalance in using her in his search for

Bainbridge. At that time he had thought Elizabeth might be involved herself; now he figured it was Vanessa. He could imagine Elizabeth's reaction should she ever learn of this; he prayed to God she didn't.

Tonight he realized that his feelings for Elizabeth Rose were more encompassing than mere lust, than even desire or passion. He cared for her — really cared. That's why he hadn't seduced her. This consideration for a woman was a new feeling for Chase. In fact, he was downright uncomfortable about it and made him regret involving her in his mission.

But now that he had tasted her sweetness he couldn't leave her alone. He must . . . he would have her.

Even as Elizabeth closed and locked the door, she knew Chase hadn't followed her . . . not this time, and she was disappointed . . . so disappointed that her stomach was churning and tears threatened. With every pore in her body she had wanted him, but like a coward, like a creature of the society in which she had been born and bred, she was unable to tell him so, unable to give herself to the moment with no thought of the morrow.

In becoming aware of her own emotions, Elizabeth was better able to understand Vanessa. She realized now that Vanessa had been neither a hypocrite nor a coward. Although Vanessa's lifestyle was not one Elizabeth respected or one that she would have chosen for herself, it was Vanessa's choice. She had known what she wanted out of life and had gone in search of it. She had been willing to pay the price and take the responsibility for her actions. To attain her goals she defied morals and conventions.

Not so Elizabeth. Deep down in the secret part of her heart she wanted Chase to pursue her, to knock down the door, and force her into submission. Gone then would be her responsibility for her actions; come the morning she would have been guiltless, her conscience appeased. Yet her longings would be satisfied, and she could place all blame for the consequences on Chase. His would be the guilt to carry.

But he hadn't fallen prey to her emotional snare. With his sweet words and reluctance in seducing her, he had lain a trap for her, such a convincing one that she was tempted to believe him. But she knew better. Life had taught her that men always used sweet words and empty promises to get what they wanted.

But, her conscience pointed out, *he didn't make any empty promises.* In all fairness to . Chase, Elizabeth had to agree. He had promised to introduce her to the wonders and delights of lovemaking, to open full the floodgate of passion and desire and bring her to ultimate fulfillment. Innately Elizabeth knew that making love with Chase would be consummate joy and fulfillment. She also knew that in making love with him, she would love him.

Elizabeth remembered the endless trail of men who had promised to show Vanessa the pleasures of love-making. They took her to bed, some staying with her longer than others, but she hadn't married one of them. Aunt Feldie always maintained they hadn't wanted to marry Vanessa. The old woman had clucked her tongue disapprovingly and said, "Why take the soiled goods, when you can have a virgin?" Elizabeth had seen Vanessa go from one to the other, and although it hadn't seemed to bother Vanessa, Elizabeth had promised herself that she would never allow that to happen to her. For Elizabeth such a life would be meaningless.

Oh, God, she thought, raising her hands to cover her face, if Corporal Man had not played that particular song which reminded her of her brother, she would have willingly given herself to Chase Daniel. She wouldn't have thought beyond the minute. Racked with guilt, at the same time eaten up with unfulfilled yearnings, she wondered how she could have allowed Chase Daniel such intimacy with her body. In two days Chase had razed all her barriers, leaving her not even the rubble for defense.

So completely was Chase enthroned in the secret chambers of her heart that not once tonight did she remember that he and his kind marched through the south leaving untold havoc and devastation in their wake. How could she so easily forget Yankees were responsible for the death of her father and Johnny; indirectly they killed her mother. Because of Yankees Vanessa had run off with a Confederate deserter and Elizabeth's life had been left in shambles.

Yet this man—of all men—was the one who turned her blood to liquid passion. Somehow she had lost sight of his being a Yankee, an enemy whom she must fight. She only thought of him as a man, mortal man made of flesh and blood, a man whom she could love and a man by whom she wanted to be loved. Her discovery was so startling she could hardly believe it: she loved Chase Daniel! And shame didn't walk hand in hand with love.

Walking across the room, she slipped out of her wrapper and laid it across the foot of the bed. She looked down at the pillow where her rose had lain and remembered that she had dropped it when she was running away from him. She pressed her hand to the slight indentation. The rose, like Chase was gone; she was alone. Before despair could wash over her, she heard Chase's words again: *Elizabeth, I desire you. I want to show you the wonders of making love.*

Not a word had he spoken about loving her!

As she squirmed into the softness of the ticking, Elizabeth was relieved that soon she would see Chase no more. At Uvalde they would part; he and his soldiers would travel on to Fort Clark; the mail coach would circle around to Eagle Pass. The parting imminent, Elizabeth promised herself that she would allow no more intimate encounters between her and Chase. She couldn't take the chance on her traitorous heart and emotions; they would betray her she knew.

And she wasn't sure that once Chase Daniel had made love to her that he would not betray her . . . heart.

Chapter Fourteen

The front of his shirt drenched in blood, Blake
Lowell hid inside the door of Vance's barn and
watched the two men who stood on the lawn talking.
He wished they would hurry on to bed, so he could
get out of here. His shoulder was hurting like hell;
he'd lost a lot of blood and was weak. He leaned his
head against the door frame in hopes the spinning
would stop. He didn't know how much longer he
could retain consciousness.

He had to have help, and he was afraid to go to the
townspeople. As jumpy as they were over the robbery, any of them would probably report him to the
sheriff who in turn would inform Major Chase Daniel of his whereabouts. A shoulder wound would be
all the evidence Chase needed to hold him for questioning. While Blake didn't fear for his life—he knew
Chase was a just man—he didn't have the time to

spare for a lengthy interrogation. He had to get to Mexico, and the sooner he got there the better. Inadvertently his eyes swept to Elizabeth's room on the second floor. She was the only one whom he could trust. He had to get to her.

Blake figured his luck had begun to change for the better the day Rod Everett came running into *Le Grande* Casino with the strong box from the Union pay wagon. Although Blake was unhappy about the needless deaths of the three soldiers, he was glad to get the money—the one commodity that gave him bargaining power—and he was glad Rod was far enough away from the casino when he was apprehended and arrested by the soldiers that he brought no suspicion to rest on him or Celeste.

Blake conceded that robbing the Union payroll wagon was a necessary evil—an evil that gave him the opportunity for which he'd been searching for a mighty long time, the opportunity to meet Roswell Bainbridge in person and to get to the brain of the Bainbridge Brigade. Blake had been associated with the organization long enough to be familiar with the Eagle Pass ranch that sat directly on the border and through which outlaws easily passed from the United States into Mexico, but he'd never been privy to meeting Bainbridge himself or to seeing the military ranch and arsenal in Mexico. Always Blake dealt with an intermediary . . . until now.

Although it was probably one of his few mistakes, Blake thought, Bainbridge had personally ordered the theft of the Union payroll. The money he said he

244

needed in order to purchase more and better weapons and to pay a new group of mercenaries he had hired. As soon as Rod left the casino that night, Blake hid the money in a safe place; then he sent word to Perry Anderson, Bainbridge's ranch manager on the American side of the border, informing him that he had it. If Bainbridge wanted the money, Blake would bring and deliver it. Blake's stipulation was that he be allowed to come to the garrison and meet Bainbridge in person.

Revealing himself to his inferiors was something Bainbridge had steadfastly refused to do since his bogus death. Only those few, trusted subordinate officers who had ridden with him during the war knew his true identity. Blake knew how much Bainbridge wanted the money when he agreed to Blake's terms. Bainbridge, however, set up the time and place of the meeting. Blake's entire future with Bainbridge's Brigade depended on his getting to Mexico with that money intact.

Time and events seemed against Blake.

Already Daniel was suspicious of him and blamed him for Everett's escape and the two deputies' death. If he ever got his hands on the man who helped Everett escape, Blake thought, he'd kill him with his own bare hands. Everett was ambushed and didn't know who shot his stomach full of lead. He'd refused to tell Blake who helped him escape from jail.

Knowing he was dying, Everett's only words had been about Vanessa. The only person whom he really trusted was Elizabeth, but he didn't know where she

245

was staying. His only link to her was Blake. Completely obsessed with getting Vanessa out of Bainbridge's clutches, Everett told Blake all he wanted to know about Bainbridge and his operation once Blake promised he would rescue her.

Everett refused to let Blake get a doctor, and although Blake and Celeste had nursed him to the best of their ability, he died. Blake had taken the body out and dumped it on the Castroville Road. Callous as his action seemed; it was also practical. Blake wanted the body found, so the search would cease. He wanted no soldiers on the road when he took off for Mexico; he couldn't afford the least little slip, nor did he have any time to lose.

What a time for the bank in Castroville to be robbed!

Blake learned of the holdup when he rode through Castroville and found the sheriff gathering a posse. Immediately he suspected some of Anderson's men, but he figured they were making haste back to the ranch and didn't contemplate running into them. The men still had presence enough of mind to erase their trail.

Quite by accident Blake stumbled onto them where they had stopped to stem the flow of blood from Norman Stone's wound. While it wasn't fatal, it slowed their escape and demanded attention. Blake was glad that he'd seen the men several times at the ranch so that they recognized him. Their code was to shoot first and ask questions later. When he told them the posse was forming and included soldiers as well as civilians, the magnitude of the situation they had created dawned on them. They became jittery and nervous and worried about the Colonel's reaction.

Blake wasn't sure what happened or what line of reasoning the men followed. Perhaps they thought their secret would be safe and punishment less likely if he were dead. He cursed himself for letting his guard down; he knew better. Survival depended on alertness and quick thinking, but he had allowed himself the luxury of being more concerned about the posse and soldiers than immediate danger. When he was mounting his horse to ride off, they turned on him and put a bullet through the shoulder. He was damned lucky they didn't know he had two saddlebags full of the Union payroll which he was taking to Mexico or they may have taken out after him to make sure they finished the job they started.

Blake pushed away from the door frame and peered through the moonlight. The talking had ceased. He saw the men walk into their rooms; he heard their doors close; still he waited to be sure no one stirred. Eventually Blake slipped out of the barn and staying in the shadows, moved across the lawn. Grasping the handrail with his uninjured hand, he slowly ascended the stairs, his dizziness increasing the more energy he expended. Each step jarred his body and racked him with excruciating pain. Fresh blood was oozing out of the wound.

He was breathing heavy when he finally leaned against the wall and knocked on Elizabeth's door.

Once. Twice. Three times. "Elizabeth," he called softly so as not to awaken the other boarders.

Elizabeth didn't hear Blake call her name, but the persistent knocking roused her. Unable to believe it was morning already, she sat up and fumbled at the foot of the bed for her dressing gown. She wasn't ready to face the day yet. She certainly wasn't ready for the long, jostling trip to Eagle Pass.

"Elizabeth." She heard Blake call as she slipped into the dressing gown. Surprised, she stopped her movements and looked blankly at the door. She had thought Lonnie Pickford was knocking. What was Blake doing at her room, particularly at this hour of the morning?

"Elizabeth," he called again, this time his voice a little more frantic, the knocks louder and more urgent.

"Just a minute. Let me get dressed."

She finished buttoning her wrapper and lit the candle. The minute Elizabeth unlocked and opened the door, Blake pushed into the room with such force she stumbled back.

"I'm sorry to bother you," he said in a tight voice, staggering for the chair in the corner, "but I had no place else to go."

Looking at his tottering steps, Elizabeth thought he was drunk, and she was angry. How dare he come to her room in such a condition as this! Ready to tear into him, she moved the candle, the arc of light following his movement, and she saw his face twisted in pain, a shock of blonde hair lying across his forehead. The resemblance to Johnny was shocking! Lower her gaze went to the wounded shoulder, the jagged hole in the material and the dark stain of blood that saturated the front of the shirt.

"My God!" she gasped, her heart leaping to her throat to choke her. "What happened?"

"On my way to Mexico . . . overtook . . . three riders . . . headed south," from afar she heard Blake's disjointed words. "They were . . . moving fast . . . and were nervous. Guess they were the ones . . . who robbed . . . the bank. I managed to escape . . . but was too weak to push on . . . to Mexico."

Gripping the candle holder tightly in one hand, Elizabeth closed her eyes and leaned against the wall, for fear she would fall down. She didn't see Blake at all. She saw Johnny's gaunt face after Watkins shot him in the chest.

"Please forgive me"—Blake's pain-filled words gritted between clenched teeth—"for coming to you, Elizabeth, but you're the only one I can trust. Couldn't come into town with a shoulder wound. The sheriff might think I was . . . one of . . . the bank . . . robbers. Castroville . . . is . . . Unionist and . . . not kind to ex-Confederates."

Elizabeth opened her eyes, swallowed the bitter taste of her memories, and pushed away from the wall. Now she was a nurse who had a patient to take care of. "There's nothing to forgive," she told him briskly. "Of course, you should have come to me."

She crossed the room to place the candle holder on the dresser, picked up her portmanteau and set it on the bed. Unlatching it, she rummaged until she found a partially filled bottle of alcohol. She placed it on the night table and began her search again, this time pulling out an old petticoat, soft and clean and easy to tear. She caught the material in both hands and ripped it into strips. She had done this so frequently during the war that she never gave her actions a thought.

"Where did this happen?" she asked in an effort to get his mind off the pain.

"Few miles . . . south of Castroville," Blake answered, leaning his head back against the chair. He closed his eyes because the room was spinning around him and he was nauseated. "Ran into three men, one of them with a flesh wound. They shot first and asked questions later."

"We'll have to inform the sheriff and Chase," Elizabeth said.

"I know," Blake murmured, "but it won't do any good. That was mid-afternoon. If the posse hasn't already found them, they're—" he knew they were headed for the ranch in Eagle Pass and were already across the border, "—safe." The word barely slipped out of his mouth before his head lolled forward and his chin rested on his chest.

Her movements quickening, Elizabeth draped the homemade bandages over her arm, moved to the dresser, and dropped several of the rags in the bowl before she filled it with water. She lifted the basin and carried it to the table by the bed. After she moved the candle to the night table, she knelt in front of him and began to unbutton his shirt. Blake groaned and stirred.

"I'm going to have to take your shirt off," she explained. When Blake tried to sit up as if to help her, Elizabeth raised her hands to his shoulders and gently pressed him back into the chair. "I'll take care of it," she told him. "You relax as much as you can."

"I'd relax better if I had a drink," he said.

"Sorry," Elizabeth murmured with a wan smile, "but I'm fresh out of liquor."

She unbuttoned the shirt and motioned him forward so she could ease it over his shoulders and down his arms. Blake winced when he moved, otherwise gave no indication of his pain. Weakened by the exertion, he collapsed against the chair, his head rolling against the back.

"How . . . bad is . . . it?" he asked.

Elizabeth picked up the candle in one hand and held it close to Blake's chest while she probed the soft, discolored flesh with her other hand.

"Pretty bad," she answered and stood to examine his back, "but pretty good. The bullet went straight through, so you won't be bothered with my having to dig for it. You've lost a lot of blood, but a little rest should be all that's required."

Elizabeth was glad for her nursing experience; otherwise, she might have been squeamish and unable to give him the care he needed. She glanced at Blake's drawn face, the black circles around his eyes. He looked like so many of the young soldiers she had nursed during the war.

251

For the next few minutes the room was quiet except for the sounds Elizabeth made as she cleaned the wound and dressed it. Again she was inundated with memories and transported back to The Rose during the war. She heard the groans of the wounded as they were brought into the house, every room a ward. She heard a man screaming as a shattered limb was amputated without the aid of anesthesia in her dining room. She smelled the stench of dried blood and rotting flesh. She saw the sunken sockets of death.

She saw Johnny's eyes sunk in death!

When Elizabeth was through doctoring Blake's wound he was so weak he could hardly sit up. "Get in bed," she instructed.

Blake stared at her from pain-darkened eyes. "What about you?" he muttered.

"I'm going to tell Chase about the outlaws."

Blake's hand banded around her arm. "Not yet."

"You're hurting me," Elizabeth said, twisting her hand out of his grasp.

"I'm sorry," Blake said and released her. "As I said before, the outlaws have too much of a head start. Chase couldn't begin to catch them."

"He still needs to know."

"Please, Elizabeth," Blake said, "give me a little time. It's very important that I get to Mexico immediately. If Chase finds out about me, I'll have to stay for questioning. Don't have time." His head rolled back, and he waited for the wave of pain to subside. "I need a few hours head start."

"I can't," Elizabeth answered.

"What if I asked you to do this for the South?"

Elizabeth shook her head and her eyes darkened. The past few years had presented her with so many dilemmas and none of the solutions were easy. "I love the South, but I can't forget all those innocent people who have lost their life savings."

Blake pushed to his feet, walked to the window and threw open the shutters with his good arm. Because he was outlined by the moonlight, Elizabeth saw him lift a hand to rub the back of his neck.

"Would you do it for your sister?"

"For Vanessa!" Elizabeth exclaimed, running to where he stood. Her heart seemed to leap into her throat. "What do you know about her?"

Blake said, "I think she's Bainbridge's mistress and she's in trouble."

"How do you know this?" Elizabeth demanded.

"Everett." Blake paused a moment before he said, "I don't know who helped Rod escape from prison, but he stumbled into the casino in the wee hours of the morning with a horrible gut wound. He knew he was dying, so he'd come to me. He asked me to get a message to Bainbridge." Deliberately Blake avoided mentioning the stolen Union payroll which he was also delivering to the outlaws. "He told me that Vanessa was Bainbridge's mistress and that she was in trouble. He wanted me to help her get out of Mexico and away from Bainbridge."

"You're lying," Elizabeth accused, not far from tears. "You're telling me this to keep me from going to Chase."

"No," Blake answered softly.

"Why didn't you tell me this yesterday?" Elizabeth asked. "Why did you wait until tonight?"

"Everett was a vindictive person," Blake replied, "and a habitual liar. I wanted to verify what he said before I told you. I didn't want to upset you unnecessarily."

"Are you working with Bainbridge?"

"I'm working for the South," Blake returned. Because his shoulder was throbbing, he lifted his left hand and grasped his right upper arm, squeezing tightly.

"Is a Confederate military base being built in Mexico?" Elizabeth persisted, determined to find out how much Blake was involved.

"Yes," Blake answered. "That's why Chase is out here. As Grant's special agent, he's investigating it."

Elizabeth moved to where he was standing. "Blake, the war's over. Get out of this while you're still alive. Go to Chase and tell him everything. Let him help you. He can help us get Vanessa out."

Blake sighed deeply. "You go to him and see how much help you'll get. I can't."

"You can if you want to."

"I'm traveling the only road possible for me," Blake answered sadly. "No matter what, I've got to ride to the very end . . . by myself." The room was still too dark for her to see his features plainly. "Something you ought to know, Elizabeth," he said. "If what Everett said is true, Vanessa's been with Bainbridge for the past three years. If she's apprehended, she'll be treated as a war criminal the same as Bainbridge. Give me enough time to get her out before Chase finds Bainbridge."

Elizabeth rubbed her forehead. Blake had pushed her into a corner and she had only one way out. "I don't have much choice, do I?" Expecting no answer, she added, "Promise me that you'll get her out safely."

"I'm going to try," he said and leaned forward to plant a fleeting kiss on her forehead.

The gesture spoke volumes to her. It confirmed what she already knew: Blake Lowell was only a friend and could never be more; his touch evoked none of the sensations that Chase's mere presence stirred up. His kiss was like that of a brother, sweet, warm, and friendly. Chase's touch was hot and wild; it created an ache deep within her body, an ache that only his love could fulfill.

Blake moved to the dresser and picked up his hat. Looking across the darkened room at Elizabeth, he said, "Thanks, Elizabeth."

With a heavy heart Elizabeth nodded and watched Blake leave. She locked the door and returned to bed. But again she didn't go to sleep. Her thoughts darted randomly. She thought about her feelings for Chase Daniel; she wondered about his feelings for her and his reasons for lying about his assignment; she contemplated Blake's visit and his strange confession. She didn't want to but she had to believe Vanessa was Bainbridge's mistress. Ever since she'd talked with Everett she had sensed Vanessa was in trouble. She only hoped that Blake was successful in getting her out safely. Although Elizabeth didn't understand the full implications of Blake's mission to Mexico and of the Confederate military garrison, she knew a web of deceit was being woven and somehow she—not Vanessa—was the center of it.

Dawn was breaking when Blake retrieved a shirt from his saddlebags and slipped into it. Afterwards he returned to the barn behind Vance's Hotel, climbed the ladder and moved around in the loft, hunting for the saddlebags he had hidden before he went to Elizabeth's room. Then he hadn't known what he was going to do with them. Now he ——
When he jumped on top of Santleben's Mail Coach, the bulging bags were slung over his right shoulder. He extracted several matches from his pocket and struck one. Holding it above the luggage, he searched until he found the trunk with the rose crest.

Quickly he unfastened the chest, lifted the lid and burrowed through the clothing until he reached the bottom of the chest. Here he dumped the content of the saddlebags. One worry taken care of, he thought. No one—especially Major Chase Daniel—would search Elizabeth's luggage for the Union payroll. If he figured right, the major was infatuated with if not madly in love with Elizabeth Rose Barrett. Hers would be the last trunk he would think of searching if it came down to searching.

Blake liked Elizabeth and hated to do this to her,

but he had no other choice. If he were to rescue Vanessa—if she really were Bainbridge's mistress—Elizabeth must become his courier; he could depend on the money's safely reaching Eagle Pass. He straightened Elizabeth's belongings as best he could, shut the trunk lid, and locked it. He prayed she wouldn't open this before he retrieved the money, but if she did, he trusted her to keep her mouth closed. If she wouldn't do it for him, she would for her sister.

The empty saddlebags over his shoulder, he climbed off the stage, exited from the barn, and in a crouch ran across the hotel lawn and down the river to a small grove of trees where he tethered his dapple-gray last night. So far so good. No one was following him.

As he slipped his foot into the stirrup, his keen ears detected the click as someone cocked a revolver. Whoever was behind him was an expert in tracking. Blake hadn't heard one tell-tale sound. Instinct told him it was Chase Daniel.

"Hello, Lowell, I thought this was your horse."

Making sure he never gave in to his wounded arm, Blake dropped his foot and slowly turned around to see Chase sitting at the foot of a large tree, leaning back against the trunk.

"I noticed him when you were riding off yesterday. Fine Arabian and that blotch of color on his flank is real distinguishing. Noticed him when I was returning to camp this morning after I washed up and wondered what you were doing in Castroville."

"I was down at the river cleaning up," Blake said.

"Yeah," Chase drawled disbelievingly. "I figured maybe you were visiting with someone."

Blake forced himself to laugh. "And who would you figure that someone to be?"

"Thought you might tell me," Chase returned.

"Nobody here, Major. This town is full of Unionists," Blake replied, taking the chance that Chase didn't know he'd been in Elizabeth's room. He asked, "Why the gun?"

"Figured I might need the added persuasion when I questioned you. You don't seem to be too cooperative."

"The war taught me to distrust Yankees," Blake returned evenly, wishing his arm didn't ache. The throbbing in his shoulder was so intense he could hardly think straight, and straight thinking was his only defense with a man as astute as Chase Daniel. "But I assure you I didn't rob the Castroville bank."

"No," Chase said, "I didn't figure you did. Whoever did that was stupid."

Blake reached up and tilted his hat back. Although dawn was streaking the darkened sky with gray, he still couldn't see the features on Chase's face; he sure as hell couldn't tell anything from the toneless modulation of his voice. "Is that a compliment, Major?"

Chase shook his head. "Nope, just a fact."

"Why all this then, if you don't think I'm involved?"

"Now, I didn't say you weren't involved, Lowell," Chase drawled. "I just said you didn't rob the bank." Chase rose in slow, easy movements and closed the distance between him and Blake. "I know you're involved in this mess, else you wouldn't be in Castroville, else you wouldn't have been playing errand boy at the jailhouse and hackney driver in San Antone. Before I'm through I intend to find out exactly how deeply involved you are. That's a promise."

Blake strained through the diminishing shadows to study Chase. He heard the resolve in Chase's iron tone; he saw it in the craggy hardness of his face. "This is more than duty, isn't it, Major? You have a personal matter to settle, don't you?"

"One of the soldiers who was killed was my best friend," Chase returned quietly.

Damn! Blake silently cursed. Of all the damned luck! He felt his insides coil tighter and tighter, until it thought he would burst. He understood the anguish Chase was feeling; he had lost his best friend during the war. The major wouldn't rest until he had captured and/or killed all of the people responsible for his friend's death.

"I'm sorry," Blake said. "I know how you feel."

"Yeah," said Chase, "I suppose you do." He wished for a moment that he and Blake were working on the same side. He admired the man. He could use the man's expertise in tracking down the murderers. Again he was assailed by that elusive feeling that he had met Blake Lowell before. So strong was the recognition that he said, "I know you from somewhere, Lowell."

Blake shrugged it aside. "Probably fought each other during the war."

259

"No," Chase said, "it was more than two enemies meeting in battle. And one of these days I'll remember when and where."

Blake smiled. "Sometimes recognition can be dangerous, Major."

"I know," Chase answered. "That's why Terry is dead today. He recognized one of the outlaws who robbed the union payroll."

"Such a senseless killing," Blake said, despising Everett for being such a fool. "For what it's worth, I want you to know that I didn't do it. Not saying that I would have any qualms about robbing a Union pay wagon, just letting you know I don't kill innocent people for no apparent reason."

After a long period of silence, Chase asked, "Can you tell me anything about the outlaws who robbed the payroll or the bank?"

"Sounds like you think the same people are responsible for both," Blake said.

"I do," Chase replied. "I think all the criminal activities in this area are masterminded by a bunch of ex-Confederates who are holed up in Mexico and enjoy the immunity of the Mexican law. Now answer my question."

Blake shook his head. "Sorry, Major, I can't tell you a thing about the payroll or the bank robbery."

"Or won't?" Chase accused.

Blake shrugged and said easily, "Same difference, the way I see it." He smiled. "Do you have any evidence on which to hold me, Major?"

Chase was silent for a long time; finally he said,

"No."

"The way I see it then, Major, is this: kill me, turn me over to the sheriff, or let me go."

Chase slipped his gun into his holster. "Murder isn't my style either, Mr. Lowell. Since I have no evidence connecting you to the crimes, I'll have to let you go." He paused before he said, "Odd how you always seem to show up at the scene of the crime."

Blake caught the brim of his hat and lowered it on his forehead. "I can say the same thing, Major. You've been present at the scene of both crimes: Everett's escape, Addison's death, and the bank robbery. Does that make you guilty? No?" He laughed and said, "Guess I'll be leaving now."

As Lowell swung into the saddle, Chase said, "Lowell, promise me that you won't see Elizabeth again."

Blake caught his breath. He wondered if Chase had seen him entering or leaving her room. "Why should I promise that?"

"I saw the way you looked at Elizabeth at the Plaza House when the stage was leaving," Chase said. "You're halfway in love with her."

"No," Blake contradicted, "not halfway, Major. I'm fully in love with her. If I thought for a minute I had a chance with her I'd be with her right now."

Chase felt jealousy wind its tentacles around his heart and squeeze until he could hardly breath. "Then leave her out of this, Blake. She's innocent and quite vulnerable. You know a... ...ll as I do if you tell her you're fighting for the South, ...'ll volunteer

261

her services with no questions asked."

"Lots of people would give themselves to create another South and to whip the North," Blake finally said.

"But you and I know that you're not creating another South. We know that under Roswell Bainbridge's leadership you've established a base in Mexico and are gathering all the criminal elements you can find on both sides of the border."

"Me, Major?" Blake lifted his uninjured arm and pointed his index finger at his chest. "You're just stabbing in the dark. You don't know that I'm involved with anything more than a brothel and gaming house in San Antonio, and right now I'm on my way to Mexico to take care of business. You know, cattle." Blake laughed. "You're beginning to sound like General Grant. Good-day, Major. Don't get too caught up in your hallucinations."

"Lowell," Chase called, "if you have any regards for Elizabeth at all, you won't involve her."

Blake turned the horse around and said in a sad voice, "I think it's too late to be concerned about Elizabeth's loyalties, Major. No matter what you or I say, she chose sides a long time ago. Politically, she's already involved, and nothing you or I do can change that."

"By damn, I will change that," Chase said, hatred for Blake Lowell almost choking him. "And I'll see you hanging from the gallows, if I find out that you had anything—anything at all to do with Terry's death. That's a promise, Blake Lowell."

Blake turned the horse around and stared through the shadowed morning at Chase. "I confessed that I'm in love with Elizabeth," he said quietly, "but you, Major, only want to bed her to satisfy your own needs and desires." Automatically Chase opened his mouth to protest, but Blake continued speaking. "When you do, know this. Elizabeth Barrett will not make love to you unless she loves you. Just hope, Major, for the sake of your—" Blake hesitated; laughed shortly, then said, "I started to say for the sake of your heart, but I don't think you have one, so I'll change that to ego and pride. Hope for the sake of your ego and pride that Elizabeth can unconditionally love a man who's against everything she stands for."

Chapter Fifteen

Her packing finished, Elizabeth set her valise by the door and walked onto the porch to watch the burst of morning color ribbon across the eastern sky. She inhaled deeply, drawing into her nostrils the fragrance of the flowers in the garden below. The sweet scent drugged her senses, and images of a lone red rose lying in the middle of her snowy white pillow case danced before her eyes. Never again would she see a rose without thinking of the man who had given that one to her.

Although she knew wisdom guided her decision not to see Chase again, she wouldn't soon forget him . . . she would never forget him. Closing her eyes and leaning her head against the cool, white porch column, she could see his face more clearly than she could see any of the portraits of her family hanging on the walls of The Rose, more than Johnny's, more than Vanessa's face on the miniature which she carried in her reticule. Chase was so real in her imagination she felt as if he were here with her.

Moments later when she heard his deep, mellow voice say, "Good morning, Elizabeth," she couldn't quite believe he was standing in the yard below. She didn't open her eyes for fear he would disappear. Her legs suddenly were the consistency of melted butter; she clung to the column to keep from dripping to the floor. Her heartbeat accelerated and pumped blood through her body at such a high speed she was heady.

"I trust you slept well last night?" he asked.

Elizabeth breathed deeply and slowly, a smile cautiously creeping across her lips. Chase was here! Her resolve not to see him again quickly vanished. She opened her eyes and dropped her head over the railing to see him standing near the garden. As if this were the first time she had seen him, she let her gaze wander at will down and up the length of his hard, muscular frame, resplendent in cavalry blue. He was one of the most handsome men she'd ever seen — not beautiful in the traditional sense of the word — but masculine. His features were too rugged and irregular for classical beauty; the nose a little crooked; the jut of his chin a little arrogant, the angle of his cheeks aggressive. But he was devastatingly attractive with his roguish smile and dancing blue eyes.

Right now his dazzling smile made her feel peculiarly breathless, as if she'd run too far and too fast. Pleasure at seeing him again rushed heat and color to her cheeks.

"I know you have a bird," Chase said, "because I

can hear him serenading us. I'm wondering if perhaps you have a cat also?" His voice was thick with gentle amusement.

Elizabeth blinked down into his face, the craggy lines and angles gentled by laughter. "A cat," she repeated.

"When you didn't answer, I thought maybe it had gotten your tongue."

Elizabeth smiled and shook her head. "No," she managed to say quite calmly in spite of the errant emotions which played havoc with her nerves, "I was just admiring the garden."

"Just the garden?" Chase lowered his head as well as his voice and reached out to pick one of the roses.

"Just the garden," Elizabeth drawled, fascinated at the way infant rays of sunlight burnished his dark curls.

His face lifted again. "And what do you think of it?" He eyed her appreciatively, his gaze touching individually each and every feature of her face, youthfully beautiful and radiantly healthy. His eyes darkened in frank pleasure at the lovely picture she made in the fitted traveling gown of forest green. A mass of luxurious curls tumbled over her shoulders to frame her lovely face in their golden web. At last the blue eyes fastened themselves to her.

"Quite beautiful," she returned, "especially the roses."

"Yes," Chase answered, "I think so, too. And always there is one rose that is more beautiful than the others." His eyes burned hotly with steel blue fires as they rested upon her. "Every time I see you, Elizabeth Rose Barrett, you're more beautiful."

"Thank you." The recurring weakness in her knees made her feel as if she were sinking to the floor despite all efforts to hang onto the pillar.

Holding up the rose to her, he said, "For you, the lady of the roses."

"Thank you," she whispered again and knew she was lost to Chase and to her own feelings. She only regretted that she could not tell him about Blake's visit last night. Her silence was out of loyalty to her sister; she must give Blake an opportunity to get Vanessa out before she was captured and tried as a war criminal—a criminal that is hated by all.

Chase was astonished at the depth of emotion Elizabeth aroused in him. He had desired women before and had taken them. But he had never been a victim of his own emotions before. He had the wildest desire to leap up the stairs by two and crush her into his arms. He wanted to cover the slender, creamy-smooth column of her throat with hungry kisses; to feel her rosy lips return the heat of his mouth with a flaming desire that matched his own.

With the pleasueable thoughts came a rush of bad ones. Chase regretted having involved Elizabeth in his search for Bainbridge. He wished he hadn't sent off to New Orleans for her records or spoken to Jack Stevens about her. He was sure now that she was innocent and knew nothing about the outlaws. No matter what Blake Lowell had intimated, Chase could not believe Elizabeth was a part of any criminal activities. He winced when his hands tightened around the stem of the rose and a thorn pricked his palm.

"I was wondering," he said, breaking the lengthy

silence, "if I could take you to breakfast before the stage leaves?"

"Yes," Elizabeth answered quickly without a second thought, without a doubt as she gazed into the boyish, almost vulnerable face. "I'll get my things."

A dreamy, faraway look in her eyes, she turned and walked into her room. She smiled when she heard Chase's boots hitting the stairs, two at a time. Then she heard him say from the door, "Do you have a trunk or anything I need to take down to be loaded onto the stage?"

She turned to see him standing in the opened doorway and laying the rose on the edge of the dresser. "No—" She would have said more but she saw him look toward the bed and felt her stomach flutter at the subtle, and perhaps unintentional, suggestion.

Chase saw the indentation in the pillow where her head had lain; he visualized Elizabeth's eyes closed in sleep, her golden lashes fluttering against her rosy cheeks; her hair tangled around her face. Breakfast was the farthest thing from his mind. His face solemn now, his eyes darkened with desire, he walked across the room and laid the rose in the exact spot where her head had lain during the night. His gaze returned to Elizabeth's face.

She gasped at the shaft of desire that spread into her stomach, and her eyes automatically moved to Chase's mouth, the firm upper lip, the full bottom one. She remembered the feel of it on hers. The hungry pressure had sent fiery tingles down to her; it had incinerated her bones, leaving her limp and powerless.

Because of his own desires, Chase was able to correctly read Elizabeth's imagination. Because he was a part of her fantasies, he understood what she was thinking and dreaming about, and wanting; he knew because he wanted it, too. To keep from touching her, to refrain from taking her into his arms was the hardest conflict he'd ever fought in his life. Never had he engaged an opponent as awesome as his own emotions. The War Between the States, the Indians, the bandits and ex-Confederate outlaws, all paled in comparison. When Elizabeth opened her mouth and rounded her lips with the tip of her moist, pink tongue, Chase knew he had lost the battle. He moved closer to her, and she felt the heat of his lean, hard body. It sent excited shivers darting through her.

"Elizabeth Rose," he murmured, and before either one of them quite knew how it happened, they were in each others arms.

Elizabeth pressed her body against his and opened her mouth to the fullness of their kiss; willingly she transformed fantasy into reality. She wanted time to be still; she wanted the world to consist of no one else but her and Chase. Gone were the strictures placed upon her by background and family and friends. In this magical place that she and Chase created she was free to make love to him and accept whatever he was willing to give to her.

She was vaguely aware of the firm pressure of his fingertips gently tracing her spine and the curves of her buttocks. They moved away from her and she felt bereft. They found her again, and she sighed her relief . . . her pleasure. She felt the cradling warmth of his calloused hands against the lushed curves of her cheeks as he held her face for yet another kiss.

The tip of his tongue urgently parted her lips and surged hotly between them to explore and taste the secret recesses of her mouth in a shocking, intimate way that once again ignited licking tongues of desire than burned deeply in her belly. Chase's kisses aroused her to the very core and left her aching for more . . . for more than kisses.

"Elizabeth, my darling," he murmured, nuzzling her neck, "I'm hungry for you, not food." He scooped her into his arms, kicked the door shut with his foot, and carried her to the bed where he gently deposited her.

Her head turned, and her cheek brushed the fragile petals of the rose; she inhaled into her nostrils the delicate scent. She knew Chase was going to make love to her and she welcomed it. She cast good intentions out the window long before he shut them and locked the door. In the golden light of morning sun that slivered into the room through the cracks in the shutters, Elizabeth gazed at him adoringly as he returned to the head of the bed. His hand went to his belt. She heard the buckle click; she saw him lay his weapons on the night table.

"Elizabeth —"

The wisp of his voice was as gentle and tantalizing to Elizabeth as was the touch of his finger tips on her cheek.

"— my rose."

When he felt her tremble beneath his fingers, fire burned through his body. His loins tightened. He sat in the chair to take off his boots and looked down to see the light playing across a familiar piece of checkered material that trailed from beneath the bed. He recognized it as the shirt Blake Lowell had worn yesterday. Anger, disappointment disgust, all three lumped together in one horrible mixture churned in his stomach. He stooped to catch the fabric in his fist and brought it up for closer observation.

Elizabeth gasped.

"Blake Lowell's shirt," he said in a wooden voice, the man's image clearly imprinted on his mind. Swiftly his head lifted and his eyes landed on Elizabeth's face, gone ashen.

Elizabeth couldn't believe she had forgotten about Blake's shirt. She recalled he hadn't worn it when he left, but she had been too tired and too confused to think about it last night. Her conscience had been too heavy. This morning as she cleaned up the room and dressed, she must have kicked it under the bed. She had never given it another thought.

She looked up to see Chase's pain-darkened eyes. She knew what he was thinking and she could understand why. Her heart came crashing to the ground. The face, that last night had been sculpted soft and silvery in the moonlight, the face that this morning had been roguish and charming was now hard and implacable, hewn out of granite. Invisible shutters had lowered over the eyes. They were pure blades of sharpest steel. Chase Daniel was a harsh, condemning judge.

"This is Blake's, isn't it?" he demanded in an edged voice, his eyes penetrating.

Harted for a fellow man — an emotion totally foreign to Chase, totally foreign to an army

271

officer who had fought through all the years of the War Between the States — surged through his veins. He hated Blake Lowell, and for just a moment he hated Elizabeth. He had thought her to be so pure — untouched by any other man. He had thought he'd be the first . . .

"Yes," said Elizabeth quietly, "but it's not what you're thinking, Chase. Let me explain."

Chase wasn't listening. "He was here last night! The bastard was here!" The accusation was sharp; it sailed across the room to pierce Elizabeth in the heart. "He came to your room after I left last night?"

"Yes." Silence, like a wool blanket in the dry, dead heat of summer, settled over the room to suffocate Elizabeth. She sat up but never took her eyes off Blake's shirt. "Chase, please let me explain."

Chase didn't hear a word she said; his imagination was running wild. He could envision Elizabeth and Lowell together, their arms wrapped around one another, their lips pressed together. What she hadn't given to him, she had given to another man. What he had refused to take last night, what he had been willing to wait and woo her for she gave to the bastard. Chase's hands balled into fists as he suppressed the anger and resentment that flowed through him.

"Dammit," he emitted between clenched teeth. "Blake Lowell was here last night. *Here in your room!*" His hand darted out; his fingers curled around her arm; he yanked her across the bed, his warm breath slightly scented with tobacco spread across her face. "I thought you were different."

"And I thought you were different," Elizabeth cried, jerking her arm from his grasp, "but you're just like the rest of the Union army. You think the worst. Without a hearing, you've already judged me."

Elizabeth was so disappointed in Chase that she wanted to cry; at the same time she wanted to lash out at him and to hurt him with equal measure—perhaps more. Most of all, she wanted to assure him that Blake Lowell was only a friend, nothing more.

"So you think me a whore again?"

"What do you expect me to think?" he countered. Without looking at the shirt, he crumpled it in his fist. "What do you expect me to think when I find his clothing in your room and learn that he spent the night with you!"

Elizabeth jerked the shirt out of his hand and held it up by both shoulders, waving the bloodied material in front of his eyes. "He was shot," she pointed out angrily. "He figured your soldiers would immediately jump to the conclusion that he was the wounded bank robber, so he came to me because he had no place else to go. I tended his wound. That's all," she shouted.

Chase looked at the ragged bullet hole and the blood stain. He looked up at Elizabeth's face, drawn with pain and hurt. Now he heard all that he hadn't heard before. "I didn't know," he murmured.

"No," Elizabeth said, her nerves frayed to the breaking point, "you didn't know, but you were ready to condemn. It's easier to condemn than it is to listen and rightly divide the truth. Just because Blake is a Southerner—"

"My feelings toward Lowell have nothing to do with his being from the South," Chase countered.

"Why do you condemn me, Major Daniel?"

Chase stared into the stormy green eyes. When he didn't immediately answer, she continued her tirade. "Not because you care about me, Major! But because your pride and ego had been deflated. You thought Blake had gotten the choice goods that you had been refused!"

Chase didn't like the portrait Elizabeth was pairing at all; his emotions were giant monsters ready to destroy everything they touched. "Elizabeth," he said and reached out to touch her.

"Don't," she said and moved to the other side of the bed.

Slowly Chase brought his hand back. "You're partly right," he admitted evenly. "I was jealous because I thought he'd taken what I had been refused, but it was more than wounded ego and pride. I was hurt because I care . . . truly care about you."

Saying nothing, Elizabeth folded her arms across her breasts and stared across the bed at him.

"Blake doesn't care about you," he ended lamely.

"Like you do?"

"Like I do," Chase quietly affirmed. "Please don't get involved with Blake?"

"Because you're jealous of him?"

"I've admitted that I'm jealous of him," Chase said, "but that's not the reason for my request. I think Blake is a dangerous man. I have reason to believe he's working with a huge outlaw ring in Mexico. One organized by Colonel Roswell Irwin Bainbridge. Do you know who I'm talking about?"

Chase watched her closely, every expression on her face and in her eyes. He had to find out if she were involved in this operation. Perhaps Everett had told her something about it . . . or Blake.

"I'd heard he was dead," Elizabeth answered dully and wondered if the war would ever end. She was tired of ghosts from the past haunting her. No matter how far she traveled, they were there awaiting her. "Didn't he die during one of the last battles?"

"We have reason to believe he's alive," Chase said. "He and his men lied about his death so he could escape into Mexico and regroup." When Elizabeth made no reply, he asked, "Can you understand my fears?"

As she watched Chase throw the shirt on the bed, she wanted to tell him that Bainbridge was alive and that he was building a military garrison in Mexico. Although she found the whole concept revolting, she couldn't say a word for fear of betraying Vanessa. She wasn't sure what Chase's reaction would be. He was the man with whom she was falling in love, but he also wore army-blue and was a Union soldier.

She had promised Blake she would give him time to rescue his sister. Loyalty and love kept her silent. She turned and walked to the dresser, her head bent, as she fiddled with the mesh chain on her purse.

She felt the gentle pressure of Chase's fingers as they curled around her shoulders; she heard his voice coming from behind. She looked up to see his reflection in the blotched mirror.

"Elizabeth, you must trust me. Your safety depends on your not having anything more to do with this man." Chase couldn't get Lowell's words out of his mind: *She's already involved.* If she were, Chase would have no alternative but to bring her to justice along with Bainbridge and his men. Knowing this tore at Chase's heart. "Leave Blake and his kind alone."

Elizabeth spun around. "I can't leave him and his kind alone," she exclaimed, her heart tearing into shreds. "Can't you understand I'm one of them."

"No," Chase replied, "you're not, and maybe one of these days you'll wake up and see that you're different."

"Maybe one of these days you'll see me for what I am," she retorted and moved away from him and his tormenting touch, "What are you going to do now that you know he's wounded?"

"Go after him." Chase picked up his belt from the night table. "I only wish I had known about his wound earlier this morning when I saw him. I would have had enough evidence to keep him here for questioning."

Just as Blake had supposed. "You saw him?" Elizabeth asked.

"When I was returning to camp after cleaning up this morning, I saw his horse tethered in a clump of trees on the other side of Vance's barn."

"It could have been anyone's horse," Elizabeth said.

"No, the markings on this horse distinguish it from all others. I'd know it anywhere."

Chase put his hat on. "If you'll excuse me, Elizabeth, I'll have to be going without breakfast. Now that I know Lowell's been wounded, I need to find him and question him more closely. He's already got several hours head start on me, so I need to get going as quickly as possible."

Her heart heavy, Elizabeth nodded and watched him walk across the room. She wanted to tell him what Blake was doing; but she couldn't. She was bound by her promise and by love to Vanessa. When Chase's hand closed around the door knob, she said, "Chase, nothing happened between Blake and me. I only tended his wound."

Chase was across the room in a few long strides and Elizabeth was in his arms; she willingly cuddled against him. His hand against her cheek, he pressed her sweet face against his chest. "I wish I didn't have to go," he muttered, his voice thick with passion, "but I have to."

"I know," she replied. "I understand."

Chase wasn't sure that he did understand any more. His feelings for Elizabeth filled him with confusion. Without conscious design she was slowly becoming the center of his world. With an aching heart he slowly put her away from him and stared into her beautiful face. His hand lifted and he tucked an errant curl behind her ear. For once Chase found duty a cumbersome burden.

Chapter Sixteen

About one o'clock the next day, Blake rode into Uvalde. He'd made good time even if it had meant traveling a day and a half and one night with little rest and no sleep. Wearily he shifted in the saddle, careful not to jar his shoulder more than was necessary. He wasn't much earlier than the stage, but this was the way he had planned his journey. He couldn't let Elizabeth get too far out of his sight; yet, he couldn't afford to be right under Chase Daniel's feet. He must avert the man's suspicions and get him off his trail. So Blake traveled parallel to them.

As he hitched the Arabian outside the Silver Dollar saloon, he gazed around the sleepy little town. Satisfied that nothing out of the ordinary was going on, he turned and moved toward the boardwalk, unconsciously reaching up and clasping his upper arm to knead the tense muscles as if that would stop the throbbing. When he dropped his gaze, he saw the dark stain on his shirt where blood had seeped through the bandages. He thought of Elizabeth, of her tender ministrations and in spite of the pain, he smiled.

He pushed on the swinging doors and entered the saloon. Waiting a moment for his eyes to grow accustomed to the dim light, his gaze swept the room and he spotted two men sitting at a table in the far corner. The older one—a leathery frontiersman who raised his hand and waved—Blake knew; the younger was a stranger.

Blake moved toward them, calling to the bartender as he passed, "Whiskey."

"Howdy, Blake," Evan Warner said, rising to shake hands. A smile touched the corners of his lips; relief flared briefly in the faded brown eyes, then subsided into blandness. He reached up to run his finger around the red-and-black bandanna he had tied around his throat. "About to give you up. Run into trouble?"

"Trouble ran into me, Evan," Blake replied easily as he pulled out a chair and sat down.

Evan's eyes moved to the blood stain, but he said nothing. The bartender was approaching with Blake's drink. When he left, Evan vented his curiosity, "What happened?"

"I was cresting a ridge when bullets started flying around me," Blake replied, hating himself because he was lying to his old friend. "Before I could take cover, one of them found a home."

"The men who robbed the bank in Castroville?"

Blake shrugged. "As nervous as they were I figure so. I caught sight of three of them, but I can't be sure that was all. They had me in a blind gully. I was lucky to get out alive."

Evan's eyes scanned the pinched features of Blake's face, then lowered to his shirt. "Bad?"

"Could be worse."

Blake looked at the stranger sitting across the table and judged him to be about in his mid twenties, about five years younger than Blake. In a gaunt sort of way the man was handsome. Black hair, long enough to brush his collar, and cold gray eyes. Killer eyes, Blake thought, recognizing the gleam of challenge. A shiver ran his spine. The man returned Blake's stare with equal measure.

"Need a doctor?" Blake heard Evan say.

He shook his head, then took a needed swallow of liquor. "No, got this woman I know to clean it out and bandage it for me. I slept over at her place. That's one of the reasons why I'm late."

The hard lines of Evan Warner's weathered face eased somewhat as he laughed. "The other?"

Instead of answering, Blake asked, "Who's this?"

"Tony Mason, one of our new recruits. Been working with Sorrell up toward the panhandle. Tony," Evan said, waving his hand toward Blake, "this here is Blake Lowell who used to be a captain in the Texas Rangers."

Blake smiled lazily at his old friend. "No longer captain, and no longer a ranger. Just a citizen."

"Glad to meet you, Lowell," Mason said. "You've got quite a reputation with the knife and gun."

Blake quaffed the remainder of his drink in one swallow. He didn't care about reputations. By the time a man acquired one in Texas, he was a legend and legends were dead. Blake wondered if this upstart was giving him a message. He set the glass down and reached up to stroke his moustache. "Where you from?"

"Augusta, Georgia," Tony drawled, his southern accent deep.

So deep, Blake wondered if it were exaggerated. He leaned back in the chair, finished off his drink, and waved for another. "What'cha doing out here?"

"What do you think I'm doing out here?" was Tony's laconic reply.

Warner rolled his eyes and shook his head; he couldn't believe the audacity of the younger man. Neither could Blake; his eyes narrowed, his voice hardened. "If I knew what you were doing out here, I wouldn't be asking." He leaned across the table and clamped his hand around Tony's neckerchief. "Even with a bullet hole in my shoulder, Mason, I'm more a man than you'll ever be. Don't you ever use this tone with me again. Do you understand?"

Tony would have sliced him to bits with his cold, gray eyes, but he couldn't. Blake Lowell had a spine made of iron, and a constitution just as strong.

Blake's hand tightened on the scarf and he yanked Tony across the table. "I said, do you understand me?"

"I understand." Mason spat the words. When Blake turned him loose, he reached up and straightened his shirt and tie. His eyes blazed his hatred for Blake Lowell and promised a reckoning.

"I'm waiting for an answer," Lowell said.

"Lost everything in the war," Tony said sullenly. "My family, the plantation." Mason shifted his bitterness and hatred from Blake to past memories. "My fiancé married a man who was wealthier than me – a scallywag—who for a pittance ended up owning my home." His lips curled upward, but he wasn't smiling. "Too bad," he said softly. "Her husband was killed by a robber, so I heard, and the house burned down with my fiancé in it."

"How'd you get a job with the Rangers?" Blake asked. He didn't like Mason, not a little bit, and he sure as hell didn't trust him.

Tony laid his revolver on the table and patted it caressingly with his right hand. "I'm good with the gun, *Captain Lowell*. Very good." With swift, fluid motion he brandished a knife. "I'm good with this, too. Since I've been out here, people keep wondering if I'm as good as you are." A harsh smile thinned his lips.

"Keep going like this, boy, and we'll soon see."

"I wouldn't mind that," Tony answered.

Blake's eyes moved from the revolver to the knife. He didn't doubt the man was good with both the revolver and the knife. Just as he had figured, Tony Mason either was or soon would be a cold-blooded killer, and Blake knew with an intuitive certainty that Tony Mason hated him. Again he felt the race of chills down his spine. He wouldn't turn his back on this man for a second.

"Have you decided to help us?" Evan asked, glad for an opportunity to change the subject. While he didn't mind Mason—in fact, he quite liked the young fellow—he knew Mason and the Captain instantly hated one another. The tension between the two of them was so strong Evan could feel it.

"Don't know yet," Blake returned. "I gave up being a ranger a long time ago, Evan."

"You can't make me believe that, Blake," Evan said. "Once a ranger, always a ranger."

"Dammit, Evan, how many times must I tell you I'm not the same man who left here to join the Confederacy?" Blake's face was as harsh as his tone. "Now quit pushing me."

Evan raised his hand and motioned for another drink. "Did you see Everett while he was in jail?" At Blake's nod, he asked, "Did he talk?"

With a shake of his head, Blake said, "He didn't talk, and he won't talk. He was a stupid man who got killed while escaping from the Bat Cave." *Dear God, he'd never run into so many stupid people as he had since he joined up with Bainbridge's men. They seemed to be begging the U.S. Army and the Texas Rangers to find them.*

"Damn!" Evan exclaimed. "He was our only lead." The three of them were silent for a minute, then Evan asked, "Did the cavalry recover their payroll?"

"Nope," Blake replied, and the image of the rose-crested trunk flashed through his mind. He only hoped Elizabeth didn't open her trunk before he retrieved his goods. But even if she did, Blake wasn't overly worried. Elizabeth thought he was slipping ex-Confederates over the border. Already he knew her well enough to know she wouldn't expose the money until she'd asked him about it.

"Hell, Blake!" The chair creaked beneath Evan as he shifted position and leaned across the table, folding his arms on the table and balancing his weight on them. "Soon we're going to have the cavalry meddling in our business."

"Not soon, Evan, they are now. The best I can

understand, a Major Chase Daniel is investigating this personally, and he thinks I had something to do with Everett's escape and murder."

"Maybe, gentlemen," Tony said quietly, joining the conversation for the first time of his own accord, "it's time we considered joining forces with Colonel Bainbridge's men in Mexico."

"For God's sake!" Evan's hand came down on the table with such force the glasses tottered on their bases. "The war's over. Furthermore, I don't hold with joining forces with common thieves and murderers, and that's all Bainbridge's men are."

"You don't know anything about these men," Tony said. "How can you make such accusations?"

Evan yanked the red-and-black bandanna from around his throat to expose a long, puffy scar. "I know as much about Colonel Bainbridge's elite force of murderers as I want to. This is what one of 'em did to me."

"War," said Tony.

"Outright attempt at murder," Evan replied. "It was Bainbridge who showed me that he and I weren't fighting on the same side. I was fighting Yankees, not raping women and plundering my own country. Bainbridge and his men did. When I tried to stop one of 'em, Bainbridge tried to kill me." Evan retied the bandanna and looked at Blake. "Captain Lowell here saved my life."

"Seems that most of Texas owes Captain Lowell a debt of gratitude now, don't they?" Tony mocked. "We ought to have a statue of him made and set up in the Main Plaza in San Antonio. Why we could even send one to Washington, D.C., to see if they would put one up there."

"For God's sake, shut you damned mouth, Mason!" Evan snapped at the end of his patience. "Always knew you were a hothead, but I thought you knew how to control it." He shook his head in puzzlement. "Don't know what's ailing you, boy, but your mouth is getting bigger than the Mississippi. You're soon gonna be in more trouble than you can get out of alive."

"What do you know about Bainbridge's operation in Mexico?" Blake asked, his gaze taking in both men.

Evan shrugged. "Nothing really. Hear things now and then. That's about all. You think these holdups are connected with it?" The brown eyes focused intently on Blake who pursed his lips and shrugged noncommittally.

"Could be." Again Blake felt remorseful that he must lie to Evan.

"Blake, you got to help us." Evan wasn't so proud that he wouldn't beg. "If we don't prove that we can handle our own domestic affairs, no telling how long them Yankees will hold the reins of our government. No telling how many innocent people are gonna be affected."

Rearing the chair back on its hind legs, Blake studied the man sitting across from him. His expression never changed, but his eyes softened and he said, "Evan, you've put in your years with the Rangers. Why don't you get out now? Get out while you're still alive. Marry Etta Sue and start that ranch you've been talking about. Have a passel of kids."

Evan's eyes narrowed as he shook his head. "Nope," he drawled. "Got one more job to do."

"Dammit!" Blake's chair hit the floor with a thud and his fist came down on the table. "Leave Bainbridge's men alone, Evan. They're killers."

"That's why I can't leave 'em alone, Blake," Evan replied, a note of disappointment in his voice. Reaching for his hat, he clamped it on his head and stood. "I remember a time when you would have felt the other way." When Blake didn't answer, Evan said to Tony, "Come on. Let's get out of here. We have work to do."

Blake walked out the door behind them, unhitched the Arabian and swung into the saddle. By the time the cry, "The mail is coming," echoed through the streets, he had disappeared.

The stage's arrival precipitated a flurry of activity. The once quiet and sleepy village came alive. Eagerly people—two of whom were Warner and Mason—gathered to meet the mail coach.

"Move back outta the way," Ingram yelled as he guided the stage around the corner and Lonnie pulled the brake, metal shrieking against metal.

By the time the coach jerked to a halt, all of the military escort but Samson had ridden in the direction of Fort Inge. Lonnie jumped down with the mail bag, and the crowd converged on him. De Witt climbed down on the other side and opened the door of the vehicle. "Uvalde," he said. "We'll be stopping overnight here. Silver Dollar Saloon is one of the best places to stay. Beds, don't know how clean, and decent food. Moderate prices. Are you gonna want to be taking off any of your luggage?" he asked.

"No," Elizabeth answered as she stiffly climbed out of the stage and swung her portmanteau in the air.

"Just this, and all I want right now is a bath and a bed." She was glad the trip was over; it had been long and tedious. Her body ached so badly, she didn't know if she'd ever get rested again. Now with her feet planted on the ground, she still felt as if she were swaying and jostling with the coach.

More than the tedium and hardship of continuous travel, Elizabeth missed Chase and found herself jealous of the attention Samson paid Joy, his riding beside the coach so that they could talk together and laugh, his picking her a bouquet of posies along the way, his singing. All this made her even lonelier, made her miss Chase all the more. Not having seen him since he left to pursue Blake, she wondered where he was.

"What about you Miss Franklin?" Ingram asked when he helped Joy out of the coach.

"Nothing for me," she answered, her baggage in hand also. She hurried up the street to meet with Samson.

Elizabeth looked around for Jefferson but couldn't see him; then she heard him call out, "Mister Doug—las Draugh—dy." She rounded the stage to see him sorting through the mail and handing it out. "Ar—nold Fer—gu—son."

Leaving him to his task, she walked into the saloon, stopped just inside the door until she grew accustomed to the dark interior, then walked to the bar. "I'd like two rooms."

"Cheaper if you share," the man said.

"I need two of them," Elizabeth answered.

"Two dollars a room," the bartender announced and waited until she had extracted the money from

287

her reticule before he reached behind for the two keys. "Through that door," he pointed to the back of the room, "down the hallway. Last two rooms on the right side. Supper and breakfast will be extra. You can pay for it whenever you eat."

"What about tub and water for a bath?" she asked.

"Either that or you can bathe in the river," he said. "It runs back of the place about a half mile."

"Tub and water in my room," Elizabeth replied dryly. After he quoted the cost, she added, "At such a rate I expect a bar of soap, towels, and wash cloths." When the man nodded his acknowledgment, Elizabeth turned from the bar and bumped into Tony Mason, the abruptness of the impact causing her to drop her luggage. "Sorry," she murmured.

Tony was momentarily dumbfounded. The woman standing in front of him was one of the most beautiful he'd ever seen. When she stepped aside as if to pass him, he quickly galvanized into action. He swept his hat off, and a large, pleasant smile chased all surliness from his face.

"It is I who should apologize, ma'am." He bent and picked up her suitcase. "May I carry this for you, ma'am?"

Elizabeth smiled. "Yes, you may, Mr. —"

"Anthony Joshua Mason, ma'am," he said. "From Augusta, Georgia."

Elizabeth extended her hand and said, "Elizabeth Barrett from New Orleans."

"I'm right proud to make your acquaintance, Miss Barrett," Tony said. "It's nice to hear the soft, feminine inflection of a Southern Lady."

The compliment was a balm to the exhausted

woman. "Thank you," she returned quietly, turned, and moved toward her room. "What are you doing out here, Mister Mason?" she asked when they reached her door.

"Not much left of my home after the war," he replied. "So I drifted out and am working with the Texas Rangers right now. What are you doing out here?"

Elizabeth shoved the door open and took her portmanteau from Tony. "The war drove my sister out here, and I'm coming to visit her."

"Maybe we'll see each other later," Tony said as she stepped across the threshold. "I'd sure enjoy talking with you some more, ma'am. Supper maybe?"

"Perhaps," Elizabeth returned.

Sitting in the post commander's bedroom at his desk, Chase folded a note and handed it to George Washington Man. "Take this to Miss Barrett." When the door closed behind the corporal, Chase stood, walked across the small room to where Evan Warner stood and extended his hand. "I'm Major Chase Daniel, Mr. Warner. Thank you for coming and for waiting so patiently."

His hands never leaving his sides, Evan looked at Chase with open hatred. "Don't thank me, Major. I came because I had to. I didn't have a choice."

Chase's eyes narrowed at the man's overt hostility — something Chase should be accustomed to by now yet wasn't. "You're working with the Texas Rangers?"

"I am."

A man thoroughly accustomed to evaluating people

and situations, Evan watched Chase's slow and deliberate movements as he laid his gun belt and weapon on the dresser, as he stripped out of his jacket.

"Cigar?" Chase offered.

"Nope."

Chase picked up a cigar and lit it. He pointed to the whiskey bottle. "Care for a drink?"

"Only drink with friends," Warner said.

Chase's eyes narrowed, but he merely nodded his head and returned the bottle to the dresser. He walked across the room and stood at the window, gazingly at the river below. Smoke spiraled into the air.

"Within the past week," Chase said, "the Union payroll and the bank in Castroville has been robbed." Evan didn't answer, but Chase hadn't expected him to. He was growing accustomed to the antagonism of the Texans. He understood; even if he didn't, he had to live with it. "We had a prisoner from the payroll robbery, but he escaped."

Holding his cigar in his hand, Chase turned to look at the weathered man who leaned indolently against the door. "This prisoner was the only lead we had, Warner. He was only a hireling, but he could have given us information about the masterminds behind the holdup.

Chase paused; still the Ranger said nothing.

"Someone saw to it that he escaped and in doing so was killed. Two deputies—former Texas Rangers, I believe, had their throats slit, Warner, by an expert. A more excellent piece of butchering I've never seen. Everett ended up with a belly full of lead." Chase paused, then said, "Addison and Thurman were the deputies."

Evan, more interested than he appeared, reached up to rub his chin. "Any suspects, Major?"

"Yes. That's why I sent Corporal Man to get you," Chase replied. At length he said, "Do you know Blake Lowell? I understand he used to be a Texas Ranger."

"Blake Lowell!" Evan exclaimed. "You can't mean that."

Glad to get a response of some kind from the Ranger, Chase nodded. "Never meant anything more."

"Major, I've known Blake for the past fifteen years. Why, he was a captain in the Rangers, and—"

"And he was also a distinguished member of the Texas Light Cavalry," Chase said dryly, tired of the locals venerating the man, "but the war's over now, Warner, and all of us soldiers have changed. Some for the better; some for the worse."

"Not Blake Lowell," Warner maintained.

"I want Blake Lowell," Chase said in hard, unyielding tones.

"I don't know where he is."

"Don't lie to me," Chase ground out, tired of this misplaced loyalty Southerners had for one another. "I know he was here. I followed his trail all the way from Castroville. He rode parallel to the stagecoach just a few hours ahead of us and did such a damn good job covering his trail I wouldn't have found it if I hadn't been headed toward Uvalde myself."

Pale, weathered eyes stared unwavering at Chase. "I never lie," Evan answered evenly. "I don't know where Blake is. I saw him a couple of hours ago, but he left before the stage got into town. I don't know where he went."

"In what direction did he ride?" Chase asked.

"Don't know," Evan answered.

"I'm going to get him," Chase promised in a low voice. "With or without your help, Ranger Warner, I'll get Blake Lowell."

"Without my help, Major. Now if you don't have anything more to say to me, I'd like to go."

The two men measured each other from across the room. Eventually, Chase nodded his head and Warner slowly ambled out of the room. As soon as the door closed behind the ranger, Chase walked to the dresser, unplugged the whiskey bottle and lifted it to his lips to take a long drag.

True, he'd lost Everett, but in light of all that had happened in the last three days that loss didn't seem so great now. Everett was only an underling, and a stupid one at that. Blake Lowell, however, was something else. If, as Chase supposed, Blake were working with Bainbridge, he was no mere underling taking orders. He would be at the top of the criminal hierarchy issuing orders.

If he played his cards right, Chase thought, Warner would be on his way to warn Lowell right now. He could trust Samson and the men to keep an eye on the ranger and to let him know where he went.

By damn, despite these Texans he would find Blake Lowell!

Chase set the whiskey bottle on the dresser. Right now, he had other matters to attend to, and at the head of the list was Elizabeth Barrett. He smiled as he thought about their evening together. Circumstances surrounding his finding Blake's shirt in Elizabeth's room dictated his wasting no time in his wooing and bedding of the southern lady. Although he would move cautiously and gently, he would make her his. During his long ride from Castroville to Uvalde he had thought of little else. He frowned as Blake's words came back to haunt him.

I don't have to involve her, Major. She chose sides a long time ago. She's already involved.

Chase figured Blake had been planting seeds of doubt; he was a highly astute man and knew Chase was infatuated with Elizabeth. Chase couldn't believe she was involved with Bainbridge . . . but she was southern and probably sympathetic to their lost causes. Maybe he didn't want to believe she was involved with Bainbridge!

Chase was a wary man, his life directed by cold reason rather than emotion. He must be careful what he told Elizabeth until he assured himself that she wasn't involved in any illegal doings. He must keep her under surveillance. Whatever else Chase may have been, he was a soldier; he was an officer, and he would do this. He wouldn't let his feelings for her override his better judgment; he wouldn't let anyone or anything jeopardize him or his men. He might be infatuated with the lady and want to go to bed with her, but as yet he didn't trust her implicitly. No one or nothing would stand in his way of finding Roswell Irwin Bainbridge.

Chapter Seventeen

Refreshed from her bath, Elizabeth put a dressing gown over her chemise and impatiently waited for Lonnie to bring in her her trunk. She smiled at her last minute decision to have dinner with Chase on his return from a meeting with the officers at Ft. Inge. She hadn't hesitated a second after receiving his note — she couldn't wait to see him. She was so engrossed in her fantasies of the coming evening with Chase, she jumped as if she had just committed a crime of grave consequences when she heard the knock on the door.

"Yes?" she called.

"It's me, Miss Barrett," Lonnie said, "with your trunk."

Feeling rather foolish over her guilty reaction to the knock, Elizabeth walked across the room to open the door.

"And me," Jefferson added when he scooted through the door ahead of Lonnie.

"Put the trunk over there." Elizabeth pointed.

"And thank you for bringing it to me."

"Anything else you going to be a'wanting me to get off the stage?" Lonnie asked, and although he wasn't curt, he showed his irritation of this last minute request by refusing to be mollified.

"No," Elizabeth replied, "that's all I need."

Lonnie nodded and tossed over his shoulder as he disappeared through the door. "I'll be up early in the morning to pick it up."

"Anything you need me to do?" Jefferson asked, peering up at her. When Elizabeth shook her head, he said. "Corporal Man asked if I could camp out again with 'em, Miss Elizabeth. He says I'm a real big help with the chores."

Elizabeth grinned. "Did Corporal Man ask you or did you ask Corporal Man?"

Jefferson returned her grin and said with assumed worldliness, "You know how some people are, Miss Elizabeth. They want you to do something but they're too shy to ask so you gotta help 'em along."

"From what I've seen of Corporal Man," Elizabeth replied, carefully concealing her laughter, "I wouldn't have thought him to be a shy man."

Pulling a long, solemn face, Jefferson nodded. "Yes'm, he really is." He paused reflectively before he said, "Way I look at it, Miss Elizabeth, if I'm going to be a Buffalo Soldier when I grow up, I need to start learning how right now."

Elizabeth lifted her brows. "Sounds reasonable to me."

"Then I can go?"

Elizabeth chuckled and nodded her head. "However," she called as Jefferson spun around. "Before you run off, I'd like to know what a Buffalo Soldier is—a soldier who chases buffalo?"

"A soldier who chases buffalo! Just wait till I tell Sgt. Liberty and Corporal Man this!" Jefferson whooped with laughter. Finally when his mirth had died, he wiped the tears from his cheeks and said, "Miss Elizabeth, a Buffalo Soldier is a black soldier."

Although she didn't understand what was so funny, Elizabeth laughed with Jefferson. "Why the name Buffalo Soldier?"

"That's what the Indians named 'em, a name we can rightly be proud of," Jefferson replied, happy to be relaying knowledge to Miss Elizabeth for a change. "Sgt. Liberty says they named the black soldiers Buffalo Soldiers cause they respect us and think we're like the buffalo. We're brave and our hair's curly." Without taking a breath, he said, "Now, can I go, Miss Elizabeth?"

"When will I see you again?" she asked.

"In the morning when the stage takes off," Jefferson returned. "And if it's all right with you," he added, "Corporal Man is gonna see if the Major can find me a horse, and I can ride along with 'em. Won't have to ride on top of the stagecoach any more."

Elizabeth felt a tinge of sadness as she saw her little ward growing up in front of her, as she saw him gradually shifting his affection from her to the black troopers. "No," she replied, "I don't mind your riding with them. I just want you to be careful and to remember that you're not a soldier yet. You still have a lot more growing up to do."

"Out here, Miss Elizabeth," Jefferson informed her, "a boy grows up quick. I reckon I'm a man now, ready to make my own decisions."

"And who's opinion is that, Thomas Jefferson?" Elizabeth asked.

"Law of the frontier," Jefferson stated simply. "That's what Sgt. Liberty says."

"I don't doubt Sgt. Liberty in the least," Elizabeth replied a little sharply, "but I promised your mother that I'd look after you until you were old enough to make it on your own. I think I'll wait another year or two before I relinquish you to your own handling. Until then you're still accountable to me. You hear me?"

Jefferson grinned. He loved it when Miss Elizabeth's green eyes sparked pure fire and she spoke just like a schoolmarm. Her voice was kind of rough and kind of tender but mostly full of care and concern. "Yep, Miss Elizabeth, reckon I do."

Elizabeth laughed softly. "Now scoot before I change my mind."

"Yes, ma'am." Jefferson's cry echoed through the long, narrow hallway long after he was gone.

Elizabeth was smiling after she closed and locked the door. With time to spare after she dressed in her yellow calico gown, she rummaged through the trunk until she found her writing case. Picking it up, she moved to the edge of the bed to sit down and open the chest. For a long time she stared at Vanessa's letter. When she thought about how close she was to finding her sister, she couldn't help but get excited. A few more days at the most! But when she thought of Vanessa's being involved with Bainbridge, her chest grew tight and her heart hurt. She hoped Blake was in time to save her. She ran her fingers over the delicate handwriting. Vanessa was her own worst enemy, and only she could save herself from herself!

While finding Vanessa was still Elizabeth's major concern, and the concern steadily turning into deep-seated worry, Elizabeth found Chase stoutly vying for time in her thoughts. At the oddest moment and most inopportune times, his face would flash before her eyes. She would hear his rumbling laugh; she would feel the heated touch of his fingers on her arms, his mouth on hers. More and more she was beginning to feel at home in this Texas wilderness.

Such intrusions troubled Elizabeth. Too easily she could love Chase Daniel, and if she did, she risked having her heart trampled. Their worlds were poles apart, and she found no common ground upon which they could base a . . . relationship. He was a man accustomed to getting what he wanted, and what he wanted from her was merely pleasure in the bed—one night, maybe more.

Beyond that Elizabeth didn't know what Chase wanted. Certainly she didn't paint marriage into the picture, and that is what she wanted. That was her greatest desire: to marry a man whom she loved, to bear his children, and to have a home to cherish.

Heaving a deep sigh, she pushed Vanessa's letter aside, opened the small bottle of ink and picked up her pen. Quickly she wrote a note to her overseer, describing her journey from San Antonio to Uvalde and apprising him that she would write again when she reached Eagle Pass. Once the letter was addressed and sealed, she locked her chest and returned it to the trunk. Picking up her reticule and parasol, she hurried out of the room.

After she posted the letter, she browsed through the general store finally to stop in front of the bolts of material and sewing accessories. So intently was she studying the ribbon, she wasn't aware of anyone's entering the store until a shadow fell across her and she heard Chase's deep, familiar voice.

"I think we'll take a length of the black. It'll look beautiful with that yellow dress you're wearing and in your golden hair."

Elizabeth dropped the card of ribbon she was holding and spun around. "Chase," she whispered, their disagreement from the previous day forgotten in the joy of seeing him again. Her fears and doubts were casually pushed aside.

"Hello," he said, his eyes hungrily sweeping over her face, visually touching and caressing each feature. He couldn't believe it had only been two days since he'd seen her; he felt as though they had been separated for years.

"What are you doing here?" As eagerly Elizabeth looked at Chase. The damp hair combed back from his freshly shaven face. The clean uniform. The hat in his hand. "I thought you were at a staff meeting."

"I'm supposed to be," he admitted. "It's been postponed until later this afternoon. I was on my way to get a room for the night and to see you." *So I could be close to you.* "You can't imagine how disappointed I was to discover you weren't in."

"But you found me."

"Yes," Chase said, his eyes somber, "I found you."

"Did you get the room?"

"Yes," said Chase.

For a moment they were lost in each other, as each

pondered the consequences of his announcement. Finally he said, "I came to tell you that I can't meet you for supper."

"Oh," Elizabeth said, disappointment taking the sparkle out of her eyes.

While he wasn't happy about not having dinner with her, Chase was glad to see her disappointment. This was a clear indication that Elizabeth was as eager to be with him as he was with her. He looked around for the elderly woman who tended the store. When he saw she was on the far side of the room straightening dry goods on a long table, he turned to clasp Elizabeth's hands firmly in his. "I know this is going to sound like an old story," he said, "but I had to see you tonight. I want to apologize for what happened yesterday morning at Vance's Hotel."

Elizabeth tried to concentrate on what he was saying, but he was too close to her; his hands sent a warm pleasure through her body. She looked down to see hers lost in the bigness of his. She felt the warmth of his breath on the back of her neck, the odor a blending of whiskey and tobacco.

As a soldier, Chase was accustomed to planning his campaigns before the battles. He always fought to win, and fighting for Elizabeth Barrett was no different. He applied the same rules to her courtship and ultimate seduction. The past two days and night in the saddle he spent charting his moves, one by one, carefully and methodically. He would have liked to move more slowly, but time and Blake Lowell were against him. He would have to hasten the wooing—which meant doing whatever was necessary to get her into bed with him.

"Although I was jealous of Blake Lowell, I had no right to misjudge you or to make false accusations." He smiled sheepishly, and the solemn blue eyes stared into hers. "Seems to be a habit where you're concerned." Again he felt a twinge of guilt as he thought about his reasons for not mentioning the ribbon he found at the jailhouse and his subsequent conversation with Jack Stevens. "I want you to know, Elizabeth, that I care for you . . . really care." While his admission was true, it was also calculated; he knew it would appease her aggrieved spirit.

Elizabeth was deliriously happy; he hadn't declared love to her, but she felt the truth of his words. His confession was like a soothing ointment that miraculously healed all hurts and wounds. "I care for you, too," she murmured. Gazing at the exhaustion written on his countenance, she said, "I wish you didn't have to go to that meeting."

"Me, too." He smiled wistfully. "But I do." He reached up to rub his tight neck muscles. "I'm not looking forward to it at all. I have nothing but bad news to relay." More as an extension of his thoughts rather than conversation with Elizabeth, he muttered, "The paymaster wagon was robbed, and although we're making provisions for the soldiers' pay, they'll have to take scrip until we receive the money." He sighed deeply as he leaned against the counter. "As if that's not enough, we now have the bank robbery on our hands."

"It's that bad?" Elizabeth quizzed.

"Worse," Chase admitted. "We could have a mutiny on our hands. The men signed up for the war, and it's over. They were ready to go home; instead they were ordered out here, and frontier conditions are bad at the best. When I tell them about the robbery of the paymaster—" Chase simply shrugged his shoulders.

Elizabeth reached out and gently touched her fingertip to the dark semicircles beneath his eyes. "You're tired," she said. "Have you had any sleep since you left Castroville?"

Chase caught her hand in his and shook his head.

"You can't continue to push yourself like this," Elizabeth chided. "You've got to get some rest."

"I couldn't stop," Chase told her. "As long as Blake was moving, I had to keep going. I couldn't take a chance on losing him."

"Did you . . . overtake him?" she asked, a strange catch in her voice as she thought about Vanessa.

The odd inflection didn't go unnoticed by Chase. As he looked at her, he cursed Blake Lowell for having planted the seeds of doubt in his mind. He couldn't help wondering if she were involved with Blake and ultimately with Bainbridge. Ironic that she always seemed to be wherever Blake was and the two of them were traveling in the same direction. She was definitely interested in Blake; he just couldn't qualify what kind of interest. Even though he hated himself for having ordered it, he'd be glad to get that report from Stevens; then perhaps some of his questions would be answered.

"I trailed him here," he finally said. "But he's either—" the soldier in Chase made him pause; the man was infatuated with the lady and wanted to trust her implicitly; the soldier was wary and would trust no one. "—gone or hiding. You haven't seen him since you arrived, have you?"

"No," Elizabeth exclaimed, her eyes rounding with surprise. "I had no idea that Blake was here in Uvalde."

Even as she said the words she could see Chase's inner conflict and knew he was wondering whether he could believe her. He had apologized because he wanted to make love to her, but he didn't trust her. Although he cared for her, she knew he didn't share the same caring for her that she did him. Hers verged on love; his, she surmised, were simply lust.

Strangely she wasn't disappointed. She was exhilarated by the challenge Major Chase Daniel had just thrown down. Before this war was over, she would have the mighty Union Cavalry officer in love with her. She wouldn't humble him; a meek man didn't suit her purposes at all. She admired Chase's will power, his strength of character, and that hint of arrogance. An enigmatic smile sparked in her eyes. She might lose a few battles along the way, but she wouldn't lose the war. She wanted Chase Daniel, and she determined to get him — on her terms. Before he knew what had happened, his lust would be transformed into love.

"That ribbon just came in," the elderly storekeeper said, coming to stand behind them. Her hands busily arranged and rearranged the bolts of material. "Mighty pretty, too. It's gonna sell really fast. Better get you some while it's here."

"I was looking for a piece of red," Elizabeth said.

"Didn't get no red this time," the woman informed her with a wave of her hand down the counter. "Just what you see."

"I'll take a length of this." Chase picked up the card

303

of black grogram and handed it to the woman.

"How much?" she asked, moving down the counter to her scissors.

"Enough to tie back a cloud of golden blonde curls," Chase leaned down to whisper in Elizabeth's ear.

"What's that?" The woman held her hand up to her ear and turned around. "I can't hear you."

"About twelve inches," Elizabeth answered as she and Chase smiled secretively at each other.

With her purchase tucked safely in her purse, Elizabeth allowed Chase to guide her outside where the afternoon was quickly turning into evening. When they stood on the boardwalk, she opened her parasol and he put his hat on.

"It may be quite late when I get out of the meeting," he told her. "May I come by and see you?"

"Yes," Elizabeth murmured, wondering at the wisdom of her answer. Being with Chase in the public like this was different; she was safe with numbers. She could control her feelings and desires. In the privacy of her own room she had no defense against her perfidious emotions, and to carry out her plans she needed a clear mind and on her part disciplined emotions.

"No matter what time," Chase iterated.

Elizabeth was fickle. Before her arguments could take residence, she swept them away as if they were of no significance. Reaching out, she curled her fingers around his lower arm. "No matter what time. I'll be waiting for you."

Chase laid his hand over hers and marveled that it could be so tiny. "I'll be there," he promised.

Elizabeth watched him mount and waved as he rode off. When he was out of sight, she slowly returned to the Silver Dollar, his promise taunting her. She had seemed so cool and in control, but she knew tonight would be a different story. Where Chase Daniel was concerned she had no will power, no desire but to please him. Yet, she must remain firm in her resolve to make the basis of their relationship more than lust if she were going to win Chase Daniel's heart, and she would settle for no less.

Chapter Eighteen

Disappointed because Chase couldn't be with her, Elizabeth pushed through the swinging doors into the cool interior of the saloon. As she fiddled with the catch of her parasol to lower it, she made her way to the bar and ordered her supper. She wasn't as much hungry as she was weak, not having had anything to eat since breakfast.

"Be about thirty minutes, ma'am," the bartender said. "Have a seat and I'll bring it out to you."

"Miss Barrett!"

When Elizabeth heard her name called out, she turned to see Anthony Mason striding toward her, a smile creasing his face.

"I hoped I'd see you again." He swept his hat from his head and bowed deeply. "Could I buy your supper, ma'am?" When he saw that she was about to protest, he said, "Please, Miss Barrett. I'd consider it an honor, and I'd sure love to spend some time talking with you. It's been a long time since I've talked to someone from down our way, and I'm mighty lonesome for news about home."

Elizabeth couldn't help but relent. The evening

without Chase would be long and lonely, and Anthony Mason was such a pleasant looking man. She could understand his desire for company. She had instantly felt that same kindred spirit with Blake. All of them, she, Anthony, and Blake, seemed to share a common heritage. Why not share a meal and a little company with him!

She smiled and said, "I'd love to have supper with you, Mr. Mason."

"Tony, ma'am," he said, his fingers lightly touching her elbow as he guided her to a table in the corner. "Please call me Tony."

"All right, Tony," Elizabeth answered. "If you'll call me Elizabeth."

For the next hour as Elizabeth and Tony ate, they talked, recalling the halcyon days of their childhood, skirting over the war years and resuming with their lives since the war. The sun set, but the saloon was ablaze with light from myriad candles and lamps. The sleepy town had turned into a den of activity and flurry, and Elizabeth was sure that most of its citizens were in the Silver Dollar.

"I came out here to get away from the Yankees," Tony said disgustedly when a group of soldiers walked into the saloon. "Seems that no matter where you go you run into them. Guess the only way a body can be rid of them is to join one of the Confederate colonies in Mexico."

"Surely you're not thinking about that," Elizabeth exclaimed, shocked. "You can't desert your own country and people."

Tony shook his head. "This isn't my country anymore, Elizabeth, and the Yankees sure aren't my people. They destroyed my life and left me a shell of a man."

"No," said Elizabeth softly, "no person, event or condition can rob you of life or your own individuality. If the South is to survive, Tony, we can't go on blaming the North for our shortcomings. We must face up to our irresponsibility and accept the consequences of our actions. We must fight against the carpetbaggers and scalawags; we must regain control of our institutions and build our governments anew for the good of everyone."

"Oh, God," Tony murmured, "you sound just like one of those over-zealous blue-bellies."

"And you sound like a coward who's running away from life. What's in Mexico for you, Tony?"

Narrow-eyed, Tony stared at her for a long time. After a while he leaned across the table and said, "Have you ever heard of Colonel Roswell Irwin Bainbridge?"

"Since I arrived in Texas I've heard of little else," Elizabeth answered dryly. "Until recently I thought he'd been killed. Now I find he's been resurrected in soul if not body."

"Rumor has it he faked his own death and is now living in Mexico," Tony said. "He's gathering an army down there, and he's planning to invade the South and drive the Yankees out."

"The war's over, Tony."

"No, it isn't," he insisted. "We're just regrouping."

"If Bainbridge is alive and is doing what you're claiming, he's our enemy not our friend. By his actions he's jeopardizing our chances of every getting out from under military occupation," Elizabeth maintained. "No matter how good his intention he's got to stop."

"He can't stop," Tony maintained. "If we'll let him, Bainbridge will be the South's savior. You don't know how many destitute families he's helped, Elizabeth. You don't know the number of people who refused to take an oath of allegiance that he's smuggled over the border. Good innocent people the Yankees have branded as enemies of the state and confiscated their property."

"So here you are," Evan Warner's voice boomed over the noisy buzz of the saloon as he pulled a chair from the table where Elizabeth and Tony sat. "Been looking for you."

Tony looked at the other ranger and grinned. "Evan Warner, I'd like for you to meet Miss Elizabeth Barrett from New Orleans, Lousiana."

Evan smiled and quickly whipped his hat off, grey hair falling across his forehead. "Glad to meet you, Miss Barrett. What are you doing this far west?"

"I'm going to visit my sister in Eagle Pass," she returned.

"What a coincidence!" Tony exclaimed. "That's where Evan and I are headed."

"Perhaps you've heard of my sister then," Elizabeth said eagerly, hoping that Vanessa had managed to get out of Mexico and was living in Eagle Pass. "Vanessa Barrett." Evan stoked his chin and murmured to himself, "Vanessa Barrett." Finally he said, "Nope! Don't reckon I've ever heard the name before, ma'am."

"Let me show you her portrait," Elizabeth said, reaching in her lap for her purse. She withdrew the miniature and handed it to the ranger.

Evan studied the dark-haired beauty carefully before he shook his head. "Sorry, ma'am, I don't recognize her either." As Tony took the miniature from him, Warner smiled gently and hastened to assure her, "Now that don't mean there ain't a Vanessa Barrett living there. Tony and I haven't been assigned to Eagle Pass very long, and I'm sure I don't know everybody what lives down there."

Elizabeth looked at Tony who raised his head. "No, ma'am," he said. "I don't reckon I know her." He grinned. "Sure wouldn't mind though. She's a beautiful woman."

Elizabeth took the portrait and returned it to her purse. She sat a little longer, talking with Tony and Evan, but the long journey was taking its toll. Finally she could stifle her yawns no longer. "Please excuse me," she said. "Your company isn't the least bit boring, but mine shall soon be. I'm extremely tired. Two days and a night in a stagecoach have robbed me of much needed sleep."

Chase pushed through the swinging doors into the smoke-hazed interior of the saloon. As he threaded his way through the tables, his gaze swept the crowd. In the corner he saw Elizabeth, sitting with two other men, and fire raced through his veins. The older one he knew: Evan Warner. The younger one—the handsome one—he didn't know. As if that boy—he didn't look old enough to be shaving—were the only person in the room, Elizabeth was laughing with him, her green eyes sparkling.

Chase felt the suffocating tentacles of jealousy as they compressed his chest. All his life he had been guided by reason and logic, but since he'd met Elizabeth his life had been turned topsy-turvy. Thinking of her when he should be thinking about his safety and that of his men. Deliberately keeping her name out of the Everett investigation.

Chase was livid with anger and jealousy every time he saw her with another man, and knowing that he had to leave for Ft. Clark within the night, he was even more conscious of the few hours they had to spend together. He didn't want to share them with anyone but her.

Long, determined strides took him across the room. He arrived at the table in time to hear Tony say, "May I see you to your room?"

"I think not," said Chase, planting himself behind Elizabeth, his hands resting possessively on her shoulders. Her gasp of pleased surprise didn't go unnoticed, but at the moment he was concentrating on the pup across the table.

Tony took one look at the cavalry uniform and leaped to his feet. In his haste he almost knocked the table over. Hatred blazed in his eyes. "Who the hell — who are you?"

"Major Chase Daniel," Chase introduced himself in a smooth tone, a dangerous quietness not unlike the eye of the storm.

"Look, soldier boy," Tony said with surly belligerence, "what right do you think you — "

Elizabeth laid a hand on Tony's lower arm and said soothingly, "It's all right. Major Daniel is a friend of mine." She turned to Evan. "Major Daniel, I'd like for you to meet Rangers Anthony Mason and Evan Warner."

Evan grabbed his hat and rose. Curtly he said, "We

already met, ma'am. Come on, Tony, guess it's time for you and me to mosey on." He smiled at Elizabeth and added, "I'm right glad to meet you, ma'am. I'm looking forward to seeing you again in Eagle Pass."

"The pleasure was all mine, Mr. Warner," she said. "Thank you for an enjoyable evening."

Evan glanced at Tony who was making no preparations to leave. "Come on, Tony," Evan said, "let's go."

Tony didn't budge; he stood glaring across the table at Chase.

Evan's hand capped his partner's shoulder. "Time for us to be moving along, boy."

"Yeah," Tony muttered, "I guess it is." His gaze shifted from Chase to Elizabeth, his expression turning from hatred to pleasure. "Thank you for having dinner with me. I also look forward to seeing you again in Eagle Pass." Without a word to Chase, Tony put his hat on and turned. Side by side, he and Evan walked out of the room.

"I didn't expect to see you so soon," Elizabeth said as she watched him sit down across the table from her.

Laying his hat in the vacant chair next to him, Chase smiled lazily. "Had I known that good-looking young pup was dancing attendance on you, I'd have been here sooner."

"You had nothing to worry about," Elizabeth returned. "We were properly chaperoned."

"Would I have anything to worry about had you not been properly chaperoned?" Chase asked.

"No," Elizabeth whispered, "absolutely nothing." She reached out to lay her hand against his cheek, the tip of her index finger resting beneath the corner of his eye and bringing her attention to the dark circles of exhaustion.

Chase covered her hand with his. "That's the answer I needed to hear." For a moment that stretched into eternity they stared into one another's eyes. "Shall we go somewhere quieter and cooler?" he asked.

A knot formed in the pit of Elizabeth's stomach as she thought of being alone with Chase. She wasn't ready for that just yet. "Later," she replied, her voice slightly husky. "Have you eaten?"

Chase shook his head. "Frankly, I don't have food on my mind."

"If you don't get some in your stomach, you won't have a mind or body for anything," she said.

"Are you suggesting something, madam?" Chase teased, his fingers sliding from her hand down her arm to send tantalizing shivers through her body.

Elizabeth's face turned a delicious shade of red. "I'm suggesting that you eat some supper, sir. Then we'll go for a stroll along the river."

"I'll eat later," he said, "and I'm not really interested in strolling by the river."

"Your health comes first," Elizabeth said, and the nurse in her wouldn't be disobeyed. "After you eat, we'll discuss strolling down the river, and if you come up with a better suggestion I'll consider it."

"Yes, ma'am," Chase answered softly, his eyes gleaming soft and warm like a placid lake on a summer day.

Being fussed over by a woman was a new and wonderful experience for Chase. It gave new dimensions to the word care; it seemed to verge on love—the one emotion Chase hadn't fully developed because it was the emotion he feared most. Yet he welcomed Elizabeth's caring, and he liked caring for her.

After he had eaten, the two of them walked out of the saloon into the cool April evening. When they sat on a large boulder on the bank of the river beneath the drooping bows of the huge tree, Chase lit a cigar. The night was peaceful, one of the most beautiful he'd spent in many a year. Even when they weren't talking, he enjoyed being with Elizabeth. Her silence was comfortable and reassuring.

Although she thoroughly relished watching the moonlight play across Chase's broad shoulders, Elizabeth yearned to touch him, to feel the warmth of his flesh beneath her hands. Compelled by her desires, she slid off the boulder and came to stand behind him, her hands biting into the tensed, knotted muscles of his shoulders and neck as she massaged.

"What are you worried about?" Her fingers firmly slid down his spine and up again.

"Got word from the commander at Ft. Clark. More trouble is brewing. I need to get there as soon as possible."

"Indians?" she asked.

"I'm not sure," Chase returned laconically, grinding the tip of the cigar into the boulder before he threw it on the ground. He let his head loll forward and gave himself to the relaxing bit of Elizabeth's fingers and hands.

"You think it's Bainbridge, don't you?"

"Could be. Both are getting more daring and more frequent in their raids from Mexico." He reached up, caught her hand in his, and pulled her so that she stood in front of him. He caught her in an embrace

314

and rested his cheek against her breast. He thrilled to the rushed, erratic beat of her heart. "Just below Ft. Clark," he said, "a trading caravan and an entire patrol was wiped out by a band of Mescaleros who were reentering Mexico. The patrol was out scouting when they heard the shots and rode to the rescue. Only one trooper escaped with his life."

"Did you know the men?" Elizabeth asked tremulously, quickly drowning in the swirling eddy of sensations created by Chase's touch.

"Yes."

"Chase," Elizabeth said quietly, tentatively, "even if Bainbridge is alive, do you think perhaps you're overestimating his ability to rally all these people in his cause?" Shyly she circled his body with her arms and began to brush her fingers through the thick hair at the nape of his neck. More firmly her fingers gently kneaded just below the cap of the skull.

"I've learned never to underestimate the enemy," Chase returned. "And I most assuredly will not underestimate Roswell Irwin Bainbridge. The man is shrewd, cunning, devious, and most of all deadly."

Elizabeth paled, more afraid for Vanessa than ever.

"Elizabeth," Chase asked tentatively, "did Everett say anything to you about the robbery?"

"No," Elizabeth replied, "we talked only of Vanessa."

"Do you think he was connected with Bainbridge?"

"I think so."

"What about Vanessa?"

"I don't know," Elizabeth murmured, hesitant yet to confide in him. "I want to think not . . . but . . . I just don't know."

Because of the rocky foundation on which their friendship was based, Elizabeth hesitated to speak to Chase about his obsession with Bainbridge, but she felt she must. She didn't want to believe Vanessa or Blake were mixed up with a man as deadly as Bainbridge seemed to be.

"Chase, have you thought perhaps your feelings for Bainbridge are based on prejudice — the feelings of an officer of the United States Cavalry to an ex-Confederate officer and a highly successful officer at that. Maybe he's not as bad as you want to believe he is."

Chase laughed shortly. "You think I'm chaffing because this man has eluded us?"

Elizabeth shrugged. "Something like that?"

"No," Chase returned, "my desire to capture this man and his band of cutthroats isn't based on prejudice of two opposing officers. I admit I'm prejudiced, but it's based on hatred for a man who preys off of other humans. And if you Southerners were not trying to make Robin Hoods or saints out of all your ex-officers, you'd realize that Bainbridge and his men are enemies of us all." He was silent for a moment.

Elizabeth felt his arms tighten about her.

"Damn! The conditions on this damned frontier are enough to get to the best of men," he said, his tone harsh and grating. "We don't have enough men, and the ones we do have don't have the experience or the proper equipment." Abruptly he set her away from him, stood and moved closer to the river. "We get what's rejected by the rest of the army — horses, clothing, weapons, and food, and we're rejected by the very people we're protecting with our lives. We're basically rejected by the army that we serve."

He whirled around to look at Elizabeth through the moonlight. "Dear God, how can we win in this no-win situation? How many men will we have to sacrifice before the government understands that we must have the cooperation of both it and the Mexicans to apprehend these criminals—both Indians and whites—who slip back and forth across the border."

Thinking only of Chase's anguish, Elizabeth rushed to where he stood, wrapped her arms around him and pressed her cheek against his shoulder.

His arms circled her small frame, and he inhaled the clean perfume of her freshly washed hair. "Or we're going to have to take matters in our own hands and go over there to destroy the scourge." He savored her warmth; his hands moved up and down her back.

"You can't do that," Elizabeth said. "Neither government will allow that. Our relationship with Mexico is tenuous at best."

"And getting more tenuous with each incursion of Indians and outlaws."

"Why don't you give up the army?" Elizabeth asked, wondering about Chase's background, worrying about his safety should he remain here on the border. "Surely you have a family back home that—"

"The army is my life," Chase returned, his tone sharper than he meant for it to be. "And I have no family. My father deserted my mother before I was born, and she died in childbirth. I was reared in a foundling's home."

"I'm sorry," Elizabeth whispered, immediately stricken with remorse at her inadvertent blunder.

"You have nothing to be sorry about, sweetheart." Chase pressed his hand against her cheek and laid his head on the crown of hers. "And I've grown accustomed to being alone and on my own. It's just that watching the men I've grown to know through the years die so needlessly—" The sentence trailed into silence.

"Captain Terrence Lee," he finally said, a husky catch of tears in his voice. "Terry and I met at the home. He was about three years older than I." Chase broke off to laugh, the sound void of any identifiable emotion. "Kids raised in an orphanage seldom know their exact age or their real birthdays." *Some of us don't even know our own names.* "So we figured Terry was about three years old than I."

Elizabeth blinked back the tears that threatened to spill down her cheeks. Chase didn't need her pity; he wanted no judgments; he only needed her to listen.

"He taught me how to take care of myself. He and Aunt Ida are the nearest to family I have . . . had."

"Who's Aunt Ida?" Elizabeth's arms tightened automatically, her words holding a hint of jealousy, her embrace gently protective and reassuring.

"Ida Owens," Chase said, a smile in his voice. "She opened her house and heart to the waifs she took in off the street." As he remembered the matron of Owens Orphanage, he laughed aloud. "She was about five foot three and as wide as she was tall. Ever since I can remember her brown hair had one streak of white, and she always wore it in a coil on the top of her head. Over her dark dresses, she always wore a bibbed apron. She's the only thing in my life that never seems to change."

"Have you seen her recently?" Elizabeth asked. She felt Chase's head move on hers as he nodded.

318

"At the close of the war, Terry and I applied for and received leave. Both of us went back to Philadephia together." Chase felt the bitter bite of tears as he thought of those two wonderful weeks that he and Terry had spent with Aunt Ida. The last time the two of them had been together.

He could still see the golden blaze in the huge fireplace in the kitchen. He felt the warmth of the fire; he felt the warmth of Aunt Ida's love. Without his being aware of talking, he told Elizabeth about his childhood in Philadelphia.

Elizabeth listened as he told her about roasting chestnuts and popping corn over the fire on cold, winter evenings. Going to school. Skimming down a snow-covered hill on a sled. Fighting. Loving. The older children had to help the younger; they also had to perform chores for other people in order to earn wages which they willingly shared with Aunt Ida and the other children.

"As best she could," Chase said, "Aunt Ida provided us with a homey atmosphere. With all her heart and soul she tried to be the mother that life denied us."

"You've never heard from your father?" Elizabeth felt Chase's chest expand and contract as he inhaled, then exhaled.

"No."

"Does Mrs. Owens know anything about him?" Elizabeth queried. "Perhaps you could find him, Chase. You could—" She pulled back and lifted her head.

"No, I know nothing. Aunt Ida said my mother was a gentle woman of good breeding, but she refused to talk about her past or her background."

Chase stared at her face, so fragile and ethereal in the wan light of the moon. "Let's not spend our precious time together discussing a man who never cared enough about me or my mother to claim us," he said.

Elizabeth was of the same inclination. Her fingers dug into the thickly muscled shoulders. She raised her lips to him. The free-will offering he gladly took. The kiss was hot and consuming, setting desire ablaze in both of them.

Elizabeth felt his hands brush down her back, his rough palms rasping against the delicate texture of her dress. Her breasts tightened with desire and throbbed against the constraining material. When she felt his hands slip under her arms to cup the swollen fullness, she pulled her mouth from Chase's and moaned softly.

Chase knew he must stop . . . if he were going to stop. He had been long without a woman, and Elizabeth aroused him quickly; her very presence drove him to distraction. Her passionate responses to his advances pushed him to the point of no return. He was standing at the edge of the precipice. But he didn't intend to make love to her here on the river bank.

"We need to go." His hands slid down her arms as he firmly set her away from him.

Disappointment knotted in Elizabeth's stomach. Lifting her starlight face to him, she said, "Let's not go in . . . just yet." Chase hadn't moved a step, but he seemed to be a million miles away.

"If we don't go in now, we won't be going in." His features were molded of granite as he peered into the moon-streaked face. Chase didn't understand himself. He had wanted her; he had intended to take her, and now that she was willing, he was the one calling a halt to it. "Do you understand what I'm telling you?"

"Yes."

Chase shook his head. "I can't, Elizabeth. I'm not willing to make you the promises you want and deserve."

He slid his hand beneath her elbow and guided her back to the saloon. Neither said a word as they walked. Both were caught up in their own thoughts. Elizabeth was struggling with herself: A part of her wanted Chase to make love to her before he left; another part was angry because she could so quickly and easily forget her virtue and resolve where this man was concerned.

Chase was furious with himself because he was getting too emotionally tied to Elizabeth. He knew he had only to lower her to ground by the river and he could make love to her. In so many words she had begged him to. But did he? No, he was suddenly stopped by a conscience he wasn't aware he possessed — a troublesome burden that he'd like to unload.

They walked through the crowded saloon, down the dimly lit hall to Elizabeth's room. Taking the key from her, Chase unlocked and opened the door, a wedge of pale light penetrating into the dark interior. He stood back and watched as she moved to the dresser and lit the oil lamp. When she turned to him, the light flickered across her face.

"I guess I'll be seeing you in the morning." Despite her growing disappointment, Elizabeth kept her voice light.

Chase watched as she laid her purse and parasol on the dresser and stripped off her gloves. "No," he said, "I'll be leaving long before the stage."

Elizabeth's head jerked up, and she stared at him. She forgot that only a few hours earlier she had resolved never to see him agin. She couldn't bear to think of life with Chase Daniel. Unable to help herself, she asked, "Will I see you again?"

"No." His hand clenched into a fist at his side. He silently cursed himself for being a fool where Elizabeth Barrett was concerned. "It's better if we don't," he said.

Swallowing her tears, Elizabeth held her back straight and continued to stare at him. "Why?" she asked.

"I've already told you," he said, hating himself for doing this to her; yet, proud that he was strong enough to consider her before himself. "I'm not willing to give you what you want or deserve in a man. Marriage isn't part of my plans."

As he stared at Elizabeth's stricken face, Chase's felt as if his heart had been thrown on the ground and trampled by a herd of stampeding cattle. He wanted to recall the words and take the pleasure that the moment offered. He wanted to make wild, passionate love to her. But he couldn't. He absolutely could not. Elizabeth wasn't that kind of woman; he wasn't that kind of man.

He turned and walked to his room—the longest journey Chase Daniel ever traveled.

Chapter Nineteen

Wrapped in a cocoon of numbness such as she hadn't experienced since Johnny's death, Elizabeth undressed, her clothes falling into a heap around her feet. She couldn't bear the thought of Chase's leaving in the morning. Probably, they would never see each other again.

Without putting on her nightgown, she slipped into her wrapper and stood in front of the dresser looking into the mottled mirror. She didn't see her pale reflection in the arc of golden light. She saw only Chase's face. She felt only his touch: his arms around her and his lips on hers. All she could think about was his leaving in the morning, of her being alone. His imminent departure made her poignantly and deeply aware of the emptiness and void in her life.

She reached up to rub one of the smudges from the smooth glass. She still wanted to find Vanessa, she wanted her out of Mexico and away from Bainbridge and out of danger, but Elizabeth was no longer obsessed with the idea of bringing her back to The Rose or of changing her life style. Much to her surprise, Elizabeth found herself thinking less and less about the plantation. Her return to New Orleans no longer seemed imperative to her happiness. It was more a wonderful memory than her reason for existing. Since she'd met Chase her whole concept of life and values had changed.

Without a doubt she loved him, but she also knew that Chase didn't love her. He cared about her, but he didn't love her. After their conversation at the river she understood why. Love frightened him. His father had deserted his mother before he was born; his mother had died soon after his birth — the two people whom he needed most in his life were denied him. As he had grown up in the orphanage he had built a barrier around his heart. If he never loved, he'd never be hurt. He was afraid to love for fear the one whom he loved would be taken from him as his parents had, and he would be left alone . . . again.

At the moment assuring Chase of her love was the most important thing in Elizabeth's life. She was going to have to make the biggest sacrifice of her life, and contrary to what Aunt Feldie and Mama had always taught her, it wasn't her virginity; she was going to have to offer Chase unconditional love that asked for and demanded no commitment. She was giving him her heart to do with as he wished.

Elizabeth realized that giving herself to Chase was an irrevocable decision and it was chancy at best. Once they made love, she would never be the same again. Once they made love, she had no guarantee of a future with him, yet a part of her would always belong to him. Without him the future seemed bleak.

Elizabeth had learned a long time ago that life was a gamble. If you never risked, you never gained. If she fought for Chase's love and lost, she would be no worse off than she was now and probably far happier than if she hadn't made the effort. At least, she would have memories — happy ones to replace all her nightmares. If she won, she would have everything.

Picking up the lamp and carrying it to the night table in front of the opened window, she stared at the starlit night before she went to bed. She smelled the aroma of tobacco and knew Chase was smoking a cigar in his room. She could imagine him gazing at the heavens as she was doing. She wondered if he were also aching with unfulfilled needs . . . if he were wishing he were with her.

Elizabeth had promised herself earlier that she was going to make Chase Daniel fall in love with her on her terms, but tonight he'd taken the initiative away from her. If she won him, she'd do it on his terms. And his terms were high, so high she wasn't sure she could pay the price. Neither could she let him ride out of her life. His love was important to her. Important enough that she would risk all and fight against all odds for it. If she lost she would know that she could have done no more.

Elizabeth leaned over and, cupping the top of the lamp chimney with her hand, blew out the wick to leave the room saturated in darkness.

Chase liked the darkness; it brought a quiet serenity that daylight never afforded. Standing in front of the opened window and wearing only his breeches, one foot hiked on the low window casement, he gazed into the heavens, the twinkling stars reminding him of

Elizabeth's eyes. He lifted the glass to his lips and quaffed the whiskey, not caring that he would soon be drunk. Tonight he welcomed the oblivion inebriation would bring. Then and only then would his body no longer be riddled by desire and his mind be free of thoughts of Elizabeth.

He reached for the bottle and was about to refill his glass. Thinking better of it, he set the glass down and lifted the bottle to his lips and drank freely. No need to waste time and energy refilling glasses, he decided. When he heard the knock on the door, he turned and grimaced. He didn't know who it was, but tonight he didn't want company . . . he wanted Elizabeth Rose Barrett; he wanted to lose himself completely in her luscious body. Long strides carried him across the room. Still holding the liquor bottle, he unlocked and opened the door to find the woman of his thoughts standing there.

"Elizabeth," he murmured, his eyes devouring her beauty, the tentative expectancy on her face, "what's wrong?"

"Nothing you can't make right," she replied quietly, seeking some sign of welcome on his countenance.

Chase's gaze moved from her face to her bodice and lower. With the hall candle to her back, her petite body was outlined through the thin material of the billowing wrapper. Chase had the wildest desire to stroke the shapely lines of her gently flaring hips that were silhouetted through the swirling folds of material; to feel her tremble beneath his hands; to partake of her virginal beauty. He was filled with lust as his eyes slowly moved up to linger on her breasts.

"Elizabeth," he whispered, reluctantly raising his

head to her face and using all his strength to control his desire.

The raucous laughter of a man and a woman teetering down the hall snapped both Elizabeth and Chase out of their magical world. Chase's free arm darted out, and his hand curled around her arm. He tugged her into his room and slammed the door.

"What in God's name are you doing out here wearing no more than that?" he demanded.

Elizabeth looked down in surprise; so intently had she been thinking about Chase she'd forgotten she was wearing only her wrapper.

"Everybody in that saloon could see you," he said sharply.

"No one saw me," Elizabeth returned, her eyes going to the half-empty liquor bottle he held to his side.

"Not because you didn't want them to," Chase lashed out, but he wasn't angry nor did he really believe his own accusation. He was frightened of the feelings he had for Elizabeth. He'd never been this vulnerable to a woman before, and he didn't like it. Sensations like this could compel a man to propose marriage.

"I wanted to be with you so desperately I didn't think about what I was wearing," she confessed.

Elizabeth could tell that Chase was hurting inside, that he, too, was caught in the same maelstrom of emotion as she and didn't know what to do. She reached out and took the liquor bottle from his hand to set it on the nearby table.

"Good, God! Elizabeth," Chase exclaimed, wondering if she knew how difficult decency was at a moment like this, at a moment when his baser side

327

was yelling for him to take her. At the moment honor felt like an unwanted garment he wanted to snatch off and cast aside. "What do you think I'm made of? Wood? Do you honestly believe you can stand in here so near naked and not make me want you desperately? Get out of here before we do something that you'll regret." He turned and strode to the window.

"If we don't do something, I'll regret it," Elizabeth said, her voice low but firm. That she was being the aggressor filled her with a strange sense of exhilaration. That she was persuading him to make love to her was strangely exciting. "That's why I'm here."

Chase didn't know how long he could keep his hands off Elizabeth, and she wasn't making his struggle any easier. The voice of his conscience was getting softer and softer—but he could still hear it. "I care about you," he said, his back still to her, "—more than anything in the world I want to take what you're offering, but," he turned, "I . . . don't love you."

"I know."

"And still you want—"

"Yes," she answered, walking toward him, "and still I want you to make love to me."

She held out her arms and watched Chase as he fought his last battle with himself. Unable to stop himself this time, unable to voice again his arguments for not making love to her, Chase was compelled by the look in her eye to move into the warm, welcoming embrace.

Elizabeth held him tightly. "If we don't make love," she said, her voice muffled against his chest, "I will regret it for the rest of my life. I want you, Chase." What she couldn't say aloud; she silently affirmed. *I want to give you the love you've never had. I want to teach you to love and to be loved, and perhaps I'll be the one whom you choose to love.*

Chase had to give her one more chance. "Elizabeth, you were right in your description of me when we first met. I am a cad, a bounder. Certainly I'm no gentleman planter, like you're accustomed to. I'm a soldier. My life is far from easy, but it's what I've chosen to do. I've never included a . . . a wife in my plans."

"I understand," Elizabeth said, blinking back the tears and squelching the disappointment. "Now you must understand, I'm not asking you to make a declaration of love or to propose marriage to me. With no strings attached, I'm asking that you make love to me." *I'll pretend that you love me; I'll pretend you're going to come a'courting and that you want to marry me.*

"You mean it?" Chase asked as if he couldn't believe what he was hearing.

"I mean it."

Chase was silent for only a minute; then happiness flowed through his blood stream. He threw back his head and laughed, a deep rumble of infectious laughter. "Elizabeth Rose Barrett," he said, "I'll give you the most wonderful night of your life."

Elizabeth smiled and stepped back out of his arms. Standing straight, she unbuttoned her dressing gown and let it fall to the floor around her feet. In the spill of moonlight she stood proudly staring at Chase, her golden hair cascading over her shoulders.

"And I, Chase Daniel, promise you a night of pleasure such as you've never experienced before and will never forget." *I will give you the gift of my love.*

Chase felt his stomach quiver as he looked at her naked body; she was indeed lovely all over. The fluid lines and hollows of her throat led down to supple shoulders and small, shapely breasts. Her waist was slender, her hips gently rounded, the saucy triangle at the pit of her stomach a riot of golden curls. In the pale light her tiny body looked as if it were a statue, sculpted by loving hands into sheer perfection.

"Is . . . something . . . wrong?" Elizabeth asked. She couldn't read Chase's expression, and her newly found wantonness flew straight-away out the window.

"No," he huskily answered, reassuring her.

"Am I —" she licked lips suddenly gone dry "— am I pretty, Chase?"

"You're beautiful." He moved to where she stood.

Unable to keep his hands off her, he ran his fingers through the silky hair that framed her face; he traced the contours of her mouth. Then his warm fingers, so strong and calloused, lightly brushed her nipples. A feeling akin to reverence filled him when he felt her tremble beneath his touch.

His hands resting lightly on her upper arms, he leaned down to kiss her, starting with her forehead and moving slowly all over her face, down the soft arch of her neck, back and forth over the collarbone. His lips tasted the skin that smelled so delicious, so clean, so fresh. His lips nibbled the fullness of her breasts, and his hand moved to lift gently one from the bottom and to urge the taut nipple into his waiting mouth.

"You are beautiful and delicious," he murmured. "Just like I knew you would be." Reverently he tasted the goodness of her body.

Elizabeth writhed; her stomach contracted with the sweet ache of desire; she caught her breath and moaned softly. Instinctively she arched, thrusting her breast more fully into Chase's mouth.

Remorse and shame locked in the deepest recesses of her mind, Elizabeth was aware only of Chase. She was attuned to his every touch and his silent commands. Willingly she gave of herself. She felt his fevered warmth; she saw the sheen of perspiration that glistened silver on his torso.

"You're driving me mad," Chase groaned. "I don't know that I'll ever have enough of you, Elizabeth Rose."

"That's what I'm hoping," she whispered. *Dear, Lord, that's what I'm hoping and praying for.*

Her fingers furrowed in the crisp, black waves, and she guided his mouth back to hers. She wanted to know again that sweet fierceness of his kiss; she fervently desired that every inch of her body be possessed by this man whom she loved so much and to whom she wanted to show love. Deep in the throes of passion, she was conscious only of the stirrings and demands of her body. Yielding to these primitive urges, she gave herself to him eagerly, freely, holding nothing back . . . hoping to receive in return.

As her lips opened to welcome the thrust of his tongue, Elizabeth closed her arms around him and her fingers dug into his shoulders. With a groan of unleashed desire, Chase lifted her to her tiptoes, grinding his mouth to hers in abandon. As he kissed her, he unknowingly filled her with the flowing of his soul and demanded the same from her.

Finally he raised his lips and lifted her into his

arms. "Now it's time to go to bed, love."

"Yes," Elizabeth murmured, happiness singing through her heart, "it's time to go to bed, love." She had no regrets. She loved Chase Daniel — loved him with all her being. And love knew no shame.

Chase carried her across the room, and laid her on the mattress. After hurriedly undressing, he slid in beside her. His mouth devoured hers hungrily. His hand traveled sensuously down the velvety plateau of her belly, his fingers gliding lower and lower over her trembling flesh with erotic calculations that made her writhe in desperate delight. Exploring fingers parted her thighs and brushed up the pliant inner columns to caress their satiny flesh with light strokes until, after endless moments of pleasurable torment, he at last reached the golden triangle at their juncture.

His hand slid through the downy softness into her inner core, unerringly seeking and finding the place he hungered for, the place that would give her the greatest joy. He felt Elizabeth tremble anew as he tenderly traced the outline of her nether lips with a teasing finger. Little whimpers broke from her parted lips, and she arched her hips to meet his probing fingers; she welcomed the sweet invasion of his hand.

A long, drawn out sigh escaped Elizabeth when she felt his fingers enter to explore lovingly her most intimate part. Delicious shivers ran her body as she went hot and cold all over. Her eyes closed, soft moans whispered through her lips, and her head rolled from side to side in pleasure.

Her delight was Chase's. Intent on giving her pleasure, his whole body joined in the amorous assault. As his hand probed, as his fingers moved inside her, his teeth teasingly grazed the fullness of her breasts to the tiny nipples and back again.

So ecstatic was her pleasure, Elizabeth writhed and cried aloud. With all he was giving to her, he hadn't given enough. She had to have more! Casting out all coherent thought, this tormenting desire for more surged through her blood and pounded in her head. Her hips began to undulate in that primeval dance as old as time itself. She arched her lower body, straining against Chase's hand, her body trembling with the force of the emotions he had unleased in her. She begged for release.

Chase's body clamored for release. His manhood was stiff and swollen, yet he deliberately held back. He fought against losing himself in the pleasure of her hot, velvety sheath. He concentrated on loving Elizabeth; his primary concern was for her.

At the very moment when she thought she could stand the torment no longer, her blood turned to molten passion, flowing hotly and thickly through her veins, obliterating conscious thought and turning her into all sensation. Her breath shortened, and her heart drummed frantically; every nerve in her body screamed for relief. All her feeling was centered in the pleasure point beneath Chase's hand.

Chase's ache turned from a dull throb of need to an acute wanting; he could restrain himself no longer, and he knew she was ready for him. So long he'd been without a woman, so long had he harbored a desire for Elizabeth, his body hurt with its need for release. Gracefully smooth, he moved so that she was beneath him. He eased his knee between her legs, opening them, spreading them apart. His hand slipped beneath her buttocks. Elizabeth welcomed the weight of his body on top of hers. Intuitively, her hand began to brush up and down the indentation of his spine, over his muscle-flexed buttocks. Her stomach contracted when she felt his manhood gently probe into the triangle of her femininity; she tensed and her hands stilled their movements.

"This is your first time," Chase asked, his breath ragged in her ear.

"Yes," she whispered.

"It will hurt a little but never again. I'll be as gentle as I can." He felt her cheek brush against his chest as she nodded. "Lie still, my darling."

As his hardness gently touched her, Elizabeth realized the enormity of her actions. Once they had made love there was no turning back, and she had no guarantee of gaining his love. She risked the chance of losing even his respect. Using her palms, she pushed against his chest in an effort to push him off her.

"No," she cried.

"Yes," Chase whispered, becoming more aggressive and locking his arms about her. He couldn't . . . he wouldn't turn back now.

His lower body ceased moving as Elizabeth became his prisoner. His mouth captured hers and he kissed her and stroked her until all resistance fled, until her hands sought and found his to draw it up and urge him to fondle her breasts. Willingly Chase caught the delicate morsel in his hand, desire splintering through him when Elizabeth moaned. He wasn't aware that he thrust forward until Elizabeth gasped and the barrier yielded easily under his tender onslaught. He caught the muffled sob of pain in his kiss and gently ran his hands up and down the sides of her body.

"That's it, sweetheart," he murmured. "The pain is over with. From now on it's only pleasure."

Chase eased deeply into her, and the tension ebbed as she melted in surrender to him. Slowly he made love to her with deep, rhythmic strokes, each one deeper than the one before. Every touch awakened her innocent woman's body gradually and sweetly and fully to the pleasure he had promised her the first night they met.

"Oh, Chase," Elizabeth moaned, tears running down her face. She knew no shame or remorse. She knew only love. She loved Chase, and this was the most natural thing they could do together. They were joined physically as well as spiritually. "I didn't know making love could be so wonderful."

Her cry touched Chase deeply; without his knowing it, Elizabeth had opened the door and entered his heart of hearts. "It's going to be even more wonderful, love," he promised.

Chase's deep and tender thrusts fanned the embers of passion until a blaze raged through her, until she feared she would be incinerated by sheer pleasure. Elizabeth slowly, rhythmically moved her hips; instinctively, her hands curled around Chase's shoulders, her legs embraced his back, and she arched upward to meet his thrusts. Now he was her prisoner. She wanted to keep him within her forever.

Passion mounted. Higher and higher Elizabeth soared until she was beyond the heavens in a world that was all hazy and golden and beautifully brilliant. Time and people had ceased to exist; all she felt were sensations. Then she was in a whirlwind, spinning and swirling even higher. She burst into a million tiny fragments of gold dust to become a part of this new, sensuous world that belonged only to her and Chase.

I love you, she silently cried. *I love you, my darling.* She would not cry the words aloud because she had given her love freely, and that's what she wanted from Chase — his love freely given.

Knowing no shame and feeling absolutely no remorse as she gently floated back to reality, Elizabeth caught his lips in a deep kiss of gratification.

Chase turned the kiss into one of deep passion, one of ultimate promise for himself. His hands tightened around her hips as he brought her closer to him. His last plunge verged on savagery and violence but was tempered with love to merge into supreme ecstasy. He shuddered in her arms.

Lying side by side, their eyes closed, Elizabeth and Chase drifted lazily in and out of the beautiful world they had created with their love. Elizabeth was aware of Chase's hand still lightly caressing her. She smiled and stretched, a sigh of contentment escaping her lips. Never had she known such satisfaction in her entire life.

Aunt Feldie and Mama had been wrong, Elizabeth decided. Making love was beautiful and wonderful and glorious. She couldn't understand why they thought it was shameful and degrading. When she felt the bed move beneath her, she opened her eyes to look into Chase's face as he leaned over her. His calloused hands brushed the love-moistened hair from her face.

"Thank you so much for loving me, Elizabeth Rose Barrett," he said.

"Thank you for loving me," she whispered and

when he lay down and squirmed so that she was pillowing her head on his shoulder. "I wish you didn't have to leave so early."

"Me, too," Chase replied absently.

As many times as he had made love during his life, he'd never found the experience as beautiful and consummate as this time. The satisfaction was more than sexual gratification; it was a peace and contentment of his soul. But then he'd never cared for a woman as he did Elizabeth Rose.

She would be a wonderful mother, he thought, visualizing her with children . . . with his children. Somehow he couldn't picture life without her. With a smile he thought of the portrait. With a smile he thought of the miniature he carried at all times of his mother—a portrait she had painted of herself and the only likeness he had of her. Elizabeth reminded him of his mother. She was when he had always imagined him mother to be: strong and couragous but soft ansd stender. A lady.

Although Elizabeth hadn't said the words aloud, he knew she loved him. She would never have given herself to him otherwise. Such a thought was awesome and humbling. He could imagine her saying to him, "I love you, Chase." The words, though mental only, overwhelmed Chase. He realized in that instant that his caring could easily transform into love.

He turned and clasped her tightly to him. She was his; she belonged to him and he to her. But Chase was afraid to love, afraid to vocalize his feelings, for fear Elizabeth would vanish. He had already lost so many whom he loved he couldn't bear to think of losing her.

Elizabeth wrapped her arms around Chase and

held him close. She spoke no words, no endearments because none were needed. She let her presence reassure him of her love. She ran her palms over his chest, enjoying the feel of moist hair and the hardened nipples. She even let her hand stray down his stomach and delighted when she felt flat muscles tense and shudder beneath her touch.

"Lady," he whispered, sliding down into the bed, dragging her with him, "you're asking for something."

"I thought I just had something," she shyly teased.

"That was just the beginning," Chase said, planting sweet little kisses over her face. "I have many wonderful secrets of love-making that I'd like to share with you. Are you ready?"

"Umhum," Elizabeth replied, totally wanton in her desires.

She lifted her lips to his, and when her mouth opened beneath his and her inviting tongue urged Chase to greater delights, she felt the tremor that ran his body. This time she slid her lips over his in a gentle suckling; she was thrilled when she heard his husky groan. She capped his head with her hands and pressed his face closer to hers.

When he finally lifted his head, he propped up on an elbow and pressed his hand against her flushed cheek. As if he had never seen her before, he looked at Elizabeth's nakedness. Slowly, leisurely he admired her beauty. Entranced, his eyes traveled downward from her graceful neck and shoulders to the sensual mounds of her small breasts. He gently cupped one creamy breast and touched the tip to see it harden with expectancy.

Elizabeth felt the piercing sweet pains of desire

sliver through her body again as if she'd never been satisfied. When she saw Chase's features take on a feral fierceness, she, too, became feline in her responses, purring her pleasure and arching her body as she pulled his head to her waiting breasts. As he tasted the sweetness of her offering, Elizabeth was inundated anew with tormenting and agonizing desire. Each caress pushed her closer and closer to the edge of the precipice of fulfillment; yet each time she thought she would find it, Chase seemed to pull her back.

Her passion liberated after so many years of tight control, Elizabeth was an urgent lover. She pressed Chase on, pulling him to her in a desperate attempt to satisfy the yearnings which she felt, searing from her breasts down her stomach to become a sweet, burning pain between her legs.

"Chase," she begged, "please take me." She wanted him again, and this time the need was as great if not greater than the first time.

"Let's not hurry," Chase replied in a passion-drugged voice. "Let's take it slow and easy, love."

He raised his head and caught her lips, his hand cupping the breast so recently abandoned by his mouth. As his tongue found entrance to her mouth, he felt her hand travel up his chest. She pressed her body to his, and her taut little nipples shot flames all the way to his manhood.

Tightening his arms around her, his lips released her mouth and showered kisses over her face, into her hair. Tracing the delicate curve of her ear with his tongue, he caught her earlobe tenderly between his teeth. His breath, like honey, was warm and thick against her skin. He felt her shudder.

With a quiver of delight and a slowness which belied the pounding fury of his heartbeat, he planted kisses in a trail down her creamy neck and shoulders, over the fullness of her breasts until he at last caught the delicate tip in his mouth.

Elizabeth's response was instantaneous and uninhibited; she arched to fill his mouth with the tender gift. As Chase's hand lightly brushed down her body, over her hips and thighs, Elizabeth caught her breath, held it, and slowly exhaled. Intense pleasure washed through her. When he shifted his body between her thighs, she slid her hand down his stomach and her fingers guided his fevered manhood to its place. He would have entered her gently, but Elizabeth would have no gentle coupling. She needed and wanted him urgently. She caught his buttocks with both hands, arched her hips and urged him deeply within her. She felt his hardness plunge to her depths, filling her emptiness.

Slowly he began to move within her, sending shimmering sparks of desire through her already highly sensitized body. As the movements gained momentum, she raised her hips to meet him over and over again. Her arms clung to his shoulders; her fingers dug into the flexed muscles of his back; her eyes clenched tightly as passion surged through her blood vessels, pounding against and finally stretching the walls until they burst and Elizabeth exploded into a magnificent burst of light.

Having held himself back until he felt Elizabeth's tremors of ecstasy Chase now concentrated on his own pleasure. Two, three deep strokes and a cry of pained-pleasure, he released his own passion inside her. As the shuddering subsided, he rolled to her side and clasped her to him in a tender embrace. They lay together, their breathing and heart beats returning to normalcy together.

Later . . . much later Elizabeth lay on the bed alone and in the candlelight watched Chase as he bathed in the tub of cold water left over from the night before. When he dried off, he looped the towel around his waist, walked over to the dresser and picked up a cigar. When he heard Elizabeth's soft laughter, he turned to the bed and raised an inquiring brow.

"How reminiscent this is of the first time we met," she said, holding out her arms to him. As he sat down on the bed beside her, she added, "Only this time I managed to seduce you."

Chase laid his cigar on the night table and took her into his arms. He held her tightly because his conscience was weighing heavy on him. He had regretted leaving women before because they had given him great pleasure, but this was a first time for his heart to be heavy. He didn't want to leave Elizabeth.

"Come to Ft. Clark with me," he said.

"No," Elizabeth whispered against his shoulder as she pressed her fingers through the moist hair on his chest, "I must go on to Eagle Pass to see if I can find Vanessa." As much as she wanted to, she couldn't go with him, not without a statement of love.

Chase felt as if his heart were breaking, yet he wouldn't say the words that would keep her by his side. He wasn't sure that he did love her, and he wouldn't speak the words idly. When he said them, he would mean them and they would be forever. Then a thought, unbidden and unwanted, ricocheted through his mind: Elizabeth could be pregnant.

The thought of her carrying his baby filled him with such joy he could hardly contain himself. He had to marry her; it mattered not that he loved her as much as she loved him. He'd be a good husband to her. Already he'd proved that he was a good lover for her. They would be good for each other.

He caught her shoulders in both hands and pulled her away so he could look into her face, his wondrous with his discovery. "Will you marry me?" he asked.

Elizabeth reached out and cradled a cheek with the palm of her hand, the tips of her fingers touching the wispy tendrils of black hair at his temples. These words should have made her the happiest woman in the world, but they didn't. To marry Chase would legally bind their lives together, but it didn't come close to touching their hearts; whereas love would bind them together spiritually forever.

"Why?" she asked.

Chase was stunned. He could only say, "Why what?"

"Why do you want to marry me?"

He reached up and pressed his hand over hers. "I want to because I care about you. I want you to be the mother of my children."

Elizabeth smiled to keep from crying. Aunt Feldie's words came to mind: Men generally have two women in their lives, a wife to have babies, and a mistress to love. Perhaps Vanessa had chosen to be loved; therefore, she was the mistress. Elizabeth wondered if her lot in life would be to be married because a man wanted her to mother his children. While that was a wonderful part of marriage, it wasn't the foundation. Sadly she shook her head; the hardest chore she'd ever performed.

"When I came to you tonight," she said in a low voice, "I knew you didn't love me. I didn't make love to you so that you would propose out of a guilty conscience. I wasn't laying a marriage trap for you."

"I'm not asking you to marry me because I feel guilty," Chase exclaimed. "I proposed because I wanted to. Because it's the right thing for us—"

"—to do," Elizabeth finished. "But it's not the right reason for us to marry."

"What if you're pregnant?" he asked.

"When and if I'm pregnant," Elizabeth answered, "I'll let you know. At that point we can discuss our choices and make our decision."

Chase stared into the beautiful, clear green eyes, filled with love—unconditionally. He saw no shame or guilt; he saw no evidence of her trying to snare him into marriage. Somehow he wished she would insist on it, that she would demand he make an honest woman out of her. He knew she had made up her mind and no amount of pleading would change it. Elizabeth made love to him only because she loved him; she would marry him only if he loved her. For her sake, he wouldn't make a mockery out of the emotion she treasured most in life.

He rose, picked up his cigar, and walked to the window. He threw open the shutters and stood there smoking for a long while before he finally said, "I asked you to marry me because I thought about your getting pregnant, and I wanted to protect you and the baby."

"I know," Elizabeth answered, pushing up in the bed and fluffing the pillows behind her.

"I want to give my child my name."

Elizabeth heard the heart-thick emotion in his voice, but she didn't completely understand the reason why.

He threw the cigar out the window and turned to face her. "But maybe I don't have a right to love, Elizabeth, or a right to propose marriage," he charged bitterly.

Elizabeth was out of the bed, across the room and in his arms. She wrapped hers about him as if in doing so she could wrap him in the security and warmth of her love. She couldn't stand the hurt that underlined his words.

Chase held her tightly, his cheek resting on the crown of her silken head. "I'm illegitimate, Elizabeth. I don't even know my own name. I don't know anything about my father other than he supposedly loved my mother but couldn't marry her. I know nothing of my mother. Although Aunt Ida took her in and kept her until I was born, my mother refused to talk about her past or her background. All she left me was two paintings, a small self-portrait of herself and the painting of—" *of Daniel* "—the man."

The painting in his room at Beck's House.

"The caption reads 'Portrait of Love' and is signed 'Daniel.' All these years I told myself that Daniel is my father," Chase said in thick tones. "But I don't know. She didn't live long enough to tell me . . . or to name me."

Elizabeth felt him shudder in her arms.

"Some days I hated her because . . . she didn't leave

me anything but questions. I don't know anything about her except her first name, April. Aunt Ida called me Danny because of the name on the portrait and the attachment my mother seemed to have for it. Later when I realized that Daniel was the closest thing to a family name I had, I wanted it to be my last name. As a child I hoped and prayed that somehow it was my father's name and that someday I would find him."

Elizabeth couldn't help the tears that flowed to moisten Chase's chest. She not only felt his grief, she gladly shared it. This was love, and at this moment she loved Chase more than she had ever loved him. She was bound to him more securely than any court of law could bind them together.

"I don't care that you're illegitimate," she said. "The only power a name has is what a person gives it." She pulled her head back and stared at him, her eyes swimming with tears. "I love the name Daniel, and I would gladly wear it and would be proud to have my children called by it."

"Yet, you turned my proposal down," he said.

"I did because you don't love me," she said, "and more than I want marriage, I want love."

"Oh, God, Elizabeth," Chase groaned. "What are we going to do?"

Elizabeth brushed her hands up and down his back in soothing motion. "You're going to Ft. Clark, and I'm going to Eagle Pass to continue the search for Vanessa. We'll give ourselves time to think through this and see what we want to do."

"I think I'm in love with you," he murmured.

Elizabeth smiled. "I think you want to be in love

with me because you know that's what I want. When and if you are, you'll know it. You won't have to think about it."

"I'll see you in Eagle Pass," Chase said.

"Come only because you want to," Elizabeth said, "not because you feel obligated."

"I promise." He swept her into his arms and carried her back to bed where he tucked her under the covers. "Now go back to sleep," he said.

"Where's your mother's portrait?" she asked.

"In my personal belongings at the camp," he replied, sitting on the edge of the bed and leaning over her.

"I would like to see it."

"All right." Chase smiled and lowered his face to kiss her forehead. "Now go to sleep."

When Elizabeth awakened later, she found a note lying on her pillow beside a yellow wild flower. Pushing up on her elbow, she picked up the sheet of paper and read: *I am leaving this for you until I can find you a length of red ribbon or a red rose. I'll see you in Eagle Pass.*

Chapter Twenty

Stooped beneath the rose-crested trunk, Lonnie led Elizabeth and Jefferson into the End-of-the-Line Saloon mid-afternoon on Friday. "Howdy, Butch," he called to the bearded bartender as he set his burden in the middle of the room and moved closer to the bar. "Got'cha a guest here, Miss Elizabeth Barrett. She's come out here to visit with her sister, Miss Vanessa Barrett." Waving his hand, he beckoned to Elizabeth. "Ma'am, this is Butch Harris, owner of this here establishment."

"Glad to meet you, Mr. Harris." Elizabeth stepped so that she was standing at the bar beside Lonnie, her eyes running is distaste over the scruffy looking man. His trousers were faded and thread-bare; his long-sleeved undershirt, a dingy red, extended below the sleeves of an equally worn shirt.

"Same here, ma'am," Butch returned, giving his wad of tobacco several good chomps and twirling the ends of his moustache. "What can I do for you?"

"Two rooms to begin with," Elizabeth answered.

"And some information." She felt the tension her words caused to fall across the room. She watched the bartender's eyes narrow as the blood-shot eyes peered intently at her. Maintaining her poise was a most difficult chore beneath such scorching scrutiny, but she managed.

"Rooms are easy to come by. Not so sure about the information." The man removed his hand from his moustache to his head. His fingers burrowed through the dull brown hair and dug into his scalp. "What'cha want to know?"

"Where's the post office?"

As quickly as the tension had fallen; it dissipated. Butch grinned to reveal stained, uneven teeth and turned. He waved his hand toward a wooden shelf of postal slots. "You're at the place, ma'am."

"Do you have any letters for me?"

"Reckon I do," he answered.

Setting her portmanteau on the floor and brushing damp strands of hair out of her dirt-streaked face, Elizabeth watched Butch pull several letters out of the small wooden slots. He riffled through them finally to say, "Yes, ma'am. Got two letters here for Barrett." He turned around and extended his hand. "One for a Vanessa, another for Elizabeth."

One for Vanessa! With a sinking heart, Elizabeth took the letters. The one she immediately recognized; she had written it to Vanessa on the day before she set out for Texas. The other was a letter for her from Elijah. They had agreed when she left that he would send all correspondence to Eagle Pass.

"Miss Vanessa hasn't been in to collect her mail?" Elizabeth asked.

The man chewed his cud quite awhile before he lowered his head over a rusty bucket that served as a spittoon. After he spit, he wiped his mouth with the back of his hand. Yet tobacco juice stained the wrinkles around his mouth. "Appears not, ma'am," he drawled dryly, "else I wouldn't still have the letter."

Elizabeth resented Butch Harris' attitude, but since she was the one in need of information and he was the one who possibly had it, she had to bear with him. Valiantly she strove for patience. "Do you know Miss Vanessa Barrett?"

"No, ma'am, sure don't. Of course now," he added, "out here it ain't uncommon for a body to go by another name, especially since the war. If you know what I mean?"

Elizabeth opened her reticule and brought out a small portrait of Vanessa. "This was painted several years ago," she said, holding it out for the bartender to see, "but I'm sure you would recognize the likeness if you were to have seen her."

Propped on his elbows, Butch leaned across the counter to take the miniature from Elizabeth. He squinted his eyes as he studied the portrait. "Sure is a beautiful woman," he said, his eyes lingering appreciatively on the dark hair that framed the elfin face with large green eyes. "If I ever saw here, reckon I'd remember it for sure. Don't know of any woman around here, going by any name that looks like her." Shaking his head, he straightened up and handed the miniature back to Elizabeth. "You might try at the Ranger's station, ma'am. Quite possible they may know something about your sister."

"Thank you, Mr. Harris. Now if you'll show me

where my rooms are."

"Right down the hall," he said, pointing to a doorless opening at the end of the bar. "Lonnie'll take you to 'em. One dollar for a room with a pallet. Two dollars with a bed. Money in advance, ma'am."

Elizabeth returned Vanessa's portrait to her reticule and pulled out her coin purse. When she opened it, she saw the dwindling roll of bills and was glad that she had finally arrived at Eagle Pass. She was quickly running out of funds. As soon as she bathed and changed clothes, she would have to go to the bank to see about a transfer of funds from her bank in New Orleans.

Without closing the coin purse, she said, "Also, Mr. Harris, I would like to have a bath in my tub."

"Two dollars if you want just the tub and water," he told her. "Three if you want a towel, wash rag, and soap."

Elizabeth unrolled the bills and laid them on the counter. "Two rooms, each with a bed, and I'd like to have one bath now, Mr. Harris. Towels, wash cloths, and soap. I'll send word when I'm ready for the second one."

"Yes, ma'am," he said and reached under the counter for the keys to her rooms. "Number 5 and 6. You'll see the numbers painted on the doors."

Taking the keys in one hand, Elizabeth bent to pick up her portmanteau. Her trunk on his back again, Lonnie led her down the dark, narrow hall to her rooms.

"I'll tell you, Miss Elizabeth," Jefferson's childish voice rang out in the deserted saloon as he sauntered behind Elizabeth swinging the bird cage in one hand, his valise in the other, "Texas is sure hot and dry. Trees out here look like bushes, and the rivers are bone dry. And it's mighty lonesome. Yes, sir, mighty lonesome."

Elizabeth couldn't have agreed more. Exhausted and sleepy, she was covered in dust and grit. Her traveling dress was soaking wet from perspiration, her hat discolored and ringed. The feather had long since broken off.

"I thought you wanted to be a soldier," she said as she reached up again to brush damp hair out of her face.

"Well, I been doing some thinking, Miss Elizabeth," the boy drawled. "Right now, like you said, I'm too little to be a soldier. I'm sorta thinking about being a doctor again. Or maybe by the time I grow up they'll have buffalo soldiers back in Louisiana."

Elizabeth chuckled. "Perhaps they will, Jefferson."

Using the rusty key the bartender had given her, Elizabeth unlocked and opened the door. She stepped aside to let Lonnie precede her in the room with the chest. Jefferson followed to set Gloria's cage on the small table beside the bed.

"Well, ma'am," Lonnie said. "Sure have enjoyed having you travel with us. I hope you find your sister."

"Thank you, Lonnie," Elizabeth returned. "I'm sure I will."

"Mr. Ingram told you when you could expect the stages to come through?" Lonnie asked as he moved toward the door. When Elizabeth nodded, he tipped his hat. "Good-bye, Miss Barrett."

After Elizabeth closed and locked the door behind Lonnie, she moved across the room to set the portmanteau on the bed. Her reticule and parasol she lay on the table that served as the dresser base. Vanessa's letter she place next to them. Elijah's letter she opened and read the terse message aloud to Jefferson: *We're all doing fine. Waiting to hear some word about Miss Vanessa. Aunt Feldie says her old bedroom is fixed up and waiting. Crops and mill are doing good. All of us miss you. Can't wait until you return with Miss Vanessa. Tell Jefferson we miss him. The house is too quiet with him gone and we don't have anyone to run our errands. God bless. Come home soon.*

"Well, Miss Elizabeth," Jefferson said, "I'll tell you the truth. I'm kinda ready to go home. I'll be glad when we find Miss Vanessa."

"Me, too," Elizabeth answered as she lay Elijah's letter on the dresser.

Because the heat was so unbearable she unfastened the top two buttons of her dress and moved close to the window in hopes a breeze was stirring. As she stood there, she gazed through the gossamer curtains at the street below and pondered about her search for Vanessa. When she had set out from New Orleans, Elizabeth had known that she was doing the right thing.

But so much had happened since she set out. She couldn't begin to imagine what all Vanessa was involved in, and Butch Harris' not knowing Vanessa indicated that she herself hadn't posted the letter here or else she had taken care that no one really saw her to recognize her. Evidently she must still be in Mexico and in danger. Elizabeth could only hope that Blake reached her in time.

"Well, Miss Elizabeth," Jefferson asked, breaking

the silence, "what are were going to do now?"

Elizabeth turned to see him perched on the edge of the chair, his elbows propped on his legs, his face cradled in his fists.

"First, we need to bathe and change clothes. Second, we need to get something to eat. Then I'm going to the bank before it closes and get some money, so we can starting hunting Miss Vanessa," she announced.

"I'm all for the eating and finding Miss Vanessa," Jefferson solemnly stated, "but I'm not so sure I need to take a bath. Mr. Mathias once told me, Miss Elizabeth, that he believed too much bathing could take the skin right off a person."

"Believe me, Thomas Jefferson," Elizabeth said dryly, "you need to take a bath, and I firmly disagree with Mr. Mathias: bathing won't take the skin right off a person. And if he bathed a little more frequently, he'd learn that it can take the dirt and stench off. And speaking of baths, go find out why Mr. Harris hasn't gotten my bath in here."

Jefferson's, "Yes, ma'am," was still lingering in the room when he returned posthaste with a wooden tub in hand. "Mr. Harris said to tell you, he was sorry but he didn't have nobody—"

"Anybody," Elizabeth automatically corrected.

Jefferson shook his head and grinned mischievously. "Mr. Harris didn't say anybody, Miss Elizabeth, he said nobody, and I'm just repeating him."

Elizabeth grinned with him. "I take it you now have a job, Thomas Jefferson?"

"Yes, ma'am. Reckon I do. Sweeping the floor and running errands for Mr. Harris. He reached into his pocket and pulled out two dollars. He said to give you this. The job comes with a small room on the bottom floor off the kitchen and meals."

Although she didn't like the man, Elizabeth did indeed thank him for the return of the money. As she reached for her reticule, she said, "Do you want me to continue to keep your money for you?"

"Yes, ma'am," he answered. "I reckon I do. I feel safer knowing you have it."

When Jefferson bounded out the room to get the water, Elizabeth decided it was time to do some washing. She opened her portmanteau and emptied its contents on the floor. Then she opened her trunk, knelt beside it, and began digging through the clothes. When she had pulled out the last garment, she saw the neatly stacked bundles of money. She picked up one of the packets and held it in her hand.

Inundated with questions, she could only stare at the money. Who? she asked. Who would have put this in her trunk? Blake, the answer whispered through her mind. Elizabeth recoiled with anger and dropped the packet of bills to the floor. All she could think was that Blake had used her; she was nothing but a pawn in this game he was playing. She rose and walked around the room, the anger slowly evaporating to be replaced with a gnawing fear. She was being involved in a web of intrigue, and she was afraid.

She had to do something with the money; she didn't dare keep it on her person. It had gotten in her trunk without her knowing about it; it wouldn't leave the same way. Rising, she picked up her portmanteau. As soon as she bathed and redressed, she would take the money to the bank and deposit it for safe keeping until Chase arrived in town. Yes, she thought, she would tell Chase. He would know what to do with it.

She was still standing in front of the dresser when Jefferson knocked and entered with two buckets in his hands, a towel and wash rag draped across each shoulder, and a bar of lye soap protruding from his pocket.

"How's this for quick service, Miss Elizabeth?" he asked.

"Very good," she returned, her lips moving into a warm smile. "You're an excellent errand boy, but—"

Thomas Jefferson Barrett tensed. Although he loved Miss Elizabeth dearly, he was thoroughly acquainted with the timbre of her voice and knew what kind of phrase would follow that *but*.

"—you make sure your chores don't interfere with your taking a bath."

"Yes, ma'am," he mumbled as he emptied the water into the tub. For ever eternal that *but!* he thought.

"And be sure to wash with soap behind your ears."

Jefferson laid the towel, wash rag, and soap on the straight chair and darted to the door. His eyes sparking absolute mischief, he said, "Yes, ma'am, Miss Elizabeth," he said. "I sure will. I'll bathe as soon as I have time."

"You make the time."

The slamming of the door was the only answer Elizabeth received. With a shake of her head and a sigh, she crossed the room and locked the door. Quickly shedding her clothes, she bathed and washed her hair. After she put on her undergarments, she brushed her hair dry and stood in front of the mottled mirror, debating whether to put it up or let it hang loose. She thought about her yellow calico dress and the length of black grogram ribbon Chase had bought for her.

Thoughts of Chase brought a smile to her face and a glitter to those green eyes. She thought about the two flowers he had given her, now pressed between sheets of stationery at the bottom of her writing chest. She thought about his words of love, of his caresses, and of his promise to come.

She desperately wanted him to come to Eagle Pass, but a small part of her wondered if he would. She couldn't help but remember Vanessa's suitors. Once they had made love to her, they left. Elizabeth's heart hurt; she couldn't stand even the thought of losing Chase. A life without him would be unbearable. Surely he wouldn't think she was a loose woman. He had to come.

Moving to the dresser she picked up the length of black ribbon and tied her hair from her face. Her golden blonde tresses hung down her back in soft, glowing waves.

She laughed at her reflection in the mirror. She felt young again, more carefree than she had since the war. And Chase was the person who had brought this happiness to her, who had given her soul new life and vigor.

Her hand brushed across the letters, and she dropped her head to gaze at them. Elijah's she must answer promptly, but Vanessa's . . . was Vanessa all right? The smile slowly faded from Elizabeth's lips. She picked up the letter and pressed it to her bosom. Vanessa was all right, she reassured herself, and Blake would find her and get her out of Mexico. He would!

Quickly Elizabeth slipped into her gown and wrote

the letter to Elijah. After she posted it, she departed the saloon, the portmanteau in hand, and headed down the dusty street to the bank.

To the young man behind the clerk's cage she said, "I'd like to deposit—my money in your bank." She opened the portmanteau and extracted the money. She must be extremely careful in what she said; she didn't want to arouse suspicion.

The man's eyes bugged out when she continued to pile the bills on the counter. In puzzlement he looked from the money to Elizabeth back to the growing mound.

"I'm Miss Elizabeth Barrett from New Orleans," Elizabeth explained, her clear, steady voice a contradiction to her inward trepidation. "I'm out here to visit with my—with my family whom I haven't seen for four years. While I'm here, I would like to know my money is safe in your bank."

She looked up and batted her eyes coyly at the young man; she certainly didn't want him to think anything was amiss nor to report the large amount of money she was carrying to the sheriff. The least attention she attracted to herself and the money, the better off she was.

She leaned over and whispered, "This is my entire—my entire inheritance. I sure wouldn't want anything to happen to it. You know a woman traveling by herself can't be too careful."

"Oh, no, ma'am," the clerk hastily agreed, his gaze locked on Elizabeth's lovely green eyes. "You sure can't be too careful. I guarantee you that we'll take good care of your money."

"Thank you, Mr.—"

"Filmore Fremont, ma'am," he sputtered, totally spellbound by the lovely creature in front of him. "I'm Filmore Fremont."

"Thank you, Mr. Fremont." Elizabeth smiled warmly. "Now if you'll count the money and give me a receipt."

"Yes, ma'am." His face turned red as he bobbed his head.

After he had put the money into the safe and was writing a receipt, Elizabeth withdrew Vanessa's portrait from the reticule and laid it on the counter. "I'm looking for my sister, Vanessa Barrett. Do you know her, Mr. Fremont?"

Filmore reached for the portrait which he cupped in the palm of his hand. He shook his head. "No, ma'am, I haven't ever seen her before. Sure would have remembered her if I had."

"Could you check to see if she's a bank customer?" Elizabeth asked.

"I'll check, Miss Barrett," Filmore answered kindly, "but I'm sure she's not. I don't recognize the name either."

The receipt safe in her reticule, Elizabeth stepped outside the bank and whisked her parasol up. She was relieved to have the money deposited in the bank, but she wondered who had posted Vanessa's letter. Evidently she hadn't been in Eagle Pass at all. Neither the postmaster nor the banker had recognized her. Elizabeth wondered if her looks could have changed so drastically during the past four years. Tilting the parasol over her shoulder, she walked down the uneven boardwalk to the Ranger's station.

The sun was beginning the dip into the west when

she entered the one room adobe building. A tall man stood by the stove, pouring himself a cup of coffee. From behind a bewhiskered face, he stared at her.

"Good afternoon," she said. "I'm Elizabeth Barrett."

"Nolan Griffin," he returned. "What can I do for you, ma'am?"

"I'm looking for my sister," she answered. "Vanessa Barrett."

Griffin waved her to the empty chair in front of his desk. "Don't know anybody by that name," he said, "but that don't mean nothing. What does she look like?" Sitting down himself, he took a long swallow of his hot, black coffee.

Again Elizabeth dug through her reticule for the portrait which she handed the ranger. The rough, work-calloused hand closed around the miniature.

"Nope," he finally announced. "Ain't never seen her." He handed the painting back to Elizabeth. "Sorry, ma'am, but I shore can't help you none. Tell you what though," he said, turning in his chair so that he could stretch his long legs out. "I'll ask about. Maybe somebody else would know her or just maybe they would have heard about her."

"Thank you, Mr. Nolan." Elizabeth stood and moved to the door. "By the way, have Rangers Warner and Mason arrived in town yet?"

Nolan shook his head. "Not yet, ma'am. When they get here, I'll be sure to let them know you asked about 'em. Mind telling me where you're staying, Miss Barrett?"

After Elizabeth told Nolan where she was staying, she departed. Dispirited, she retraced her steps to the

359

End-of-the-Line and walked down the narrow corridor. When she reached her room, the door was ajar. Immediately she sensed that something was wrong. Perspiration beaded on her upper lips, and try as she may she couldn't regulate her quickened heartbeat. She curled her hand into a fist and nervously rubbed her fingers against her palm.

Chapter Twenty-one

Elizabeth let her parasol down and gripped the handle as if it were a club. Standing well in the corridor, she pushed the door open and gazed around the room to see Blake standing there. She breathed a sigh of relief, entered the room, and closed the door.

"I've been expecting you," she said.

Without preamble Blake asked, "You found my money?"

"You mean the Union payroll money," she countered shortly as she laid her parasol and reticule on the dresser. Blake shrugged, and she was irritated that he would treat the matter as if it were of no consequence. "Yes, I found it. When did you hide it there?"

"The night I was wounded," he answered. When she made no comment, he said, "I guess you're wondering why I didn't tell you about it?"

"No, I've had time to figure that out," she answered. "You're taking the money to Bainbridge. You didn't let me know about it because you knew I would have turned it over to Chase."

Blake reached up and tilted his hat back. "I couldn't let you do that because it's my key to see Bainbridge."

Remembering the three soldiers who had died protecting the money, remembering Chase's dead friend, Elizabeth asked, "Did you have anything to do with the robbery?"

Blake sighed and shook his head. "Rod Everett and a group straight from Bainbridge in Mexico robbed the pay wagon. After the hold-up, Rod headed for San Antonio rather than back to the border. In a double-cross, he was going to use the money to buy Vanessa's freedom."

"How do you know this?" Elizabeth demanded.

"I've just returned from seeing one of Bainbridge's men. I learned that Everett was killed because Bainbridge discovered his double-cross. I learned that Bainbridge does have a mistress who goes by the name of *La Mariposa,* and in Spanish that means the butterfly."

"Vanessa," Elizabeth whispered. "Vanessa also means butterfly."

"I have an appointment to meet with the man himself day after tomorrow at his hacienda in Mexico." He pushed away from the wall. "I have to have the money, Elizabeth, or I don't get in."

"I don't have the money," Elizabeth answered.

Blake looked at her incredulously. He had to have the money. Without it all his planning and scheming was for naught. "What have you done with it?" he demanded, his voice hardening perceptibly.

"I put it in the bank," she replied.

For a moment Blake was disappointed; then he breathed a sigh of relief. Perhaps it would work out for the better like this. He didn't trust Bainbridge or his greedy men. Not having the money on his person might assure him of longer life. No one would think of its being in the bank at Eagle Pass. Surely his movements were being monitored, but none of Bainbridge's stooges would think to connect him with Elizabeth. Blake had been careful. His training in the secret service had taught him to be.

"If you don't mind," he said, "leave it there for awhile. I'll make arrangements to come back for it later."

"Dammit, Chase," Captain Wilcox threw his hands up in the air in frustration as he paced the floor of his office, "what am I going to do?" Without waiting for Chase to answer, the commander of Ft. Clark said, "My latest scouting expedition under the leadership of a Lipan guide was massacred. Massacred because the guide led them into an ambush. Without guides my soldiers can't possibly apprehend the Indians, and with guides who are traitors they're being apprehended."

"On top of that," Wilcox walked to his desk and riffled through the mass of papers, "I've received so many citizen complaints that I can't begin to address them, and Brackettville is nothing but a devil's den. They want us soldiers here, their very existence depends on us, but they take advantage of my men. On payday my troopers "troop" across the way to debauch in liquor, women, and cocaine. The next day the majority of them are in the stockade, no good to me, to themselves, to the citizens of Brackettville, or anybody else."

Chase shifted his position in the straight chair in which he sat. He understood his friend's frustration; he felt it himself, but his frustration today had nothing to do with duty. He was thinking about Elizabeth; he was missing her. He could hardly wait until he could see her again. Never had time seemed to move so slowly. They had parted in Uvalde only two weeks ago; but Chase thought it was more like an eternity.

Wilcox sighed deeply and waved a sheet of paper through the air. "This is my latest news. One of my primary duties is to see to the education of the incoming black troopers. A chaplin is to be assigned to each regiment as a teacher. In this instance, I have been blessed. I've been assigned a black teacher along with the chaplin. Hell, Chase," Wilcox exploded, "how can one chaplin and one schoolmarm be expected to do all this? You know the regiments are going to be divided between the forts. Furthermore, when will the soldiers have time to learn? We have to build us a place to live; we're forever chasing the Indians and bandits who disappear at will across the border." Wilcox turned to Chase. "What are we going to do?"

"For one thing," Chase replied, pulling his thoughts from Elizabeth to business at hand, "we're going to convince General Phil Sheridan that the government needs to open more forts along the border to stop this flow of undesirable traffic back and forth across the Rio Grande. When I go to Eagle Pass, I'm going to check out Ft. Duncan. Then I'm going to make a written report to send to Colonel Hatch concerning its reestablishment."

"Which he'll promptly file away."

"And which I will keep sending until they do something about it."

"More than likely they'll do something with you first," Wilcox muttered.

Chase laughed as he stood and moved across the room to slap his friend on the back. "Probably so."

"Does the general have any clues on the payroll holdup?" Wilcox asked abruptly, his mind skittering back and forth from one problem to the next.

Chase didn't immediately answer as his thoughts once more returned to Elizabeth. Because of him she was the only lead in the case—if she were a lead. Again Chase chastised himself for having involved her. If only he had waited . . . but he hadn't. His goal then had been to capture Roswell Bainbridge, no matter what the cost. Right now, Chase felt like the cost might be more than he was willing to pay.

"Chase?" he heard Wilcox say.

Snapping out of his reverie, Chase shook his head. "Not a clue."

"The damned murderers slipped across the border," Wilcox said, "knowing that we can't touch them. Safe and sound in Mexico, they're laughing and making fun of us. What are we going to do about paying the men?"

"The General's taking care of that," Chase returned. "He's made arrangements for a temporary loan with a bank in San Antonio."

Wilcox nodded and reached up to rub his temple. "When are you leaving for Ft. Duncan?"

"In the morning," Chase returned.

"Getting your men out of Brackettville for the weekend," Wilcox said.

Chase grinned. "Wasn't really thinking of it that way. Just wanted to get to Eagle Pass as soon as possible."

"Sounds like it's more than the ruins of an old fort that you're going to see."

Chase's eyes twinkled. "See you when I get back."

Chase returned to the Las Moras Creek where his men were camped and went to bed early. He spread his bedroll and lying beneath the branches of the huge tree, he listened to the gentle rush of water in the creek and to the wind soughing through the leaves. Yes, his going to Eagle Pass was more than an inspection trip. He thought about Elizabeth and finally fell asleep to dream about elusive green eyes.

Before daybreak Chase and his troopers were in the saddle, headed for Ft. Duncan. Although they were constantly on the lookout for Indians, Chase didn't push his men. They rode leisurely and took the time to study the countryside. He wanted them thoroughly familiar with the natural landmarks, such as rivers and rock formations; this knowledge would help their changes of survival in this lonely land.

Sunday morning they reached their destination. The men quickly set up camp and under Chase's orders began an inspection of the ruins. Chase was inspecting a building on the far side of the fort when he came face to face with a stranger. At first glance Chase thought the man was a Negro, but a second look made him wonder. He was dressed like an Indian; he moved and carried himself like one, but he had negroid features. The two of them stared at each other for a long time as if waiting for the other to speak first.

Finally Chase extended his hand and introduced himself. Expressionless, the man looked down at Chase's hand, but he didn't speak nor did he offer to shake. Thinking perhaps the man didn't understand English, Chase began to speak in Spanish. Still the stranger stared blankly at him. When Chase's troopers began to gather and gawk curiously, the man turned and walked away. They watched as he mounted his horse and rode into the desert, leaving only a trail of dust.

"Who was that, Major?" Sgt. Liberty asked, pushing his hat back on his head and peering at the retreating figure.

"Don't know." Chase also kept his eyes trained on the receding figure.

"As for me," Corporal Man said, "I want to know which he was? Indian or Negro?"

"Way he's dressed and handles that horse," Chase said, "I'd say he's an Indian."

"Yep, that's true, sir," Man replied, holding his hand over his eyes and straining at the horizon into which the stranger was disappearing. "But I have a feeling he's got some Negro blood in his veins, too, sir."

The stranger was still on Chase's mind when he rode into Eagle Pass that afternoon and stopped at the ranger's station. Nolan Griffin was standing outside, leaning against the building. Even though his hat was pulled low over his forehead, he squinted his eyes against the glare as he watched the approaching officer.

Chase swung off the horse and said, "Major Chase Daniel."

"Nolan Griffin," the ranger said. "What brings you down our way, major?"

"Checking out Ft. Duncan." Chase tied his horse to the hitching post.

Griffin tilted his head upward and scratched his throat. "Is the army thinking about opening it up again?"

"Thinking about it," Chase replied. "Have you had any undesirables around lately?"

Griffin shrugged offhandedly. "Depends on what you consider undesirable. Around here, Major, if a man's got money he's desirable. If he's broke, he's undesirable. Law's kinda different on the frontier and the Mexican border."

Chase could believe that.

"I see a lot of men passing through town," Griffin said. "Here today and gone tomorrow, if you know what I mean. Don't know who they are, where they come from, or where they're going. None I could identify for certain as outlaws, but I have my suspicions."

"I ran across a suspicious looking fellow today," Chase said. "Looked like he was a black man, but he was dressed and acted like an Indian."

Griffin reached up and rubbed his fingers from the corner of his mouth down his chin. "Reckon that was one of them Seminole Negroes. They live down in Mexico." He pushed away from the wall and walked into the building. "Ever hear of 'em?"

"Can't say that I have," Chase said. He followed the

ranger to the door where he leaned against the casement.

"Most folks figure they was run away slaves who took up with the Seminole Indians in Florida and became their slaves. About 1842, I think it was, they was taken to Indian Territory along with the Seminoles, but the Seminole didn't fare any better there; Creeks and other tribes tried to take their slaves from them. So the Seminoles moved again, taking their black brothers with them. This time to Naciemiento." Griffin waved the coffee pot at Chase. "Care for a cup?"

"No, thanks." Chase watched the ranger fill his tin cup with the tepid, black liquid.

"Well, in Mexico the Negroes multiplied and to a certain extent intermixed with the Seminoles until they outnumbered their masters," Griffin continued. "They learned the ways of the Indians, but they haven't forgotten the ways of the white man. Pretty smart people. Besides speaking their own language, these Seminole Negroes speak the languages of several border tribes. They're about the best scouts and hunters in the territory. As familiar with the countryside as they are the backs of their hands. Know all about the methods of Indian warfare."

"How do I go about talking with them?" Chase asked, his interest piqued.

"Well, now," Griffin muse, "I'll have to give that some thought." He set his cup down and reached up to rub his chin. After a while, he said, "Reckon I could get one of the Mexican traders to deliver a message for us. If the Indians are interested in talking with you, they'll set up a parley."

"I'd appreciate your doing that for me," Chase said.

"Where you staying so I can get word to you?" Griffin asked.

"My men are camped at Ft. Duncan," Chase replied, "but I'll be staying in town. Can you recommend a hotel?"

"End-of-the-Line is about one of the best," Griffin replied. "Certainly the cheapest."

"Then that's where I'll be," Chase answered. He pushed away from the casement and asked, "You wouldn't happen to know if a Miss Elizabeth Barrett is in town, would you?"

Griffin turned, a smile teasing the corners of his mouth. "So happens, I do, Major. I always happen to know when a woman's in town."

"Where's she staying?"

"Same place you'll be staying, End-of-the-Line Saloon. Can't miss it," Griffin said. "Just head on down Main Street. You'll come to the barber shop first. Then a couple of buildings down you'll see the saloon."

"Thanks."

Chase unhitched his horse and rode down the street to the barber shop. He had a few things he wanted to do before he saw Elizabeth, one of which was to clean up. After his haircut, shave, and bath, he stopped at the general store. A few minutes later he came out, a package wrapped in brown paper tucked under his arm. Whistling softly, he walked to the saloon.

"Howdy," Butch called when the major stepped through the door. "What can I get for you?"

"I'm looking for Miss Elizabeth Barrett," Chase said.

Harris's eyes flicked up and down Chase's uniformed body before they returned to his face. "Number five down the hall." He pointed. "If you'll wait here, I'll send my boy to see if she's in."

"Thanks," Chase said. "I'll check for myself." Before Harris could respond, Chase was walking toward Elizabeth's room. When he reached the door, he knocked.

"Yes. Who's there?" she answered.

Chase smiled. "Open the door and see."

"Chase," he heard her muffled exclamation.

The door opened and Elizabeth threw herself into his arms. She lifted her face as he lowered his, their lips coming together in an urgent kiss that quickly eradicated the loneliness of the past two weeks that they had been separated. Chase filled the sweet, soft cavity with his probing tongue. As he explored all the tender interior, his lips moved over hers, burning her with the intensity of his passion. At the same time, his fingers capped the back of her head, and his other hand dropped down her back to cup her buttocks.

Elizabeth surrendered to the fiery passion that engulfed them. Her hands moved up his chest to lock around the base of his neck. The sensations that rushed through her body were tormentingly familiar. They filled her anew with excitement and longing.

Chase's mouth finally released hers, but his lips continued to nip hers, moving around her mouth, butterflying across her cheeks back to her mouth. "I missed you so much," he breathed, lifting his face to look into hers.

"I missed you," Elizabeth confessed.

Chase looked down the hall to see Harris lounging

in the hallway, watching them. He gently shoved Elizabeth into her room and closed the door.

"When a week passed and you didn't write or come, I thought maybe you'd forgotten about me," Elizabeth said, her hands moving in loving fury from his face to his shoulders down his arms. She couldn't believe he was here in person. So many nights without him, so many nights of loneliness and wondering if her gamble had been worth it.

"I didn't write because I knew I would beat a letter," he told her. "And you can always depend on me to keep my word. I said I was coming, and I meant it." His arms slipped around her, and he gazed into her face. "Nothing could have kept me away."

"I'm glad," Elizabeth whispered.

His lips fastened on hers in another long kiss that ended in a trail of tiny kisses all over her face. "I brought you something," he eventually said, unwrapping an arm and holding the package out to her.

"What is it?" She was as excited and giddy as a child receiving a present on a special occasion. "What did you bring me?"

Chase laughed. "Open it."

With trembling hand Elizabeth ripped the paper aside. "Oh, Chase," she cried and held up the length of the red ribbon, "you remembered."

"I remembered," he agreed and moved so that he stood in front of her. He pulled the pins from her chignon, letting them drop to the floor. After he finger-combed her hair, he caught her shoulders and guided her to the mirror. "Your hair is beautiful," he said. "I noticed it the first time I saw you, gleaming golden in the lamp light. You looked like an angel."

Elizabeth stared at their reflections. They looked so perfect together that tears of happiness spiked her lashes.

"We were apart only two weeks, but they seemed like an eternity. This is the way I kept remembering you," he said. Twinging the ribbon through her hair, he tied it into a lopsided bow, but Elizabeth didn't mind. She thought it was beautiful.

She turned in his arms and buried her face in his chest. "Oh, Chase, I'm so glad you're here. I've been so lonely . . . and frightened."

Chase heard the desperation in her voice. "You haven't been able to find Vanessa?"

"No one has heard of her or seen her. No one recognizes her portrait."

Elizabeth wanted to tell Chase about the stolen payroll money, but she couldn't. As Blake had said earlier it was his key into the Bainbridge Brigade. She had to give him time to find out about Vanessa. She couldn't do anything that would further endanger her sister's life. Her conscience was weighing her down; she could barely hold up beneath the load.

"She's—she's probably still in Mexico. Maybe she never meant for me to find her."

Chase silently agreed with Elizabeth that Vanessa was in Mexico; he also figured she was part of Bainbridge's community. He held Elizabeth tightly and said, "You said the letter you received was posted Eagle Pass?" When he felt Elizabeth's cheek brush his chest as she nodded her head, he said, "Vanessa wants to be found; otherwise, she wouldn't have sent you the letter. I have a hunch she's close by."

"You really think so?" Elizabeth exclaimed, pulling

back to look into his face.

"I think so, and I promise we'll find her. Now," his hand slipped down her back to cup her buttocks again, "I'd like to find all the sweet secrets of Miss Elizabeth Rose Barrett."

Chapter Twenty-two

Without Elizabeth's really knowing or caring how, she was divested of her clothes and lying in bed. Chase was standing beside the bed naked also, the evening sun filtering in through the cracks of the shutters to glimmer over him and to accentuate the sleek hardness of his body.

"It's been too long," Chase groaned as he lowered himself on the bed beside her, his hand tangling in her silky hair. "I'm finding that one taste of you isn't enough. Not nearly enough."

As hungry for the taste of him as he was for her, Elizabeth's lips nipped at his, tracing the fullness, playing at the corners. "That's part of the grand design," she murmured between the caressive bites.

Refusing to be tormented by the loving foreplay no longer, Chase turned his head and his mouth captured hers in a searing kiss that rocked them both to their souls. His hands roved her body hungrily as did his lips. He released her lips to claim her face, strewing kisses wherever his mouth moved, down her neck

375

across her collar bones but always returned to her welcome lips for the sustenance he'd been denied for the past week.

"Beautiful, tiny and sweet. Oh, so sweet," Chase murmured, his words a worshipful litany. His head lowered, and his lips gently tasted a rose-tipped nipple. Elizabeth arched her breasts forward and threw her head back, her golden hair pooling on the pillow. She was utterly lost in the passion that flowed from Chase through her. His hand gently parted her thighs and moved up to stroke boldly beneath the folds of her femininity.

"You don't know how many times I've dreamed of this during the past week," he murmured, his tongue trailing along her neck to the sensual curve of her shoulder. Delicately he cupped her breast in his hand and moved his palm lightly across the nipple. He marveled at the instant swelling and peaking beneath his touch. His mouth paid homage to the other breast.

When both breasts had been thoroughly adored, he nibbled his way along her ribs, his hair brushed tantalizingly on her sensitized breasts. A low guttural groan escaped from deep in Elizabeth's throat when his mouth stopped at her naval, and his warm breath oozed across her taut and flat but quivering stomach. He rested his cheek against her skin and felt the rising and falling of her body with each ragged breath she drew.

He flattened his hand on her stomach and again thought of her carrying his child. Pleasure raced through him, and he knew he would marry Elizabeth.

He would love her; he would make her a good husband. The tips of his fingers, resting in the mound of golden curls at the top of her thighs, began to wiggle erotically.

Elizabeth's hands burrowed into Chase's thick black hair and she pulled his head back to hers. "Now," she murmured, "take me now, Chase."

He moved over her, captured her mouth in a searing kiss and plunged his strength into her, gloving himself snugly within the hallowed warmth of her womanhood. Elizabeth received him easily this time and took him deeply within her. Moving together as one, they rose and fell with frenzied desperation, losing all reason and concept of time or place.

They climbed higher and higher as Chase delved deeper and deeper into her velvety warmth. Together they reached the pinnacle of ultimate pleasure; they cried their victory together, the vibrations causing the entire universe to shake. With the wondrous moment over, Elizabeth slid her hands around Chase's neck and held him tightly. She burrowed her cheeks against his moist chest.

"I didn't know it kept getting better and better."

Chase chuckled at her innocence and wondered at his surprise. "I didn't know it could be this wonderful," he admitted. He wrapped his arms tightly around her and snuggled his face in the curve of her shoulder. He, too, sensed the wonder of this particular coupling, the oneness they shared.

As only lovers do, they created a beautiful world out of the dingy room and lay there, talking until the evening breeze began to filter through the shutters.

"Woman," Chase finally said, running his hand over her hips and down her thigh, "if we don't get up from here, we won't get up because I'm already thinking about something other than food."

Elizabeth lifted her arms above her head and stretched sensuously. "I'm totally in agreement with you, Major Daniel. I'll follow whatever plan of action you wish to implement."

Chase moved and laid his cheek on Elizabeth's belly, his fingers trailing up and down her smooth legs. When he heard her stomach growl, he laughed. "I think, love, the old saying is quite true. The spirit is willing, but the body is weak." He sat up and gently swatted the creamy globes of her buttocks. "I think we need to be getting us something to eat. We'll return to this battlefield later this evening."

"That's a promise," Elizabeth said.

"That's a promise," Chase agreed, swinging his legs over the bed. As he slipped his into his clothes, he asked, "Where shall we eat?"

"I've been eating at *Señora* Delgado's," Elizabeth answered. "The food is marvelous and the prices are great." Thinking of her quickly depleting supply of money, she unconsciously sighed.

"What's wrong?" Chase asked, instantly attuned to her every movement and sound.

"Nothing really," Elizabeth answered. "I'm going to have to have a transfer made from my bank in New Orleans if I don't find Vanessa soon. My money is running low."

"I'll give you some," Chase said.

"No," Elizabeth quickly answered. She couldn't accept money from Chase; that would change their relationship into something unsavory. She would feel like she was a kept woman. While she was willing to give him her love unconditionally, she wasn't willing to become his mistress. A fine line of difference . . . but one nevertheless.

As if he had followed her thoughts, Chase moved to her, tucked his fingers under her chin and lifted it. For a long time he stared into the depth of her eyes; he saw the beauty of her soul. He saw himself reflected in those lovely irises. He loved Elizabeth Rose Barrett; he loved her more than life itself. He opened his mouth to tell her so, but he couldn't force the words from his lips.

Elizabeth could see the battle he was fighting. He wanted to admit his feelings for her but couldn't. He could show her, but he couldn't tell her. Having never spoken them in his life and perhaps never having had them spoken to him, he didn't know how to communicate emotions.

Finally he said, "Wear the red ribbon for me tonight."

Elizabeth nodded her head. She wasn't disappointed with his request; she was disappointed that he wouldn't admit his love for her. Moving away from him, she walked to the dresser to brush her hair and tie it off her face with the length of red ribbon.

At dusk, enjoying the cool of the evening, Chase and Elizabeth walked out of the saloon. As they crossed the street on their way to the restaurant, Elizabeth glanced up to see a rider coming into town. He was a dirty looking man, his clothes ill-fitted and ragged. The crown of his battered hat was rounded and sat low on his head, the brim shelved on his eyebrows. He slouched in the saddle, his head swinging from side to side as if he were looking for someone or something.

"Where are your men staying?" Elizabeth asked, her attention going back to Chase.

"At Ft. Duncan," he replied, and in answer to her raised eyebrows, he added, "a fort that hasn't been activated since the war."

"Is the army thinking about activating it," she asked.

Chase grinned. "I am."

As Chase discussed with her the reasons why he wanted more forts opened along the frontier line, they quickly traversed the few blocks to the restaurant. When they entered, a lovely Mexican woman greeted them.

"Elizabeth," she said in a soft Spanish accent, a smile curing her full lips, "you are late tonight, no?" When Elizabeth's face colored, Elena laughed. "I am so glad to see you, and you bring a guest with you tonight, yes?"

The woman was voluptuously built, her white blouse and full skirt, showing her figure to its best advantage. Her thick black hair was braided and coiled into a chignon on the crown of her head. Long gold earrings dangled from each ear.

"Yes, I do," Elizabeth returned. "Elena Delgado, this is Major Chase Daniel of the United State Cavalry."

"I am glad to meet you, Major Daniel," Elena said,

her black eyes sparkling. "And I am glad you have come. Already you have given color to the *señorita*'s cheeks and a luster to her eyes, no?"

Chase reached out to lay his hand over Elizabeth's and smiled into her face. "I'm not sure I can take credit for her beauty, *señora,* but I'd like to think it's because of me."

"I will bring each of you a glass of the finest wine in town," she said. "You can drink that while you wait for your dinner."

Not long after Elena set their drinks on the table, Nolan Griffin and another man entered the room. When Griffin saw them, he waved and moved in their direction.

As they approached, Chase studied the man following Griffin. He was small and wiry with a broad chest that narrowed into a slim waist and hips. His round face and dark features were almost obscured in the shadows provided by the large sombrero which he wore. When he swept the hat from his head, black, straight hair fell across the forehead, hair the same burnished color as the thick moustache that topped his upper lip.

"Major Daniel," Griffin said, nearing the table. "Just the person I was looking for. I'd like to introduce you to Isidor Moreno — one of the Mexican traders I was telling you about."

Chase rose and extended his hand to the Mexican, their eyes instantly locking as each studied the other. "Mister Moreno," Chase said, "I'm happy to make your acquaintance."

"And I yours, *señor,*" Moreno returned.

His sparkling eyes turned from Chase to Elizabeth as Griffin said, "This, *Señor* Moreno, is Miss Elizabeth Barrett."

"*Señorita* Barrett." Moreno bowed low and caught her hand in his. In a completely innocent but gallant gesture, he brushed his lips over her fingers. "How delighted I am to meet you, *señorita.*"

"Thank you, sir," Elizabeth answered.

With a smile that revealed beautiful white teeth, Isidor released Elizabeth's hand. Slowly, he returned his attention to Chase. When he saw the jealous glint in the depth of those expressive blue eyes, Isidor's smile widened. He had thought the man invincible, but the woman was his Achilles heel. This was good to remember for future reference.

"*Señor* Griffin tells me that you would like to meet with the Seminole Negroes who live in Naciemiento."

"Yes, I would," Chase answered, irritated because the Mexican was too astute and had learned more than Chase wished for him to know. But if he were to meet with the Seminole Negroes, he had to have the man's help. "Shall we discuss this over supper?"

"*Si, señor,*" Moreno replied silkily. "This would be an excellent time for us to talk, no?"

"I've been asking around about your sister, Miss Barrett," the ranger said as they sat down, "but so far I haven't come up with anything."

"Thank you, Mr. Griffin," Elizabeth said.

"Who is this sister whom you're hunting, *señorita?*" Isidor asked. "Perhaps I know of her."

"Vanessa Barrett," Elizabeth replied.

Isidor's forehead furrowed as he pondered. "I do

not know the name," he finally said. "Perhaps if you could give me a description I might recognize her."

"Will this do?" Elizabeth asked, opening her purse and withdrawing the portrait.

Isidor clasped the miniature in the palm of his hand and studied the exquisite features of Elizabeth's younger sister. "She is indeed a lovely woman," he said. Lifting his head, he stared into Elizabeth's face. "You and she have many features which are the same," he observed. "Your eyes and the shape of your faces. But if the artist has captured the true essence of *Señorita* Vanessa, I would say that you are more spirited than she."

Elizabeth laughed as Isidor returned the portrait to her. "I would have to say that Vanessa is the more spirited, sir. After all she is the one who left home in search of a new life and excitement. I stayed to build something out of the ruins."

"Phoenix," Isidor said softly. "As I said, *señorita,* you are the most spirited. You didn't escape your destiny."

Shivers ran up Elizabeth's spine as she looked deeply into the black eyes of the Mexican trader. She wasn't afraid of him, but his soft, prophetic utterances frightened her. She felt as if he had the ability to see the scrolls of her soul and was revealing these secrets for all and sundry to see. She dropped her gaze and played with the napkin in her lap.

"*Señor* Griffin," Elena Delgado exclaimed when she came bustling out of the kitchen, her brightly colored skirt swirling around dainty ankles. "How glad I am to see you."

"And what about me, *Señora* Elena?" Isidor asked, those twinkling eyes moving to the comely woman that approached their table.

Elena smiled tenderly, almost shyly. "I am glad to see you, *Señor* Isidor. It has been a long time since you come to my restaurant."

"My trip into Mexico took me much longer than I anticipated," Moreno answered. "I met with many setbacks this time."

"Elena," Griffin said, "I'm right near starved. What have you got for supper tonight."

"Ah, *señor,*" Elena said, "I have your favorite. Beef stew and homemade bread." She continued with the oral recitation of her menu, quickly going into the Mexican dishes. As soon as each had ordered, Elena disappeared into the kitchen.

Isidor looked across the table at Chase. "What do you wish me say to these Seminole Negroes, Major?"

"I only want you to arrange a meeting," Chase replied. "I'll do my own talking."

Moreno held both hands up in a gesture of surrender. "*Señor,* I am not prying into your business," he said, "but I know these people quite well. They won't agree to see you unless you make known before hand your reasons for wanting to meet with them." He picked up the napkin and tucked into the collar of his shirt. "Without that information I can deliver all the messages in the world for you, but you will receive no answer."

Again blue eyes clashed with black, but Chase saw only the truth reflected in Moreno's. "I want to hire some of these men to scout for me," he finally said.

"For the U.S. Cavalry?" Morena asked.

Chase nodded his head.

"You're asking a lot of these people, Major. You're asking them to work for the same government that drove them from their home in Florida and is responsible for their plight into Mexico."

"I can't excuse what the government did to them nearly thirty years ago, Mr. Moreno. Neither can I be held to blame for the same action. I'm not responsible for their plight," Chase answered. "However, I am offering them a job, and I'll pay them for services rendered." The blue eyes firmly met the black ones. "Conditions, Mr. Moreno, that I'll discuss only with the Seminole Negroes."

"I will deliver your message, *señor,*" Moreno announced. "You will be here in Eagle Pass?"

"My men and I are camped at Ft. Duncan," Chase replied.

"Is your government perhaps thinking of reopening the garrison?" Isidor questioned.

"We're thinking about it," Chase answered.

Openly curious, Moreno asked, "Why? Surely you are not expecting trouble from the *Mexicanos?*"

Chase leaned back in his chair and gave the Mexican a long, appraising look. "We have reason to believe that an ex-Confederate war criminal, Roswell Bainbridge, is living in Mexico, Mr. Moreno."

"You think my government has given this man political asylum?"

"I certainly hope not," Chase replied. "If so, it has in effect given him permission to amass an army of

385

outlaws to launch criminal attacks on the United States."

"You have evidence of this?" Moreno asked, his eyes mere slits in his face.

"Not yet," Chase replied.

Moreno waved his hands through the air expressively, "Then you are guessing, *no?*"

"No," Chase answered softly.

Moreno dropped his arms to the table and leaned closer to Chase, studying the implacable lines and angles of the major's face. "Are you proposing to use this guide to cross the Mexican border to search for this man, *señor?*"

"I have told you all that I intend to tell you," Chase replied curtly.

"A military incursion into Mexico would be a most unfortunate incident, *señor,* if my government were to learn of it. We would consider it an act of war and would react accordingly."

"That's the way we Americans feel about the incursions of Roswell Bainbridge and his pack of cutthroats," Chase returned. Now he was the one scrutinizing the face across from him. "Have you no knowledge of such a person as this, *señor?*"

Moreno lifted a hand to twirl his moustache. Finally he shrugged and drawled in a heavy accent — one that Chase felt was affected for the occasion, "We have many *Americanos* who have taken shelter in our land since the ending of the war. It is possible that this man lives in Mexico. I do not know."

With the arrival of the food, the conversation shifted from Bainbridge to Elizabeth. Moreno, quite

386

interested in her and her background, plied her with questions which she willingly answered. During the meal Elizabeth looked up to see a most unsavory character peering in the window at them. His beard was unkempt, the crown of his battered hat rounded so that the brim rode low on his face. His eyes were barely discernible. When he realized Elizabeth had seen him, he hastily ducked out of sight.

Elizabeth returned her gaze to her plate, but she was no longer hungry. A shiver ran up her spine as she thought about the man. Every so often she would dart a glance at the window to make sure he wasn't watching them again.

Chapter Twenty-three

As she and Chase returned to their room after dinner, Elizabeth pondered the conversation Chase and Moreno had had. Finally she asked, "Are you planning to go into Mexico after Bainbridge?"

"I'm going to get Bainbridge," Chase told her. "I'm not sure how, but I'm going to get him."

"This has become rather personal to you because of Terry's death, hasn't it?"

"Yes," Chase admitted freely, "it's as much personal as a duty."

In front of the saloon Elizabeth stopped walking and turned to look at him in the dull light that spilled through the open window. "Chase, I'm frightened. Give this up." She laid her palms on his chest. "You're much too involved. You can't be objective about Bainbridge anymore. You've become obsessed with finding him. You're going to put yourself in danger."

Chase caught her hands in his and laughed her fears away. "Don't worry your pretty little head," he told her. "I'm going to be just fine. My troopers are the finest in the world, and though we're only ten in number, we work together as a finely fit unit." His eyes twinkled devilishly as he leaned his head close to her ear and whispered, "I propose, madam, that we return to our room and work together as a finely fit unit."

Pleasure winged through Elizabeth's body at his suggestion. "You, sir," she teased, "are a cad."

"No," he returned softly, his eyes suddenly gone somber, "I'm a man who wants to make love to the most beautiful woman in the entire world."

These were not the words Elizabeth wanted to hear, but she was certain that Chase loved her. Perhaps in time Chase would be able to vocalize his feelings, perhaps never. Staring into Chase's eyes, Elizabeth was unaware of the man moving down the boardwalk until he bumped into her and jostled her against the wall.

"Excuse me, ma'am," he hastily apologized, yanking his hat off his head. "I tripped. Didn't mean you no harm."

"It's . . . quite all right," Elizabeth murmured as she looked into the face of the man who had been peering through the restaurant window.

"You ain't hurt, are you?" he asked, his eyes darting back and forth between hers and Chase's face.

"No," Elizabeth said with a slight shake of her head, "I'm fine, thank you."

The man clamped the hat back on his head and pushed through the swinging doors into the saloon, soon lost in the noisy crowd of night revelers. More slowly Chase and Elizabeth followed the man, treading their way through the tables to their room.

"Miss Barrett."

Elizabeth heard someone call her name and turned to see Evan Warner walking toward her.

"Howdy, ma'am," he said, quickly removing his hat, thin gray hair looping over his forehead.

"Ranger Warner," Elizabeth greeted, her face lighting up with pleasure, "how nice to see you. I was getting worried about you."

"Just took our time," Evan replied. "Had a lot of territory we wanted to scout out before we reported in to Nolan." Warner's glance strayed from Elizabeth to Chase. "Evening, major," he said coolly. "What brings you down this way?" His eyes shifted back to Elizabeth suggestively.

"Ft. Duncan," Chase replied easily, his eyes scanning the crowd for a sign of Mason.

Evan pursed his lips and nodded his head. "Thinking about reopening it?"

"Thinking about it," Chase returned.

"Seems like a reasonable good thing to do," Warner conceded. "Help us keep some of this riffraff from crossing the border at will."

Remembering the ranger's hatred of and aversion to him in Uvalde, Chase was surprised at this tolerable reception. "Have you seen any suspicious riffraff in your travels?" Chase asked.

"Nope, not a thing. Not one little thing." Evan flipped his hat back on his head and said, "Well, guess I'd better get going. Hope to see Nolan before he turns in for the night."

"We just left him at *Señora* Delgado's restaurant," Chase answered. "If you hurry, you'll be able to catch him."

"Where's Ranger Mason?" Elizabeth asked before Evan could turn away.

Evan's lips curled into a crooked smile that transformed his face into wrinkled friendliness. "He'd around somewhere, ma'am. He's a mighty sociable young man."

Elizabeth and Chase were still smiling when they walked down the corridor to her room. As she waited for Chase to unlock the door, she glanced up the corridor into the saloon to see the man who had peered into the window at the restaurant and who had bumped into them on the boardwalk watching them. Shivers of apprehension ran down Elizabeth's spine.

"She tugged Chase's arm. "Look," she said, pointing. "That man who bumped into us is staring at us."

As Chase threw open the door, he glanced up the hallway. "Nothing to be worried about," he assured her with a laugh. "He's gawking because you're a beautiful woman, a sight he's probably never seen in his life."

Elizabeth looked down the hall at the strange man one last time before she entered the room. His being here was no mere coincidence; she felt that in her bones. Hardly had the door closed behind them before Chase enveloped her with his arms. He didn't know how much longer he could stay in Eagle Pass with her; already he felt the pinch of time.

As greedily in love as Chase and totally unsated for all their couplings, Elizabeth lifted her face for his kisses. She would feast at passion's table as long as she could. Their coming together earlier had been swift and urgent and desperate. This one would be slow and leisurely. They would fill the night with their sensual banqueting. She would savor each delicate morsel with ultimate pleasure.

Chase's dark head dipped as his lips trailed over a smooth and rounded shoulder and lower to nuzzle the satin flesh of Elizabeth's breasts with little caresses and kisses that sent quivers of renewed longing flickering through her loins.

"I love you," Chase whispered to her, overwhelmed by the depth of his feelings. Her warm, seductive body in his arms filled him with renewed passion; at the same time his heart was filled with the desire to protect her and to fight all her battles for her . . . and if not for her, at least, he would fight at her side.

The words washed Elizabeth with a joy that she didn't recall ever having experienced before, a joy that filled her completely body and soul. She laced her fingers in the crisp black curls at the base of his neck and pulled his face down for her kiss that quickly turned into their kiss. Ardently she clung to him and gloried in the broad rough strength of his chest pressed against her breasts. His lips and tongue tip explored her mouth in a way that made her pulses leap and desire rippled through her slight frame.

"Chase," Elizabeth sighed her passion when Chase

paused in his kisses.

Her fingertips drifted down across the tanned width of his shoulders, relishing the powerful feel of corded muscle beneath smooth flesh. Indulging himself in loving her, he stroked her body, learning each curve, each plane and tiny hollow anew. She gasped in delight when he parted her thighs and touched the font of her womanhood ever so gently with his work-hardened hands.

His eyes were aflame with burning desire when at long length he filled her with his throbbing hardness. Slowly and beautifully they moved together in that age-old dance of love. They kissed; they touched; they whispered endearments to one another, until passion expelled conscious thought and they became an extension of their sensations.

When her hands dug into his shoulders and he felt those first tentative contractions against his shaft, Chase thrust deeply and urgently and deliberately, making sure he carried her to the highest plane of fulfillment. He knew he had succeeded when she shuddered in his arms and gasped her pleasure over and over again. Gathering her into his arms, he thrust deeply once more, his lips heatedly covering hers as the dam burst and the pleasure of fulfillment rushed through him. He groaned in delight, then lay quite still on top of her for a long time before he rolled over.

Later, they fell into an exhausted but sated sleep, limbs tangled, heads resting side by side upon the pillows, the golden against jet black. Sometime during the wee hours of the morning Chase was awakened by a noise in the hallway, no doubt a drunk making his way to his room. Unable to go back to sleep immediately, Chase slipped out of bed and lit a cigar. He moved to the window and hitching his foot on the casement, stood there smoking and thinking.

He had realized earlier that he loved Elizabeth, and he wanted to marry her. Now he was more sure than ever. He finally understood what Aunt Ida had been telling him all these years, what poets had been singing for eons. A man is far richer with having loved and lost than in not having loved at all. Life itself was a gamble; so was love, and he was willing to take his chances with it. He realized how much Elizabeth had gambled on his falling in love with her when she had given herself to him.

He stubbed the cigar against the casement and threw it out the window. When he turned, his thigh hit the night table and he knocked Elizabeth's purse off, the latch opening and the contents splaying across the floor.

Elizabeth roused and mumbled, "What's wrong?"

"Nothing," he answered. "I got up for a smoke and hit the table. Go back to sleep."

"Are you coming back to bed," she asked, squirming her head into the pillow.

"As soon as I pick this up," he said. By the time he lit the candle and set it on the floor, Elizabeth was asleep again. He raked her things together and dropped them into her purse. When he picked up the sheet of paper, his eyes inadvertently scanned the name of the local bank and the amount of the deposit.

Feeling as if he'd been hit squarely in the gut and all the wind knocked out of his body, Chase sat back and stared at the receipt. Elizabeth had deposited in the bank the exact amount of money that had been stolen from the Union pay wagon. All this guilt he had been carrying around was for naught. Blake had been right all along. Elizabeth was involved with Bainbridge.

God, but he was sick. He felt as if he were going to vomit. Yet he had enough presence of mind to return all her belongings to her purse and return it to the night table. He dressed and regardless of what she might think when she awoke, he left the room and stood in front of the saloon.

Chase was accustomed to making split second decisions but he'd never felt the weight of any as he did the one he must make now. He was in love with Elizabeth, but now he wondered if she were in love with him. Perhaps she had been using him all along. That would explain why she wasn't all that interested in getting married.

Giving her virginity wouldn't be too great a price for her to pay for her beloved South and her old way of life!

Such a thought was bitter gall to Chase, but he was a man beyond reason at the moment. He had finally given his heart to a woman, and she seemed to be trampling it under feet. If Elizabeth had trusted him, if she had loved him as she declared, she would have told him about the money. She would have confessed her part in this operation.

Again the question that he had pushed to the back of his mind resurfaced and demanded an answer. What was he going to do?

He really didn't have too many alternatives. He had few people whom he could trust. The majority of the people in this area were either outlaws or southern sympathizers or both. He had thought Everett was the key to unlock the mysteries of the Bainbridge operation, but it wasn't Everett. All along Blake Lowell had been the key.

Chase was sure he had met Blake Lowell before. When or where he didn't know, but he understood the man too thoroughly for it to be mere coincidence. He must concentrate and pull up that elusive tag that would put the label on Blake Lowell that he recognized.

By the time the sun peeked above the horizon, Chase had made his decision. He returned to the room and sat down on the edge of the bed. If Elizabeth wanted to play games, he would play. Only this time he understood the rules. He would take what she offered without any qualms, any tender words of love or any promises of marriage. When time came for them to part, he would do so without any regrets.

Even as he brushed the golden tangles from her cheeks, Chase knew he was lying to himself. He loved Elizabeth with every fiber of his being. She was imbedded in his heart for life, perhaps longer.

He leaned over and kissed the end of her nose.

"Wake up, sleepy head," he said. Then he slid off the bed and pulled the scarf from Gloria's cage. Within minutes the room was filled with the bird's cheerful warble.

"Must we get up so early?" Elizabeth asked, rubbing her eyes with the back of her hands.

"We must," Chase answered. "We have a full day ahead of us."

"Doing what?" she asked, propping up on an elbow, unmindful that the sheet slid down her body to reveal her breasts.

"We're going to spend the day at Ft. Duncan," he said. "We'll have a picnic. How about that?"

Elizabeth grinned. "That's marvelous. When shall I be ready?"

Chase walked to the dresser and picked up his watch. His back to her, he held it in the palm of his hand to look at it and said, "While you're getting dressed, I'll go ask Elena to pack us some food and tell Nolan where we're going to be in case he needs to get in touch with me. Then on our way out of town we'll stop by the bank and see about getting you some money transferred in from New Orleans."

Through the mirror he watched Elizabeth's reaction to his suggestion. Her head turned and her eyes darted to her purse.

"We don't need to take up our time going by the bank," she said, wishing she could tell him the truth. With all that money deposited in her name, she didn't dare go in and ask for a transfer of funds without raising suspicion. She'd be glad when Blake came for it, and she was no longer involved with his plot. But she had had no other alternative but to help Vanessa, Elizabeth reasoned to herself. She was the only family she had. "I'll do that one day when you're not here."

Chase hid his disappointment. "I'll go on over to Elena's then and the ranger's station. I'll be back here for you in an hour and a half. That'll give me time to rent a buggy." He picked up his hat.

"Aren't you forgetting something?" Elizabeth called, slipping out of bed and running across the room. "A good morning kiss." Wrapping her arms around his neck, she pressed her mouth to his in a moist and warm greeting.

The hat slid from Chase's clutch as his hands smoothed down her back to rest on the gentle flare of her buttocks. He twisted his mouth from hers and laid his cheeks on her head. Dear God, but he loved her. He had to get her out of this mess she was involved in, but could he? He didn't know if she wanted to be rescued.

"Chase," Elizabeth said tentatively, "will you show me the portrait of your mother today?" Although Chase never changed position, Elizabeth felt him tense in her arms.

Finally he said, "Yes, I'll show you."

When Elizabeth stepped out of his embrace, she wondered about his hesitancy to show her the painting. His family was such a delicate subject with him that she should have waited for him to mention it again. Perhaps he considered this an intrusion of his privacy. "Chase, if you don't want me to . . . if you don't want to show me—"

"I want to show you," Chase answered and pulled back to look searching into her face. "I'm also frightened."

"Of what?" Elizabeth asked.

"Of losing you," he whispered.

"You're not going to lose me," Elizabeth managed in a thick voice.

Chase didn't take her into his arms again because he knew they'd never leave the room. He reached out and touched her face; he brushed a strand behind her ear; he ran a finger across her cheek. "Promise."

"I promise."

With all his heart Chase wanted to believe her; he needed to believe her. "I'll be back in a moment," he said.

"Tell Mr. Harris I would like to have a bath on your way out."

As he walked through the saloon Chase saw Jefferson sweeping the floor. "Good morning," he called. "Miss Elizabeth would like to have a bath brought to her room."

"Yes, sir, Major," Jefferson answered. "I'll get it for her as soon as I finish this."

Chase walked out of the saloon and down the street to the barber shop. After he'd bathed and shaved, he headed for Elena's and put in an order for a picnic lunch. From there he went to the ranger's station and let Nolan know he'd be at Ft. Duncan should Moreno need to get in touch with him. At the livery stable he rented a buggy and drove down Main Street to stop in front of the bank.

For a long time he sat and stared at the building. He watched as the employees unlocked the front door and entered. Moments later the shades came up; the closed sign was taken out of the window, and the door was opened.

Still Chase at in the buckboard and stared.

Chapter Twenty-four

Lying on his back beneath the shade of the tree, his hands twined together under his head, Chase watched Elizabeth with a certain amount of puzzlement as she picked up their eating utensils and returned them to the basket Elena had prepared for them earlier. She smiled and hummed as she worked and seemed not to have a care in the world.

She had casually skirted the opportunities he had given her to tall him about the money at the bank. At different times during the day he had mentioned the robbery, Blake, Everett, and Bainbridge. Always Elizabeth listened to what he was saying and made suitable comment, then deftly veered the conversation in another channel. He marveled that she could be so cool, acting as if nothing were amiss.

"You told Ranger Griffin that we'd be out here today?" she said, breaking the silence as she tucked the table cloth over the dirty dishes.

"Umhum," Chase drawled. "Said he'd send a message if Moreno contacted him."

Shoving the basket out of the way, Elizabeth stretched out beside Chase, nuzzling her face against his chest when he moved his arm to receive her. For a long time they lay together, neither speaking. Elizabeth was enraptured with the wonder of her growing love for Chase; he was worried about her involvement with Blake and Bainbridge.

"After one gets accustomed to the desert qualities, this part of Texas is beautiful," Elizabeth murmured, playing with the buttons on his shirt. She slipped a button through the opening and slid her fingers beneath the material to touch his warm flesh. The tip of her nail scored his nipple to send a shudder of pleasure through his body. "And after one" — she lowered her voice so that Chase had to strain to here her words — "has become accustomed to making love, she finds she's rather greedy and cannot get her fill."

For the moment Chase allowed his love and desire to push the tormenting thoughts aside. He chuckled and rolled over to prop on an elbow. He caught her hand in his and looked into her delicate face framed with a mass of golden curls. His other hand gently cradled the tiny jawline.

"On hearing my confession," she asked, "do you find me wanton?"

Chase's eyes darkened until the irises were a deep blue, outlined with indigo. "I find you extremely wanton, Miss Barrett," he admitted, "but delightfully so. If we were in a more secluded place, I'd see if I could not sate that avaricious appetite you've so recently developed."

"What an arrogant assumption," Elizabeth teased. "How do you know it's so recent?

"It better be, and I better be the only man who can sate it," Chase growled possessively, then added, "You've created the same hunger within me, woman." He guided her hand downward and laid it over his thigh. "See what you do to me."

Elizabeth spread her hand over the hardness that strained against his breeches. Chase lowered his face and his lips gently touched hers, lightly brushing back and forth before they finally settled into a kiss. When he felt her mouth open beneath his and the pressure of her hand on his manhood turn into gentle massage, he ran the tip of his tongue over her lips then ducked into the honeyed interior to savor the sweetness.

"I love you," Elizabeth murmured moments later as he raised his head and she cradled it with both hands to gaze into his eyes.

So innocent! So beautiful! Chase thought, and her confession brought him a modicum of pleasure, but recurring memories of the bank receipt diminished his joy. He wondered if her admission was a ploy, another calculated move in this game of espionage they were playing. Again he wanted to confront her, but again he refrained. He would play by her rules. He would wait; he had never been one to rush a situation prematurely.

"Major," Corporal Man yelled as he came running in their direction, "a man just came with a message from Ranger Griffin."

Elizabeth rolled away from Chase, sat up and began to straighten her clothes. Chase, smiling at the faint coloring in her cheeks, moved also but more slowly.

"The meeting has been set up with the Seminole Negroes and you're to be at the ranger's headquarters as soon as you can get there," the trooper ended, slightly winded.

"Has the messenger left?" Chase asked.

"No, sir. He's waiting for an answer."

Chase nodded and donned his hat. "Tell him to tell Ranger Griffin that we're leaving within the next thirty minutes, and I'll come directly to the ranger station."

Elizabeth was on her feet by now, flapping the blanket through the air to free it of twigs and dirt. While she folded it, Chase picked up the basket and replaced it in the buckboard. "I'll be right back," he told her. "I need to leave some orders with Sgt. Liberty before we leave."

Elizabeth nodded and leaned against the tree trunk to wait for him in the shade. She watched Chase while he talked with the sergeant. He seemed different today—preoccupied and moody. She wanted to see his mother's portrait before she left the camp, but after his hesitancy this morning she was leary of asking again.

At times today she had felt as if he were a thousand miles away. She surmised that he was tense about this coming meeting with the Seminole Negroes. Still she had enjoyed the day immeasurably and was sorry to see it come to an end. Elizabeth saw Chase look at her, his expression almost brooding, and after Sgt.

Liberty walked away from him, Chase remained where he was standing. He turned and ducked into the tent behind him.

When he existed and walked in her direction, Elizabeth pushed away from the tree and moved to the buckboard where she waited for him.

"You wanted to see my mother," he said without preamble and held out his hand.

As Elizabeth took the small painting in her hand and studied it, Chase watched her expression. At the moment he was the most vulnerable he'd ever been; he was sharing with Elizabeth parts of his life that only Aunt Ida and Terry had known heretofore. And he wasn't sure of Elizabeth's love or her motives, but he . . . loved . . . her.

"Your mother is beautiful," Elizabeth said.

"I think so."

"And you look so much like her," Elizabeth exclaimed, raising her head and scrutinizing Chase's face. "The color of your hair. The shape of your face. Your eyes." She dropped her gaze to the portrait and looked at it a moment longer before she returned it to Chase. "She really is beautiful. You must love her very much."

"I do," Chase answered.

When he returned from the tent the second time, he asked, "Are you ready?"

"No," Elizabeth answered quietly, "but I suppose we must go."

Understanding how Elizabeth felt, he caught her hands in his and squeezed. Out here they could forget

405

about the ideologies that separated them. They were simply a man and a woman who were in love. When they returned to town, each would walk on the opposite side of an invisible line.

He himself was fighting all the demons of hell. Only by sheer willpower did he constrain himself from confronting her. But he had decided last night to wait to see what transpired, and he would do just that. If his hunch was right, Blake would be meeting with her soon to arrange for a transfer of the funds into Mexico.

Chase nodded his head and said sadly, "We must." His hands caught her tiny waist and he swung her aboard the buggy.

When Chase and Elizabeth arrived in town, he squinted against the afternoon sun as he scanned both sides of the street for unusual or suspicious activity—a habit so deeply ingrained that he did it without conscious thought. All was quiet and peaceful. He stopped in front of the saloon and assisted Elizabeth from the buckboard.

Untying her bonnet and pushing it off her head, Elizabeth peered into his face. "When will you be back?" she asked, again trying to read this complex man whom she loved more than life itself.

Chase shrugged. "I don't know. Moreno's the leader. He's setting up the meeting. I'll wait at the ranger's station until he sends word." Inadvertently his eyes swept over to the bank building. "What are you going to do this afternoon?"

"Nothing nearly so exciting," she said, refusing to

follow the trail his eyes blazed. "Elena has been letting me use her tubs to wash my clothes, and today is wash day, so—" Her shrug and smile sufficed to end her sentence. "If you come back early and I'm not at the hotel, check at Elena's."

"I will."

Elizabeth hated to see him leave. Something was wrong, and she was losing him. He hadn't gone anywhere but suddenly they were separated by a yawning and invisible gulf that seemed to be getting larger by the second. When he leaned over to kiss her good-bye, she threw her arms around him and clutched him to her. She had no pride left when it came to Chase. She had to keep him.

"Chase," she breathed against his chest.

His arms slowly circled her and he held her tightly against him. He, too, felt the same barrier between them and feared they were losing one another.

"I love you so much. So very much."

"I love you," he answered.

She pulled back and lifted her face for his kiss. When he lifted his lips from hers, she said, "Hurry back, my darling. I'll be waiting."

Chase held her for a precious moment longer and gazed into her face. Then he lowered his head and gave her a quick kiss and a pat on the backside before he rounded the buckboard and hopped into the seat. Elizabeth watched as he turned it around and rumbled down the street toward the ranger's headquarters. They waved, smiled, and threw a kiss. Then Elizabeth walked into the saloon to be greeted by

Jefferson, who was swinging a huge mop with both hands and wearing a white apron that was so long it dragged the floor.

"Miss Elizabeth," his eyes darted around the room to make sure they were alone, "I have a note for you. Mr. Lowell came earlier today when you was—" He propped the mop handle against the wall.

"—were," Elizabeth automatically corrected.

"—gone on that picnic with Major Daniel," Jefferson continued. He had no time to stop for a grammar lesson today. Mr. Lowell had given him a whole dollar to make sure he delivered this message to Miss Elizabeth the minute she arrived at the saloon. He dug into his pocket and pulled out a crumpled piece of paper. "He said for me to give you this."

"Thank you, Jefferson," Elizabeth said and took the note. She hurried to her room and waited until she was safely behind closed door to unfold the paper.

Dear Elizabeth, it read, *the meeting has been set up. Bainbridge is sending someone to get me tonight. I'll need the money as quickly as possible. I'm across the street where I can see you. Whenever you can, slip out, and I'll join you at the bank.*

Relieved that this secrecy would soon be over, Elizabeth put her bonnet back on and exited from the saloon. She stood for a long while in front of the building to make sure Blake saw her—wherever he was—then she looked both ways down the street to make sure Chase didn't see her. Out of the corner of her eye she saw the stranger who had bumped into her on the boardwalk. He was hunched up against the

408

building across the street.

Again that shiver of apprehension ran up Elizabeth's spine as she crossed the thoroughfare and walked into the bank. When she reached the counter, she unfastened her purse and searched for the receipt.

"Good afternoon, Miss Barrett," Filmore greeted her, a pleasant smile on his thin face. "It's nice to see you again."

"Thank you, Mr. Fremont," she said and laid the piece of paper in front of him. "I've come to withdraw my money."

"You've found your sister I take it?" he said, as he picked up the receipt and glanced at it.

"Well . . . yes . . . I have," Elizabeth answered, reasoning to herself that she wasn't telling an outright lie. She had found Vanessa. Elizabeth couldn't remember a time when she'd been so ensnared by intrigue and deception. She turned when she heard the door open and saw Blake enter the bank. "My sister is married to a Mexican and is living in Mexico now. My friend, Mr. Lowell, is going to deliver the money to her."

"I see," Filmore said in a disinterested voice. He gave Blake the once-over. "Give me a few minutes, Miss Barrett. The safe is in the back room, and it'll take me a little while."

Elizabeth nodded. She was glad Chase had gone to meet Moreno. At least, by the time he found out about the money Blake would have it and be across the border. Then she could explain to Chase why she had acted as she did, and it would be too late for him to object. She felt guilty about what she was doing, but she had no other alternative, she told herself. Chase was an official of their government, and he had no authority to let Blake have the money when he stood to loose all of it. She loved Chase, but she knew he would be unbending when it came to the letter of the law. He wasn't unjust, but he didn't bend the rules. He went by them strictly. She prayed he would forgive her when she confessed.

"Did you tell Daniel about this?" Blake asked in an undertone.

"Of course not," Elizabeth snapped. "What do you take me for? A fool?" Before he could answer, she said, "While I don't agree with your strategies, I do want to save Vanessa."

"Did you have any problems getting away from him?" he asked, his eyes peeled to the door.

"No, he's at a meeting at the ranger's headquarters."

"Miss Barrett," Filmore called from the door of the back room. "If you don't mind, step back this way. I'll prepare a receipt while you count the money. Then I'll sack it up for you."

"Certainly," Elizabeth said, moving through the gate that Blake held open for her. "Is it all right if Mr. Lowell comes with me?"

Filmore nodded. "Of course."

Elizabeth followed him into the office and looked at the pile of money on the desk. She listened as Fremont counted the money, but he could have cheated her for all the attention she was paying. She was nervous and wanted to get out of the room; it seemed to be closing in on her. The sooner Blake had the money, the better. She sighed when Fremont dropped the last bundle of bills into the sack and slid a sheet of paper across the desk.

After he dipped the pen into the inkwell, the banker handed it to her. With the other hand he thumped the page. "Will you sign for it right here, Miss Barrett?"

"Certainly," Elizabeth answered, writing her name at the bottom of the transaction. Her hand closed over the handle of the sack and she stood, smiling down at the young man. "Thank you, Mr. Fremont, for everything. Mr. Lowell and I will be going now."

The door opened. "I don't think you'll be going anywhere." Chase entered the room, his revolver drawn and pointed directly at her and Blake.

Shock drained the color from Elizabeth's face as the gunny sack slipped from her hands to the floor. Not Chase! Not when she was so close to being out of this entanglement. She collapsed into the chair she had so recently vacated. She unconsciously wrung her hands. Before this hers and Chase's relationship had been tenous. She could only imagine what it would be now.

Neither Blake's stance nor his expression changed. He would have gone for his gun, but when he saw the weapon in Chase's hand he knew that would be foolish of him.

"Mr. Fremont," Chase said, "I would appreciate it if you would leave the room and close the door behind you."

Elizabeth didn't hear the man say, "Yes, sir," before he quietly exited the room. Because she was shaking, she held her hands together in her lap. While she didn't know what the outcome of Chase's finding out about the money would be in terms of their future, she was relieved that he knew. A weight lifted from her shoulders, but her heart was sad. She had to get her sister out of Mexico. Her life was in danger.

The door closing behind Fremont's retreating figure jarred Elizabeth and made her aware that the three of them were alone. She lifted her head and looked into Chase's face. She could hardly stand the disappointment she saw reflected in his eyes.

"How did you know?" she asked.

"Last night when I got up to smoke, I accidentally knocked your purse off the night table." His eyes never left Blake. "The contents spilled to the floor and among them was the receipt. This morning I came to the bank and ordered Mr. Filmore to inform me the minute the money was withdrawn."

"You've known all day, yet you said nothing." Elizabeth couldn't keep the hurt from clouding her eyes. Once before he had trusted her enough to come to her; this time he had laid a trap. Now she understood his preoccupation and moodiness this morning. Still she was hurt because she felt that like Blake he had used her. She was nothing but a pawn to each of them in their quest to get to Bainbridge—albeit their reasons for finding him were different.

Chase raised a brow, refusing to feel guilty. "Come now, Elizabeth! Are you pointing a finger at me in hopes I'll forget you're mixed up in this mess?"

"She's innocent of anything except wanting to save her sister." Blake was quick to come to Elizabeth's defense. "I put the money into her chest in Castroville. She didn't know about it until she arrived her and went through her trunk. I'm the one you want, not her."

"You slipped up, Lowell," Chase said. "I wouldn't have figured you to be sloppy."

"That's part of the game," Blake returned blandly. "I didn't have many options open at the time and took a desperate chance. I lost, but at least I gained some time. Otherwise, I may have been apprehended in Castroville. If you'd found the money on me then, I'd have been charged with three counts of murder, and I doubt any of you would have believed my innocence." He bent, picked up the money sack, and laid it on the desk. "I know you're going to arrest me, and for what it's worth I didn't rob the Union payroll. I didn't help Everett escape nor did I murder Addison or Thurman."

"I don't figure you did," Chase said, moving across the room and easing down into the chair behind the desk. "None of that is characteristic of you, Private W. Black."

"You remembered?" Blake said, not in the least surprised. "I knew if I hung around you long enough, you would."

Elizabeth looked at both men in amazement. She had no idea what they were talking about. Yet she sensed that each respected, if not admired, the other.

413

Chase nodded. "I'd almost forgotten. You've changed quite a bit since you were a private in my unit. You colored your hair and wore a beard then which made you look older. When I checked out the hotels and saloons this morning to see who had registered, I knew as soon as I saw the name White on the roster." Chase said reflectively, "A case where Black may be White. You were one of the Confederate's top secret service agents, so good you slipped into and out of my unit before I knew you'd even been there. I can't imagine why you're in with a cutthroat like Bainbridge."

"The war changes all of us," Blake said, still disinclined to discuss the reasons for his actions.

"Not someone like you," Chase said. "You're not a criminal. You were a soldier fighting for a cause you believed in." Chase slid the gun into his holster.

"You can't be sure that I'm not one of Bainbridge's men," Blake said.

"I'm sure," Chase replied without a thread of doubt. "You're not a murderer. Why didn't you tell me that you were after Bainbridge? We could have worked together."

"I didn't want your help," Blake said. "You want to bring Bainbridge and his men back to the States to stand trial for their crimes. I don't. Bainbridge is mine, all mine. I intend to kill him with my own bare hands."

Chase picked up the bag by its bottom and emptied the contents on the desk. "And this was your key to Bainbridge?"

414

Blake nodded.

"How does Vanessa fit into the picture?"

"According to Everett, she's Bainbridge's mistress. Things are getting rough and she wants out, but Bainbridge refuses to let her. She knows too much. She was part of the deal I cut with him," Blake said. "When I give Bainbridge the money, he's agreed to let her go."

Chase looked at the pale woman who still sat in the chair. He understood the role she played in the episode. He was relieved that she wasn't a part of Bainbridge's organization, and he was also glad that Blake wasn't. Blake was the kind of man he wanted to fight beside not against.

"You accused me of being personally involved in this case," Chase said. "What about you? What's your interest?"

"Bainbridge raped and killed my mother and my sister," he said in a toneless voice. "He stole everything of value from our home and burned it to the ground. He left the bodies of my mother and sister lying out where anyone who passed would see them and for the buzzards to pick. Faithful servants buried them for me. I've been hunting him ever since I received the report of his death. That's why Celeste and I opened *Le Grande* Casino; it was my cover. I infiltrated the ring as much as I could but had to deal with intermediaries and could get no farther than the ranch in Eagle Pass."

Blake reached up lifted his hat and ran his fingers through his hair before he resettled the hat. "It's sort of a clearing house for outlaws. Bainbridge is a clever man who wouldn't reveal himself to anyone but the men who had served under him during the war. When the officer — your friend — recognized Everett as being one of Bainbridge's original men, Everett shot him. He left the money at the casino with me for safe keeping."

"Have you seen their setup?" Chase asked.

"Several nights ago I was taken to the Mexican garrison for the first time," Blake answered. "But I can't get you there; I was blindfolded, and I'm not sure I'd recognize it from the outside in the daytime."

"Is that the arsenal also?" Chase asked.

Blake nodded. "Tonight I'm carrying them the first half of the money, and they're supposed to let Vanessa return to the States with me. Tomorrow night I'm to bring the other half."

"You're getting slouchy in your old age," Chase said. "To trust a man like him to keep his word."

"Desperation made me slip, but I'm not getting old, major, and I'm not slouchy." Blake looked at Elizabeth. "Just sentimental. For one of the few times in my life, I've allowed myself to be influenced by a woman. Trying to get Vanessa out for Elizabeth has thrown all kinds of kinks into my plans." He smiled. "However, my goal is to kill Bainbridge. I've never made any personal plans beyond that."

"No, Blake," Elizabeth exclaimed, "you can't give your life for a man like him."

Although Chase grudgingly admired Blake and was coming to like him more, and although he knew Elizabeth did not love Blake, he still felt a twinge of jealousy at her quick defense of the man. "We could still work together," he said.

"We could," Blake agreed, "but it would be your way or nothing."

Chase nodded his head. "My way is better than nothing, isn't it? At least, we'll bring Bainbridge to justice."

Blake folded his arms across his chest and contemplated the younger man sitting behind the desk. "I don't want justice. I want revenge; I want Bainbridge dead. Your way is bound to be too soft for me."

"I can arrest you," Chase said.

Blake grinned. "But you won't because I'm more valuable to you loose than in jail."

"What about Vanessa?" Elizabeth cried. She had listened to Chase and Blake talk long enough; each of them was obsessed with finding Bainbridge to the exclusion of everything and everybody else. "The two of you are more concerned about your own personal interests than you are about Vanessa. We've got to get her out of there."

Simultaneously both men, grins plastered to their faces, turned to look at Elizabeth.

"You're accusing us of being more concerned with our personal interests?" Chase chided gently.

Elizabeth tilted her chin and said, "Well, I'm probably the more righteous of the three. At least, I'm wanting to save someone. The two of you are after scalps."

The knock on the door prevented more conversation.

"Major Daniel," Fremont called. "Ranger Warner is—"

The door opened and Evan Warner pushed past the smaller man to stomp into the room. "We've just arrested one of the bank robbers," he said. "A fellow by the name of Chester Stone. He's drunk and was in the saloon, shooting it up. When we arrested him, we found a piece of the jewelry on him that was in the Castroville bank." Warner paused, darting a puzzled glance from Chase to Blake and back to Chase, then said, "He was also boasting about the South rising again, Major. Said something about an army sweeping up from Mexico. Thought you might want to question him."

Chase rose. "I do. Where is he?"

"At the ranger's headquarters."

"What are you going to do about me?" Blake asked.

"You'll go with me," Chase answered. "Consider yourself under arrest and in my custody from now on."

"First chance I get, I'll be on my way," Blake promised.

Chase laughed. "Not without the money. You're life wouldn't be worth the bullet it'll take Bainbridge to kill you with." He turned to the banker. "Mr. Fremont, put this money back in the safe and give me the receipt."

The man nodded and while he was sitting at the desk making the receipt, Chase turned to Elizabeth.

Catching her hands in his, he said, "Go on back to the saloon," he said. "I'll be there as soon as I question the prisoner. We have a lot to discuss."

"Chase, I'm sorry about not telling you about the money," she said.

"It's all right. We'll talk about it later," he said, pressing a finger against her lips. He couldn't be too angry at her, he thought. After all, he hadn't trusted her either. He'd ordered an investigation of her in New Orleans. "While I'm disappointed that you didn't confide in me, I understand." He lowered his voice and said, "I love you."

"I love you," she murmured, her eyes never straying from his face. "And from now on I'll trust you. I promise."

His hands lifted and he cupped her face. "I'll be back as soon as I can."

Elizabeth grinned. "Do you think I'll have time to do such a mundane chore as my washing?"

Chase returned the grin and nodded.

"If I'm not at the room, I'll be at Elena's doing the wash," she promised.

Tiptoeing, she kissed Chase chastely on the mouth before she slipped out of the bank. Walking toward the saloon, she surreptitiously looked toward the building where the man had been hunkered before. When she saw that he was gone, she drew in a breath of relief. Her steps hastened and she rushed through the saloon into her room. As she piled her soiled garments into the basket, she heard a knock on the door. When she opened it, she saw the unsavory char-

419

acter who had been shadowing her for the past few days.

"Miss Elizabeth Barrett?" the man asked.

"What do you want?" she demanded, refusing to answer his question or to open the door any wider than a crack. She felt extremely apprehensive of him, and from where she stood she could smell the whiskey on his breath. She was shaking with fright, but she outwardly remained poised.

"I'm Johnny Muskrat," he said, his eyes darting from the door to the corridor entrance. "I have a message for you from your sister."

Elizabeth's heart leaped at the announcement, but she kept her expression bland. Excitement somewhat diminished fear but not caution. "How do you know about my sister?" she asked.

"You been asking around for her," the man said, "and word got down to Mexico. She sent me up here to fetch you."

"How do I know that?" Elizabeth asked. "Do you have a note from her or any kind of identification."

The man grinned and reached into his shirt pocket to pull out a ragged piece of paper which he held out for her to see. *"La Mariposa,"* he said and pointed at the drawing.

Elizabeth stared at the butterfly. She wanted to believe him yet was afraid to. "Why have you waited so long to tell me?"

"She wanted to make sure you didn't bring that army major with you."

Of course, Elizabeth thought, Vanessa wouldn't

420

want Chase to know about her.

"Pack your things," Johnny said. "We need to leave right away. *La Mariposa's* buckboard is waiting on the other side of the border."

"Leave right now?" Elizabeth exclaimed. "I need some time to get ready. My clothes—" she looked at the basket on the floor.

"*La Mariposa* is very ill, ma'am. She wants you to come right away."

Remembering Vanessa's letter and the wispy scrawl, Elizabeth believed the man when he said Vanessa was ill, and she had no alternative but to believe him when he said she must come immediately. But she would not go without telling Chase first. He wouldn't want her to go, but she would. Neither he nor Blake had seemed interested in helping Vanessa. They were thinking only of getting Bainbridge.

"I'll go with you," she told Johnny, "but I won't leave without telling Major Daniel. You may return in thirty minutes and I'll be ready to go."

"No, ma'am." The Muskrat pulled his revolver from the holster and held it against her stomach to push her into the room. "I don't reckon I can let you do that." He forced her to sit down in the chair. "Don't make one sound, ma'am because I won't hesitate to shoot you. Wouldn't want to but I will."

Elizabeth heard footsteps thundering down the hall, then saw a shaggy head poking around the door frame.

"What's wrong?" He entered with a rope coiled around his arm.

"She was going to tell the major, Dalton," Johnny replied. "Shut the door and get in here and gag her."

"What about Chester?" the man asked as he picked up Gloria's night scarf from the small table by the bed and tied it over Elizabeth's mouth, the rough cloth biting into her tender flesh. She flinched but the man didn't care. "What about my brother?"

"We'll worry about him later," Johnny answered, the revolver still pointed at Elizabeth as a reminder. "Nothing's going to happen to him right now. He's worth more alive than dead to the major."

"I don't know that this was such a good idea," Dalton grumbled. "I wish the Colonel could of come up with another idea. It's dangerous Chester setting hisself up to get caught so's we could separate the major and the woman."

"Doesn't matter if this was a good idea or not," Johnny said. "The Colonel said do it. This little lady is what the Colonel wants, and she's what he's gonna get."

Tears burned Elizabeth eyes when the rope cut into her wrists, but she bit back any sound of pain.

"As soon as we get her tied up and in the wagon, we can find out what the Colonel wants us to do next. Then we can rescue Chester."

Elizabeth found the conversation strange but illuminating. The Colonel had sent for her, not Vanessa. What could Roswell Bainbridge want with her?

Chapter Twenty-five

"You're making a mistake, Major Daniel!" Leaning over Fremont's desk and bracing his weight on both palms, Evan Warner glared into Chase's face. His eyes were rounded, his face red with anger. "I don't care how much evidence is piled up against him, Blake Lowell ain't no outlaw. And you know it, too."

Not a trace of his inner thoughts revealed on his face, Chase reared back on the hind legs of the chair, folded his arms across his chest, and stared at the veteran ranger.

"Now I want to know what the hell is going on," Warner shouted and pointed at Blake. "I'm the one who dried him off behind the ears. I can't be closer to him if he was my own son."

"Evan, stay out of this," Blake said. Evan Warner was the closest thing to a family Blake had; he liked and trusted him, and he didn't want to involve the old man in his quest for revenge. Most of the time vendettas like this had only one ending.

"Hell, no! I'm not staying out of this, and I mean it, Blake," Evan warned, not caring that his voice thundered through the small office or carried into the outer lobby. "Ever since the war was over, you've had me going in circles, wondering about you and your sudden change of attitude. Running that saloon and whore house! It's high time you told me the truth. And you"—he wagged his index finger at Chase—"it's about time you Yankees started working with us Rangers. We're all a part of the same country. Ya'll was sure-fired determined to keep us, so let's start acting like it."

Chase grinned at Warner; then he looked at Blake. "I think you ought to tell him," he said.

Still Blake hesitated.

"I'm listening, Blake," Warner said, straddling his legs and folding his arms across his chest.

Blake shrugged and began to talk quietly, revealing to Evan what he had only recently told Chase about the atrocities his mother and sister had suffered at the hands of Bainbridge. Only his eyes communicated his hatred.

"I should of knowed it," Evan said when Blake concluded. "I should of knowed you was doing something about that piece of scum. Just wasn't like you Blake to be so disinterested." He clapped his arm around Blake's shoulder and hugged him.

"What can I do to help you, son?" he asked.

"Stay out of it," Blake repeated. "For God's sake, Evan, stay out of this. This is my battle not yours."

"Ain't no use trying to talk me out of it," Warner said and lifted his hand to his bandanna, the mere thought of Bainbridge causing his throat to hurt. "I want Bainbridge as much as you do. You should have told me a long time ago what you were doing and I would have joined you."

"I know," Blake sighed. "That's why I didn't tell you. I don't want you to die because of my quarrels."

"It's my quarrel, too," Warner told him, a certain tenderness beneath his gruff tones. "I wouldn't mind giving them a whole lot of what they gave me a little of."

Chase looked at Warner. "I'm going to arrest Blake for the Union payroll robbery and at least three counts of murder. The money is on deposit in this bank under the name of the U.S. Cavalry." He nodded his head toward the main lobby of the bank. "I would imagine I can count on Mr. Fremont to spread what he's seen and heard today."

Warner nodded his head. "That's for sure, but are you sure that's what you want to do? Word's bound to get back to—" Evan stopped talking when he realized Chase's plan. "You want this to get all over town, so it'll get back to Bainbridge."

"That I do, Mr. Warner." Chase walked to the

door and opened it. "Mr. Fremont," he called, and the young man came scurrying into the room, "I'll be back tomorrow morning to pick up the money and to take it back to San Antonio. Meanwhile I'll post some of my men to guard the bank through the night."

Relieved the burden of protection for that large a sum of money would be taken from his shoulder, Fremont nodded his head. "What about him, sir?" he asked and looked at Blake.

"He's under arrest. I'm taking him to the ranger's headquarter's right now."

Fremont watched the three men walk out, and as soon as the door closed behind them, he ran to the window to press his face against the pane. He followed their journey all the way to the two room adobe building down the street. Without looking at his watch, he rushed behind the counter to pick up his hat and coat. When they were on, he placed the closed sign in the window, pulled the shades, and went out, locking the door behind him.

He smiled to himself. He'd get quite a few free drinks tonight because he had a story worth telling, and he witnessed it first hand. He sashayed across the street, pushed open the door and entered the End-of-the-Line.

"Howdy, Butch," he called, lifting his hand in greeting. He nodded to the man standing in front of the bar. "Pete. Guess what happened over at the bank today!" His exclamation drew a curious crowd to circle him and with great flourish and a tolerable measure of exaggeration he told the tale of Blake Lowell's apprehension and subsequent arrest by Major Chase Daniel for the Union payroll robbery. "Why, right now," he said, lifting his mug of beer up to take a deep drag, "the major's locking him up."

"Hell, Fremont," Butch drawled as he leaned his head over the rusted bucket and spit, "that ain't nothing. One of them outlaws what hit the bank in Castroville showed up in here today and two rangers arrested him. They got him in jail, too."

His hands on his hips, Mason stood in the office at ranger's headquarters and stared through the door into the adjoining room where the cells were. "What's the great Captain Blake Lowell of the Texas Rangers doing in here?" he threw over his shoulder at Chase. Mason hadn't liked Blake from the minute he met him and was rather pleased to see him in jail. Maybe now Warner would quit thinking of him as being a god of some sort.

"Robbing the Union payroll and killing three soldiers," Chase answered. "Also he used an innocent woman to carry the stolen goods. Miss Barrett could easily have been implicated in this."

Griffin sat in the corner of the office with the

heel of his boots propped up on the edge of his desk and whittled. The pile of wood shavings, growing by the minute, was larger than the small tree branch that he held in his hand. His right hand dexterously snipped around the piece of wood, but as of yet no particular shape had emerged and none seemed to be forthcoming.

Chase threw the ring of keys over Griffin's legs onto the desk. "I reckon he could be Rod Everett's accomplice. If so, he's also responsible for the death of the two deputies and Everett himself. Probably a double cross."

"Gotta prove it first," Warner said, refusing to look into the other room where his protege was incarcerated. "Just a bunch of hot air as far as I'm concerned."

Mason rubbed his hands together with great delight. "We made quite a catch today, major. Probably find our name in the papers in the near future. I'm planning on starting for Castroville with Stone tomorrow. Heard there's a reporter there from the East. He should be interested in this story. Might even write a book about us. You want me to take Lowell with me?"

"Just might," Chase answered evasively, wanting a little more time to mull the situation and find the best solution. "In the meantime I'm going to question Mr. Stone. I have reason to believe he's working with an ex-Confederate colonel who's operating out of Mexico."

428

"Colonel Bainbridge!" Tony said the name with a reverent awe that didn't go unnoticed by Chase. The young man's eyes glittered with sudden interest and excitement. "He's really in Mexico."

"I think so," Chase replied, glad he'd decided not to trust anyone else but Warner. This pup was definitely in the traces of misguided patriotism, an easy prey for Bainbridge and his group.

"What are you going to do with Lowell?" Mason asked. He didn't fail to notice the searching glance Chase bestowed on Evan Warner.

"He'll stay here until tomorrow, then I'll take both him and the money back to San Antonio with me," Chase said as he walked into the other room and unlocked the cell. "Right now I want to talk with the prisoner. Mr. Stone" — Chase waved his hand toward the office — "if you'll come in here I have a few questions I want to ask you."

Grinning, the man stood and shuffled out of the cell. "I ain't never been one for too much talking," he said.

"Me, either," Chase answered, closing the door to the cell room. "So it shouldn't take us too long. Sit down over there. Now, gentlemen," Chase turned to the other rangers, "will you please step outside the building but don't leave in case our guest decides he doesn't like our hospitality and wants to leave. I'd like to talk with Mr. Stone in private."

When the two men were alone, Chase said,

"You're in a lot of trouble, Mr. Stone, but I can help you if you'll cooperate with me."

"You're wrong, major," Stone returned. "I ain't in no trouble. A feller sold me that necklace."

"What about the South rising again and sweeping up from Mexico."

"That's right, major, the South's gonna rise again," Stone said with a grin.

"Who are you working for?"

Stone dropped his head and started to crack the knuckles on his right hand, each snap sounding through the room louder than a clap of thunder.

"Bainbridge?" Chase asked.

Without looking up, Stone started popping the knuckles on his left hand.

"Why the bank robbery?"

Question after question Chase threw at the man, but Chester Stone remained impassive and silent. When he was through popping his knuckles, he cleaned his fingernails. Then he looked all around the room. Chase was not only furious; he was uneasy. The man was far too calm and assured, and Chase didn't judge him to be the serene type. His eyes were far too shifty.

When Chase returned Stone to the cell, he said to Blake, "Now it's your turn, Mr. Lowell." Once they were by themselves in the office, Chase asked, "Has he said anything to you?"

Blake leaned back in the chair and grinned. "Quite a bit but none that bears repeating and nothing important. You don't really expect anything worthwhile to flow from a mind like that, did you?"

Chase was in no mood for comedy. "Don't play games with me, Lowell."

Blake shrugged.

"Something worries me about Stone," Chase said. "He's acting much too cocky; he's too calm and assured. It's as if he's waiting for someone to come get him."

"Probably, because he's certainly not the calm type." Blake shifted in the chair and recounted for Chase his last encounter with the Stone brothers outside Castroville several hours after the holdup. "In fact, Chester's the one who shot me."

Sitting on the edge of Griffin's desk, Chase reached into his pocket for a cigar. After he lit it and took a few drags, he asked, "Why would Bainbridge order the Castroville bank to be robbed?"

"Didn't," Blake replied, making sure he kept his voice down so Stone couldn't overhear them. "Chester, his brother and the Muskrat work at the ranch on the American side. The ranch manager, Perry Anderson, is more interested in women than he is in controlling the men and seeing that they are gainfully employed on the ranch. He wasn't aware that the three of them had slipped off until much later. Bainbridge was furious when he found out. He doesn't want the U.S. Cavalry snooping

431

right now. He's waiting for a big shipment of weapons. That's what the Union payroll is for."

"And you would have given it to him?" Chase asked.

"I figured he'd be dead and couldn't do anything about it," Blake returned. "I might have brought the money back." He grinned again. "You never can tell."

"Reckon Bainbridge will rescue Stone?"

Blake shrugged. "About like he did Everett."

"Does Stone know Bainbridge?"

"No."

Unable to find the answers to his questions, Chase returned Blake to the cell a few minutes later and opened the front door to admit the rangers.

"Find out anything?" Mason asked.

"Nothing," Chase replied. "Give them some more time and they'll break."

"You're sure?"

"I'm sure," Chase replied. "I'm quite a professional when it comes to interrogation, Mr. Mason. I understand what makes men talk."

Mason hiked a brow and looked at Chase skeptically; Warner glowered, and Griffin resettled himself in the chair in front of the desk to begin his whittling again.

"Good afternoon, *señores!*" Isidor Moreno, wearing his sombrero and a colorful serape, stood at the door of the office, a hand on each side of the casement. "What are you having in here? A *fiesta?*"

"Nope," Griffin said. "Just a parley. Arrested us a couple of crooks."

Moreno's gaze swept over to the door that led to the cells.

"I'd invite you in," Griffin said, his knife never missing a lick on the wood, "but as you can see the office is overcrowded as it is. Even the cells are filled."

Isidor nodded his head vigorously, the broad brim of the sombrero waving through the air. "*Si, señor,* the room is indeed crowded. Thank you for the invitation, but I must be on my way. I have wagons of goods which I wish to load and get to San Antonio. I stopped by, Major Daniel, to tell you I have arranged for you to meet with Billy August, the Seminole Negro whom you saw yesterday. He will meet you sometime this afternoon at your camp."

"Do I need an interpreter?" Chase asked. "He wouldn't talk to me yesterday."

Moreno grinned and shook his head. "He speaks English fluently, Major. Yesterday he had no desire to meet you. Today he has great curiosity and will be willing to converse with you."

"Thank you, *Señor* Moreno," Chase said.

"You have been busy today, yes?"

"I have been busy today, yes," Chase answered. "I have reason to believe, *señor*, these men are

433

working for Bainbridge out of Mexico."

Moreno lowered his lids until his eyes were mere slits, their expression skillfully hidden. He ducked his head so that the brim of his hat shadowed the lower part of his face and concealed it from observation also. "You insist on believing this man is in my country, *señor*, but I think you are wrong. Now I go. Remember, Billy August will meet you this afternoon at the ruins of Ft. Duncan." He stepped back, the serape billowing around his lithe body.

"Mr. Griffin, I'll send some of my troopers back to help you guard the prisoners," Chase said. "Until then I'll have to count on you."

"It's my job, major," Griffin answered, "and so far I've done it pretty good." He leaned forward and swung his legs through the air. By the time the chair thumped heavily to the floor, the ranger was on his feet. "Do you want one of us to stay at the bank?"

Chase nodded. "I'd appreciate that, too."

"Warner." Griffin barked the order in one word.

"Nolan," Warner said, "you ain't gonna let the major keep Blake in jail, are you?"

"Ain't much I can do about it," Griffin returned. "The major came by earlier today and told me about the money. He caught Blake with it fair and square."

Griffin walked to the window and spit his cud of tobacco out. He returned to the drinking pail,

434

picked up the dipper and took a swallow of water which he sloshed around in his mouth. After he spewed this through the window, he dropped the dipper into the bucket with a splash.

" 'Sides, Evan," Griffin continued, "Blake implicated the little lady, Miss Barrett. That don't sit none too well with me. Tell you what, I'll send you to San Antone with them to make sure he gets a fair trial."

"Ain't no such thing as a fair trial with them Yankee soldiers and carpetbaggers in power," Warner complained.

"I'll guarantee that he'll get a fair trial," Chase said.

"Like I said," Warner repeated, walking out of the room onto the boardwalk, "with them Yankee soldiers and carpetbaggers in power, there ain't so such a thing as a fair trial."

Chase stepped out of the building behind Warner and Mason followed to lounge in the opened door. After the veteran ranger was out of hearing distance, Mason said, "Don't mind Evan, major. He and Blake are friends from way back."

"Yeah," Chase drawled, then tossed over his shoulder, "Mr. Griffin, if you need me, you'll find me at the camp with my men."

Griffin kicked through the shavings and settled back down in his chair with knife and diminishing piece of wood. "All right, Major."

Chase walked over to Elena's, but the restaurant

was closed. He walked around to the back entrance, but the women were nowhere to be found. Thinking Elizabeth may have returned to her room, he headed for the saloon. She wasn't there either. Standing in the door, he gave the room a cursory sweep. The shutters were open and sunshine poured in. Gloria was atop his perch, preening himself. The basket of soiled clothes was still there, but Elizabeth's reticule and parasol were gone. She had taken the time to clean off the dresser, Chase observed, because nothing was on it except the tin holder; lying beside it was the new candle. No telling where Elizabeth and Elena were, and he didn't have the time to hunt them. Disappointed, he turned and walked down the hall.

When he reentered the saloon, Butch called, "Howdy, Major. Got a letter for you. Looks mighty important. Arrived by stage a few minutes ago."

"Thanks," Chase said and moved toward the counter. "Do you know where Miss Barrett is?"

"No, sir," Butch answered, "I sure don't. I haven't seen her since she came in about mid-day. Guess she went out without me seeing her."

"What about Jefferson?"

"He's out running some errands for me, Major. He should be back directly. Want me to send him to you?"

"No," Chase answered, opening the envelope. "I just thought he might know where Elizabeth was."

"Don't reckon so. He's been out most all day."

Chase pulled out the letter, excitement rushing through him when he saw that it was Jack Stevens' report on Elizabeth. The first page was a repeat of the story she had told him about Watkins attempt to rape her and the murder of her brother.

But there was more! A military tribunal under the authority of General Butler, acquitted Major Emery Watkins and branded Elizabeth a whore. Watkins had been transferred, but further investigation revealed that he indeed raped and killed a woman at his new post. Before he could be arrested and tried for murder, he deserted the army. As a result of the report on Watkins that was filed in New Orleans, the new military government of the state reviewed Elizabeth's file and cleared her of all charges.

"Good news?" Butch asked, observing the changing expressions on Chase's face.

"Very good," Chase replied, folding the letter and inserting it into his pocket. "When Miss Barrett returns, tell her that I'm at Ft. Duncan. I'll be back as soon as I can."

Butch bobbed his head. "Sure will, Major. Heard tell you arrested Blake Lowell."

"You heard right."

"What'cha gonna do with him?"

"Take him back to San Antonio and turn him over to the proper military authorities for trial," Chase returned.

"What about the money he stole?"

"That goes back, too."

"Sure had a lot going on today," Butch said, shaking his head. "Lowell arrested for stealing the Union payroll, and Stone for robbing the Castroville bank. Makes a body tired just thinking about it."

"Reckon so," Chase replied absently, already moving toward the door.

When he arrived in camp, Chase sent two troopers to the bank and two to the ranger station as guards. Then Chase went into his tent and wrote Jack a letter of thanks for his investigative report on Elizabeth, then turned his attention to his paperwork. Ever so often he would stand and walk outside the tent to scan the horizon in search of the Seminole Negro. Time after time he returned to his desk and the papers. When he was through, the sun was dipping low in the west. He stood and stretched, then moved outside the tent to watch the men as they prepared supper.

He despaired of seeing the Seminole Negro when he heard one of the troopers shout, "Somebody's coming."

Chase saw two riders approaching their camp. The large sombrero announced one of the visitors as Isidor Moreno. Chase assumed, and correctly so, that the other was Billy August. He walked to the edge of the camp to meet them.

The two men dismounted, and the Mexican

spoke. "Major Daniel, this is Billy August."

"Thank you for coming, Mr. August," Chase said and extended his hand.

This time the Seminole Negro grasped and shook it. "What have you to say to Billy August, Major?"

"I would like to hire some of your people to be guides for our troops," Chase answered. "Before we talk, may I offer you some supper?" he asked.

The Seminole Negro nodded, and he and Moreno followed Chase to the campfire. After they ate, they lingered over a second cup of coffee and listened to Corporal Man play several songs on his harmonica for them.

"You ask me and my men to be scouts for your government?" August asked.

"Yes," Chase answered. "I am."

Billy's eyes shadowed. "My people do not feel kindly toward Americans."

"I'm sorry about the past," Chase said. "I would have it different, but I have no power to restore your lands or to change history. I do want to hire several of you to be scouts for me and my men. I have heard that you know this country as well as you know the back of your hand."

"Perhaps better," August agreed. "I look at it much more than I do my hand." He closed his eyes and sat quietly for a long time, then said, "I must consider all you have said, Major Daniel, before I make my decision." After another long period of silence, he rose. "I go now. I will return."

"I am leaving to take my prisoner to San Antonio in the morning," Chase said.

"I will find you," August said and walked to his horse and mounted.

"Thank you for the supper, *señor*," Isidor said, swinging his sombrero on his head. "I will be leaving now. I must get my wagons to San Antonio."

"You're welcome to travel with us," Chase said.

Isidor shook his head. "I think not, *señor*. I will be safer by myself than with you. The goods which you are carrying are much too tempting to thieves and bandits."

"You know something," Chase said.

Isidor's hand slipped beneath the folds of his serape and he withdrew a dagger. "Do not move, *señor*," he ordered quietly. His arms whipped up, his hand poised, and the knife whined through the wind to hit the earth with a discernible thud. Chase turned to see a writhing rattle snake.

Moreno walked over and picked up his knife. He ran both sides of the blade against the sole of his boot and cleaned off the blood. "I have never learned to use the revolver," he said, holding the dagger up. "This is my weapon, *señor*. Unlike a gun that barks and announces my presence to the whole world, my knife is silent and swift. She betrays me to no one." He slipped his hand beneath the serape.

"Who are you Moreno?" Chase asked. The way the man handled a knife was more than impressive; it was startling and deadly and called to mind the murders of Addison and Thurman.

"I am a trader, *señor,*" Moreno answered simply. "I trade whatever I can to make money. Also I am a smart man who has learned to protect himself. I deal with men who would slit your throat without thinking twice." He smiled. "Now I return to town. Thank you for your hospitality."

Night had fallen by the time Chase returned to Eagle Pass. When he rode down Main Street, he gave the ranger's station a swift glance. Light spilled out the window onto the boardwalk. Sitting inside the building was Private Joseph Jacob Lincoln. Chase smiled; he really liked that boy. He was a fine soldier.

As he drew abreast the bank Chase was again assailed by troubled thoughts. Innately, he knew Bainbridge would come after the money. Already six men—at least—had been killed for it; a few more wouldn't make any difference. Chase only wondered when the colonel would strike. Like Blake, Chase had his doubts that Bainbridge would rescue Stone. People were expendable and easily replaced. Money wasn't.

Chase stopped outside the saloon and tied his horse to the hitching post. When he walked in, he waved at Butch who shook his head and shouted, "Miss Barrett ain't been in since you left, Major."

Nodding his head, Chase retraced his steps and headed for the restaurant. Elizabeth had to be with Elena. When two women get together and start talking, they lose all count of time. He peered through the window but didn't see either woman. Opening the door, he entered as Elena came out of the kitchen.

"Chase," she called, "how nice to see you. Where's Elizabeth?"

"I thought you could tell me," he answered. He was getting worried, and something didn't feel right. He remembered how neat the room had looked when he checked on her earlier. Nothing out of place. "I haven't seen her since early afternoon."

Elena was shaking her head. "I haven't seen her since last night."

"She was going to come over and do her washing." Chase remembered how naked the dresser looked without her brushes and hand mirror and ribbons.

"Not today," Elena said.

Chase turned and rushed back to the saloon, down the hall, and into Elizabeth's room. He fumbled on the dresser until he found a match. With shaking hands he picked up the candle and set it in the holder, then lit it. His eyes quickly surveyed the room. Now he knew what was wrong. Her portmanteau was missing. Elizabeth was gone.

"Major," Warner's footsteps thundered down the

442

hall, "come quick."

The anxiety in the man's voice caused Chase to spin around.

"The ranger's station. Stone's escaped."

The two men ran out of the room, Chase quickly out-distancing the older man. When he arrived, Corporal Man was sitting with a faraway look in his eyes. Two cups of coffee sat on the desk in front of him.

"What happened?" Chase demanded.

"Me and Joe wanted some coffee real bad, sir, so I went to the saloon to get us some," the corporal said dully. "I wasn't gone more than fifteen minutes, sir, and when I returned I found this. Joe, he was lying here in a pool of blood. Dead, sir."

"What about Lowell?" Chase demanded and knelt beside the body of the private.

"I'm all right," Blake called from the other room. "They weren't inclined to release me and didn't kill me for some reason. They just gave me a good tap on the head that knocked me out for a few minutes."

"Who was it?" Chase asked.

"They wore bandannas over their faces, but from the smell of them, I'd say it was Chester and The Muskrat."

When Chase caught Private Lincoln's shoulders and turned him over, he saw the horrible slash running from one side of his neck to the other.

Pinned to his chest with a gold filigree brooch in the shape of a rose was a note. With hands he could hardly keep from shaking Chase unfolded the note.

At the moment Elizabeth Barrett is alive. If you wish her to remain so, you will send Blake Lowell to Colonel Roswell Bainbridge with the union payroll money. Lowell knows the meeting point.

Fear gripped Chase's heart with a strangling hold as he crumpled the note in one hand and looked at the rose brooch that lay in the palm of the other. Bainbridge had been close enough to Eagle Pass that he knew what was going on. When he learned Blake had been arrested and the money was taken into custody by the U.S. Cavalry, he had used Stone as a decoy to get Chase away from Elizabeth. She was being held hostage for the money, and Blake had been left in jail so he could be the intermediary. Chase swore softly. Elizabeth wasn't safe with a man like Bainbridge, and he didn't trust him to keep his word to free her once he received the money.

Chase dropped his hand to his side and stared at the dead body of his trooper—Private Joseph Jacob Lincoln. He remembered the day the boy had chosen his name.

"I choose Joseph for my first name, sir"—his lips curled back in a full smile, and the black eyes glittered like polished ebony—"because he was sold into bondage but got his freedom and rose up to

444

be second only to the king. And I choose Jacob for my middle name because he made many mistakes but he never forgot his goal; he got that birthright." The eyes had twinkled. "And Lincoln suits me just fine for my last name, sir, cause Abraham Lincoln is the man what set us free, sir."

Chase reached down to pick up his cap and lay it over the trooper's face. The boy had attained part of his goal; he had tasted freedom and could hold his head high as a free man — a man who was willing to put his life on the line for people who didn't appreciate his services.

"I'm sorry, sir," Corporal Man said. "I didn't —"

Chase shook his head as he stood. "It's not your fault. Probably you're being gone saved your life. I figure the killer was someone the private knew and had no reason to fear. Otherwise, he wouldn't have gotten into the room. Go to the saloon and get a blanket to wrap his body in and take him back to camp for burial. Tell Sgt. Liberty I want the guard doubled at the bank as soon as you've buried the body."

"I'll tell him, sir," Corporal Man said and turned to rush up the street to the End-of-the-Line.

"You can leave if you want to," Chase said to Warner. "I'll stay here with Blake. We're not going to have any more action tonight."

"I don't mind staying," Warner said.

Chase shook his head. "I'm not going to be doing any sleeping any way."

445

Warner shrugged. "I'll be at the bank if you need me."

Chase picked up the keys from Griffin's desk and walked into the room where Blake was jailed. He unlocked the door and threw it open. "The same man who murdered Addison and Thurman murdered my soldier." The weight of all the world settling heavily on his shoulders, he handed Blake the note. "Bainbridge outsmarted me. Stone was a decoy to get my attention off Elizabeth and he could snatch her."

Blake read Bainbridge's message and lifted his head. "Looks like I'll be going after Bainbridge after all."

"We'll go together."

"You can't."

"I can," Chase vowed, "and I am."

"How long will it take you to get it cleared?"

"Never, so I'm not going to ask."

"Do you have a plan?"

Chase shook his head. "I thought I'd let you help me. You know more about the Bainbridge Brigade than I do."

Blake held his hand out and Chase gripped it. A kinship, stronger than any blood binding, was born between the two men as they looked deeply and thoughtfully into one another's eyes.

"And I'll give you fair warning," Chase said, "if you find Bainbridge first you'd better kill him because if I see him first I promise you I'll kill him."

A shadow fell across the cell and Chase turned to see Billy August who had entered so quietly neither Chase nor Blake knew he was there. "I am sorry about the death of your trooper," the Seminole Negro said. "I have come to tell you that I will ride with you and your men. Do you wish me to track the man who killed the young soldier?"

"No," Chase answered, "I want you to lead us to the *La Mariposa* Hacienda in Mexico. Do you know where it is?"

Billy nodded.

"Good," Chase said.

"I also know where the *Americanos* have built a fort to store weapons—many weapons," Billy quietly added. "These men have been coming to *Mejico* since the ending of the War Between the States."

Dumbfounded, Chase stared at the Seminole Negro for a full minute before he said incredulously, "You know where the arsenal is?" Chase whirled to Blake. "You know what this means?" Blake hadn't nodded his head before Chase strode into the office and searched through Griffin's desk for paper and pencil. Sitting at the desk, the only sound in the building the scratch of lead on paper, Chase said, "Take this to Ranger Warner at the bank. Tell him to get me all these supplies and to load them on mules. Be ready to pull out in one hour."

Looking over Chase's shoulder at the growing

list, Blake said, "It looks like we're waging war, Major."

"We are, Captain Lowell. We are indeed." Turning to the corporal, Chase said, "Take care of Private Lincoln's body and burial. Also go by the saloon and get Jefferson. I want him in camp with you at all times."

Ten minutes later the three men walked out of the adobe building. Billy August moved to the bank; Chase and Blake mounted their horses and headed for the camp at Ft. Duncan. The ride was silent as each man retreated into his own personal thoughts.

Often Chase had known fear . . . an emotion he learned to harness and to use to his best advantage; it had become of his most prized weapons because he had a firm grip on it. Now he'd lost his grip and fear had caught hold of him.

He knew he could face life without Elizabeth, but he didn't want to.

Chapter Twenty-six

The elderly maid inserted the last pin in Elizabeth's hair and stepped back to allow her to admire herself in front of the full length glided mirror. While Trinidad was totally indifferent to the *Americana,* she had to admit she was beautiful now that she was no longer the tangled mess she was when she had been brought to the hacienda earlier in the day.

Elizabeth's hair was brushed into an elegant chignon of curls atop her head. The bodice of her gown, forest green satin, was cut low and tight to reveal the fullness of her breasts and to emphasize the smallness of her waist. Her tiara, necklace and earrings were exquisite clusters of emeralds and diamonds, designed by a master craftsman — all gifts of *El Patron.*

Yes, Trinidad thought, as she withdrew from the room and locked to door, *El Patron* would like this young beauty. Down the hall the woman

449

walked until she stopped in front of another door. She unlocked it and stepped inside. The reds and blacks were bold and aggressive. She looked at the flimsy black undergarments — especially made for *El Patron's* pleasure — lying on the red satin bedspread. Beside them lay *El Patron's* whip, black leather with small, sharp slivers of gold woven into the strand. On the dresser was the rope and the silver chain. Satisfied that everything was prepared according to his instructions, Trinidad departed, careful to lock the door behind her.

Elizabeth, unable to appreciate her appearance for thinking of her imprisonment, walked to the barred window to peer into the patio below. She had been at the hacienda all day, locked in this room on the second floor, seeing no one but Trinidad, talking to no one but herself for the most part.

Earlier when she had questioned Trinidad about Vanessa, the old woman looked at her with lackluster black eyes that saw everything but recalled having seen nothing.

"I do not know a *Señora* Vanessa," Trinidad replied in her heavily accented English. "Tonight at dinner you will meet *El Patron*. You can ask him your questions. He will have the answers."

From that day so many months ago when she received Vanessa's strange letter, Elizabeth had been plagued with questions, their number increasing by the day. Unceasingly and diligently she searched for the answers. Now that she was so

450

close to finding them she was frightened, probably more frightened than she had ever been before in her life. She was afraid of the colonel, but more she was afraid the answers she would learn to her questions and doubts about Vanessa were not those which she wished to hear.

She twined her fingers together nervously and wondered what fate awaited her when she joined Colonel Roswell Irwin Bainbridge for dinner tonight. An anxious shudder racked her small body. Someone had told her that he had a penchant for lovely young women. She didn't dare think about it. She wished Chase were here. How she needed him. He would come and get her. She knew he would . . . what if he couldn't find her?

She refused to give way to such negative thoughts. She squeezed her eyes tightly together and dammed the tears that threatened to overflow. Crying wouldn't help; it would only worsen the situation. She had learned never to let the enemy see her vanquished. Conquered, yes. Vanquished, never! Breathing deeply and slowly, she straightened her shoulders. Yet, when she heard the key grate in the lock, her heart skipped a beat and her body grew clammy. She had to hold her hands together to keep them from shaking.

The door opened and Trinidad entered. "Come with me. *El Patron* is waiting."

Elizabeth turned and slowly walked to the dresser to pick up her ecru lace gloves. She put on one, taking her time to straighten the seams and smooth the wrinkles; then she put on the other, taking as much time and care as with the first. She saw the frown dig deeper into the old woman's forehead, but she didn't rush her movements. She lifted her ivory and gold fan and swirled it in her hand, fanning her face delicately as Mama had taught her.

"I'm ready," she announced with a smile as if she had not a care in the world and swept out of the room ahead of Trinidad.

She moved down the hall but stopped at the landing of the circular staircase to await the servant. Trinidad led her down the stairs through several large rooms into an elegant salon, richly decorated with furniture more Continental in design than Spanish or Mexican. Numerous candelabrum graced the room, casting their brilliant light into every corner and giving a false sense of gaiety, but behind the facade Elizabeth felt darkness and evil lurking.

She jumped when the door slammed and she was left alone. For minutes that seemed more like hours she stood in the middle of the room, staring at the painting that hung over the fireplace. Vanessa. Slowly Elizabeth advanced until she could read the caption on the gold frame. *La Mariposa*. Beside it was the engraving of a tiny butterfly. In her maturity Vanessa was startlingly beautiful. The hair was yet so brown as to be black and the eyes were a vibrant green . . . but they were cool and aloof.

When the door opened, Elizabeth didn't turn. She didn't have to; she knew who entered. *El Patron.* But knowing that Bainbridge was the one who entered didn't keep her heart from racing. She listened to the marked, decidedly military cadence of the footfalls that grew louder and nearer. Finally Elizabeth could stand the suspense no longer; the time to turn was now. She would look Colonel Roswell Irwin Bainbridge straight in the face. She whirled about, her gaze fastening on the man. Her eyes widened in disbelief. She was living in a nightmare.

"Watkins," she whispered. So fast did the room spin about her, she thought she would faint.

"Hello, Elizabeth."

But Elizabeth didn't faint. She didn't even swoon. She cringed when the nauseating nasal whine grated across her overly exposed nerves, and the color seeped from her face. Inundated with feelings long repressed, she inwardly shrank from the man, but outwardly she remained poised and calm. She fought the waves of nausea that threatened to make her vomit. She was no longer an innocent young woman in the throes of grief over the death of her family and the loss of her wealth, and she wouldn't act like one. She was a woman filled with loathing and hatred for the man standing in front of her.

Watkins rubbed his hand across the gray waistcoat that stretched over his protruding stomach, and his watery eyes attached themselves to the creamy skin of her breasts. "You're surprised to see me?"

He started to take another step but his eyes caught hers, and he saw the fire of anger burning in them. He could see the challenge in her stance and her demeanor. His hand fidgeted with the buttons on his waistcoat as he contemplated his next action, but he remained where he was.

"What are you doing here?" Elizabeth asked.

Watkins was a little disturbed by this new Elizabeth. She was more confident and authoritative than the younger one had been. She was sure of herself. He should have expected her to change, but still it surprised him. Her straight forward question disconcerted him; he had expected fear, shock, surprise, anything but this calm defiance.

"I'm sure you're wondering about Vanessa," he said.

"You're certainly not adept at mind reading," Elizabeth said, delicately fanning her face, "or you would know that I'm thinking about the question I asked you. Had I wanted to know about Vanessa I would have asked."

Elizabeth spoke with far more assurance than she felt, and she lied. She did want to know about Vanessa, but she would never let this miserable excuse for a person know her true thoughts.

Disconcerted, Watkins clasped his hands behind his back and walked the width of the room to a large table where he poured himself a glass of whiskey from a crystal decanter. "Would you care for a drink?" he asked.

"No."

He took several swallows before he turned around to face her again. The whiskey gave him a certain amount of bravado. "Vanessa is away on a trip," he said. "You'll see her as soon as she returns."

"Why are you here?" Elizabeth repeated, deliberately refusing to recognize him by addressing him by name.

Watkins took another gulp of whiskey and swallowed. "I'm here, Elizabeth, because the army didn't appreciate or understand me and we parted ways. Through — through a friend of mine I met Bainbridge and we found that although we're from different parts of the country, each of us has the same cause."

"Greed," Elizabeth said.

Watkins' weak eyes cut in her direction. He didn't like this Elizabeth at all. He would have to show her who was the master and who was the slave. With her golden coloring she would look lovely in red and black, he thought. He could see her most intimate secrets revealed through frothy undergarments. Her creamy buttocks beneath his touch, whip marks across them that he could kiss and caress. His loins tightened at the thought. He would have a most pleasurable time tonight. Trinidad had assured him the room was ready.

"To some," he said, resuming the thread of conversation, "I guess our cause is greed. As you can see, our relationship has been quite profitable and promises even more."

The pale blue eyes circled the room, visually caressing each material possession, before they returned to rest on Elizabeth.

"Now I have you . . . and I have always meant to have your virginal beauty. It's taken a lot of time and a lot of planning, but it's come to pass, and nothing is going to stop me from taking you this time, my dear, in my own way . . . ways." Heat rushed through his body to settle in his groin.

Elizabeth was shaking so badly inside she felt as if she couldn't remain standing, but she locked her knees and willed herself to stand in front of this repugnant man. All the hatred she had ever felt for him resurfaced with tidal proportions to sweep through her and to give her renewed strength and courage. She remembered her promise to the man, and she would keep it. This time she would kill him.

"I'm no longer a virgin," she announced and tilted her chin.

"I was afraid of that," Watkins sighed, "and while I'm sorry that I shan't be the first, I'll still enjoy taking you."

"I'll have something to say about that," Elizabeth said.

"No," Emery returned, setting the empty glass on the silver tray beside the decanter so he could reach into his pocket for a handkerchief. "You're the slave, Elizabeth, I'm the master.   n *El Patron* around here, and the sooner you learn that the better you'll be."

"I thought Bainbridge was *El Patron*."

"Not here," Watkins said and slapped his handkerchief through the air. "This part of the estate is mine. Bainbridge stays at the garrison most of the time, making love to his arsenal." Watkins smiled and cupped his belly with both hands. "I stay here and make love to," he smiled, "to people."

Looking him straight in the eye, Elizabeth said, "You may call yourself *El Patron*, but I'll never be your slave, and I'll never consider you *El Patron*. The first opportunity I have, I'll kill you."

"Ah, yes," Emery said, dabbing at his watering eyes, "you did promise to kill me, didn't you. But I think not. You see, the servants in this house are my servants, Elizabeth. Since I have been here, I've made sure that their loyalty belongs only to me. Not Bainbridge. Not Vanessa. But me. They do my bidding. Without me they have no *dinero*. They live a comfortable life here and won't give it up for a woman who's destined for the whore houses of Mexico . . . unless she pleases me enough that I'll keep her. If she pleases me, when I tire of her I'll see that she's well placed." He slowly, menacingly walked toward her.

A contemptuous smile on Elizabeth's lips stopped him dead in his tracks.

"I'd take the worst whore house in the world before I'd give you pleasure."

"You'll regret this," Watkins hissed, his entire body shaking from anger. "You'll regret that you ever spoke to me like this." He didn't come any closer to her, but he pointed a pudgy finger at her. "And I will have my pleasure."

The door swept open and both Elizabeth and Emery looked up to see Vanessa standing defiantly in the door in her riding habit, her crop to her side, her dark hair flowing unrestricted down her back. For an instant she and Elizabeth looked at one another. While Elizabeth's thoughts were mirrored in her face for her younger sister to read, Vanessa's face seemed to be etched in stone.

Not so her spirit. Vanessa had never been so glad to see anyone in her life as she was to see Elizabeth. Fear for her sister's safety kept her demeanor cool and aloof. When she had written that letter to Elizabeth, Vanessa had thought she was dying and she wanted to make restitution with Elizabeth; perhaps she had been making an unconscious plea for her sister to find her. Rod had tried to reason with her, but Vanessa wouldn't listen. Later she had realized the stupidity of her action. Now because of her Elizabeth was implicated in this mess.

Vanessa knew that Roswell and Watkins had an ulterior motive for bringing Elizabeth here. They didn't have her best interests or happiness at heart. The only way she could defend her sister was to pretend no interest at all, and this was a difficult task for Vanessa when she looked into Elizabeth's face to see love and warmth and finally puzzlement and question.

Out of the corner of her eye Vanessa saw Watkins watching her, and she smiled coolly at Elizabeth and lowered in invisible shield over her eyes. Vanessa's green eyes, frosty with anger, quickly moved from Elizabeth to Watkins.

"After all I've done for you, how could you do this to me?" she accused. "I'm the one who talked Roswell into letting you join our organization, and you promised that you'd never reveal my identity and that you'd leave Elizabeth alone. Dear God, Emery, have you forgotten how large Elizabeth's conscience is? She'll be nothing but trouble for all of us."

Elizabeth recoiled from the lash of Vanessa's words. This wasn't her sister. This was a cold and hard woman. Elizabeth understood what Roderick had tried to tell her that day at the Bat Cave. The Vanessa she knew was gone.

"For the most part, I kept my word," Watkins said. "I did tell Roswell who you were, but I didn't contact Elizabeth. I most assuredly didn't involve her. You did, my dear, when you sent her that letter. Of course, when I intercepted it, I could have refused to let Roderick mail it, but I didn't. You see, I was quite ready for Elizabeth to come join us."

He lifted his hand and brushed his fingers through the hair at his temples. "In fact, you're responsible for Roderick's death also. Roswell and

I decided to eliminate him when we learned that he had a greater loyalty for you than for us. You were getting out of control, and we thought we needed some leverage."

"Let Elizabeth go, Emery," Vanessa said. "You have no reason to keep her."

"Contrary to what you think," Emery said, "I have every reason to keep her. I intend to make her my mistress."

Vanessa's face blanched. "No, you can't," she whispered in shock. Her hand against her breast she backed up. "I'll tell Roswell," she said. "He won't let you do this to her."

Watkins laughed. "Roswell needs me far more than he needs you. Mistresses are easy to come by, not soldiers, not men who are dedicated to their cause and willing to do anything to see it espoused by all, and I, dear Mariposa, am the one responsible for getting the weapons Roswell needs for his campaign."

"I'll kill you," she threatened, her eyes blazing.

"I doubt it," Watkins said, not in the least terrified of her. "Besides your sister has already promised herself that pleasure."

"Good evening, Emery," a strange masculine voice said from the door way.

Elizabeth looked up to see a slender man in his early fifties enter the salon. Tall, suave, and well dressed, he carried himself like a gentleman. His reddish-brown hair was combed straight back from his face and brushed the collar of his camel-colored coat. His full moustache, the same color as his hair, drooped over the corners of his mouth and gave his lips a sensuousness they would have otherwise lacked. He smiled and moved in Elizabeth's direction.

"You must be Mariposa's sister," he said and bowed deeply. "I'm Colonel Bainbridge. I'm so glad to make your acquaintance."

"Why did you bring me here?" With one question Elizabeth brushed the amenities aside.

Roswell's eyes narrowed, but the smile never left his lips. "You're rather like your sister." He looked at Watkins and said, "Pour me a glass of whiskey."

To Elizabeth he said, "I really didn't intend to involve you in this, but Mariposa was getting ideas of her own. She was getting greedy and wanted more than her share of the spoils. Watkins and I decided that you were the answer. And you fit into our plans . . . even more so when I learned that Blake Lowell had been arrested and the Union payroll was in the custody of the U.S. Cavalry. You see, my source in Eagle Pass tells me that you and the Major are—" He furrowed his brow in pretended thought. "How shall we say it? You are quite friendly." He took the drink Watkins handed to him. "You are going to be my guest until Major Daniel gives me the Union payroll."

Elizabeth stared at Bainbridge in stunned silence, his words slowly sinking in. He and Watkins expected Major Chase Daniel to give them the Union payroll in exchange for her! Finally she

461

started to laugh, the sound more hysterical than humorous. Vanessa, worried about her sister, ran to the liquor table and filled a glass with brandy. Then she rushed to Elizabeth.

"Drink this," she ordered coldly, masking her concern, and held it up to Elizabeth's mouth. "I don't want you to make a fool of yourself in front of everyone."

Elizabeth coughed as she swallowed the fiery liquid. She wiped a drop of the brandy from her lips and looked at Bainbridge. "You've underestimated the major," she finally said, her voice raspy from the liquor. "He's not an Emery Watkins, Colonel, or a Roderick Everett. He goes by the book, strictly by the letter of the law." Elizabeth was pleased to see the glimmer of worry enter the colonel's eyes.

"You're saying the major doesn't love you?" he parried.

Elizabeth had regained her aplomb now. "Whatever the major's feelings are," she said, "they are not so great that he would go against the government he serves. To him duty and honor are the greatest of virtues."

Bainbridge sighed deeply and took a swallow of his drink. "I've seen men like that," he finally said, walking around the room and stopping at a far window, his back to Elizabeth. He looked at her over his shoulder. "It's a shame, my dear. I guess I'll have to send him another note and be more graphic of the consequences should he not

462

give me the money."

Trinidad appeared at the door. "Dinner is served."

"We'll finish our discussion later," Watkins said. "Come now, let us eat."

Now that Bainbridge was here, Watkins felt braver. He moved to Elizabeth's side and cupped her elbow with his hand. When she jerked away from his touch, he grimaced and silently promised retribution. For now, he only smiled.

Elizabeth sat at the table but she couldn't eat a bit of food. She wondered about the graphic consequences Bainbridge promised as she listened to the men indulge in banal conversation as if nothing were amiss or different. Vanessa sat across from Elizabeth, but her expression was closed. She talked only when spoken to.

Elizabeth had ceased to be afraid for herself. She had decided that nothing could be worse than becoming Watkins' mistress. Now she was preoccupied with escaping and was worried about Chase. She had lied to Roswell. She knew full well that Chase would try to rescue her. She had no doubt that he would give the money in exchange for her and suffer the consequences. Perhaps mouthing the words of love had been difficult for Chase, but he had accepted her with his heart and that was a deeper commitment than mere words. That he would come she never doubted. The greeting he would receive when he came terrified her.

Over her wine glass she looked at Vanessa and

wondered what kind of person she had become. She had always been self-centered, but this woman seemed to be totally unfeeling. Not once had she given Elizabeth more than a cursory glance. She allowed no emotion to show on her face or in her eyes. Elizabeth doubted Vanessa would help her escape or that she would send word to Chase to tell him where she was or to warn him about Bainbridge and Watkins.

Before dinner was over, Trinidad entered the room and whispered something in Roswell's ear. He nodded and stood. "Ladies, you'll have to excuse us. Emery and I have some business to attend to. Our source has arrived with some news. Mariposa, I'm going to let you visit with your sister in her room for awhile."

Vanessa looked at Elizabeth and shrugged her shoulders. "I would rather be with you."

Roswell reached out and touched her chin with his fingers. "Thank you, sweet," he replied, "but not tonight."

"You used to include me in all your plans," Vanessa pouted.

"That was before you and Everett tried to double-cross me," Roswell answered. "I still enjoy your body, but I don't trust you." He turned to Trinidad and said, "Take them to Elizabeth's room."

"Do I lock the door?" the servant asked.

"No," Roswell answered and looked directly at Elizabeth. "Guards are posted all around the house. Their orders are to shoot first and ask questions later. That includes any of us who venture out. Need I say more?"

Neither Elizabeth nor Vanessa answered as they followed Trinidad out of the dining room through the salon and up to the room where Elizabeth was staying. Elizabeth moved to the dresser and laid her fan down; then she took off her gloves. Through the mirror she studied her sister who leaned back against the door. The silence was long and heavy.

Finally Vanessa said, "I guess you're wondering why I treated you so coldly down there?"

"Yes, I am."

Vanessa's eyes glittered with tears, and her voice broke when she cried, "Oh, Elizabeth, I'm so glad you're here, but I'm so frightened for you." She rushed across the room and threw herself into her sister's arms. "I shouldn't have sent that letter, but I was so sick. I thought I was dying. I was sure Roswell was poisoning me." Tears ran down her cheeks. "I didn't mean to get you involved in this."

Elizabeth held Vanessa close. "You didn't. I came because I wanted to."

Vanessa pulled back and said, "Johnny. How is he?"

Elizabeth led Vanessa to the sofa and the two of them sat down as Elizabeth quietly told her about Watkins and of Johnny's death, and she talked about The Rose. Aunt Feldie. Uncle Wally. Elijah. Finally when that initial explosion of catching up

465

on the years was over, the questions asked and answered, the two girls sat quietly digesting all they had heard.

Vanessa finally jumped to her feet and cried, "I didn't know Watkins tried to rape you, Elizabeth. I swear to God, I wouldn't have helped him. I didn't know he killed Johnny. He never told me." Her hand curled into a tight fist. "I swear I'll kill him."

"I want him dead, too," Elizabeth said, "but right now we need to concentrate on escaping."

"There is no way," Vanessa said. "Roswell has guards and spies everywhere. He was not lying, Elizabeth. If you walk out of the house, you'll be shot. What about this Major Daniel Roswell was talking about? Do you think he'll bring the cavalry down here and rescue you?"

"I don't know," Elizabeth said. "I'd like to be-lieve he's coming, but—"

"You're in love with him?" Vanessa asked.

"Yes," Elizabeth answered, "I'm in love with him."

"You're going to be married?"

"Yes, we're going to be married," Elizabeth said and indulged for a second in happy thoughts. Quickly she pushed such ruminations aside and concentrated on the situation at hand. She must learn as much information as she could. When Chase came—he would come—she must tell him.

"What do you know about the weapons Bain-bridge is having smuggled in?" Elizabeth asked.

466

Vanessa shook her head. "Nothing. Ever since he discovered that I wanted out, he has told me nothing. I know no more about their business now than you do."

Both looked up when the door opened and Roswell entered without knocking. neither was sure if he had overheard their conversation, and his bland expression did not give his thoughts away.

"Vanessa, it is time for you and me to go."

"What about Elizabeth?" she asked, retreating behind her facade of cool indifference.

"She's going to stay here," Roswell answered.

"Not alone with Watkins! You know how he is."

"He's going with us," Roswell explained, a strange expression in his eye. "We've received word that our new supply of weapons is going to be delivered across the border tonight. I want all of us to be at the arsenal when they arrive. Also word has come that Lowell is bringing the money."

When Roswell mentioned Blake's name, Elizabeth's head jerked in his direction.

The colonel smiled. "Your major has decided to cooperate with us, Elizabeth. He's sending the money as I requested."

"You're going to free Elizabeth?" Vanessa said.

Roswell smiled. "Not to worry, sweet little butterfly. I'll take care of you and your sister."

Elizabeth couldn't help the shiver than ran down her body. The man's promise was fraught with evil intent. Vanessa turned her head, and the two of them stared at each other for a moment. Elizabeth

467

could read the fear in her sister's eyes.

"Come, Mariposa," Roswell's hand banded around Vanessa's upper arm and he pulled her out of the room with him, "we must be on our way. You can visit with your sister later."

Elizabeth heard the key grate in the lock after Vanessa and Roswell left and knew she was once again imprisoned within these four walls. And she knew that Roswell didn't intend to free her. She was here for Watkins' perverted pleasure. Restlessly she moved around the room, the width and breadth of it getting smaller by the minute. Time was of the essence; she couldn't sit back and do nothing but wait for Chase to rescue her. She had to get out of here. She needed to warn Chase about the weapons they were smuggling across the border.

Hours passed and no plan formulated. Finally she walked to the bed and lay down, but she didn't go to sleep or did she extinguish the candle. She didn't want to be in the dark. She lay there thinking about Chase and all the things they hadn't gotten to do. She wondered if she were pregnant with his child. Just the thought sent a delightful flutter through her stomach. To be his wife and the mother of his children.

She heard the key inserted in the lock and the grinding as it turned. When the door opened, Emery Watkins stepped into the room.

Elizabeth sat up, holding the sheet beneath her chin. "What are you doing here?"

468

He laughed. "You should have to ask, Elizabeth?"

"I thought you were going with Bainbridge and Vanessa."

"Roswell told her that to get her away without a fight. You belong to me, Elizabeth. Roswell gave me to you as repayment for my getting the weapons for him." Watkins laughed. "I own every bit of you, body and soul. Knowing that you wouldn't obey me willingly," he said, waving a revolver at her, "I brought this. Now come along. I have a special room prepared for you and me."

Elizabeth knew if she wished to remain alive resistance was foolish at the moment. As she stood, she said, "You may force yourself on my body, but you'll never touch my soul. I own that, and it belongs to me exclusively."

"We'll see." Watkins' laughed as waved her out of the room. "Turn to the left he said and go down to the third door. It's closed but unlocked."

Slowly Elizabeth walked down the hall and stopped in front of the designated door. Fear paralyzed her, and she couldn't reach out to turn the knob. The man was insane; she had to get away from him. She turned her head, seeking an avenue of escape, but felt the gun barrel against her back.

"Don't do anything," Watkins warned. "Even if you succeed in getting away from me now, you'd have the servants to get past and the guards outside. If they catch you alive, they'll all take you before they kill you. Those are the house rules."

He laughed shortly. "You can't win."

He reached around her, caught the knob, twisted and threw open the door. Elizabeth gazed in horror at the room that looked so reminiscent of a dungeon. The drapes were drawn and candles gleamed from all over, the reflection of the light intensified by the many mirrors that decorated the wall. It caught and glimmered in the gold that was so intricately woven into the many black fixtures. Whips. Chains. Ropes. Watkins pushed her, and she stumbled into the room. He slammed and locked the door, dropping the key into the pocket of his waistcoat. Keeping the gun in hand, he shoved her toward the bed.

"Put these on," he said and pointed to the flimsy undergarments.

"No," Elizabeth said, "I won't." She looked from the bed to the wall across from her and stared at her reflection in one of the mirrors.

So accustomed to the mirrors as to be unaware of them, Watkins held the gun to her head and cocked it. "Yes, Elizabeth, you will if you wish to live."

Elizabeth was sick at the thought of Watkins' touching her body, but she was also determined that he wouldn't kill her. She planned to do that to him. She picked up the material and discovered it was hardly large enough to cover her breasts. She threw it down.

Watkins pressed the revolver barrel into her back. "Undress now, Elizabeth. I'm loosing patience with you."

"El Patron." Trinidad's voice and knock sounded through the room. "You have a guest."

"Damn!" Watkins swore and involuntarily turned his head toward the door.

When Elizabeth saw that his attention had wandered from her, she saw her opportunity to escape—possibly the only one she would have. She knew she must act fast. She was a small woman and would be no match for Watkins' strength. Surprise and swiftness were her only weapons. She doubled her arm and gouged him in the stomach with her elbow, ducking and swinging around to knock the gun out of his hand. Taking him by surprise, she had a momentary edge. Before he quite knew what was happening she reached under the bed to grip the revolver.

"El Patron," Trinidad called.

"Unlock the door and help me," Watkins called as he rushed across the room and grabbed the whip from the dresser.

"I can't, Trinidad answered. "You are the only one with the key."

"Go get Sancho and have him knock the door down."

From the other side of the bed, Watkins saw Elizabeth rise with the revolver in her hand. His hand jerked back, and the whip snapped through the air, but coiled around the bed post rather than Elizabeth. The sharp gold slivers bit deeply into the mahogany and defied all Watkins' efforts to free them.

Elizabeth slowly walked to where he was cowering.

"Don't shoot me," he cried, dropping the whip at his feet. "Please don't shoot me."

In the shortness of time that it takes lightening to streak across the sky and dissipate into nothingness, Elizabeth relived those minutes years ago when Watkins had tried to rape her in the linen closet. She remembered Johnny's death as vividly as if it had just occurred. The same sensations inundated her body. She cocked the hammer and tightened on the trigger, but she didn't shoot him.

"*El Patron,* we are here," Trinidad called, and the butting against the door began, rhythmic thuds resounding through the room.

Elizabeth didn't turn toward the noise, but Watkins knew she was distracted. He slid his hand along the dresser his fingers curling around the long length of chain. When a board in the door cracked, Watkins brought his hand back and swung the chain through the air. It circled Elizabeth's upper body, the rough edges where the links were pressed together cut into her shoulders, arms and breasts. The pain was so intense, she cried out, but she didn't drop the gun.

She pulled the trigger again and again and again.

As the chain slipped down her body, scratching into her tender flesh, she watched the surprise on Watkins' face give way to horror. He clutched his stomach, the blood oozing through his fingers. He stared at her for a few seconds before he fell to the floor.

Emery Watkins was dead and Elizabeth felt no remorse.

Chapter Twenty-seven

Dawn was a myriad of color behind Chase as he stood on the banks of a small creek deep in Mexican territory and talked to the sixteen men who clustered around him. Among them were his eight troopers; Billy August and three other Seminole Indian scouts whom he recruited. Blake Lowell. Evan Warner. Nolan Griffin. Anthony Mason.

"At Eagle Pass when I recruited you," Chase said, "I told you the mission was on a voluntary basis because it was dangerous. One, our crossing the Mexican border can be construed as a military invasion of this country—an incident that neither country would approve. No matter what the outcome don't expect medals of honor from either government. Two, we're going to rescue Miss Elizabeth Barrett and her sister, and we're going to capture a notorious outlaw and as many of his followers as we can."

"Is this Colonel Bainbridge?" Griffin asked.

"It is," Chase answered. "First, we'll get the women out, then we'll give the other occupants an opportunity to surrender; then we're going to blow this place to oblivion. Sgt. Liberty, Nolan, you know what to do." Chase's gaze moved to the pack mules, staked out close to the water.

"Yes, sir," both men answered simultaneously. "We have everything ready. We just need to scout out the area and get the explosives set up."

Chase looked at Billy and his three scouts. "Two of you will go with each group."

The Seminole Negro scout nodded.

"Major," Tony was frowning and scratching the nape of his neck, "don't you think you're placing the women in a great deal of danger? If Bainbridge is the kind of man you and Warner have described him to be, he's not going to release the women simply because you're making the demand."

Chase gave the young ranger a thin smile. "Each man has a tragic flaw, so I'm told, Mr. Mason. I think Roswell Bainbridge's is his greed. It's my understanding that he's receiving a shipment of weapons today—a shipment that demands cash."

"The Union payroll money," Mason said.

Chase nodded his head.

"How do you know he has the women in here?" Griffin asked, fishing in his pocket for his chewing tobacco. "We could be at the wrong place for all we know."

"We don't," Chase answered, "but Captain Lowell and I agreed that if we're going to rescue Elizabeth we have to pick the time and place. We're turning our defensiveness into an offensive maneuver. Bainbridge then becomes responsible for running around the countryside. If Elizabeth isn't here, we'll make him get her."

Again Chase allowed his eyes to move over each member of the patrol. "This is the day we're going to do it. Bainbridge isn't expecting us to be here and before he's aware of our presence we're going to completely surround the garrison. Sgt. Liberty and Griffin are in charge of those two details. You men know which one you're working with."

A low murmur of acknowledgement went up from the group.

"Warner, Mason and I will remain here in this strategic position with the money. We'll know who's going in and out of the garrison. Lowell will ride in and issue our demands."

"You're sure putting a lot of trust in a man who robbed your payroll and killed God only knows how many men in the process," Tony accused.

"Yes," Chase agreed, "I'm putting a lot of trust in him, Mr. Mason. While I don't agree with Lowell's methods, I do agree with his purpose. I want Elizabeth out of there, and I want Bainbridge . . . dead or alive. Now, any more questions?" Chase asked.

"No question," Tony said, "but I'd like to make a request. I'd like to go with the men to set up the explosives. You don't need me here with you and Evan."

"When you volunteered your services," Chase said in a voice laced with steel, "you agreed to work under my command. I say what we need or don't need, Mr. Mason. Is that clear?"

Tony nodded, but Chase could tell that he was displeased. At the moment Chase couldn't have cared less. While he was glad to have an extra gun along, he didn't quite trust Mason and wanted him to be close by so he could keep an eye on him. Chase knew for sure Blake didn't like or trust the ranger, and Chase respected Blake's judgment.

"All right, men," Chase said, "you know what to do so do it. Good luck."

Quickly and quietly the camp split into two groups, one following Samson Liberty, the other following Griffin. Chase, throwing the two sets of saddlebags that contained the money over his shoulder, walked Blake to his horse, leaving Mason and Warner sitting together near the creek.

Chase said, "Now, for the most dangerous part of the expedition."

Blake smiled and tugged the brim of his hat a little lower. "But one that I wouldn't give up for all the world, Major. I've waited for this moment for many years now." He paused and looked at Warner and Mason. "If I were you, I'd keep an eye on Mason, Chase. Don't turn your back on him. Something isn't right with him, and I don't trust him at all. He admires Bainbridge too much." Blake swung into the saddle and moved the horse through the grove of trees.

Searching through the maze of rocks, Chase found a place to hide the saddlebags and marked it before he returned to where Warner and Mason were sitting. The older ranger was lying on the bank, his hands twined together to pillow his head, his hat pulled over his face. Mason sat next to him, idly drawing in the sand with a twig.

"I'm going to keep watch on the compound," Chase said. "The two of you remain here to keep a watch on the horses and be here if any of the men need you. Evan, I want you to relieve me in two hours."

Warner grunted; Mason grumbled. "I didn't come out here to sit with horses. I want in on some of the action."

"There's going to be plenty of action if we lose those mounts," Chase reprimanded shortly, disgusted with Mason.

Picking up his binoculars, Chase returned to the boulder and found himself a hidden spot where the sun wouldn't reflect on the lenses to give him away. Shortly he saw Blake moving down the narrow path toward the entrance of Bainbridge's garrison.

"Give me those," Bainbridge shouted, grabbing the binoculars from the guard. He pressed them against his face and watched as Blake Lowell rode toward the gate. "Damn it," he swore. "How did he know where to find me? He was supposed to be in Eagle Pass."

Vanessa, standing at his side, smiled. "Blake Lowell is a smart man, Roswell. I always told you that you underestimated him." She reached for the binoculars and lifted them to her eyes.

"What do you want us to do?" the guard asked. "Shoot him."

"Hell, no, you idiot!" Bainbridge exclaimed. "I need the money."

"Do you think he's foolish enough to have brought it with him?" Vanessa asked, her eyes running appreciatively over Blake's muscular body.

"We'll soon find out what he wants," Bainbridge answered. "Open the gate and let him come in." His hand banded around Vanessa's arm and he dragged her along with him as he descended the steps of the parapet and headed across the compound. By the time he and Vanessa stood in front of the small adobe building that served as his headquarters, the gate had been shut and barred and Blake was dismounting.

"Well, Mr. Lowell," Bainbridge said smoothly as if nothing were out of the way, "what a surprise to see you here."

"The surprise is all mine," Blake returned, his gaze centered on Vanessa. "As well as the pleasure."

Roswell looked at Vanessa also and smiled. "Mr. Lowell, I'd like for you to meet my . . . my busi-

479

ness associate, *Señora* Mariposa DeSilva."

"Señora DeSilva," Blake said, his brown eyes caressing the beautiful woman in front of him, "I'm glad to make your acquaintance."

Vanessa held her hand out. "And I yours, Mr. Lowell."

Blake held the hand much longer than was necessary but neither he nor Vanessa was inclined to turn the other loose. They stared deeply into one another's eyes. Roswell, aware of the attraction between them, determined to use it to his advantage.

"Won't you come inside," he invited and moved through the door. "We can talk without being disturbed."

Blake followed Bainbridge and Vanessa inside the building and smiled when he saw how elegantly the office was furnished. He watched Bainbridge move to a long table against the far wall.

"Whiskey?" the host offered.

"No, thanks," Blake answered. "I don't drink when I'm working."

Vanessa chuckled. "A conscientious man, I take it, Mr. Lowell."

Blake smiled at her. "Cautious and accustomed to taking care of myself to the very best of my ability."

Although Bainbridge was displeased with Blake's being here and with Vanessa's apparent infatuation with the man, he determined to turn the situation into his advantage. He was yet to be bested by a man like Blake Lowell.

"I'm sure you didn't bring the money with you, Mr. Lowell."

"No."

"That was my stipulation for the release of Miss Barrett."

"Where is Miss Barrett?" Blake asked, pointedly looking around the room. "I'd like to see and talk with her before we begin to discuss money."

Bainbridge's fingers tightened around the glass. He had set up the terms of the exchange, and he didn't for a minute like Lowell's taking the initiative away from him. "She's at the Hacienda de *la Mariposa*."

Blake smiled. "No Miss Barrett. No money."

"Vanessa will vouch that Miss Barrett is quite well and unharmed."

Blake shook his head. "I want to see her with my own pretty little brown eyes." He smiled when he saw the perspiration beading on Bainbridge's forehead. He knew at the moment he had the decided advantage. How long that would last he didn't know.

"I'll have one of my men take you to the hacienda to see her," Bainbridge said.

"No," Blake said softly but firmly. "You will bring her here and release her into my custody."

Bainbridge laughed. "If you think I'm going to hand her over to you before I receive the money, you're crazy."

Blake shrugged. "One of us has to give, and the one who's going to give is the one who has the most to lose." He rocked back on his heels and shoved his hands into his hip pockets. "The way I see it, Bainbridge, I figure you're the one who's wanting the most. You need the money to pay for that shipment you're receiving today. If you don't have the cash, it goes on to Mexico City to another buyer who does have the cash."

"What about Elizabeth Barrett?"

"What about her?" Blake asked, hiding his concern behind a mask of indifference.

"Didn't you come to rescue her and Vanessa?"

Blake's glance wandered lazily to the woman who stood in front of the window, the sunlight playing on her dark brown hair. "I like women," Blake admitted, "but they're not the reason why I'm here, Bainbridge. Originally I negotiated for Vanessa's freedom because of a deathbed promise I made to Rod Everett. I'm here negotiating for Elizabeth because you named me in your message. I have no personal interest in either woman," he lied smoothly.

"Yet, you were bargaining first for Vanessa's release," Bainbridge smugly pointed out.

"I wanted her out of the way because I saw the complications that were arising." His brown eyes lifted and moved across the room until they rested on Vanessa. Slowly his gaze slid down her body, lingering on the voluptuous curve of her breasts and hips. "Women are good at dividing into asunder that which man creates."

Bainbridge smiled and his eyes narrowed. He

had to admire the man's gumption and his honesty and ingenuity. He lifted a hand and stroked his moustache. "You're right at that," he finally conceded. "I did have to get rid of a good man because of Vanessa."

"I want both of them out of here; then you and I can talk."

"Are you working with the major?" Bainbridge questioned.

"He's the one who gave me the money," Blake answered. "But my purpose in coming has nothing to do with him. He's interested in the release of Elizabeth Barrett to the exclusion of everything else."

Bainbridge laughed softly. "You think once he has Elizabeth, he's going to forget all about me."

"No, he won't forget about you. He'll probably think about you the rest of his life. He didn't trust me with the money, so he and that motley band of soldiers who ride with him crossed the border at Eagle Pass. They're waiting there for me to return with Elizabeth. I would imagine by the time he reaches the border and safely deposits Elizabeth on American soil, he's going to find himself arrested by the same government that he serves."

"Arrested for what?" Bainbridge asked, his interest thoroughly piqued now.

"Military invasion of Mexico."

"And how are the American authorities going to know that he's been over here?"

"Word has a way of getting around," Blake

483

equivocated, "especially when it has a little help. Look how quickly you learned about Chase's arresting me and taking possession of the payroll. Now if you want to deal, get Elizabeth over here. We don't have any time to spare. The major is a smart man and he's only going to give me so many hours." Blake paused then said, "The Mexican authorities would be in debt to the person who informed them that American soldiers were on their soil."

Bainbridge hesitated only long enough to scrutinize the man who stood in front in him. Yes, he thought, this man was intelligent and had class and breeding. He would be a valuable asset to the organization . . . if he could be trusted. At the moment Bainbridge decided he had no alternative but to trust him. And he had time. He was safe here in the garrison.

He walked to the door and opened it. "Sibley," he shouted to his second in command, "go to the hacienda, get Miss Barrett, and bring her back here. And be quick about it."

Chase watched the gate open and the rider leave. He jumped to his feet and took a few steps in the direction where Mason and Warner were sitting. He thought about ordering one of them to follow the man but decided against it. He stopped walking and returned to the shelter of the rock. Too much was at stake. He couldn't risk Elizabeth's life any more than it already was.

Chase leaned against the huge boulder, laid his head on his arm, and closed his eyes. He felt so helpless and was worried sick; he could hardly think about what he was going to do next for worrying about Elizabeth. He reached into his pocket and closed his hand over the rose brooch. He had to get her out of here.

Her face swam before him, the beautiful smile that curved her full lips, the twinkling green eyes, the strains of her soft, husky laughter wrapped around his heart and squeezed until his eyes burned with tears.

Oh, God, he prayed, keep her safe.

He stepped back to his lookout and lifted the binoculars. Activity within the compound was nil. Blake, Bainbridge and the woman—Elizabeth's sister, Chase surmised—were still inside the building. Chase circled the glasses around the garrison to see if he could spot his men; he found none. He looked at the sun. About time for Warner to relieve him.

When he heard the crunch of approaching footsteps, he turned. "Mason," he said in surprise as the young ranger came into view, "where's Warner?"

Mason grinned. "He said if it was all right with you, he'd like for me to take the first watch. Said the ride had tuckered him out."

Chase pushed back his hat and looked at Mason. He wasn't pleased with the idea of Mason's relieving him at all.

"You give the money to Blake?" Mason asked.

"The money is my concern," Chase answered shortly.

Mason laughed. "I didn't figure you'd give it to Blake. That's army property, and you're army up one side and down the other. You never intended to exchange it for Elizabeth did you?" He looked around him. "It's bound to be hidden somewhere out here. You had the saddlebags when you left." Mason turned his back to Chase while he peered around the boulder at the compound below.

"What's your interest in the money?" Chase asked. His growing apprehension caused him to ease away from Mason.

"This," Mason said, abruptly turning to face Chase, his knife gleaming in his hand.

Chase's hand automatically went to his gun.

"Can't do that," Mason mocked. "Shooting would arouse the Colonel and his men and they'd know something was amiss."

"You want the money for yourself?" Chase asked.

"No," Mason answered, "I want it for the Colonel."

Things began to make sense to Chase; Tony had been the colonel's link with all that was going on in Texas. "You've been working with them all along."

Tony nodded. "I rode with the Colonel during the war."

"The man's inhuman," Chase said. "How can you work for him?"

"I believe in his cause," Tony said, an impassioned gleam in his eyes. "We're going to take back what's ours. You Yankees took everything away from us, but we're going to take it back."

"You may be dedicated to the South, Tony," Chase said, "but the Colonel isn't. He's nothing but an outlaw and murderer. His only cause is himself." Chase was silent as he continued to look at the knife. Again he saw Addison and Thurman and Corporal Lincoln, their throats slit. "You're the one who helped Everett escape, aren't you?"

Tony nodded.

"I knew it had to be someone these men trusted."

"I didn't want to kill them," Tony said, not the least repentant, "but they refused to turn Everett over to me. I had no choice."

"What about Everett?"

"He was a liability," Tony answered. "He and Mariposa, or whatever her name is, were double-crossing the Colonel."

"So you killed him? And Private Lincoln?"

"Yeah," Tony replied proudly, almost arrogantly.

"Murder, Tony," Chase said, disgusted at the cold admission. He couldn't believe anyone was so hardhearted. "You're committing murder for this man."

"Not murder," Tony replied. "It's war, major. Now stop the sermonizing and tell me where the money is."

"No," Chase answered.

They were at a stalemate. Chase wouldn't create an outburst because it would serve as a warning to Bainbridge that all was not well. Mason couldn't kill him because only Chase knew where the money was hidden. Tony's eyes darted about as if he were searching for a sign of the money. Chase took advantage of his distraction.

With a forceful lunge he lowered his head and butted Tony in the stomach. Winded, Tony dropped the knife and stumbled back but didn't fall. He caught Chase, twisted him and threw him off balance. As Chase buckled, Tony brought his knee up, the crushing blow tearing Chase's lips and smashing his nose as it sent him reeling to the ground. Blood coursed down Chase's chin.

Tony grabbed his knife and fell to the ground beside Chase, his hand raised, the knife headed straight for Chase's heart. Chase swung his legs into the air, ankles first, levering his torso up and flipping Tony aside. Quickly Chase jumped to his feet and wiped the blood and dirt out of his eyes.

With a growl, Tony leaped to his feet and swept an arc through the air with his knife, grazing Chase across the ribs. Grunting his pleasure, Tony pulled his arm back, again aiming for the death blow. With lightening fast movement Chase kicked Tony in the groin. With a scream of agony Tony dropped the knife and doubled over. Chase grasped the knife.

"Give up," Chase ordered, dragging in deep gulps of air. "It's over, Tony."

"Never." Tony snarled the words. "I'll see you in hell first."

He lunged at Chase, grabbing his hand and falling down with him as he tried to wrest the knife from him. They rolled in the dirt several times until Tony finally had Chase on his back. Holding Chase's hand he forced the knife toward Chase's stomach, but the major's fingers closed around the younger man's wrist. Thinking the blade was pointed toward Chase, Tony fell on top of him.

Tony grunted as the blade pierced his stomach; then he collapsed on top of Chase. Chase slowly moved from under the lifeless body and rolled it over. Blood dribbled from Tony's mouth and the knife protruded from his sternum. Chase pushed to his knees, spitting out blood, heaving deep gulps of air into his lungs. Pulling the knife from Tony's body, he stumbled back to the creek.

"My God!" Warner exclaimed, "what happened to you."

Chase tossed the knife at his feet. "Tony," he said, still breathing heavily. "He . . . was one of . . . Bainbridge's men."

"Tony," Warner said and shook his head. "No, he couldn't have been. Why, he was nothing but a boy. He and I have been riding together for the past two years."

Chase leaned over the creek and washed his face. "He's been passing information on to the

colonel. That's why Bainbridge's been so successful. He knew exactly what, when and where something was happening. He was also the Colonel's
personal assassin. Addison, Thurman, Everett, Private Lincoln." Chase took his shirt off and dipped
it into the creek. When he wrung it out, he
dabbed his wound. "And he tried to include me in
the number."

"That's why he wanted to relieve you," Evan
said musingly. "He was going to get the money
and kill you." After a few minutes he asked, "Get
some rest. I'll stand guard for awhile."

Weak from the loss of blood, Chase didn't ar-
gue with the ranger; he was grateful for a few
minutes rest. He found a shady place and lay
down. Now all the pieces were rightly fitting together to create the full picture. But Chase found
that he was no longer obsessed with getting Bainbridge. His main concern — his only concern — was
Elizabeth.

Wondering where they were taking her, Elizabeth
rode between the two men. She had changed cap-
tors three times during the course of the day. First
Watkins. Then after Trinidad and Sancho found
Watkins dead, she became their prisoner. Now
Bainbridge had sent for her.

Elizabeth wondered if Chase had brought the
ransom. While the thought thrilled her; it also
worried her. She knew Bainbridge didn't intend to

let her go free anymore than he would the person who brought the Union payroll. He could figure they knew too much about his operation and his whereabouts.

But, she thought with a smile, Chase was smarter than Bainbridge. If he came, if he had found her, he would have a plan. And he would come . . . find her . . . and have a plan. That was Chase Daniel.

Feeling better and happier, Elizabeth reached up and brushed an errant curl out of her eyes. She scanned the horizon to see nothing but barren rocks and desert. The early afternoon sun beat down upon her; her face was burning and her dress, already wet with perspiration, clung to her body.

Then in the distance she saw a rock fortress — the arsenal, she thought. This is where Bainbridge and Vanessa were awaiting the shipment of weapons. The compound was small but looked sturdy. As they neared, the gates opened, and they entered the compound. They stopped in front of an adobe building and dismounted.

"Get down," Sibley ordered, "and come with me."

Elizabeth dismounted and followed him into the building. When they entered, she saw Blake, Vanessa and Bainbridge sitting around a large table. From the looks of the table, they had just finished the midday meal. When Elizabeth looked at Vanessa, she saw the worried and anxious expression. Elizabeth saw the question in her sister's eyes; she smiled and shook her head. No, Emery Watkins hadn't touched her.

"Colonel," Sibley said, pushing around Elizabeth, "got some bad news for you."

Bainbridge raised a brow.

"Major Emery Watkins is dead, sir." Sibley pointed to Elizabeth. "She killed him last night."

Blake's blood went cold when he heard Watkins name. He remembered it from the letter Chase showed him. Watkins was the man who had tried to rape Elizabeth in New Orleans, the man who had killed her brother. No telling what he'd done to Elizabeth before she killed him. His eyes searched her face, but he kept his countenance cool and emotionless.

Vanessa looked at Elizabeth and smiled; her eyes flashed their approval and blessing.

"Told you," Blake tossed over his shoulder to Bainbridge, "you can't trust these women. They do cut asunder, Colonel."

"Yes," Bainbridge mused, "these two seem to have complicated the picture somewhat. Emery's death is a shame. Despite his bad habits, he did have connections when it came to getting the weapons we needed." The colonel looked at his man. "Thank you, Sibley. You and Murdoch may go now."

Bainbridge lifted his wine glass to Elizabeth. "Well, Elizabeth, Providence has smiled on you today. Blake Lowell is going to give me the money

492

in exchange for your freedom."

Now Elizabeth looked at Blake and gave him a small smile. While she was glad to see him, she was also disappointed. She wanted to see Chase. She wanted him to be the one who came for her. But he couldn't, she consoled herself. He's a major in the U.S. Cavalry; he couldn't cross the border no matter what the reason!

Seeing the sadness in her eyes and no outwardly change in her expression, Blake was concerned. He rose and walked to where she stood. "Are you all right?" he asked, catching her hands in his. The blue eyes searched hers. "You haven't been harmed in any way, have you?"

"I'm all right," she whispered, fighting back the tears. *I was raped emotionally, almost raped physically, and I killed a man. But I'm all right.* "I haven't been harmed."

Bainbridge said, "Now, Blake it's time for you to get the money. I've produced Elizabeth."

"You wouldn't consider letting her go with me, would you?" Blake asked.

"No, I wouldn't," Bainbridge answered.

Blake nodded. "Give me two hours."

"One," Bainbridge said. "If by then you haven't returned I will shoot both Elizabeth and Vanessa and leave their beautiful bodies for the vultures to pick."

Although Blake was worried about their safety, he didn't let Bainbridge see his consternation. He smiled and shrugged. "Whatever pleases you."

Blake walked out of the building and mounted his horse, but he rode through the compound slowly, looking around without moving his head. He memorized the layout and remembered the position of each guard. He and Chase had one hour in which to rescue the women and blow this powder keg up. Thus, every minute counted.

Chapter Twenty-eight

"Aren't you worried about what's going to happen?" Vanessa asked Bainbridge as she slowly walked across the room to stand in front of him.

"No," he replied, refilling his glass with wine. "I have no need to be worried. If anything were amiss, I'm sure Tony would have gotten me word. And nothing will happen until Elizabeth is safely out of the garrison."

"Tony!" Elizabeth exclaimed. "Do you mean Tony Mason?"

Bainbridge laughed. "None other than Anthony Mason, Miss Barrett. Does that surprise you?"

"It does." Her voice was slack. "But it shouldn't. I should have known from the beginning, the way he was talking at Uvalde."

"He's kept me informed of all your movements since he met you and learned that you were Vanessa's sister. How nice that you carry her portrait with you. Otherwise, I shouldn't have known of your presence quite so soon —" he looked reprovingly at Vanessa" — since your sister never told me her real name. Luckily Tony recognized her from the portrait. Else you wouldn't have been able to include you in our little party." He stood and looked at his watch. "Pardon me, ladies, but I think I shall go outside for a while." At the door he said, "As an extra precaution, I'm sure you won't mind being locked in."

Both women were, in fact, relieved when Bainbridge walked out of the room.

"I'm glad you killed Watkins," Vanessa said without preamble as soon as the door closed behind Bainbridge.

Elizabeth walked over to the window and gazed at the empty compound. "He . . . took me to that room, Vanessa." Elizabeth knew Vanessa was called Mariposa here, but she couldn't bring herself to use the name. "It was — it was —"

"I know," Vanessa said softly. "You don't have to tell me. I've heard about it."

Elizabeth whirled around. "You and he . . . you didn't — didn't do those kinds of things together."

"No," Vanessa said. "Although I slept with him when he was at The Rose, he wasn't into that kind of sex or, at least, I didn't know about it. When he arrived out here, I was already living with . . . Roswell."

"How did you meet Bainbridge?" Elizabeth

asked, unable to fathom how her sister had managed to become involved with such unsavory characters.

"I thought he was really fighting for the South," Vanessa answered. "At first I thought I loved him. When I found out what he was, I was too deeply involved to get out . . . or so I thought. Rod was the only friend I had. He was going to get me out."

Elizabeth nodded. "He loved you to the end. He made Blake promise that he'd—"

"I know," Vanessa said softly. "Blake told me. He's a nice person."

"Extremely nice," Elizabeth returned, a small smile touching the corners of her mouth.

"I wish I could have found someone like him to love, Elizabeth," Vanessa said. "All my life I've been looking for a husband and love, instead I attract lovers and lust."

Elizabeth moved to where her younger sister stood and took her into her arms. "You'll find love, darling."

"No decent man will want to marry me now," she said. "First Emery, then Bainbridge." Then as if she were embarrassed over her confession, she pushed away from Elizabeth and asked, "Do you think we'll get out of this alive?"

"Yes," Elizabeth answered, "we will."

Tired because she'd gotten little sleep the night before and knowing that Vanessa wanted time to be to herself, Elizabeth went into the bedroom and lay down. She wondered where Chase was and what he was doing. She closed her eyes and his image flashed through her mind. Her heart ached because she wanted him so much . . . so very much. She had so much she wanted to tell him, so many things she wanted to do with him.

She had just dozed off when she heard the explosion and bolted up. She leaped off the bed and ran into the outer room. "What's happening?" she shouted.

"The compound is blowing up," Vanessa cried.

Another explosion rend the air. Debris broke the glass in the window and flew into the room, forcing the women into the far corner where they huddled together. The door burst open and Bainbridge rushed in, his revolver drawn.

"The fool," he shouted. "He thinks he can double-cross me. I'll show him." He grabbed Elizabeth by the arm.

"No," Vanessa screamed. She clawed at Bainbridge's fingers trying to free Elizabeth.

Bainbridge drew his free hand back and slapped Vanessa across the face with the gun. Stunned, she fell to the floor. Then, before Elizabeth was aware of his intention, Bainbridge shot Vanessa through the chest. Elizabeth screamed at him when she saw blood ooze out to circle darkly the small hole. She thought she saw the rise and fall of Vanessa's chest, but she wasn't sure. She twisted her arm and dug her feet into the floor as she made the effort to stay with Vanessa. Bainbridge's fingers cut into the tender flesh of her upper arms, and he dragged her screaming and fighting from the room across the compound. He threw her down in front of a wagon.

"Murdoch," Bainbridge called, "tie her to the lead wagon so Lowell, or anyone else for that matter, can see her. Then gather your men and get them out of here with the wagons. You know where to go and what to do?"

"La Mariposa," Murdoch answered with a nod. "What are you going to do?"

"Sibley and I are going to create a diversion to allow you time to get out of here."

Having contemplated previously all eventualities of attack and having planned for them, Bainbridge issued orders methodically, oblivious to all the destruction going on around him. Like a mushroom, a huge cloud of black smoke billowed above the garrison as room after room of munitions exploded. The air was filled with shrapnel, gunfire, and screams of pure agony. Men ran from one side of the compound to the other as they salvaged as much of their munitions as they could and grouped together under Murdoch's command.

After the first charge of explosives, Chase and Blake entered the compound through a hole in the rear wall. When Blake saw Bainbridge, he took out after him. Chase went directly for Elizabeth. Sneaking through the burning rubble, he arrived at the headquarters building to see one of Bainbridge's men tying Elizabeth to the lead wagon. Also strapped to her were sticks of dynamite.

Chase's heart contracted; his stomach churned, and his entire body trembled. He had to get her out of that wagon. A stray bullet or spark of fire could ignite the dynamite and blow her up. Fear for her life galvanized Chase into action. Taking advantage of the commotion within the compound, Chase raced to the wagon and climbed into the rear. Unsheathing his knife, he slowly crept through the crates. Murdoch, hearing a noise, turned to see Chase. Before he could react, Chase fell on him, but the man was sufficiently warned so that he dodged the swing of the knife.

Tears filled Elizabeth's eyes when she saw Chase. She was glad to see him, grateful that he'd come to rescue her himself; but, her thoughts weren't for her safety, they were for his. She watched as both men, a tangle of arms and legs, tumbled from the seat of the wagon, hit the horse's rump and slid to the ground.

Murdoch landed on top of Chase. He drew his arm back and smashed a stunning blow in the face. When Chase, through bleary eyes, saw Murdoch leap to his feet, he drew back his arm and with the flick of his wrist threw the knife at the same moment Murdoch pulled his gun from the holster. The man, wide-eyed, stared at him for a moment before the gun fell from his hand and he toppled, face forward, into the dirt.

Chase jumped to his feet and jerked the knife from Murdoch's chest, wiping the blade on his trousers as he climbed into the wagon. As he deftly snipped the dynamite from Elizabeth's body, they stared into each other's eyes, silently declaring their love. Chase threw the explosive into the back of the wagon and untied Elizabeth's gag.

"Oh, Chase," she cried, tears of joy running down her cheeks. "I've never been so glad to see someone in all my life."

"You don't know how happy I was to see you alive, too, lady," Chase said, his voice husky. "Where's your sister?"

"She's inside the building," Elizabeth replied. "Bainbridge shot her."

He cut the ropes and jerked them from around her body. "Is she dead?"

"I don't think so," Elizabeth answered, bringing her hands in front of her and rubbing her wrists.

After Chase resheathed his knife, he leaped from the wagon and reached for her. He swung her to the ground and stood there a moment holding her, to assure himself that she was all right.

"Major Chase Daniel, I presume?"

Although both Elizabeth and Chase turned, Elizabeth cried, "Bainbridge!"

"Major Chase Daniel," Chase replied, slowly pushing Elizabeth away from him and looking into the barrel of Bainbridge's revolver. "I take it you're

Roswell I. Bainbridge."

"Colonel Roswell Irwin Bainbridge," the man answered smoothly, totally ignoring the battle that was raging around them. He smiled. "I see that I'm going to get to kill my most dedicated foe after all. I'd begun to despair of ever meeting you, major." Bainbridge's gaze moved to Elizabeth. "You can rest assured that I'll take good care of Elizabeth after you're gone."

Anger surged through Chase at the man's insinuation. Never had he wanted to kill someone more than he wanted to kill the man who stood in front of him.

"Come, Elizabeth," Bainbridge said, crooking his fingers and beckoning to her.

Elizabeth didn't move. Her gaze was focused on a point beyond Bainbridge. She watched Blake dash across the compound and thread through the wagons until he stood behind the colonel.

"I said, come here," Bainbridge repeated in a hard voice.

"Bainbridge!" Blake shouted.

Bainbridge whirled to see Blake emerge from between two of the wagons. He aimed and pulled the trigger, but Blake was faster. His bullet hit Bainbridge in the heart. The man tumbled to the ground, an inglorious heap in death.

Elizabeth turned to see the headquarters building going up in a blaze. "Vanessa," she cried. "We've got to get Vanessa out."

"I'll get her," Blake shouted, racing past her and Chase.

He threw open the door to stagger back when black, fiery clouds billowed from the room. He pulled his handkerchief from his pocket and wrapped it over his face. Then he charged into the burning building in search of Vanessa.

When Elizabeth saw him next, he was coming out with Vanessa in his arms. Now she relaxed in Chase's arms and lifted her face to him.

"Major Daniel, would you please take me home and make an honest woman out of me?"

"Miss Barrett," he said, his voice so thick with tears of happiness he didn't know if he could keep from crying, "I intended to do that with or without your permission."

He looked up to see Sgt. Liberty and his men riding into the compound. "Round up Bainbridge's men," he ordered. "What's left of them, Sergeant, and gather up all the munitions. We'll be taking these wagons home with us tonight."

Chapter Twenty-nine

Wearing a white diaphanous nightgown, Elizabeth stood at the edge of her bed at The Rose, looking down at the yellow bud that lay on her pillow. With trembling hands she picked it up and held it to her face, inhaling the delicate scent and feeling the soft petals against her cheeks. The lamplight danced off the wide gold band she wore on her left hand. Only this morning in the garden beneath an arched trellis of climbing roses in full bloom she had married Chase Daniel.

When she heard the door open, she turned to see her husband enter the room. His dark hair, long since defying comb and brush, was waving profusely around his handsome and smiling face. His white shirt, tucked into his trousers, was unbuttoned part way to reveal a wedge of muscled chest covered in dark hair.

He was mesmerized with Elizabeth. Her nightgown cast her in virginal beauty and provocatively revealed the secrets of which only he had partaken. His heart thudded fast and heavy. Although he'd made love to her many times, he felt as if this were the first. She was so tiny . . . so beautiful. His eyes landed on the yellow rose . . . she was so delicate.

"Am I too early?" he asked.

"No," she murmured, "if anything, too late, my love."

Smiling at her, he walked to the slipper rocker, sat down, and pulled off his shoes and socks. Standing, he unbuckled his belt and shucked his trousers, then his undergarments. Naked, he stood and both of them stared at one another.

Elizabeth lay her rose on the night table and with beautiful, fluid motions reached down and caught her nightgown by the hem and slipped it over her head to bear completely her perfectly sculpted body for him to see. She tossed it across the room, unmindful of where it landed. She ran across the room to throw herself into Chase's arms.

"My husband," she whispered as his lips lowered to hers.

"My wife," he murmured, the words becoming the essence of their kiss.

Elizabeth cupped the back of his head with her hands and brushed the skin of his abdomen with her breasts, each stroke of her flesh against him like the stroke of flint against a rock. Sparks shot off from each of them, creating the roaring blaze of desire that would surely flame around both of them.

"I love you," he whispered when he finally released Elizabeth's lips and began a low, tantalizing journey down her body.

"I love you," Elizabeth moaned as his mouth moved down that hollow arch under her chin, on her neck, across her collarbone.

His lips tasted and sipped of the delicacies that she presented to him on the platter of love, the same delicacies he had sampled time and time again, but never had they tasted this good to him. Never had he craved anyone as much as he craved Elizabeth.

In the sensual dance of mating, Chase caught Elizabeth into his arms and carried her to the bed. When he laid her down, he stretched out beside her, his hands running the length of her legs, his mouth tenderly touching the succulent flesh of her body. As he took his pleasure, however, he freely gave her pleasure. Every touch, every murmur, every gaze was shared. And he delighted to feel her hands as they touched him with loving strokes; he joyed to the whispered words of love that flowed from her lips in between their heated and fevered kisses.

His hands worshipped her, reverently sweeping to the gateway of her femininity, and his lips adored the beautiful roundness of her breasts, his tongue inciting the sensitive tips.

"Elizabeth," he murmured, his warm breath arousing her desires even more, "you're wonderful to love."

"And so are you, my darling."

Elizabeth guided Chase's mouth to hers, needing to fill her void, wanting her mouth full of the moist warmth of his and wanting her lower body filled with the firmness of his manhood. Motivated by passion, tempered with love, she held his face between her hands, and she invited the sweet spearing of his tongue into her mouth as his hand prepared her for the thrusting invasion of his lower body.

Tenderly the big man made love to the tiny woman, carrying her slowly beyond illusions and daydreams, beyond the bounds of memory to the highest pinnacle of joy and completeness. Their climax was the most fulfilling of all they had shared together, their souls had mated and wed.

They lay on the bed, their breathing quietly slowing as they listened to the wind sough through the huge trees outside The Rose. A tranquility permeated both of them, surrounding them with serene hush. They didn't speak; they only clasped hands. Yet they communicated as the melody of love flowed from one of them through the other.

When later, he turned to her again, Elizabeth welcomed him into her arms and her body.

* * *

Wearing a beautiful white morning gown, her hair hanging in a cascade of golden waves down her back, Elizabeth Rose Daniel stood in front of a trellis of climbing roses at The Rose. She was carefully clipping the blooms and filling her basket. When she heard the approaching steps she turned to see her husband. She held her hands out and smiled.

"Good morning, darling," she greeted. "Did you sleep well?"

Chase grinned. "I did damn little sleeping, Mrs. Daniel, and you know that." He pulled her into his arms and brushed his hands down her back until they rested against her buttocks. "You know full well that you kept me awake most of the night."

Devilment gleaming in her eyes, Elizabeth teased, "Should I promise not to act in this manner again, my husband?"

"You'd better promise never to act differently," he said gruffly, his head coming down as his lips captured hers in a totally satisfying kiss.

"I left your letter on the hall table, did you get it?"

Chase nodded.

"Well, Major Daniel," she said, "where is our next tour of duty going to be?"

Chase couldn't credit himself with hearing correctly. He'd been afraid to mention his career or his coming tour of duty. He knew what the plantation meant to Elizabeth and how hard she had worked to reestablish it. Now by her using the pronoun, "our," she was including herself in his life and his career.

"In two weeks," he said, "I'm to report to the Texas frontier to reopen Ft. Duncan."

"That doesn't give me much time to pack, does it?" Elizabeth said lightly.

"I know how much you hate to leave The Rose," Chase said, "and I did consider resigning my commission, but . . . I'm not a southern planter. I'm a cavalryman by profession, and I don't want to be anything else."

"I know, my darling," Elizabeth answered, "and I'm not asking you to be anything else. You're my life, Chase Daniel, and wherever your career takes us, that's where we'll go. We'll create our own destiny."

"What about The Rose?" Chase asked.

"I've already discussed that with Vanessa," Elizabeth replied with a smile. "She's ready to come home; she wants to stay here and run it. You and I can always come back for visits."

Chase pulled Elizabeth into his arms and again captured the sweet essence of her lips. His kiss was not passionate or lustful; it was tender thanks for the wonderful gift of her love. When he raised his head, he saw Vanessa and Blake, horseback riding in the distance.

"I have a feeling The Rose will have its southern planter after all," he said.

"Umhum," Elizabeth agreed, her gaze sweeping the horizon to land on her sister and Blake. "I think so, too." She smiled and lifted dreamy eyes up to Chase. "Hasn't this been a wonderful year? Samson and Joy getting married. You and me. And Blake and Vanessa, don't you think?"

"I think," Chase answered, then asked, "What are you going to do about Jefferson?"

"He really wants to live with Samson and Joy, doesn't he?" Elizabeth said, a sad note in her voice.

"He does, and they want him."

Elizabeth laughed softly. "I'm glad you had Corporal Man take Jefferson back to Ft. Clark. He had those troopers wrapped around his little finger, but Joy saw right through his glibness from the beginning."

"I think it would be a good idea to let Joy and Samson adopt him."

"So does Jefferson," Elizabeth murmured.

"What about you?"

"If they were to adopt Jefferson, his name would be Thomas Jefferson Liberty," she said and tilted her head. "A good solid name."

"Does that mean yes?"

"That means yes," she answered. "Thomas Jefferson Liberty does have a certain ring about it."

Chase chuckled with her.

"Just like Daniel," she added, her eyes softening. "It has a wonderful sound."

"Yes," Chase agreed, "Daniel is a beautiful name."

While Chase knew he would always wonder about his parents and would always be searching for another painting with the name Daniel in the corner, he no longer felt that he was incomplete because he didn't know who his parents were. He had learned that worth comes from within not without. A name and birthright do not make the man. A person is what he believes himself to be. Acceptance and rejection come for within.

"I'm glad that I've chosen Daniel to be my name."

Elizabeth smiled up at her husband, her green eyes twinkling. "I'm glad that I've chosen it to be mine."